THE THIRTEENTH CHILD

Also by Erin A. Craig

House of Salt and Sorrows

Small Favors

House of Roots and Ruin

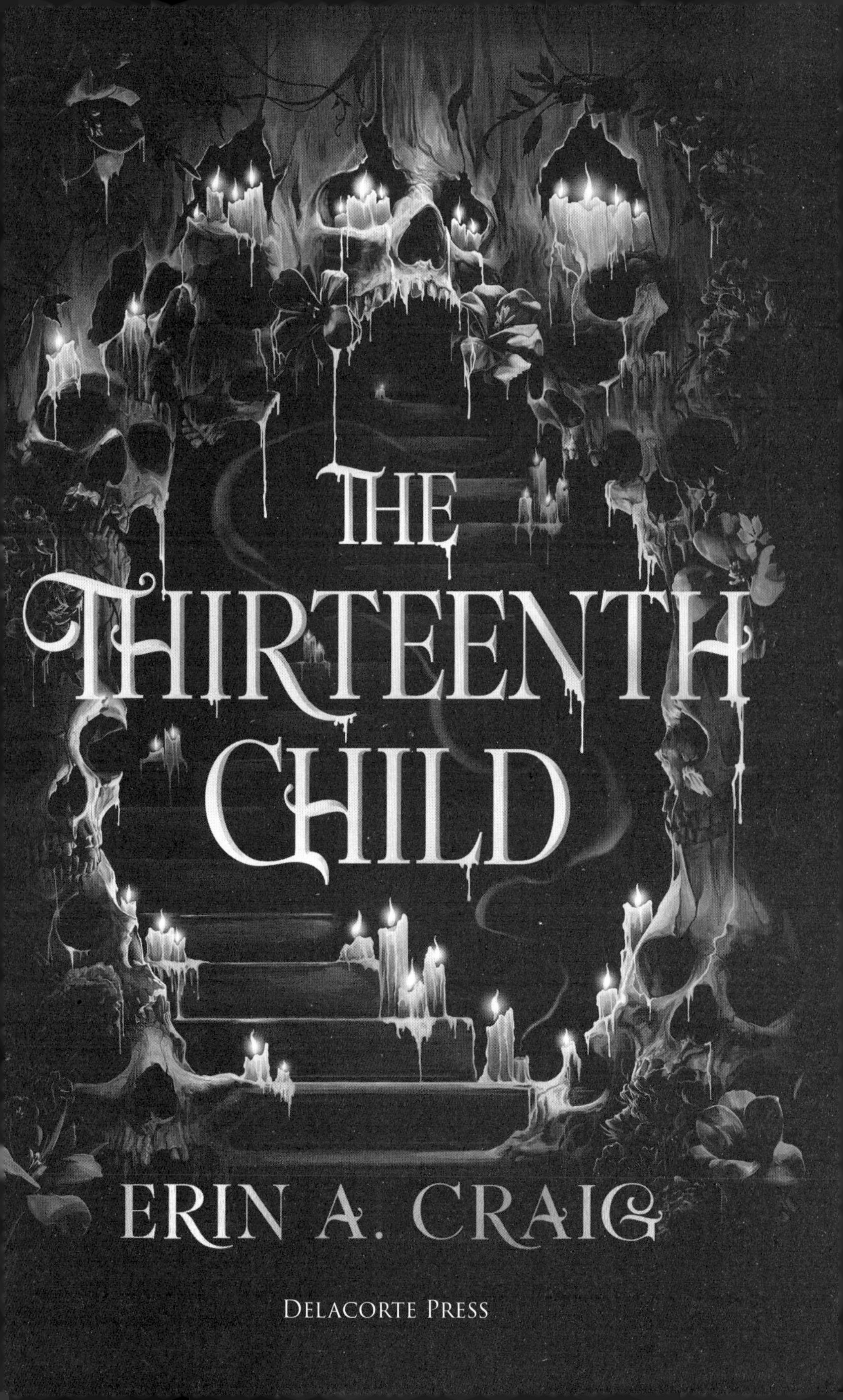
THE
THIRTEENTH
CHILD
ERIN A. CRAIG
DELACORTE PRESS

This is a work of fiction. Names, characters, places, and incidents either are the product of the author's imagination or are used fictitiously. Any resemblance to actual persons, living or dead, events, or locales is entirely coincidental.

ISBN 978-0-593-48258-2

The text of this book is set in 11-point Adobe Garamond Pro.
Interior design by Cathy Bobak
Interior smoke art by Sandaru/stock.adobe.com
Single candle ornament art by Ldarro/stock.adobe.com
Interior textured background and vine art used under license from Shutterstock.com

Printed in the United States of America

For Grace.
In the tapestry of my life,
you will always be my brightest thread.

The Birthday Story

With a punch of sharp sulfur, the little match snapped to life, flame biting at its wooden stump, hungry for a wick to feed on.

My godfather's voice rose out of the dark like a ghoul crawling from its crypt, all rustling leaves and the smoky taste of autumn.

"There once was a very foolish huntsman who lived at the heart of the Gravia Forest."

The match's flame was nearly at his fingertips, eager to singe his skin, the wooden stick all but spent, but he paid no mind.

"We don't have to do this, you know," I said, and offered him a long taper to light. It was amber in color, rich and golden and warm and lovely.

The candle cast dancing shadows across my cottage as the flame grew stronger, more resolute. I met Merrick's eyes—a strange combination of silver and red irises surrounded by a void of pure black—and smiled. I could recite this story by heart, but I let him tell it. It was his favorite part of my birthday.

"Throughout his life, this very foolish huntsman made series after series of very foolish decisions, until at long last, on one particular night, he finally made one very clever choice." With a swift snap of his elongated, knobby fingers, the match went out, and a curl of silvery smoke wafted into the rafters. "The huntsman, you see, though very poor and very foolish, had somehow found himself a very pretty, very young wife."

"And we all know what happens when very poor men have very pretty wives," I cut in, unable to help myself.

"They're blessed with lots of pretty children," Merrick intoned testily. "Are you telling this story or am I?"

Turning from him, I peeked into the oven, checking on the bread. Birthday tradition or not, we both needed to eat—well, *I* needed to eat—and supper wouldn't prepare itself.

"Sorry, sorry," I said, grabbing for the loaf pan with towel-covered hands. "Go on."

"Now, where was I?" he asked with practiced theatricality. "Oh yes, the children. The many, *many* pretty children. First one or two, then, before you know it, four, five, six, and so on and on, until you come to a complete dozen. Twelve lovely, perfect, and pretty children. Most men would have stopped long before, but I do believe I've already quite established that this huntsman was particularly foolish."

"You have," I agreed, as I always did.

He looked pleased. "I have. And so the years went by—as years so often do—and the very foolish huntsman got older—as mortals also so often do. More villages and towns sprouted up along the edge of the Gravia, and the forest was no longer as plentiful as it had been in the days of the huntsman's youth. Without game to sell and with so many mouths to feed, the very foolish huntsman despaired, wondering how much longer he could support his ever-growing family."

"And then one day—"

"And then one *night,*" my godfather corrected me, peevish. "Really, Hazel, if you insist upon interrupting my narrative flow, you might at least make sure your details are right." He tapped my nose with a disappointed *tsk.* "And then one night, while in bed, the very foolish huntsman's very pretty wife told him she was carrying yet another child.

" 'Thirteen children!' he cried. 'How will I ever provide for thirteen children?' "

This was the part of the story I most hated, but Merrick never seemed to notice my discomfort. He always threw himself with gusto into the role of the very pretty wife, his usually graveled voice rising to an acute falsetto, hands clasped with girlish affectation.

" 'We could get rid of it as soon as it's born,' the very pretty wife offered. 'Drop it into the river and let it fend for itself. Someone is sure to find it. Someone is sure to hear the cries. And if they don't . . .' She shrugged and the huntsman gaped at her, suddenly frightened. How had he failed to notice his wife's black heart?

" 'We could leave it at one of the temples in town,' he suggested instead."

I pictured myself as a baby, swaddled among the reeds and clay mud of a riverbank as frigid water seeped into my basket, rising higher and higher. Or at a temple's orphanage, one of dozens of children jostling for every scrap of food or ounce of attention, crying louder and louder but never truly heard.

Merrick held up his pointer finger. It was so much longer than his others, crooked at the knuckles like the limb of a contorted beech tree. " 'Or you could consider giving her to me,' called a soft and silvery voice from deep within the cabin.

" 'Who . . . who is there?' the huntsman dared to ask. His voice trembled as his wife tried to push him from their bed to ward off the intruder."

"And who should stroll out from those dark and shadowy depths but the Holy First," I said, now in the dining room, smoothing the creases in my floral tablecloth.

Merrick rolled his eyes. "Of course it was the First, and of course she promised to take and raise the hapless babe, nurturing her into a good and beautiful child, a postulant of perfect devotion and grace.

" 'Who are you to offer such a thing?' demanded the very pretty wife, feeling not quite as pretty as usual as she faced the beatific goddess.

" 'Do you really not know me, mortal?' the goddess asked, tilting her head with curiosity, her eyes burning like opals behind her gauzy veil."

Merrick cleared his throat, relishing the narration.

"The very foolish huntsman pushed his wife aside. 'Of course we know you,' he clamored. 'But we would not welcome you as godmother to this child. You are the Holy First, all love and light and things of beauty. But your love has brought nothing but poverty to my wife and me. Twelve children in as many years, with another on the way! Our thirteenth will manage just fine without you.' "

I lit three more candles and set them on the table, letting their happy glow warm the dark room.

What would my life have been like if my father had accepted the Holy First's offer? I pictured swanning about in the Ivory Temple, in the diaphanous, shimmering robes of the First's postulants. My light brown hair would be long, with lush curls, and my skin as perfect and freckle-free as a porcelain doll's. I would be reverent and devout. It would be a peaceful life, a beautiful one. One without shame or regret.

A glance at the line of dirt beneath my nails—always there no matter how hard I scrubbed—was enough to curdle that daydream.

"The Holy First left, and the huntsman and his wife somehow went back to sleep," Merrick continued. "Until . . . there was a crashing boom of thunder!" He clapped his hands together, creating the sound effect.

" 'Who's there now?' called the very pretty wife, anger coloring her tone. 'We're trying to sleep.'

" 'And we're trying to help you,' answered a sly and slippery voice. A long, thin figure stretched out from a shadow, slinking into the candlelight. 'Give your child to us and we shall raise her into a woman of great power and wealth. She will know fortune beyond measure, beyond calculation, and—' The god stopped.

"The wife leaned forward. 'And? Yes? Fortune and?' "

Merrick chuckled darkly, now pantomiming the movements of each of the characters. He threw his hand over his forehead with trumped despair.

" 'No!' cried the very foolish huntsman, for though he was very foolish, he still recognized the deity for who it was."

"Who *they* were," I corrected him.

"The Divided Ones stared down at the pair, regarding the husband and wife from one eye each, shared on the same face. And when they asked why the very foolish huntsman had declined their offer, they did it with two voices from one throat.

" 'You are the Divided Ones,' the huntsman began. 'You may

promise to give this child wealth and power and fortune, but fortunes can turn'—he snapped his fingers—'in the split of a second, like the split of your face. What will happen to our child then?'

"The Divided Ones cocked their head, studying the very foolish huntsman with wary respect. 'This is your final answer?' they asked, and their voices were so many strong. So many, yet only one.

"The huntsman nodded, even as his wife struck him, and the Divided Ones disappeared in a flash of lightning and shadow and mischief.

"The couple did not return to sleep, wondering what dreadful thing might befall them next. They huddled together against the darkness until the wee hours of morning, just before sunrise, when the night is at its blackest. Only then were they visited by a third god." Merrick's smile turned indulgent, the sharp tips of his teeth winking in the firelight. "Me."

Merrick paused, looking about the kitchen, then let out a noise of dismay. "The cake!"

He took out canisters of flour and sugar. Scooping up handfuls of each, he let the powders sort through his fingers. The white granules transformed as they fell, turning into layers of cake, dense and golden brown.

When Merrick blew the last of the sugar away, it turned into pale pink icing so delicate that tiers of the cake could still be seen underneath. A dusting of gold leaf shimmered across the top. From thin air, Merrick plucked a peony, frilly and fragrant and just about to burst into bloom. He laid it across the top of the cake, where tiny tapers had suddenly sprouted, an identical pink to the peony's petals.

It was exquisite, over-the-top in its magnificence, and so terribly Merrick.

"How's that?" he asked, admiring his work before leaning over to kiss the top of my head with fatherly affection. He smelled superficially of warm cardamom and clove, vanilla, and molasses, but a darker, somewhat unpleasant scent lurked beneath. It was something no pomander, however strong, could completely mask. Iron, copper, and the funk of meat sat out too long and on the verge of turning.

"You know, I'll never forget the first time I saw you, all those birthdays ago. So scrunched and squalling. Such a fragile, tiny creature. I hardly knew what to do when you were foisted into my arms."

My smile faltered, dimming. I knew exactly what Merrick had done: he'd handed me right back to my mother and turned tail, disappearing for years. But I let him tell the story the way he remembered it. My birthday had always meant much more to him than it had to me.

"I had a mind to name you Joy, because your arrival brought such delight to my heart." His forehead furrowed as he struggled to hold back a swell of emotion. "But then you opened your eyes and I was struck dumb, completely smitten. Such depth and intelligence pooling in those hazel wonders." Merrick released a shaky breath. "I'm very proud to call you mine and am grateful to celebrate this day with you."

As I watched my godfather, my heart panged with affection. He was not an attractive figure, not by half. Certainly not a being to whom most parents would willingly give their child.

Merrick had no nose, only a hollowed-out cavity shaped like an upside-down heart, and his deep obsidian skin rippled back painfully tight across his cheeks, causing his expression to read as a scowl of menace, no matter how happy he might be. He was extraordinarily gaunt and tall. Even with the high gabled peaks of my cottage, he had to stoop low under the rafters, forever ducking to avoid the bunches of flowers and herbs hung up to dry. And the fullness of his thick, dark robes couldn't hide the skeletal ridges of his figure. The black wool hung in strange shapes from the bony angles of his spine and shoulder blades, nearly giving him the appearance of having wings, much like a bat.

No. Most parents would not hand their child over to someone like Merrick.

Then again, my parents weren't like most.

And to me, his was not a face to be feared. His was the face of the Dreaded End, the god who loved me. Who'd saved me, eventually. A god who had raised me when my own flesh and blood cast me aside. This was the face of my salvation, however unearned, however unasked for.

Merrick raised his glass toward mine. "To this birthday and to all the many, many more to come."

Our goblets clinked together, and I pushed aside his words with an uneasy smile.

So many, many more to come.

"Now," he said, eyeing his pink confection with glee, unaware of my inner turmoil.

Always, always unaware.

"Shall we start with cake?"

CHAPTER 1

THE EIGHTH BIRTHDAY

"ANOTHER YEAR, ANOTHER YEAR, ANOTHER YEAR HAS come," sang the children gathered about the long table. Their voices rose, both in pitch and volume, as the final verse wound to a merciful end. "You are one year older now, so shout 'Hooray!' You're done!"

The room filled with shrieks and giggles as Bertie, the day's star, jumped on top of his chair and gave a great cheer of triumph before leaning in to blow out the nine candles topping the small nut cake.

"Start with me, Mama? Start with me?" he begged, his little voice piercing through the room's tumult with far more clarity than it had any right to.

"Yes, yes," our mother answered, pushing through the clamoring crowd of my siblings to the table's edge with a practiced nudge of her hips. "After Papa, of course."

She pulled the platter toward her and, with swift slices of the butter knife, cut a scant sliver of cake. She deposited it on a plate and pushed it down the length of the table to where our father sat watching the evening's festivities play out with glassy eyes.

He'd opened a new cask of ale for the occasion and was already three mugs in. He grunted in acknowledgment as the first piece of cake—the biggest there would be, if my eyes calculated correctly—landed in front of him. Without waiting for the rest of us to be served, Papa picked up his fork and began shoveling it into his mouth.

My siblings began to wriggle with impatience. Every eye was on Mama as she sliced the remainder of the cake.

As it *was* his birthday, Bertie got the next piece, and he crowed over its size, reckoning it was nearly as big as Papa's.

Remy came next, then Genevieve, then Emmeline, and I began to lose interest. Mama was serving down the line of us, in birth order, and I was bound to be waiting for a long time to come.

Sometimes it felt as though I was fated to spend my entire life waiting.

Everyone began to eat their fill as soon as the plates appeared before them, noisily exclaiming how good it tasted, how rich and moist the cake was, how sweet the frosting.

As Mathilde—the third youngest—got her piece, I glanced over with interest at the remaining wedgelette, and a stupid spark of hope kindled inside me. My mouth watered as I dared to imagine how nutty my bites would taste. It didn't matter that my serving would be not even half what Bertie was afforded, didn't matter that there was barely a covering of icing on its surface; I would still receive a sample.

But Mama picked up the last piece and popped it between her lips without even bothering to serve it up on a plate first.

Bertie, who had been watching the rest of the portioning with greedy eyes, hoping he might somehow snag a second helping, had the decency to remark upon it. "Mama, you forgot Hazel!"

Mama glanced down the long table and she did look surprised, as though she might have well and truly forgotten me, wedged away in the farthest corner, rubbing elbows with Mathilde and the cracked plaster wall.

"Oh, Hazel!" she exclaimed, and then raised her shoulders, not exactly with a look of apology, but more with an expression of "Well, what am I to do about it now?"

My lips tightened. It wasn't a smile of forgiveness, only a grim acknowledgment of understanding. She hadn't forgotten me and we both knew it, just like I also knew that there was nothing I could say or do that would cause her a moment of remorse, a pang of repentance.

"May I be excused?" I asked, my feet already swinging as I readied to jump down from a bench cut too tall for my tiny frame.

"Have you finished your chores?" Papa asked, startling, as if he had just noticed my presence. I didn't doubt he *had* forgotten about me. I took up a scant amount of room in both his house and his thoughts, little more than a footnote in the great, bloated volume of his life's memoir.

The thirteenth child. The daughter never meant to have been his.

"No, Papa," I lied, keeping my gaze downward, more on his hands than his face. Even direct eye contact with me took more energy than he was usually willing to spend.

"Then what are you doing in here, dawdling like a lazy wench?" he snapped.

"It's my birthday, Papa," Bertie interrupted, his blond eyebrows furrowed.

"So it is, so it is."

"Hazel couldn't miss my birthday!" he exclaimed with indignation.

A blush of pride crept over my cheeks as my brother stood up—stood up to Papa!—for me.

Papa's jaw worked, as though he was chewing on a wad of tobacco, even though he'd not been able to buy a tin of it in months. "Dinner is done. The cake is gone," he finally said. "Your birthday is well and truly celebrated. Hazel needs to go off and do her chores."

I nodded, my two brown braids brushing the tops of my shoulders. I scooted off the back of the bench and gave a little curtsy to Papa. Before I hurried out of the crowded dining room, I dared to pause, looking back at Bertie to offer him the tiniest grin.

"Happy birthday, Bertie."

With a twirl of my pinafore, I rushed out of the house and into the chilly spring air. Twilight was just about to give way to true and proper night, the time of shadow-men and woodland creatures with limbs too long and mouths full of teeth, and my heart raced with an uneasy thrill as I imagined one of them stumbling across me on my way to the barn.

With a grunt of effort, I pulled the big sliding door shut and made my way to the back worktable. It was dark, but I knew the route by heart. I found Papa's tin of matches and lit my oil lamp, casting weak golden light into the darkened stalls.

My chores *had* been done long before dinner—I'd even managed to do some of Bertie's for him in lieu of a gift. I knew it was wrong to lie to Papa—Mama was always going on and on about keeping yourself free of sin, somehow only ever cuffing *me* on the back of the head during her admonishments—but if I stayed in that happy, celebratory chaos for a second longer, my walls would crack and tears would begin to roll free.

And nothing put Mama or Papa in a worse mood than seeing me cry.

With care, I climbed the ladder to the loft, balancing the lantern precariously on one arm as I made my way up to my bedroom.

I'd been sleeping in the barn ever since I'd outgrown the exhausted little cradle that had held all thirteen of us as babies. The cabin's attic could fit only four beds—my brothers and sisters slept three to a mattress—and there was simply no space for me.

I found my quilt and curled it over my shoulders, snuggling into its decadence. It was the one thing I had that proved my godfather actually existed, that he had come for me once and would maybe one day return.

It was also an enormous sore spot between Papa and Mama.

Mama wanted to sell it off at market, arguing that the silk velvet alone would bring in at least three years' worth of coins. Papa said that selling off the Dreaded End's gift would bring an unholy mess of perdition upon the family and forbade her to touch it.

I traced the swirls of gold thread—real gold, Bertie had often murmured in wondered admiration—that spelled out my name.

HAZEL.

This was not a blanket that belonged in a barn, on a bed of straw. It didn't belong with a family of too many mouths and too few rations, too much noise and too few hugs.

But neither did the little girl whose shoulders it now covered.

"Oh, Godfather," I whispered, sending my plea out into the dark night. "Will this be the year? Will tomorrow be the day?"

I listened to the sounds of the barn, waiting and wishing for him to respond. Waiting as I did every year on this night, the night before my birthday.

Waiting.

I drifted in and out of sleep peppered with bad dreams.

Down in the valley, in Rouxbouillet, the little village skirting our forest, the bells of the Holy First's temple chimed, waking me.

Once, twice . . . seven times, then eight, and so on, until they struck their twelfth note.

Twelve.

The hours of sunlight.

The months of a year.

An even dozen.

I saw my siblings lined up from biggest to smallest, their smiles bright, their faces so lovely and shining and beaming.

A perfect set. The perfect number.

And then there was me. Small, dark, freckled, miserably mismatched me.

As the last of the twelfth chime died away in the clear midnight air, I breathed in the first moments of my eighth year. I waited to feel different, but nothing had changed. I raised my hands, spreading the fingers as wide as they would go, wondering if they looked older. I stared at the end of my nose, hoping my freckles had somehow miraculously disappeared from the swell of my cheeks.

I hadn't grown up.

Would the Dreaded End care?

"Another year, another year, another year has come," I sang to myself, nestling into the straw and velvet. My voice sounded small within the great space of the barn. "You are one year older now, so shout 'Hooray!' You're done."

I paused once more, straining my ears for any sign of my godfather's approach. Still nothing.

"Hooray," I muttered, then turned over to sleep.

CHAPTER 2

ON MY FIRST DAY OF MY EIGHTH YEAR, THE ENTIRE household descended into complete chaos as Mama readied us to go into Rouxbouillet for the spectacle of the king's holy pilgrimage.

In truth, we rarely thought of the royal family—King Marnaigne, Queen Aurélie, Princess Bellatrice, and Crown Prince Leopold—in our workaday lives. Fists were occasionally shaken as farmers railed against some new edict or unjust taxation called down from on high by "that man," but for the most part, we went about our business giving very little consideration to the crowned elite who made the sprawling palace in Châtellerault their home.

But every few years, as the last vestiges of winter tipped to spring, the royal family went on progress, visiting every temple and monastery in Martissienes as they prayed to the gods for good weather, healthy livestock, and an abundant harvest in the growing season to come.

Mama spent the morning tutting over the state of our clothing, our faces, and the entirety of our manners and temperaments, fretting over the poor impressions we were bound to make.

"You really think Queen Aurélie is going to give you a second glance?" Papa scoffed, sneaking a quick nip of spirits from his flask as he commanded our wagon down the winding road to the valley below. "You'll be lucky to get even a first, you daft woman."

"I'll have you know, I've held a private audience with her before," Mama began, laying into Papa with a story we all knew by heart.

When Mama had been a young woman, looking so different from now—beautiful and carefree and not yet saddled with a husband or children—she'd caught the eye of the queen—then princess—and it had been the most glorious day of her life.

The holy pilgrimage had looked different then too. The royal family had comprised the old king and queen—now both dead—Crown Prince René and his new bride, and the prince's older brother, Baudouin, the bastard. The younger royals were seen everywhere together then, sharing carriages and meals and smiles with one another as if to prove that all the swirling rumors about strife and conflict within the Marnaigne family were patently false.

Their carriage had stopped along the street where Mama had been stationed, waiting, hoping for a glimpse of the famed trio. While the king and queen visited the temples, the younger royals were meant to be handing out coins in the villages, little acts of charity prescribed by reverents of the Holy First. The princess, reaching Mama's spot in the crowd, pressed a few bits of copper into her hand, murmuring some rote blessing and wishes for a prosperous year. Then she'd said she liked Mama's hat.

Mama had never forgotten the encounter.

Papa always assured her that the princess had.

"Do you suppose you'll see her today, Mama?" Mathilde asked, raising her voice to be heard over the clatter of the wheels.

Mama didn't even bother to look into the back of the wagon, where we were squashed together like sardines in a tin. "I expect so," she responded with a regal tilt of her hat. Its velvet trim was nothing but tatters, and the swoop of plumage arcing over the brim was more air than actual feathers, but she wore it each pilgrimage, hoping the royal memory was strong. "If we ever make it there, that is," she added snippily. "By the time Joseph gets us to town, the royal family will be long gone and the snow will have begun to fly."

Papa snorted, working up his protest, but one look from Mama made him swallow it back, and he clicked instead at our beleaguered mules.

When we arrived in Rouxbouillet, the streets were already teeming with onlookers, and Mama insisted we be dropped off before Papa took the wagon to the blacksmith so that we might find the best vantage points to begin her scheme.

"Now remember," she instructed us all, hastily passing out the armful of colorful caps and bonnets she'd borrowed from our nearest neighbors. "They'll go down the streets slowly, handing out their alms. Make sure to change at least your hat as you move ahead of them."

My siblings nodded, familiar with the routine. Last pilgrimage, Didier had managed to get coins from Bellatrice, her aunt, and her nursemaid, by changing vests, hats, and even his gait, staggering toward the tiny princess with a painful-looking limp.

I'd never brought home a coin. I'd been five during the king's last holy progress and had been so scared of being trampled by the throngs of people pressing about the carriages that I'd not even tried.

"Hurry now," Mama said, shooing us away like a flock of sparrows. "They're already the next side street over!"

We scattered, each choosing our own spot to await the Marnaignes' arrival.

Bertie grabbed my hand and tugged me toward an apothecary shop farther up the road, saying he was certain one of the family would stop there.

"Why are you so sure?" I asked, feeling disagreeable. The streets were packed, and the early-spring sun beat down with surprising vigor. I could feel my freckles doubling, tripling their count under its rays.

My brother pointed to the painted mark above the shop's door. "The Divided Ones' eyes," he intoned with as much solemnity as a nine-year-old boy could muster. "They'll want to make sure the gods see all their good works."

I peered up at the disjointed eyes. They pointed in opposite directions, as if keeping the entire square under their watchful gaze. Their unblinking stare set my flesh to shivers, even in the heat.

"I hope I can get even one coin this year," I fretted. "Mama will give me such a lashing if I come back with nothing again."

"She won't," Bertie said, as if it was a given. He'd brought home two coins last time. "Besides, it's your birthday."

I snorted. In all the haste to leave the house that morning, not a single person had stopped to wish me happy returns. "What does that have to do with anything?"

"No one can be mad at someone on their birthday," he reasoned blithely. "Yesterday I accidentally knocked over the last of the milk." He shrugged. "Nothing happened. It was my birthday."

"Of course something happened, you great idiot," I muttered, straining my neck to peer down the street as a wave of cheering grew.

A spangled carriage was turning the corner, sparkling in the midday sun. "I went without milk!"

"Did you?"

I could hear the surprise in his voice. Had he really not noticed? His obliviousness pinched at me.

Mama and Papa often told my brothers and sisters the story of my godfather and the terrible fix he'd put them all in. My siblings were never bothered when dinner was a portion short and I went without. They didn't tighten ranks to make space for me in their beds. It was all right if my hand-me-downs were too long, too big, and worn to the point of falling apart. I wasn't supposed to have stayed with them for as long as I had, so how could I possibly ask for anything more?

The carriage fully rounded the corner, a dazzling show of gilded wheels and stately black satin cushions. The family sigil, a charging bull, was emblazoned in sharp relief across the horses' ceremonial bridles, giving the midnight-colored stallions the odd appearance of having two faces. Chips of rubies winked in the bulls' eyes, and I marveled that a single horse could be adorned with furnishings costlier than my family would see in our lives.

"Should we head up that way, to get closer?" I asked, fretting. I picked at a hangnail, anxious. Both Mama and Papa were in such foul moods this morning; I could not afford to fail this year.

Bertie shook his head. "They're going to stop here," he insisted. "I can feel it. The eyes are too big to be ignored."

Sure enough, the carriage continued past the crowds at the beginning of the street, its passengers rolling by with a series of tired waves and half-formed smiles. Rouxbouillet was one of their final stops of the pilgrimage. I couldn't begin to imagine how exhausted they all must be.

"It's the prince and princess!" I exclaimed, spotting the two smaller figures pressed to the windows. "And the queen?"

Bertie shook his head. "A governess, or great-aunt, or someone, I reckon. The queen goes with the king to the temples. They have to be sure to make nice with all the priests and prophets and whoever." He waved his hand with a roll of his eyes, as if he couldn't be bothered to keep all of the religions' hierarchies in order.

My family wasn't particularly devoted to any of the Exalted. Time was money, according to my mother, and she said we had little enough of either to squander in a temple four times a week. She did drag us into town for the festivals and feast days, though, never wanting to miss the opportunity for a free meal or monetary blessing.

"Look at that!" Bertie went on, pointing at the carriage as it slowed to a halt in front of us. "I told you!"

Once the horses had settled into comfortable stances, the footman hurried down from his perch and opened the coach's door.

The older woman stepped out first and made broad sweeping gestures with her hands, driving back the clamoring throng as she tried to make space enough for the royal children to emerge. Heavy bracelets clustered with onyx gems clacked around her wrist, and her flaxen dress was as bright as the noon sun. This was no governess.

"Come on, then," she said to the pair still inside, and after the sounds of a quick squabble, Princess Bellatrice came out.

I'd never seen her this close before and was surprised to find she was so young, probably eleven or twelve, like my sisters Jeanne and Annette. She wore an enormous hoop skirt and jacket in the pale green of new celery shoots. It was edged in swags of pink rosettes and dozens of yards of chiffon ribbon. Her hair was jet-black and left long and loose, a shimmering curtain reaching down her back.

She gave the crowds a worried glance before opening her bag

of coins and was instantly swarmed by a dozen children and some adults, all reaching out their hands, ostensibly for a blessing, though everyone knew it was the coins we'd gathered for.

"Leopold!" the older woman hissed, rapping her knuckles against the coach's side.

The prince slunk out with his jacket unbuttoned and askew, heaving the most forlorn sigh I'd ever heard. His suit was made to look just like one of a highly decorated military captain, with a sash, fringed epaulettes, embroidered bands, and more medals than he could possibly hope to be awarded in this life or the next. His hair was lighter than his sister's, a burnished gold, and his blue eyes gazed over the assembled without interest.

"I don't want that," he said, chiding the older woman as she tried to hand him a black velvet bag.

"Leopold," she snapped, her voice dark with warning.

"I don't want that," he said flatly. "You're fifth in line, Aunt Manon. You can't *make* me do that."

Crown Prince or not, the boy found himself yanked to the side with a force so sudden, I winced in knowing commiseration. I couldn't hear exactly how his aunt berated him, but when she loosened her grip, he buttoned his suit jacket and begrudgingly began giving out coins.

"Remember," Bertie instructed as he led me closer. "You don't want to catch their eye. Don't give them reason to recognize you at their next stop."

I nodded determinedly.

This was it: I would get a coin of my own.

I could already imagine presenting Mama with it—no, not it but *them,* multiples, a whole handful, so many they'd tumble from her grasp, spilling to the ground with a cacophony of merry jingles.

Bertie approached Bellatrice first, holding out his hands in a subservient scoop, keeping his eyes downcast and appropriately humble.

"I wish such blessings and such joys upon you," the princess intoned, giving away a single copper. Her hands were covered in lace gloves the same shade of pink as the trim of her dress, and I wondered if she wore them as a stylish accessory or as a precautionary guard against accidentally touching any of us gathered around her.

"Good blessing to you, milady," Bertie mumbled, then bumped me forward.

"I wish such blessings and such joys upon you," she repeated, already sounding entirely bored with her sacred endeavors. Though she faced me, she fixed her green eyes on a space somewhere over my left shoulder, unwilling to meet my gaze. Then she reached into the reticule—the same green satin as her skirts—and removed another coin. I wanted to crow as she dropped it into my cupped hands. It was not a twin to Bertie's copper. Mine was silver and weighed more than any money I'd ever had cause to handle before.

"Bertie!" I squealed with excitement before remembering my manners. "Thank you, Princess. Many blessings to you."

She'd already moved on to the next person, reciting her platitude, her eyes never quite meeting theirs either.

Bertie elbowed me in the ribs. "There's the prince," he whispered, nodding to the right. "Let's try him and then head down the street."

"But we haven't changed yet," I worried.

"None of them are even looking at us. He'll never know."

"But—"

My protest was silenced as Bertie pushed me toward the queue forming before Prince Leopold.

He wasn't much older than me, I realized.

Though the suit fit him well, undoubtedly tailor-made to his exact measurements, he moved oddly within it, as if he were deeply uncomfortable. It was strange to see a boy so stilted, so encumbered, and I had a sudden vision of him running free in a field, playing pétanque or jeu de la barbichette. In my imagination, Leopold was not dressed as a prince but wore simpler clothes and had the most enormous smile stretched over his face. And when he laughed—

"You've already been to my sister," he snapped, jarring me from the daydream as quickly as a dunk in the ice-cold bucket of water Mama had forced upon us earlier that morning.

"I . . . What?" I fumbled, acutely feeling the uncertainty of my position.

"You were just with my sister. She gave you a silver coin, if I'm not mistaken. And now you've come to me, wanting more."

I could feel the weight of everyone around us staring at me.

I licked my lips, struggling to come up with a coherent thought, one explanation that would get me out of this mess and let me escape unscathed.

"I—well. No. Well," I stammered at last.

My cheeks burned.

"Do you think me a fool?" he went on, taking a step closer. The gathered crowd shuffled back, suddenly eager to be away from this indignant Marnaigne, however small he might be. Even Bertie seemed to have deserted me. I could no longer sense him at my back and had never felt so thoroughly and miserably on my own.

"No! No, of course not, Leopold." Sharp breaths were drawn at my mistake. "Your Majesty. Your Highness? Sir." Oh, what was the title I was supposed to use?

He narrowed his eyes. "What do you need all these coins for, anyway? It doesn't cost much money to look as poor as you."

His voice held such a lofty, imperious lilt that fiery prickles of anger licked up my spine.

"What do *you* need them for?" I threw back before I could think better of it. "You live in grand palaces and are fed and clothed with the very best of everything. We don't have even a fraction of what you've been blessed with. But your father asks more and more from us, taxing and taking and never giving back until he feels like the gods are watching, and then you come and offer out a single coin?"

Leopold's mouth fell open. He looked at a loss for words, a sensation I guessed he was unfamiliar with. The moment drew out long, and as the silence grew, so too did the crowd's expectation for an answer. Two dots of hot red stained his cheeks.

Finally, he reached into his bag and withdrew a whole fistful of money. "You want coins?" he asked, all but snarling as he held them out. "Here's one for every freckle on your face!"

Leopold threw the money at me, and it was as if he'd tossed a match upon piles of dry kindling. Everyone leapt forward, eager to retrieve the coins, which had fallen to the cobblestones and were now rolling down the street.

I was pushed to the side by an older boy twice both my age and size, and I tumbled to the ground. I tried to stop the fall but only scraped the palms of my hands raw. Someone stepped on my foot and I had to roll out of the way to avoid being trampled.

Palace guards, hidden somewhere along the procession route, raced forward and swept all three of the Marnaignes back into the coach. The driver cracked the whip, urging the stallions into motion, but there were too many people swarming the carriage. One horse reared on its hind legs, screaming a whinny into the sky.

"Get them out of the way!" the driver shouted at the guards.

They began tossing people to the side without care, acting as if we were nothing more than obstacles to be removed. I saw an older woman fall on the cobblestones and grab her hip, howling. The royal coach raced by her without bothering to stop.

Good blessings and joys indeed.

I felt my shoulders dip; I was disappointed to not have gotten in a final volley of words with the prince. They burned at the back of my mouth, wanting to be spat out at someone in excoriating fury. I swallowed the words down but could feel their heat all the way to my belly. I wondered if they would always remain there, forever unsaid, left to fester and grow.

Somehow, Bertie found me in the madness and helped me to my feet. He all but dragged me into an alleyway. "Are you all right?"

I could feel blood trickling down my leg and knew my stockings, my best pair, had been torn in the fall. In truth, they were now made more of darning than actual knit wool, but they were soft and sagged only a bit in the knees and were the prettiest shade of dove-gray. I thought they'd been pink once, when Annette had first worn them, but I loved them still. And now they were in shreds.

Even worse, my silver coin was gone, somehow snatched in the chaos.

Mama was going to be so mad.

"Why did you make me talk to him?" I wailed, fighting the urge to smack my older brother. "We were supposed to change hats. He wasn't supposed to recognize me! Mama is going to give me such a beating!"

"I'll tell her it was my fault," he offered.

"It *was*!" I said, swatting at his ridiculous magnanimous gesture.

We walked up the next street, listening for the royal coach even though it would have been impossible to beg for blessings now. I kept my eyes on the ground, hoping against all hope that I might find a coin caught between cobblestones, abandoned and forgotten.

Shadows began to grow long and turn as purple as a bruise.

"Bertie! Hazel! Where are you?" We both turned to see Etienne jogging down the street.

"Mama says you're to come back now!"

I bit my lip, wondering if she'd already heard what had happened. "Is she . . . is she upset?"

Etienne just shrugged.

"Where are they?" Bertie asked, patting his pocket, reassuring himself of the copper's presence. Of course he still had his coin.

"Papa has the wagon ready, the next street over. They said we're needed at the temple."

"The temple?" Bertie groaned. "Can't we go to the tavern? I got a copper. We could have a meat pie!"

"Mama says we can't dawdle. The temple is expecting us."

My breath caught, and all the day's previous troubles vanished in an instant. "Which temple?" I managed to squeak out.

"Don't know. Not the First's. We were just there. The queen went right by Mama. Didn't even glance her way!" Etienne laughed, unaware of the revelation erupting in my chest.

Bertie's eyes, so surprised and blue, met mine, and I felt pinned in place.

I could tell he'd jumped to the same thought I had, the one making my blood race and my heart pound so heavily I could see my pulse in the corner of my eyes. I was suddenly clammy, damp with fevered chills, and my throat seemed too dry to swallow properly.

"Do you think he finally . . . ?"

"Maybe," I hedged. I didn't need him to finish the thought to know exactly what he meant. *Who* he meant.

My godfather.

"It *is* your birthday," Bertie said, and I was touched to hear the trace of sadness in his voice.

I felt stuck in place. I'd spent so much time dreaming of the day my godfather would return that I'd never stopped to consider what would happen the day *after* he did.

Or the day after that.

Where would he take me? Where would I live?

The temple in Rouxbouillet was his in name only. It was a small courtyard with a solitary monolith that no one had ever taken credit for sculpting. A candle, somehow forever burning, rested in front of the plinth. There was no building, no other structure. It was no place to raise a child, to raise me. As far as I knew, he didn't have even a single postulant. No one, it seemed, wanted to devote their life to the lord of death.

"Mama's going to spit flames if we're late. Come on!" Etienne snapped before turning down the street.

"Come on," Bertie echoed, gentler, and offered his hand to me.

I didn't want to take it.

If I took it, then we'd find Mama, and go to his temple, and he was sure to be there, waiting for me.

My godfather.

In the Holy First's sanctum, there were stained-glass windows on three sides of the hall. At the front, just behind the altar, perfectly situated toward the east to best catch the morning sunlight, was a rendering of the Holy First in all her lustrous beauty. Swirls of iridescent glass were pieced together to make up her veiled but undoubtedly radiant face, her long wavy tresses, and her flowing gown.

To her right were the Divided Ones. Thick leading segmented their face so you could easily tell that though they shared one body, they were made up of many.

And to the left was the Dreaded End. His window was less a portrait and more a mosaic, suggesting at a hint of a being, not a perfectly rendered form. It was made up of various triangles, all in dark grays and rich plums. The glass had been so heavily stained with those bruise-colored dyes that light could barely pass through it. Even on the sunniest of days, the Dreaded End's window was a mottled mess of gloom and gloam.

So when I tried to picture him . . . the Dreaded End, my godfather . . . when I tried to picture *that,* I couldn't do it.

I couldn't see him there, a figure, a being, a person. I could see the window, the dark hues, the swirling mess of fog and mist and grim finality.

I only could see the death, not my life.

"Come on." Bertie beckoned again, jangling the hand in front of me as though the only reason I'd not yet taken it was simply because I hadn't noticed its presence. "If we're really meeting him, if he's really come back, than Mama won't even mind the tear." He beamed at this stroke of unbelievably good fortune. "See? Everything is working out."

Without warning, I threw my arms around Bertie's neck, pulling him against me with a strength that surprised us both. "I'm going to miss you the most," I whispered. I could feel my body trembling as he hugged me back.

"I'm sure he'll let you visit," he said softly. "And I'll write to you every week, I swear it."

"You hate writing," I reminded him. The tears that fell down my cheeks splashed hot and wet.

"I'll learn to like it, just for you," he swore fervently.

My hand found his then. I seized hold of it and clutched him tightly all the way back to the wagon.

But it wasn't my godfather's temple we were headed to.

CHAPTER 3

"I NEED YOU TO LINE UP NOW, PLEASE, ALL OF YOU," THE reverent said with a voice so soft that you nearly missed the hard edge lying in wait. Beneath the sweep of her wide headdress—studded with five jagged peaks, each holding a swag of tulle—cool blue eyes regarded us with measured curiosity.

My family was outside the temple of the Divided Ones, in the courtyard, and my brothers and sisters wandered about the space, gaping at the stone walls, the mosaics, and the great urns that dotted the perimeter. Each of the vases had been smashed apart only to be soldered back together. Everything felt fractured, yet whole, just like the gods it represented, and I found that the angry, jagged lines made my head ache.

"Sister Ines will not ask again," snapped a young girl beside the reverent. She wore the yellow and green robe of a novice, and though she didn't look any older than Bertie, there was a hardening around her edges, a child forced into adulthood at far too young an age. Her brown eyes regarded us with open disdain. "Do as she says!"

We hurried to comply, and I fell into place at the end of my siblings' line, brushing shoulders with Bertie as we exchanged glances in confused silence.

"Maybe she'll be the one to take you to him?" Bertie whispered from the side of his mouth.

I shook my head. A reverent from one god would not carry out errands for another. My godfather had let another year pass without collecting me, I knew it in my heart.

Mama and Papa offered no answers. They stood in front of the wagon, watching the proceedings as though audience members at a theater. The action onstage—taking place out here in the courtyard—had nothing to do with them. They were separated from us by an invisible fourth wall, content to observe everything from their place beyond the proscenium.

Sister Ines stepped forward to inspect us. The younger girl followed her, making tutting sounds of disapproval, *tsk*ing over the state of Jeanne's boots and chiding Yves for the curve of his posture.

Only when the revenant approached me did Mama step forward. "Actually—"

She stopped short as the sister raised her hand, indicating that she did not wish to be interrupted. A look of irritation clouded Mama's face, but to her credit, she held her tongue.

"Look at me, please?" the sister ordered me, snatching away my attention from my mother.

I felt like a hare caught in one of Remy's traps, frozen with fear, my heart hammering so fast I was certain its pounding was visible in my chest.

"She has potential," Sister Ines murmured to herself, and I wanted to squirm. What did she see in me that marked me as different from my siblings?

"She doesn't look all that special to me," the younger girl snapped, then scowled at me as she was given a sharp look from the sister.

Sister Ines looked down our line once more, counting and nodding. "A thirteenth child. You don't see many of those."

Mama dared to step forward, laughing, though nothing seemed particularly funny. "Just another mouth to feed. So, so many mouths to feed. Her father and I should have stopped after ten. Well . . . three, even . . . one, truly."

My siblings squirmed.

"We can't be all *that* rare," said the girl, frowning as she breezed past my mother's nervous admission, and I caught her use of the word *we*. Was this why she so disliked me? Was she another thirteenth child?

"What's your name, girl?"

My throat was too thick for me to answer Ines, and I was ashamed to feel my lower lip quiver.

"That's Hazel," Bertie said, daring to take a step forward.

Sister Ines's blue gaze fell on Bertie once more. "Thank you." She turned back to Mama. Her fine robes were stiff with starch and their folds hung from her back like the wings of a moth. "Hazel will do," she declared.

"That's impossible," Mama began.

"Nothing is impossible for They who demand it so," the sister said, her eyes narrowing. There was a strange quality to her voice now that made it seem as if she was speaking in two pitches at the same time.

Stories were whispered throughout Rouxbouillet about those who chose to leave their lives behind to follow the Divided Ones. Some said the followers trained for days and weeks on end, singing the same holy songs over and over as they attempted to hit two notes at once. Others said this disconcerting talent was due to arcane rituals and surgeries most severe. Everyone agreed that the Divided Ones' revenants all went a little mad, breaking their minds into as many pieces as there were gods to serve.

"Well?" Sister Ines asked, both her voices reverberating with impatience.

Papa cleared his throat, looking uneasy. He crossed the courtyard and whispered into her ear. Though I couldn't hear exactly what he said, I did register the moment she understood his tale. Her eyes darted from Papa to me with alarm. Disgust settled over her features like a fine veil.

"I see," she said archly, taking a noticeable step from my father.

"Get out of line, Hazel," Mama snapped. "You shouldn't even be here."

Though I knew she meant *here* as *now,* in this moment, her words sliced deep. I shouldn't have been here—in this family—now or ever.

"What's happening?" I dared to whisper. It was unnerving to be on this side of the courtyard, seeing all my brothers and sisters staring at me. I kept a careful distance from Mama. She tended to speak with her hands when agitated, and since my presence so often went unregistered, I'd learned it was best to stay out of striking distance.

"Your father has accumulated a bit of debt in town, the idiot," she muttered. Her teeth were pressed so tightly together I feared she'd turn them to powder. "More than any pilgrimage coins could cover. So we need to find payment where we might."

"Payment," I echoed, my brow furrowing. I swept my eyes around the courtyard, trying to imagine what we were meant to be selling in the temple. We'd left all our bundles of firewood and tanned hides at home.

Bertie's eyes landed on me, silently asking what I'd learned.

I gasped as understanding dawned on me. "No. You can't!"

Mama's nostrils flared. "I shouldn't have to," she corrected me bitterly. "But you're still here, taking up space and money that we can't afford *not* to give you. So now, one of my children—one of my *real* children," she snuck in, her snide addition as sharp as a dagger, "will be torn from their home. One of my children will be gone, forced to worship a god I hate. A god I should have given you to long ago."

"You can't," I repeated, feeling small and stupid and unable to come up with a better argument. "You just can't."

Mama grabbed the collar of my dress and yanked me closer. Her spittle wet my lips, and I cringed from the sudden force of her fury. "You'd be surprised just what I can do for a handful of coins. Never forget that, little Hazel. Never!"

"I do believe we're done here," Sister Ines said, speaking as loudly as her twin voices would carry. "Here's your silver." She handed Papa a small purse of yellow and green twill.

He weighed it in the palm of his hand, hefting it up and down as if that was all it took to count it, then nodded. "Which one?" he dared to ask, and every muscle within me tensed.

The sister sighed, as if her selection had already disappointed her. "The boy," she said, and nodded to the two men standing at the temple's entrance.

They stepped forward and hoisted Bertie from the end of the line as he kicked and squirmed.

"No!" I shrieked, and tumbled toward them, but the men were too big and too efficient, and by the time I'd raced across the courtyard, Bertie had already been taken inside. Before the door slammed shut, I saw the younger girl, the novice, clamp a set of bronze shackles around his skinny wrists, and he screamed.

CHAPTER 4

The Twelfth Birthday

"ANOTHER YEAR, ANOTHER YEAR," MY MOTHER SANG off-key as she picked her way through the barn. Her gait was unsteady; I could tell she was already in her cups, even at this early hour. "Another year . . . and you're still here."

The irony of her words, a cruel mimicry of the usually cheerful birthday song, was not lost on me. My middle ached as I remembered the last time anyone had wished me a happy birthday.

Bertie.

It had been four years—*four years to the day,* I reminded myself—since we'd seen him.

All novices—especially those conscripted away from their homes most unwillingly—were sent off to their god's monastery for their first few years of service. We'd heard that Bertie had been forced to take a vow of silence for an entire twelve months, to better prepare his mind and spirit for his new life of devotion, but as no contact with the outside world was allowed, we never knew if that was the truth or only rumor.

"Where are you?" Mama mumbled, prowling through the stalls. I could smell her even before she rounded the corner, the stink of rye heavy on her breath and clothes. It even seemed to waft from her pores these days.

I poked my head out from the stall I occupied. I'd been up since before dawn, milking the cows, milking the goats, mucking out their soiled stalls and laying fresh hay from the bales I'd hauled down from the loft myself.

Since Bertie had been taken away—taken away screaming and crying, his face full of tears and snots and *stop thinking of that, Hazel*—five of my other siblings had left home too: Genevieve, Armand, Emmeline, Josephine, and Didier, gone in quick succession.

Genevieve, the oldest and loveliest of all us girls, had had her pick of marriage proposals. She'd taken up the butcher's son's offer and occasionally sent us a side of pork fat with a note saying she'd visit soon. She never did.

Armand left the day he turned seventeen, lying about his age so he might enlist in the army.

Emmeline and Josephine followed, finding a pair of twin brothers two towns over. They were cobblers and made the most beautiful court heels for my sisters to wear at their double wedding.

And Didier . . . Didier disappeared one day, without warning or note, and though the surrounding woods were searched, not a trace of him was ever found.

Though in his twenty-fourth year, Remy was still at home, often taking over on days when Papa had made himself too sick on spirits to shoot his bow and arrows. Remy was a dedicated hunter, often going out as the sun rose and not returning until nightfall, but all the earnestness in the world could not make up for his poor eyesight and terrible aim.

Though Papa bemoaned it, Mama still sent my remaining siblings to the schoolhouse in Rouxbouillet. Not because she believed they would do anything with their educations, but because it was free, and how many things in the world could you say that about?

Free or not, school was off-limits for me.

Mama claimed it was because we never knew when my godfather might finally return, but I knew she needed help with all the chores she didn't care to take on and Papa was too drunk to do.

I didn't mind much. The barn was quiet and the animals were kind.

Since that day with Bertie, the relationships I'd once enjoyed with my brothers and sisters had soured, growing strained and sometimes downright hostile. I alone—not Papa, or his debts—was blamed for Bertie's conscription. I was the one regarded with wary suspicion, as if they were fearful of what proximity to me might bring next.

Their turning stung, but it also made what I knew was coming that much easier.

In one year's time, I was going to leave Rouxbouillet.

I would be thirteen by then.

Some might think it too young to be out on your own, making your way in the world, but I was no stranger to hard work or independence. I spent most of my days alone. Once chores were done, I'd roam the forest, hunting for mushrooms and flowers.

There was an old woman I'd come across a year before, who lived even deeper in the Gravia then we did. She was said to be a miracle worker, always knowing the exact remedies needed to cure anything from a bad cold to infertility. She could even mend things that weren't of a physiological nature, like old feuds and broken hearts.

Papa called her a witch and forbade any of us to venture past the rushing stream that divided our land from hers. But I'd stumbled across her one day while out foraging in the brambles for late-summer berries. She had slipped on a moss-covered rock while trying to pick her way across a creek, and had twisted her ankle too badly to return home on her own. I'd helped her up and, using every bit of my strength, all but carried her back to her cottage, her long, wispy white braid batting me in the face as I acted as her crutch.

She'd chatted away the whole trip home, pointing out various plants, sharing what secret medicinal powers they possessed and how best to harvest them. Her name was Celeste Alarie, and she'd lived in the Gravia her entire life. Her grandmother had been born in that cottage, as had her mother, as had she, and she assured me she intended to die there as well.

Once Celeste had plunked into her rocking chair, despairing over the state of her ankle, she'd let it slip that she had been gathering supplies for a love spell, commissioned by the mayor's wife for their oldest daughter. Celeste had fretted over how she would harvest the flowers needed, and when I'd offered to do it for her, she'd brightened and promised to pay me three copper coins if I did a good job.

From then on, I visited her every fortnight, performing more of her errands throughout the forest. She praised my ability to scramble up rocks and trees no longer accessible to her and said what a fine miracle woman I'd one day make myself. I had the uncanny ability to spot even the most camouflaged of treasures hidden on the forest floor.

I'd been saving up every coin she gave me and by next year would have enough to buy myself passage out of Rouxbouillet, out of the Gravia, out of even Martissienes itself.

I couldn't remain at home, forever waiting for a godfather who would not come.

I was done waiting.

I needed action.

I needed purpose.

I just needed a few more coppers. . . .

"There you are," Mama said, spotting me in the last stall. She was slurring and looked as though she might tip over. "What . . . what are you even doing back here?"

"Milking Rosie," I said, gesturing to the bucket at my feet.

Mama squinted. I'd filled the pail nearly to the top, and her lips twisted as though she was disappointed to have nothing to chastise me for.

"It's your birthday," she said, surprising me. Without Bertie's to celebrate, I hadn't been sure she bothered to keep track of mine.

I nodded, unsure of the right way to respond.

"I remember that day like it was only hours ago," she murmured, and her eyes drifted, gazing at something above me with a dreamy unfocused distraction. "You were so little. You're still so little," she fretted, rubbing her thumb over the lip of the liquor bottle she held. "And he . . . he was so very big. But when he held you . . ." She trailed off for a moment, lost in the daydream. She didn't have to say my godfather's name aloud. Papa had never held me, not even once. "You looked as though you belonged together. With him."

She took a long swig. The liquor smelled astringent, burning my nostrils, and I didn't see how she could bear to drink it.

"I never could understand why he left you behind."

"I . . . I'm sorry," I said. It was the first time I'd ever dared to imagine how the situation must have looked from her side, the first time I ever felt the injustice she had lived with every day since my arrival. She'd been promised I'd be taken care of. She'd been promised she'd never have to deal with me.

But here I was, twelve years later.

"Oh, my head," she muttered, wincing suddenly.

I pressed my lips together, feeling an odd sense of tenderness toward my mother, toward this woman who had been dealt an unfair hand so many times throughout her life. "I saw some feverfew edging the garden. Their leaves can help with aches, however strong. I could make you a tea," I offered, then bit the inside of my cheek, worried she'd ask how I knew this information.

But she only blinked, swaying unsteadily. "That would be very kind, Hazel."

I knew this softness would not last. It was the drink talking, not her. But maybe if I tried, maybe if I tried so hard, it could linger for a little while longer.

"I ought . . ." She paused, rubbing the back of her hand over her forehead. "I ought to make you a cake this year. I don't think I . . ." She wavered, and her eyes seemed to cross for a moment. She blinked heavily, trying to focus on me, but her pupils couldn't find the right spot. She kept looking just off to my left, as though she was seeing double. "I don't think I've ever made you a cake before. Not one of your own," she corrected herself.

"It's okay, Mama," I said, forgiving her in an instant as she cupped my cheek, showering me with more affection in this single beat than in every other moment of my life combined.

"Another year, another year, another year has come," she sang softly, and a happy warmth radiated through me at this abrupt change in her demeanor. I didn't know what had brought about this shift, didn't understand it, but I couldn't stop to wonder on it now.

My mind raced with a dozen dreams for the future. I pictured us walking back to the house together, hand in hand. I'd brew a pot of the feverfew tea as she made a cake, and after dinner, she'd tell me not to go back to the barn. She'd say I should sleep inside the house with the rest of the family, in a bed of my own, and she would tuck me in, drawing my velvet quilt up to my chin before bending down to give me a loving kiss on the cheek, and I would fall asleep basking in the warmth of her love.

People made mistakes. It happened every day.

But Mama had finally come around, finally saw me as her daughter, as a child to be fondly thought of, a child who was all hers, her flesh, her blood.

"You are one year older now," she continued. Her crooning wasn't quite on pitch, her tempo just shy of right.

"So shout 'Hooray,' " a voice said from the threshold of the stall, taking over the song. We both startled and turned to stare at the dark, towering figure of my godfather. "You're done."

CHAPTER 5

THE MOMENT THAT FOLLOWED SEEMED AN ETERNITY.

I knew I was staring, knew my mouth was open, hanging agape, knew I needed to say something—a salutation, a greeting, *anything*—but I found it impossible to form words. His presence—he *was* tall; Mama had never said just how tall he was—filled me with both wonder and absolute dread.

The stained-glass window at the village temple was wrong, all wrong. He was not a dark shadow, a smattering of grays and purples, navy and ebony. He was as black as a moonless sky, a void completely absent of light.

He cast no shadow, I noted, staring at the ground behind him where my lantern should have thrown even some soft pattern of gray.

He *was* the shadow. He was all shadows, every dark thought, every bleak moment. He was god of departures and the departed, lord of endings and the grave.

He was the Dreaded End.

My benefactor.

My savior, I supposed.

"Godfather," I said, finding my voice and dipping into a curtsy that felt patently ridiculous but also somehow right. If you were supposed to show deference to King Marnaigne—a mere mortal with a funny hat—you should do at least that for a god.

I paused before rising.

Should I have bowed?

I should have bowed.

I should have knelt down and humbled my skinny form prostrate before his robes of midnight, pressing my forehead to the ground, pressing my entire body to the ground, into the ground, a worm at his feet.

An errant thought crossed my mind and I wondered what type of shoes the Dreaded End wore. Sandals, maybe? Boots for stomping to dust the souls of people who dared to think such irreverent thoughts in the face of his unholy magnitude?

I was struck with the terrible urge to laugh and clapped my hands over my mouth lest a giggle slip out and damn us all.

"Hazel," he greeted me, and the corners of his mouth rose, his lips pulling back to reveal a line of sharp, pointed teeth.

Was he . . . was that a smile?

"Happy birthday," he continued. "I . . . I brought you a gift." He drew back a corner of his cloak, but it was as if the dark fabric swallowed every bit of the lantern's light. I couldn't see anything tucked away in such shadowy depths.

"Perhaps we should go outside?" he suggested, and I was surprised to hear his tone quaver.

Was he nervous? This great, hulking, all-powerful *god*? Nervous? Before me?

I wanted to laugh. Again.

Who was I?

A no one.

A nobody.

And yet I couldn't deny what I'd heard. He was uncertain. He had offered a question, not a command.

The Dreaded End swayed back and forth on feet restless with apprehension.

What was he worried about? Did he believe I would say no? Did he truly think it in me to disagree with a god?

"Yes, Godfather," I said, and waited for him to turn. For all the newfound bravado coursing through my veins, I didn't think I could be the one to make the first move, the one to walk past him, brushing too near his cloak, too close to his strangely elongated form.

He seemed to pick up on my reticence and backed out of the stall. He filled the narrow hall, blocking every sunbeam cast through the barn door, a literal eclipse.

It was only then that I remembered Mama.

She'd gone terribly pale, the sickly yellowish color of goat's milk, and there was a damp sheen coating her forehead.

"Are you all right, Mama?" I asked, feeling indecision tear at me. My body wanted to approach her, feel her temple, make sure she was all right—she looked so *not* all right—but my feet shifted toward the stall door.

"I . . ." Her cheeks puffed as if she was about to throw up, and I wondered just how much liquor she'd already had.

"Hazel?"

The uncertainty filling his one word spurred me into action.

"Come on, Mama," I said, and slipped out of the stall, out of the barn, after the Dreaded End.

He waited for me in the yard, an incongruous smear of black against the white linens dancing from the clothesline as they dried in the early-spring breeze. The robes made it nearly impossible to be certain, but I had the distinct impression his shoulders were hunched tightly against his frame, as if he was expecting to receive some sort of harsh words from me, or even a physical blow. After a moment of pained silence between us, his eyes—red and silver and so very strange—brightened as he remembered there was something he could do.

"Your gift," he said, as if he were reminding himself as much as me. He reached into his cloak and removed a beautiful box. It was tufted with velvet and was the loveliest shade of lilac I'd ever seen, like mist rising over the lavender fields on a moody morning, when the earth was finally warm and the air smelled sweet and new.

"I . . . I wasn't quite sure what you'd like," he apologized, stumbling over the words. "But I imagined you wouldn't have anything like this."

A cry escaped me as I opened the tiny box and the sun hit the treasure nestled within.

"It's a necklace," he explained unnecessarily. "Gold. It's probably a touch extravagant for a girl of ten, but—"

"Twelve," I corrected him thoughtlessly, trailing one fingertip over the thin chain. It was finer craftsmanship than anything I'd ever seen my mother or sisters wear, each link sparkling. A small stone hung from its middle, caught in a net of gold and winking brightly, neither green nor yellow.

"It reminded me of your eyes," he said, his voice rounding out with fondness. "Everyone always says babies have blue eyes, but when you first looked at me . . ."

He trailed off, clearing his throat, and I could hear Mama finally making her way out from the barn.

"What is it, Hazel?" she asked, tottering unsteadily.

"A necklace," I said, turning to show her the box.

She swiped the present away from me, raking one of her fingernails across the back of my hand. She didn't notice my wince of pain. "You brought this for a child?" she asked, and her eyes were sharp and hard as she looked up at my godfather.

"Not just any child," he said, the corners of his lips turning downward as he took it from her. He lifted it up and fastened it round my neck. "My child."

"Yours," she repeated, and there was something about her tone that charged the air around them, electrifying the space between us. It was as distinctly felt as an approaching summer storm. The oppressive might of it rolled over me, a weighty foreboding.

My godfather didn't reply but studied my mother with fresh interest. There was a slight tilt to his head that reminded me a little of Bertie, when we would roam the river basin, searching for berries. He'd spot a sleek green lizard or a little snake winding its way through the brush and stop everything he was doing to watch it, his eyes wide with curiosity, seeking to understand how this tiny creature functioned.

That was how my godfather looked at Mama, as if she were a little tiny something that would normally carry out its life beyond the notice of someone such as him but that he found fascinating now that he had stopped to take note.

Such rapt focus made my insides quiver like a bow screeching over the strings of a violin. It felt decidedly wrong to have the full weight of a god's attention on me.

"Mine," he finally said, his agreement given most begrudgingly.

"If that's so, where have you been all this time? All these years? You were meant to collect her when she was a babe. You were here on the day she was born, and then you just . . ." Mama made a gesture of something flittering away, nearly losing hold of her bottle.

My heart beat heavily in the hollow of my throat. Her audacity shocked me, but I found myself hoping he would answer her. These were the same questions that had filled my thoughts for years—when would he come again, why had he ever left me behind at all.

"I've returned," he said, offering no further explanation.

Mama made a noise of disgusted dismissal. "What good does that do us now? She's nearly grown. We raised her in your stead. We cared for her, clothed her, fed her. All the things you promised you would do. All the things you swore you'd pay for."

I winced.

She sounded so hard, so full of condemnation. It didn't seem as though she was speaking to a god at all, more like she was chastising the village butcher over a bad cut of meat.

I expected his anger to rise, for lightning and thunder to strike us down, for the earth to tremble and part beneath our feet and swallow us whole.

But none of those things happened. Instead, my godfather nodded carefully, consideringly.

"I suppose you did, Madame. What would you estimate all your care and effort to be worth?"

Mama frowned skeptically. "What?"

"How much money do you suppose Hazel has cost you over the years? That's what you desire, is it not? A reimbursement? A settling of the books? Go on. Name your price. What has Hazel's first ten—twelve"—he corrected himself, his silvery red eyes darting toward mine—"years cost you?"

Mama's eyes drifted across the yard toward the house, oddly unfocused. "I . . . I couldn't begin to—"

"What do you think is a fair price, Hazel?" my godfather asked, turning toward me.

My mouth dried as terror spiked up my throat. My chest felt as though it would split in two. Where did my allegiance lie? With the mother who had raised me, most begrudgingly, or with the godfather who claimed to care but had only just arrived? "I . . . I don't know." I looked helplessly toward my mother, but she didn't notice.

"Would five gold coins be enough?" he asked, his attention whipping back to Mama. "A year? Five gold coins for each year of care? That makes sixty. Do you believe that enough, Madame?"

"Sixty gold coins?" Mama repeated, her eyes suddenly growing sharp. She sucked in a breath of air and it whistled through the crooked gap between her front teeth. "Do you mean it? Truly?"

The Dreaded End snapped his fingers and the coins fell out of the sky, conjured into existence midair. "As you say, I owe you. And you're right, of course. I do. So let's double it." More coins fell. "Triple, even." Another snap and the golden disks rained down, showering the ground where Mama stood. "Do you think it enough, Madame? Is this sufficient payment for the care and keeping of your own flesh and blood?"

Part of me longed for Mama to say no, to say that she'd changed her mind and no amount of money in the world was enough to ease the pain of losing her daughter.

I held my breath, wishing, waiting.

After a painful pause, she nodded.

"Good," he said, and then held out his hand to me. His fingers were too long, too long and dotted with too many joints. They bent into impossible angles, like the strangely segmented walking sticks found deep in our woods.

"Come, Hazel," he said as though we were about to go for an afternoon stroll, as if he wasn't about to take me away from my home, away from my entire life, all my knowns and certainties, however painful they could sometimes be.

I glanced back to my mother.

Surely she was going to stop this.

Surely she would protest.

She couldn't just let me leave home with a complete stranger, however venerable he might be.

"Go on, Hazel," she said instead. "You always knew this day would come."

Had I?

I'd been told of it often enough. I'd heard my parents rail and lament each year he did not come. But with every year that passed, the story grew a little less defined, less a promise and more a concept, an event that might never occur.

I turned to the Dreaded End.

"Where are we going?"

"Home."

My feet instinctively took a treacherous step toward the little cottage behind me that had never been mine. My pulse felt funny in my veins, racing in thready tempos, and I suddenly feared I could not draw breath.

"Our home," he clarified.

I looked over his broad shoulders as if I might somehow spot it behind him. "Is it far?"

"You could say that," he said, his tone gentling. "And yet the trip won't take but a second."

His hand raised and I stepped toward him, frightened he'd snap those terrible fingers before I could stop him.

"Wait! I . . . I'll need to pack," I said, nearly shouting in my haste.

His gaze drifted—not to the house behind me, but to the barn. He knew my possessions were there. He knew that was where I slept. Shame burned hot.

"Anything you require can be replaced once we're away," he said, offering his hand once more.

Away.

The word scared me in ways I'd never known before.

I'd never been away. Not anywhere farther than the village market. Not anywhere past Celeste Alarie's cottage, deep in the Gravia.

I'd spent years imagining life *away,* but faced with the very real threat of it now, I'd never felt more rooted to our little patch of land. Never felt more pulled to the tiny little cabin, never so longed for the family who alternatively ignored and despised me.

"My quilt," I said, grasping on to the flimsy excuse. I needed time, time to think, time to worry through my doubts. Black dots danced over my vision and I felt as though I might throw up. "The one you gave me. I don't . . . I don't want to leave that behind."

His fingers did snap then, and in an instant, the tattered velvet quilt was in his hands. He looked over the worn fabric, undoubtedly taking note of the tears I'd tried to mend, the stains I couldn't remove. It showed its age, showed its use. It was shabby and small, all traces of its sacred luster long gone.

My godfather traced a line of my clumsy stitching, his two-toned eyes inscrutable.

"Anything else?" he finally asked.

I could feel my control of the situation slipping away from me, like grains of sand pulled back into the sea by relentless waves.

"Can't I . . . can't I at least say goodbye?" My throat felt tight, swollen with painful burrs closing off my air supply. I couldn't draw breath, couldn't breathe. My lower lip trembled with the force of any attempt.

"Say goodbye, Hazel," he instructed, nodding toward Mama.

"And to everyone else! Papa and Remy are out hunting. Am I not allowed to say goodbye to them?"

His brow furrowed as he pondered my distress. "You'll see them again," he finally said, deciding on a way to comfort me.

"I will?"

It had never occurred to me that I would.

It had never occurred to me that I would want to.

Not really.

But now, when offered a promise to return, I felt my heart thud with bright hope, and my departure didn't seem nearly as forbidding.

My godfather smiled again, sunlight catching on those strange teeth, making them seem sharper. "I'm not spiriting you away forever." He let out a sound that was almost a laugh. "That was never part of the plan."

"The plan," I echoed. "No one has ever told me the plan."

"That changes today," he promised, and offered his elbow, as if he were a gallant gentleman at court and I a lady in a fine gown. "Shall we, then?"

I nodded, feeling suddenly happier.

I was leaving, but I would return.

"I'll see you soon, Mama," I said, tucking my arm through my godfather's. The shadowy cloak was the softest thing I'd ever felt, a cut of wool impossibly fine, impeccably smooth. "I . . . I love you."

Mama stared at me with watery eyes and bobbed her head once, taking my affection in without response.

"You'll want to be sure to collect all those coins, Madame," my godfather told her, adjusting the quilt under his other arm. "After all, you've earned each and every one of them."

Without hesitation or shame, Mama dropped to the ground and began scooping them into her dirty apron. They clinked with more merriment than seemed appropriate for the moment.

"Ready?" my godfather asked me.

I stared at Mama, willing her to look up at me, willing her to say something, *anything*. But she didn't, too fixed on her foraging, lest any coin escape her count.

That warm rush of affection I'd felt just moments before began to harden inside my heart. It was tiny, just the size of a kernel for now, but as pointed as a barb.

I nodded. "Ready."

Tucking me close to the swelling heft of his robes, my godfather, the god of death, snapped his fingers, and we disappeared into the void.

CHAPTER 6

I SCRUNCHED MY EYES SHUT AGAINST THE SUDDEN CHAOS that wrapped around us. The air pushed and pulled with such force I was powerless to do anything but withstand the onslaught. It roared in my ears, a swirling whoosh of so much noise my head couldn't take it all in, couldn't discern what the sounds were, what was happening around me. I could only dig my fingers tightly into the sleeve of my godfather's robe and pray to survive the journey.

But just as quickly as it began, the rushing mayhem stopped, and I nearly fell to my knees, tugged by a whirl of momentum.

The Dreaded End caught me, gripping my elbows as he sought to keep me upright.

"I told you it wouldn't take any time at all," he said, amusement coloring his voice.

When I finally dared to open my eyes, straightening from my protective hunch, I gasped. "Where . . . what is this place?"

We were in the center of a valley, surrounded on three sides by wickedly jagged cuts of stone rising so high they seemed to blend into the black sky above. There was a bright sheen to the rocks, an almost translucent reflection, like panes of smoked glass.

There was a peculiar quality to the light. Above us was night, around us were dark rocks, yet I could see everything in crystalline detail, as if it were a bright summer day. I'd never known there were so many shades and shapes in the shadows.

But my godfather was almost indiscernible from the landscape, a black smudge on a black background. I could only make out the gleam of his eyes, shining with otherworldly luminescence, when lightning jumped from cloud to cloud overhead. They reminded me of the glowing eyes of cats that would often prowl the barn at night, searching for rodents to pounce upon and eat. The bobbing green lights had terrorized me when I'd been smaller and certain they were the eyes of tiny creeping cauchemars, scurrying about the barn on gnarled tiptoes to sit on my chest and drain the life from me while I slept.

"This is the Between."

"Between," I echoed, glancing about the darkened valley. "What exactly are we between?"

His lips raised again in that strange approximation of a smile. "Many things. Here and there." He gestured from one rocky cliff to the opposite. "Life and death." He pointed to two other mountain faces, as if these concepts were actual, physical locations. "Your world"—he nodded to the hillside behind me, then tipped his head toward the one behind him—"and mine."

"That's . . . is that where the gods live?" I squinted up at the summit, but low-lying storm clouds cut off any chance of glimpsing the peak.

"Some of them."

He blinked at me.

I turned slowly, taking in the land around us. There were no trees, no shrubs or bushes or any forms of life beside us. The stark barrenness of it all made my chest ache.

The Gravia was a harsh forest to live in—full of bears larger than our horses, howling packs of wolves, mushrooms and berries and all manner of vegetation most beautiful but saturated with so many poisons that even a bite could kill you.

But here . . .

There was none of that here. No green growing things, no sparks of life.

There was just my godfather: ageless, eternal. I couldn't know if there was a heart beating within that monstrous chest of his, but I guessed not.

Why would a god need a heart?

Which left only me, and the realization of my singularity folded over me like a hand closing into a fist.

"You live here?" I asked, looking up at him. It was a strain on my neck, trying to meet his eyes.

"As much as one of us ever lives anywhere, yes."

"All alone?"

"Not alone," he corrected me, and I scanned the wasteland again, hopeful I'd missed something. "Not anymore." He patted my shoulder with an awkward attempt at affection. "Now I have you."

"Oh."

My godfather looked out over the valley with a frown. "I see now, though, that this might not be the best environment for a growing girl such as yourself. It's a bit . . ."

"Desolate?" I supplied, and was surprised to hear him chuckle.

His laughter was a rich baritone and warm as spiced cider. It was not the laugh you'd expect from the Dreaded End.

"Yes, I suppose it must seem that way to you. What would help? Whatever you want, it's yours, you only need name it."

I pressed my lips together, awestruck by the sudden power given to me. No one had ever asked what I wanted, at least not in the way my godfather was. Sometimes Papa would say "Do you want me to box your ears?" but I was certain this was different.

"How about . . . a tree?" I said, deciding.

Surprise colored the Dreaded End's face. "A tree?"

I nodded.

"What kind were you thinking?"

My shoulders raised. "I don't know. . . . I've only ever seen the ones that grow in our forests—pines and firs and alders. They're very nice, but . . ." I struggled to find the words as my insides filled with a sudden hunger. Not for breakfast or lunch, though I'd missed both of those in all the day's events. I was hungry for something bigger. I wanted to see something more than just the Gravia. Something strange. Something new.

"That sounds very green."

My godfather spoke in that voice some adults use when forced to converse with children they're never around. It could have been irritating, but I thought it endearing instead. Of course the Dreaded End wouldn't be practiced in the art of conversation.

"It is," I confided, as if it were a secret.

He laughed again. "Then, Hazel, my dear, I think you shall quite enjoy this."

He gestured toward a patch of level ground atop the embankment across from us.

At first, I didn't see anything and felt disappointment twinge in my chest. Perhaps there were limitations to even the Dreaded End's powers.

But then: a sliver of movement, sly and snaking. There was a sprig of green pushing its way free of the glassy basalt ground, breaking the stone around it as it climbed higher and higher, growing first in inches, then feet, widening from a little shoot to a sapling, growing bark and limbs, twigs and leaves. It grew taller than me, taller than my godfather, filling the space with a lush and proud canopy. The leaves were slick and glossy, and I gasped as flowers began to form. Not the tiny pastels of our meadows, but ones bright and bold and wider than my fingers could spread. They burst open like the frothy skirts of dancing women, and the pink of those petals left me breathless with wonder. I'd never seen such a vibrant hue. It was warm and wild and made me wonder what marvels lay outside the Gravia, what spectacles the world must hold.

Again, that hunger in my stomach began to rumble.

When the tree finished expanding, it gave itself a little shake, as if stretching, before falling back into wondrous placidity.

"Do you like it?" my godfather asked, worry ringing in his question.

"It's the most marvelous thing I've ever seen," I said, climbing the embankment for a closer look. "What is it called?"

He shrugged. "It's the first of its kind. What would you like to name it?"

I'd been on tiptoe, reaching up to touch a blossom, but his words brought me to a sudden halt. "What do you mean?"

"I tried thinking up what sort of thing would most appeal to you and—" He fluttered his fingers.

I looked up the dark trunk to the twisting branches above. "This is the only tree like it?"

"In all the world," he said, looking pleased with his creation.

I felt as if a battering ram had struck me in the chest. "It's all alone."

My words hung in the air, impossibly small and sad.

I knew what it was like to be unique, a thing different from the rest of your brothers and sisters. Hand-selected by a god, but not. It set you apart, made you unable to fit into any space you occupied.

His eyes softened, as if he instantly understood my distress. "It doesn't have to be," he said hastily, and snapped his fingers, once, twice, three times. Enough snaps for a whole orchard, enough trees to ensure that the original was never alone.

When he was finished, the hillside was covered in wondrous shades of green and pink. The flowers danced in the breeze my godfather himself had stirred, working as a master artist might before a blank canvas.

"It's so magical," I whispered. My arms were outstretched and my head was thrown back as I spun in circles, trying to capture every beautiful detail of this newly created grove.

"Not magic," my godfather corrected me, sounding sharper than I'd ever heard him.

The swift change in tone was so abrupt, I stumbled in my dance, coming to a stop.

"Power," he said. "There's a difference between the two, don't you see?"

I didn't, not truly. I had never experienced magic and had never held power of my own. I couldn't begin to think what differences there were between the two. Both seemed far, far away from anything I could ever attain.

He wandered over to a nearby boulder and perched on its edge.

His dark robes spread out over the onyx surface, wafting from him like so many layers of mist. He gestured for me to join him and I did, my feet moving most reluctantly toward this old god.

"Magic is nothing—a trick of the mind, a sleight of hand. It's mechanical and perfunctory. A skill performed well, but a simple maneuver nonetheless." I nearly jumped out of my skin when he reached up and plucked a gold coin from behind my ear. "See? The coin was always here." The disc tumbled across the ridges of his first knuckles and he tucked it neatly between his fingers, secreting it away with deft grace.

"Is that what you gave Mama?" I asked, taking the money from him and trying to replicate the trick. "Hidden coins?"

He made a thoughtful noise as he considered my question. "Yes and no."

"I guess I don't understand, then," I admitted, letting the coin come to rest in my palm. I couldn't hide it as easily as he did. Every time I raised my hand to pull it from thin air, it rolled free, dropping to the hard ground with a clink.

"Those coins already existed, but they weren't hidden between my fingers or squirreled away in any pockets in this." He lifted his shoulders, letting the swell of fabric rise and fall around him.

"It does look like a really good place to hide things," I told him, and he let out a loud laugh.

"It is, Hazel. It truly is."

"If this is 'magic,'" I said, dismissing the word in an echo of my godfather's scorn as I waved the coin back and forth, "what's that?" I nodded toward the trees.

"That's power. Real power. Creation." He held out his hand and we watched another green shoot form. It wasn't as full as the trees; it was only a little flower. Wide, waxy leaves unfurled around a single stalk. The petals were a deep purple and shaped like an upside-down bell. "And destruction."

The petals darkened, turning themselves and the leaves black. They dried into raspy husks before crumbling like ash.

"That flower didn't exist anywhere until I made it. And it only disappeared when I willed it."

"That seems awfully magical to me," I admitted, tracing my fingertip over his palm. The sooty remains of the flower, indiscernible against his skin, stained my fingers with stark contrast.

"I suppose to a mortal it must," he allowed. "We'll mull over these concepts a great deal, I think."

"We will?"

I looked across the grove of shimmering pink trees as I tried to picture what my life here would be like, what my days with my godfather—with this *god*—would look like. How everything would be.

He offered a gentle smile. "Yes. You see, Hazel, I have for you another birthday gift."

CHAPTER 7

HIS WORDS WERE WEIGHTED WITH A SOLEMNITY that made me guess the gift was something far more important than a pretty bauble.

"Like the necklace?" I asked anyway, glancing at his hands. They held no box, but the Dreaded End obviously was not bound by the usual laws of gift delivery.

"Not at all like the necklace."

And then, for the first time, my godfather told me of the night he'd visited my parents, of the night they'd agreed to his bargain, of the night I was given away.

His version differed from my parents'. In his, he was the hero, coming to rescue a poor, unborn babe—*me,* I realized with wonder—from a life with parents who didn't care whether she lived or died.

I hadn't known the other gods had come first.

I hadn't known my parents had been strong enough—or foolish enough, I supposed—to resist them.

When his tale was over, my head felt too full of new thoughts to parse through, and we sat for a long time in silence as I tried to untangle them. I kicked my feet back and forth, thudding the heels of my boots on the rock with a comforting repetition as I mulled over his story, pondering the words he hadn't said.

"What did you say to convince Papa?" I finally asked. My lips felt raw, my throat parched, and I badly wanted to ask for a glass of water but was too scared. I'd never felt so wholly mortal as I did in this god's presence. I was as fragile and needy as the flower he'd held in his palm and just as easily crushed.

He tilted his head, unsure of what I was getting at.

"You mentioned all the things the Holy First and the Divided Ones offered . . . all the promises of what my life would be like with them. What did you tell Papa you would do?"

He was as motionless as the gargoyles dotting the village temples back in Rouxbouillet, but then I saw the length of his throat bob up and down as he swallowed.

"Well . . . ," he began. "That's the gift I was getting to."

"The gift that is not a necklace," I said, desperate to understand the full meaning of every word he spoke.

He smiled indulgently. "The gift that is far greater than any necklace." He reached out as if about to cup my cheek with a fond affection I couldn't begin to imagine him possessing, but he stopped short, sensing my reticence to be touched. His expression softened with understanding. "I told the very foolish huntsman, 'Give the babe to me and she will never know want or hunger. Let me godfather her and she will live lifetimes, learning the secrets and mysteries of the universe. She'll be a brilliant healer, the most powerful in the land, with the power to hold back sickness, disease, and even me with her hands.' "

I scrunched my face, unsure of what the dazzling words and

promises were meant to convey. "What? What does any of that mean?"

He laughed. "You, Hazel, my dear, my goddaughter, shall become a healer."

I blinked, certain I hadn't heard him right. "A . . . healer?"

He nodded.

"But that . . . that sounds so . . . Are you sure?"

My godfather chuckled. "We all have to make our way through this world somehow, Hazel. Do you find displeasure with the profession?"

I shook my head, unable to articulate my confusion. "No. Nothing like that . . . I'm actually very good at making salves and teas from things in our garden."

"Of course you are." He smiled, leaving me to wonder just how I'd come to acquire my talents.

"It's just that . . . you . . . you're the Dreaded End. Why would you . . ." I bit my lip, wishing he could discern my meaning without me having to come out and say it. "Why would you want someone to heal sick people? Don't you . . . don't you want us all to die?"

His laughter rang out brightly over the rocky landscape. "Do all mortals truly think so little of me?" He dabbed at the corner of his eye, wiping away a tear of mirth. "I don't *wish* for people to die. It's just . . . death is a part of the journey, isn't it? A balance. If you have a beginning—birth—you must have an ending—me. Do you see?"

I shrugged. "Not many people see it that way, I would guess."

"I suppose you're right," he mused. "But it's true even so. If you were to ask the Holy First, she'd tell you the same."

"Can I?" I asked, interest sparking within me. "Speak to the Holy First?"

"Eventually, I'm sure," he said. "Once you're settled. Once your training is underway."

"Training?"

"All healers must learn anatomy, physiology, botany, chemistry. They need to know how a body operates, what things can go wrong with it, and how to correct them when they do." He peered down at me and his silvery red eyes were as wide as an owl's. "Would *you* want to go to a healer who hadn't learned all that?"

I squirmed. "No, of course not. It just . . . it sounds like an awful lot of work."

"It will be," he agreed. "But you're up for the challenge. And . . . ," he added after a sly pause, "my second gift will help you along the way. You are going to become a great healer, Hazel. A powerful one. The best this kingdom, this world even, has ever seen. You will cure princes and their brides. Kings will ask for you by name."

"They will?"

His words stirred a sudden unfamiliar sensation within me. It licked fiery flames up my middle, fortifying my spine and squaring the set of my shoulders.

It felt like . . .

Ambition.

I could picture myself doing the things my godfather said. I wanted them with an intense, sharp hunger. I ached for the chance to do them, to do them all, to prove myself, to show my family—my parents—that I was so much more capable than they ever thought I was. I could be useful; I could be worth something.

"You really think I can do that?" I asked, looking up at my godfather, elation racing through me, stirring my blood and making this moment feel important and fated.

"You will," he promised. "With my help."

He raised his hand once more, hesitating for only the smallest fraction of a moment before placing it upon my forehead. It reminded me of feast days, when the Holy First's reverents would parade through the streets, finding children to give their blessings to. All my brothers and sisters received theirs year after year, but I never did. When one of the priestesses had tried to grant me favor once, Mama had pushed aside her tattooed hands with an irreverent swish.

"You fool," she'd snapped. "This child has already been spoken for and does not need your goddess's blessings."

My godfather's hand was a pleasant weight upon me now, and for all the embarrassment and shame Mama's words had caused me then, she had been right: I *was* spoken for. I did belong to the Dreaded End. I could feel parts of myself reaching out toward him, like called to like.

When he spoke, his words reverberated down my sternum, imprinting themselves on my bones, sinking into the marrow, where they would forever reside.

"I give you the gift of insight, Hazel Trépas, the power of discernment. Henceforth you shall know everything that ails a person and how best to treat them. Your hands shall bring relief, prolong and improve lives. Your touch will soothe and correct. Your name will be spoken with reverence and awe. You'll gain acclaim, fame, everything your heart has ever desired, all because of this gift. My gift to you. You shall use this gift all throughout your long and happy life."

He removed his hand, and the loss of his touch filled me with a strange ache. My family wasn't prone to bursts of physical affection. I couldn't remember the last time I'd been voluntarily touched. Bertie, perhaps. He'd always given his hugs with sweet abandonment.

But as my mother was so quick to remind me, it had been a long, long time since we'd seen Bertie.

"Trépas?" I questioned, pushing thoughts of my brother aside. My family's surname was Lafitte.

"You're not theirs any longer," he intoned.

"I don't feel any different," I admitted after a pause, waiting for some spark of awareness to filter through me. The moment we'd shared had been important, of that I was most certain, but now that it was over, I just felt like . . . me.

My godfather smiled down at me with a strange combination of paternal beatific grace and amusement. "No, I don't expect you would. Remember the coin?"

I nodded.

"It was always there. It only needed the right person to come along and reveal the trick." His eyes twinkled like bloodied rubies. "You've always had your gift, Hazel. It's been with you since even before you were born, knitted into your bones, running through your blood. You just needed the right person—"

"The right god," I interjected, offering him a shy smile.

He beamed with agreement. "The right god—to come along and reveal it."

"So I'm the coin," I said slowly, "and you're the magician."

He nodded.

I arched one eyebrow. "So it *is* magic."

His head tipped back as he laughed, and I marveled at that. I, little Hazel Trépas—that would take some getting used to—the last and least of all my family, was here in the Between, making the Dreaded End laugh.

"It is," he agreed. "And it isn't. But for today . . . yes."

He waved his hand over the orchard and stones began to tumble loose from the surrounding hillside, rolling together into stacks as they formed a structure. A house.

It was a tiny cottage, perfect for someone my size. I watched in amazement as open windows were glazed over with leaded glass panes. A thatched roof sprouted, smelling of sweet straw. A chimney poked its way through, with curls of smoke wafting into the air. A door, of curved wood and boasting a crescent moon–shaped window, swung open, inviting me inside.

"I must take my leave of you for now, Hazel," my godfather said. "There's work I must attend to, and I'm certain you'd like—"

"You're leaving me?" I asked, leaping off the rock in alarm. "Here? By myself?"

I glanced from the orchard to the house, up the sweeping mountains surrounding us.

"You can't—you can't leave me."

He studied me with curious amusement. "This is all yours. The house was made for you. Anything you could possibly need is in it."

"But there's no one here."

"Do you require company?" His head tilted. "I was given to understand you slept alone, in a barn."

"Well . . . yes," I hedged.

"I think you'll find your cottage far more comfortable . . . and much better smelling." His eyes lit up with remembrance. "And your quilt." He handed it to me. "There," he said, looking pleased. "You should be all set."

"But . . . but what if something happens to me while you're gone? What if I . . ." I trailed off as my eyes darted about the valley, seeing all the dangers that could befall me in the strange and isolated place.

His brow furrowed skeptically. "Hazel, I just promised you

lifetimes long and happy. Do you think I would ever let harm come to you?"

I squirmed under his scrutiny. "I suppose not. I only . . . How long will you be gone?" I asked as resignation filled me.

"It's difficult to say . . . but you needn't worry. There's plenty of food inside. Books I'd like you to begin reading—you *do* know how to read, don't you?"

I nodded meekly.

"Excellent. Read what you can and we'll discuss it when I return. All right?"

I bit my lip, sensing further argument would be in vain.

He stood. "I will see you soon, Hazel," he promised, and turned to go.

"Wait!" I called, stopping him in his tracks. "You . . . you never said what I should call you. The Dreaded End? Godfather?"

He blinked, considering my question. "Neither sounds particularly right, does it? You may call me . . . Merrick. Yes. Merrick."

I swallowed, knowing he was going to turn around again. The very air of the Between seemed to press in closer, and I prayed he'd thought to stock the cottage with lanterns and candles. "Goodbye, Merrick. But only just for now?"

He smiled, his form already dissipating into the gloom, one black bleeding into another. "Only just for now," he echoed, and was gone.

CHAPTER 8

THERE *WERE* LANTERNS.

Half a dozen perched on shelves and tables throughout the cottage, and a fire roared merrily in the hearth, though I couldn't understand how it was lit. There was no wood, nothing that the flames seemed to be consuming. There was only . . . light. It illuminated the cottage as brightly as a summer sun, leaving no corners of darkness, no pools of shadows where my mind could uneasily linger, imagining whole hosts of unwanted horrors.

The inside of the cottage was open and airy, though not terribly spacious. Sections of the room bled from one to another. My bed was near the hearth, which was near an overstuffed chair, which nearly took over the little kitchen, where a tall wooden table served as a place to both work and eat.

In the center of the table was a birthday cake.

It was small—the perfect size for my party of one—and impossibly ornate, the prettiest cake I'd ever seen. Golden webs of spun sugar covered the pale pink frosting, and candied flowers circled its base. It looked too lovely to eat, a perfect work of art, though I spotted a silver-handled fork resting beside the tiny platter, indicating that eating it was exactly what I was meant to do.

The first bite was all sweetness. I'd never had anything like it before, light as air with a cloying aftertaste that reminded me of Mama's rose garden. I took another bite, intrigued by the experience but not sure if I actually liked it.

While I ate, I studied the rest of my new home.

The kitchen shelves were stocked with earthen jars, pots, a kettle, and exactly one plate, cup, and set of flatware, causing me to wonder if Merrick ever planned on dining with me.

Did gods eat?

I turned from the kitchen, my eyes skimming over a water pump and sink. There was a large copper hip tub—unspeakably nicer than the galvanized tin basin we all used in turn the morning before temple visits—and a small armoire wedged into the corner of the room. Opening it, I gasped.

There were dresses and skirts, pinafores and blouses, nightgowns and cloaks, all cut from the finest cloths. There were soft wools in colors I'd never dreamed of, voiles and twills with immaculate pintucks, and beautiful floral cotton lawns, all trimmed with perfect embroidered stitches, tiny scallops of real lace, or ruffled eyelet. Lining the bottom of the cupboard were rows of boots—black ones, brown ones, some in soft gray, and one pair in the finest red leather I'd ever seen. Everything gleamed bright and new, without a scuff or stain, and I was absolutely certain everything was my size.

Eagerly, I pulled a cream-colored nightgown off its hanger and laid it across my bed to marvel at its beauty.

I'd never had a nightgown before. Back at home, I alternated between three dresses and slept in whichever one I'd worn throughout the day.

But this . . .

It was perfect. The voile was impossibly thin and edged in chains of roses and ivy. It was a nightdress fit for a dauphine or an infanta.

And it was mine.

I wanted to shimmy out of my tattered skirt and sagging stockings and put it on then and there. I wanted to dance around the room, letting the full skirts twirl like puffs of meringue, giggling at the wild turn my life had just taken.

But then I caught sight of the books on my nightstand.

And the books lined alongside my bed.

I turned slowly, taking in the cottage once more. Nearly every flat surface within it was covered with them: big books, small books, books made of leather, stacks of paper bound with glue and thread. Titles in gold foil winked in the firelight, and other tomes seemed to have no name at all. There were texts and treatises, manuals and instructions. I flipped through the pages of a large one near me and my stomach curdled.

It was an anatomy book, chock-full of illustrations and diagrams. There were striated muscles rendered in lurid shades of red ink; drawings of the human eye, pulled back layer by layer; and a tangled mess of squiggly lines I couldn't identify. The thought of them being somewhere inside me made my throat clench, fighting back a wave of nausea, and I suddenly regretted eating any of the cake at all.

I quickly shut that tome and scanned the room, trying to take stock of the sheer volume but failing. Did my godfather—did *Merrick,* I corrected myself—truly expect me to read these, and not only *read* them but be able to *understand* them and *discuss* what I'd learned?

The cottage felt too full, as if every one of the words on every one of the pages in each and every one of the books was suddenly before me, physical beings demanding to be noticed. I could feel the weight of their ink and importance piling up like stones, a wall of them, a tower, an entire mountain's worth of ideas.

It was too tall, this mountain of knowledge, too big to last. Stones rolled from its summit, raining down, catching on others, and causing them to shift until there was an avalanche headed straight at me and I was too dumbstruck to do anything but stare at my approaching destruction.

I would be struck by it, buried and battered, and there was nothing I could do.

I'd never learn it all.

It seemed wildly unfair.

It seemed . . .

My eyes blinked heavily. Time moved in funny circles in the Between. Just hours before, I'd been doing my morning chores, but now it felt impossibly late, well after midnight.

I couldn't keep my eyes open any longer; I couldn't keep wondering and worrying.

But I could collapse onto the splendid mattress Merrick had left for me.

That I could do.

I sank into its softness and wished its sumptuous down feathers would swallow me whole. I couldn't find the energy to put on the nightgown, couldn't even slip beneath the sheets. I simply pulled my velvet quilt over me, vaguely aware that it had somehow grown cleaner in Merrick's hands, the stains removed, the patches mended out of existence.

I closed my eyes and wished for the same to happen to me.

CHAPTER 9

TERROR SEIZED ME AS I WOKE.

My eyes darted around, trying to find the familiar lines of the barn. My ears strained, listening for the rustle of animals shifting in their stalls. They weren't there. They weren't here.

I didn't even know where *here* was.

I sat up with a sharp gasp and the little cottage came into focus as I remembered everything that had happened yesterday. At least, I thought it was yesterday.

Outside, the Between was still painted in its wash of grays and blacks. Lightning bolts continued dancing from cloud to cloud, never breaking free to strike the earth, offering only their sporadic flickers.

After years of waiting for him, my godfather had finally come. He'd taken me away. He'd brought me here. Showered me with generosity—necklaces and trees and a cottage of my own and the promise of a bright future. It wasn't necessarily one I'd have chosen for myself, had I been asked. But I was only twelve, a poor girl from a poor family, and Merrick's version of my future was better than anything I would have had in the Gravia with my parents.

I blinked.

My parents.

I hadn't given them much thought since arriving in the Between, too overwhelmed by everything here to look backward. Now, in the quiet of this new maybe-morning, I wondered what they were doing, how they were. I waited for the first stirrings of homesickness to quicken within me, but they did not come. I remembered how swiftly Mama had stooped down, eager to grab all those gold coins. She hadn't even looked at me to say goodbye.

That stung more than I wanted it to.

So I pushed my legs out of the bed and stood up, appraising the little cottage with fresh eyes. Merrick hadn't said when he would return, and I was at a loss for a way to spend the first full day in my new home.

The copper tub caught my attention, and I was suddenly aware of how my scent filled the small space, the warm funk of oil in my stringy hair, an unpleasant musk under my arms. I couldn't remember the last time I'd had a proper bath, and I suddenly wanted to wash away every bit of my old life. I wanted to scour my skin raw, scrub off that old version of me, watch it swirl down the drain, and be done with it.

There was a hand-pump faucet in the kitchen, and I set to work, filling bucket after bucket to heat near the fire, before dumping the boiling water in the tub. I peeled off my soiled, stinking dress and stockings before casting them into the fireplace. I would clothe myself in dresses of Merrick's making and never have to wear one of my sisters' threadbare hand-me-downs again.

The tub was large enough that I could dunk myself under the

water, and I did frequently, scrubbing my hair, rubbing a bristled brush all along my limbs until I felt as smooth and sleek as a seal. I stayed in the bath until the water cooled, causing an army of goose bumps to rise on my skin, and my fingers and toes were as wrinkled as prunes.

Wrapped in a soft bath sheet, I made my way to the armoire and studied its contents, eventually choosing a pretty dress of ochre twill. Tiny white daisies were stitched along its collar, and I marveled at all the details Merrick had so thoughtfully included in every aspect of my new life in the Between. He hadn't needed to fill the armoire with such fine clothing, furnish the bed with so many pillows and throws. The sparsest accommodations would have pleased me. He'd chosen to enchant.

Breakfast was toasted bread and a slice of dark orange cheese, wonderfully cold from the ice chest. I nibbled at it, perched in an armchair, looking about the cottage and wondering how I should spend my day.

From the corner of my eye, I caught a flash of movement, but when I turned, I couldn't tell what had shifted. Everything was still. Then, on the other side of the room, another something stirred.

I knew I was alone. There was no one else here. Not in the cottage, not in the whole of the Between.

But then . . . Again. Another movement, just far enough from my focus that my gaze didn't quite catch it. I strained my ears, listening to the quiet. Was it mice?

The thought didn't horrify me. It might be nice to have a bit of company here in this strange solitude, even if it was tufted with fur and whiskered.

I heard a soft rustle behind me and turned just in time to see one of the books move.

Its cover opened, pushed by unseen hands, before a flurry of pages flipped by, stopping on the first chapter. I glanced about and noticed that many of the other books around the room had also been opened, gentle prompts to do as my godfather had asked me.

I turned away from them.

I didn't want to see those pictures again. Didn't want to fill my head with words like *cauterization, debriding,* or *trepanning.* I had liked helping the miracle woman in the woods with her tasks, I'd liked hearing her whisper about the best time to harvest echinacea—under the light of a new autumn moon, when the roots were at their most potent—but I didn't like the thought of learning like this.

With books and big words I didn't know.

Without guidance.

Without instruction.

I made up my mind to go outside—perhaps the trees Merrick had conjured would have some sort of healing magic I could show him later. But as my palm grazed the doorknob—an octagon of green cut glass, faceted and dazzling—the wind kicked up, tearing through the valley and past my little cottage with such force that the windowpanes rattled in their casings. It screamed with a sharp pitch, keening and howling and sending shivers through my limbs.

When I pulled my hand back from the door, the gale died just as quickly as it had come on.

Narrowing my eyes, I seized hold of the glass knob once more and swung the door open. A sudden volley of freezing raindrops lashed at my face, so stinging and wicked I was forced to slam the door shut, gasping at the effort it took to push it closed against the wind.

Again, the storm silenced.

My fingers hovered over the doorknob, but I could feel the wild chaos that lingered on the other side of the door, waiting with bated breath, and I dropped my hand.

"Fine," I called to my godfather, certain he could hear me, present or not. "You've made your point."

With a peevish sigh, I flopped into the armchair and grabbed the first book I spotted.

A Treatise on the Physicks of Human Anatomy, read the spine.

Kicking my legs over the chair's arm, I settled in, opened the book, and began to read.

I read for hours.

I read till my limbs grew heavy with sleep.

I read through the pins and needles as they woke.

I read until the words no longer made sense, then stood, stretching, and searched the little cottage for a medical dictionary I was certain I'd spotted the night before.

I looked up the words I'd had trouble pronouncing, let alone understanding, and went back to the first book, determined to reread those sections with fresh eyes.

I read and consulted my dictionary and read again, and slowly—very, very slowly—the text began to make sense, solidifying into something I could remember, something I would be able to recall at a moment's notice, something I could explain and, most importantly, *use.* I only set the book aside when my stomach let out a grumble so loud it broke my concentration.

There was no clock in the cottage, and without a sun—the windows were still dark as pitch—I had no way of guessing what time it was.

But it felt like lunch, so lunch I had.

In the ice chest was a plate of ham I'd somehow overlooked earlier, already cut into thick slices, and I layered it on the ends of the bread loaf. No one was there to stop me, so I dipped the corners of the sandwich directly into a pot of mustard, again and again, reveling in my new ability to do whatever I wanted, to grab and take without considering anything but my own pleasure.

The mustard was a rich yellow, full of whole seeds that stuck between my teeth, and I nearly groaned at its perfection.

I ate one sandwich, then another, to my gluttonous satisfaction. My stomach had never felt so full. It stretched painfully taut, poking out past the jut of my hipbones. I ran my sticky fingers over it with fascinated wonder, staining my pretty frock.

"Ilium," I murmured aloud, recalling the name of the bone as I touched my hip. I'd read the word earlier and was pleased I'd remembered it.

I ran my hands down my legs, reciting each bone the anatomy book had introduced to me. After I'd reached my toes, I did the same with my arms, talking my way from the clavicle and acromion to the humerus and ulna, down to the metacarpals and the phalanges.

I'd done it.

I remembered them all.

I couldn't wait to tell Merrick, and drummed my fingers on the countertop, wondering when he might return.

"Soon, surely," I said out loud, just to have the sound of something ring out in the cottage. I glanced at the stack of books teetering on the edge of the worktable, reading their spines.

Bad Blood and Medical Interventions, read the third from the top, and I shrugged. It was the most interesting-sounding of the lot, and I had no doubt that if I tried to go on an afternoon stroll, a storm would rise again, dashing any plans but those Merrick had expressly laid for me.

Using the hand pump, I filled the kettle and set it to boil on the strange ball of flames still blazing in the fireplace. Then I curled up in the tufted velvet armchair, opened the book, and began reading.

I awoke with a start, once again disoriented, and with a strange taste in my mouth. It must have fallen open as I slept, because my tongue felt impossibly dry and a little furry.

What time was it?

It felt late, terribly late, as though I should have been in bed, not napping in an armchair.

How long had I slept?

Merrick had left me last night, and though there was no clock to back me up, I was certain I'd slept long and deep. I'd been out for at least ten hours. Maybe twelve. Maybe even more. Then the bath, breakfast, all that reading, lunch. Then more reading. Hours and hours passed in silence and solitude.

It had been at least a whole day.

Where had Merrick gone? What was he doing? How did gods spend their days?

"Merrick?" I called, hoping he could somehow hear me.

Nothing stirred. No one answered.

"Merrick?" I said again, a little louder. I paused, indecision twisting my insides. "Godfather?"

I glanced out the nearest window, squinting at the darkened landscape. I couldn't see anyone, but that didn't mean a thing, did it?

Weren't the gods always there, watching, judging? We were taught to pray to them—all of them—told that they were forever listening, ready to hear us.

So where was Merrick now?

I didn't *truly* need him, I tried to tell myself as worry prodded at my middle. I had food, shelter, heat. All my needs were taken care of. He'd seen to that.

So why did the thought that Merrick might have wandered off and forgotten me make me want to crouch down and throw up?

I wanted to laugh my panic away. He wouldn't have taken me from home, from my family, to the Between and created this house and all these lovely things—the dresses, the books, the trees—just to leave me. I was his goddaughter. Everything he'd done here proved that I meant something to him, that I was important, that I was treasured.

"He wouldn't forget me," I decided out loud. It seemed reasonable, my logic sound.

"Wouldn't he?" a terrible little voice whispered in my mind.

For a moment, it sounded so real I glanced about the cabin to see if someone had truly spoken.

"No," I said, trying to firmly banish the treacherous thought. It *was* a thought, I decided. I was here by myself, so that voice was nothing more than a thought.

My thoughts—how I prayed they were thoughts—laughed at me. "He would."

"He wouldn't," I insisted, wondering if I'd lost my mind.

"He has before."

I fell silent, unable to argue.

He *had* left me before. Back when I was tiny and small and had needed him most. He'd come and he'd gone and it had taken him twelve long years to remember to come back.

I pushed myself up, nearly falling out of the chair, my body stiff with disuse. Never before had I spent a day so idly, still but for the turning of pages, the lifting of a teacup. I ached in ways I wasn't accustomed to and had the sudden and startling horror that I had been in this cottage, asleep, for far longer than one afternoon. I felt as though I had wandered into a strange and liminal space where so much time had passed, too much time. Merrick had been gone not for a day but for years, decades, millennia. I was no longer a young girl of twelve, nimble and lithe. I was a crone, ancient and eternal, and in that moment, something broke within my mind.

I found I could scarcely draw breath. There was a band of pressure across my rib cage, squeezing and tightening. I could feel it building in my chest, climbing higher and higher, until I was certain my eyes were about to pop from my skull.

"From my orbital sockets," I murmured, and the phrase, learned only hours before, acted as a spell, lulling me from my panic, allowing me to breathe, to think, to hear things other than the racing of my blood, the pounding of my heart.

He couldn't do this. He couldn't keep me here in the cottage, as a captive, jumping to perform whatever task he required. I was not some mindless automaton that would carry out his orders, silent and without protest.

I was his goddaughter, and I was tired of being forgotten.

Without thinking, I threw open the door and greeted the storm, which, predictably, rose to a frightening pitch.

The wind howled.

The rain fell.

If Merrick summoned the storms, conjuring them up whenever I dared to disobey, I wanted him to know that they would no longer hold me back.

I walked into the storm.

The rain drenched me within seconds, soaking my dress, my under layers, my boots. It was colder than I'd thought it would be, colder than the warm spring rains that had begun to shower the Gravia.

I shivered, but I did not let it stop me.

I made my way into the orchard, watching as lightning skittered overhead, hopping and sizzling but somehow never striking here on land.

The wind raced through the branches above me with a persistent low growl that brought to mind stories Remy would tell around the hearth on winter nights, stories of those who would change with the phases of the moon, becoming more beast than man, animalistic and impossibly hungry—the loup-garou.

"I went out anyway," I called, raising my voice to be heard over the wind, over the rain. I shouted my rebellion as loudly as I could, wanting to make sure Merrick heard me. "You can't lock me away in a cottage and forget about me for another twelve years!"

The wind tugged my hair loose from its braids. It whipped across my face, stinging my eyes. My body trembled against the force of it, ransacked with gooseflesh. My teeth chattered; I would undoubtedly come down with pneumonia.

I didn't care.

"I'm not scared of this," I continued, screaming now. "Do you hear me, Merrick? I'm not afraid!"

"Oh, little mortal," the hissing, sly voice said again.

In the cabin I'd convinced myself that it was only my thoughts, but it was not. It was most decidedly not because I suddenly saw a figure whose voice it was.

Here.

With me.

In the orchard.

Lightning flashed and I could make out a face. A broken face of too many gods sharing a single body.

"You should be."

CHAPTER 10

MY MOUTH FELL OPEN AND I INSTANTLY PLUMmeted to the ground, kneeling in alarm before the Divided Ones.

Swathed in lengths of gleaming golden linen, they weren't as tall as Merrick but still made a formidable figure against the mottled grays of the Between. Though only the two most dominant gods, Félicité and Calamité, presented themselves, there were untold hundreds of gods of chance and fortune within the one body. Félicité and Calamité had their own sets of arms and hands, capable of carrying out whatever task they wished, often working in opposition to one another. Their cluster of long limbs reminded me of the giant wolf spiders that loved hiding in fallen trees within the Gravia. But their face was split down the middle, each god getting one even half.

Félicité, the kinder of the pair, reached out for me now, though Calamité tilted their head, studying me with an icy blue eye. Neither of the gods had pupils, and their irises pulsed with an otherworldly flicker as their interest was caught and lost.

"He actually brought her here," they said, both voices speaking in unison, like leaves pulled atop a swirling current.

"Look at the mess he's gone and made for her," said one of them, and I couldn't explain how I knew, but I was certain it was Calamité.

They shook their head even as Félicité reached up to pluck one of the flowers from Merrick's trees.

"What a peculiar thing to go and do," she mused, and I wasn't sure if she meant the trees or me.

"Do . . . do you know where Merrick might be?" I asked, looking up from my bow so I could study them better. I pulled one of my knees to my chest, and my fingers dug into my calf as I awaited their answer.

"Merrick?" they echoed, and turned toward the cottage. Their movements were slow and dreamy, as though they were moving at half speed. Their grace was mesmerizing, and I could feel myself tugged along as if in a trance. I didn't notice my damp clothes or dripping hair, didn't care about the painfully hard basalt pressing into my legs; I only had eyes for them.

"He told you to call him Merrick?" Félicité wondered aloud.

"And he's not here?" Calamité asked, nearly on top of his twin. "He's left you alone? Again?"

I nodded and the gods began to laugh.

"What a life you might have had, little mortal, if your parents had not been so entirely foolish," Félicité fretted. "Did you know we wanted you first?"

"Not first," Calamité said, even before Félicité had stopped speaking. "Not exactly."

It was difficult to follow the conversation, as their words slipped and slid over each other. My ears felt clogged, as though I were underwater, my senses muffled and indistinct.

Félicité's side of their mouth frowned. "Well, yes. Not first. Not quite. But still." She twirled the pink flower thoughtfully. "The things I could have given you."

Calamité raised his eyebrow with delicate deliberation. "You took the words straight out of my mouth, Sister."

"Why *did* you want me?" I dared to ask. "And Merrick? And the Holy First? I can't see . . . why would a god want a mortal child?"

"Not just any child," Calamité singsonged. "A thirteenth child."

"Don't you know how rare those are?" Félicité asked. "How precious?"

"How powerful," Calamité added, eye gleaming. "Thirteenth children can do things even we cannot, can leave impacts on the mortal world, touching it with hands better suited to . . ." He paused, musing so dreamily that I wasn't sure if he was going to continue. He flicked his fingers, as if swatting at a flying bug. ". . . well, better suited to *mortal* things. I know what *I* would have done with you, but . . . what did you call him? Merrick? *Merrick.*" He snorted. "I can't—"

"*We* can't," Félicité corrected him, and her voice joined her brother's, uniting the two tones into one off-key pitch that suddenly made me remember the reverent who'd taken Bertie away.

"—fathom what dear old *Merrick* is up to."

"He said I'm to be a healer." It sounded so small, and as the Divided Ones stared down at me, tilting their head too far in one direction, like an owl, I regretted saying anything at all.

"A healer?" Félicité questioned. "How delightful. How—"

"Odd," Calamité finished. "How very, very odd."

Though I agreed with them, it seemed disloyal to Merrick to admit it aloud.

"It will be most intriguing to watch this all play out, don't you think, Brother?"

Calamité cocked their head up, studying the canopy of branches above them. "Trees in the Between," he murmured. "Most peculiar indeed."

"Do you know where he might be?" I asked again, wanting to steer the strange conversation back to something useful. "Or when he might return?"

Félicité's eyebrow furrowed, her expression truly remorseful. "That is impossible to say."

"After all." Calamité took over, his voice melodiously low. "What is time to a god?"

"It's just . . . he's left me here, and I don't think he wanted me out wandering about but I just couldn't stay in the cabin a moment longer, and—"

"Is that what all this is about?" Calamité asked, holding out one hand, catching raindrops. "Imagine our surprise and consternation as our evening constitution was interrupted with such unnecessary fuss. And all because dear old *Merrick* hasn't gotten his way?" He rolled his eye, though Félicité's remained fixed upon me. "Sister, won't you?"

With a swish of her hand, the storm died away. A crack of light split open the void and broke apart the dark, revealing a glowing pink night sky beyond. Cheery beams of starlight bathed the world in lustrous pastel hues, giving everything they touched a hint of iridescence. Merrick's trees shimmered, and dustings of radiance sparkled on every surface, even the Divided Ones.

I held out my hands in wonder, watching as the opalescence made my own skin glisten.

Félicité beamed, admiring her changes. "Good fortune indeed."

"Did he give you instruction?" Calamité asked. "Before he left? You must have done something wrong to create such a storm."

"He . . . he wanted me to read."

"Read?" Félicité echoed with bewilderment.

"He filled the cottage with books. To study."

"Then study them I would," quipped Calamité.

"I did. I was," I stammered. "But it's just . . . I got tired of it. I finished nearly two books," I added hastily. Why did everything I said to these gods sound so insignificant?

"Two books." The Divided Ones looked less than impressed. I suddenly knew exactly how a frog must feel before being eaten by a heron.

I gulped. "They were very big books."

"If *I* were Merrick," Félicité began, "I wouldn't return until my ward had done as I asked."

"Until my ward had done *everything* exactly as I asked," Calamité corrected her, speaking over her until their words echoed.

"But there are so many."

The gods shrugged, all four of their arms rising and falling in unison.

"Could you contact him?" I asked, trying a different tactic. I knew I was wheedling and sounding every bit of my twelve years, but I couldn't stop. "Maybe you could pass along a message for me?"

"We could," Calamité said.

"We're capable of anything," Félicité murmured on top of his words.

"But no," they said together.

"What Merrick wants of you is no business of ours," Félicité said. She glanced to the bright pink sky. "But at least you have better weather now."

Calamité brightened. "You ought to read outside," he suggested. "Soak up all this holy starshine while you can."

Despair washed over me. "Read outside? That's your suggestion?"

They shrugged again, turning to leave the orchard.

"Wait!" I called out. "My brother—Bertie Lafitte—he's at your temple in Rouxbouillet. He's served you for four years now. Do you know him?"

Calamité twisted their head back toward me, allowing only his profile to be seen. "Do you know how many postulants we have? You can't possibly expect us to keep track of each and every one of them."

"He was taken from my family," I admitted. "Sold to the temple to pay for my father's debts. He didn't exactly go willingly."

"How many children do your parents plan on sending off to the gods?" Félicité wondered aloud, still unseen.

"I just wanted to know if . . . do you know if he's happy?"

The Divided Ones' body turned all the way around to face me, and after one sickeningly long moment, their head followed suit. "He serves us," they intoned, suddenly sounding so much larger than just two voices. They were a horde, a legion, every single one of the gods contained within speaking together at once. "How could he be anything but?"

I cowered under the weight of their direct attention. They were so much bigger than they'd been only moments before, as if the additional voices required more body space to contain them. I watched in horror as other eyes opened up across their face and forearms, regarding me with hostile suspicion, intense curiosity, and utter disdain.

Just how many gods were trapped in there?

"Go back to your studies now, mortal," the gods hissed, rasping my eardrums. There were so many of them speaking. "And thank your stars that reading is all Merrick requires of you."

With a flash of Félicité's pink light, they were gone, leaving me alone in the orchard once more.

I took a deep, shaky breath. My fingers were trembling, and for a long moment I stood there, waiting for the Divided Ones to return and shower me with their wrath. I waited for the earth to open up and eat me, waited for the sky to turn ugly and bruised and drown me in a torrent of rain.

But none of those things happened, and eventually I straightened and did the only thing I could think of: I returned to the cottage, opened a new book, and began to read.

CHAPTER 11

I READ FOR MONTHS, MARKING EACH DAY WITH A LITTLE check in a notebook I kept on my bedside table.

Félicité's pink starshine never faltered or faded, so when I grew tired of reading in the armchair or hunched over the worktable in the kitchen, I took my books outdoors. I'd spread out my velvet quilt in the center of the orchard and while the day away, studying charts of bones and ligaments, tendons and musculature.

Three months went by, then four, five, six, in a flash and flurry of pages.

I'd expected the Divided Ones to return, hoping they might be interested in my progress. I was eager to show them, to show *anyone,* how I was coming along. I yearned for a bit of encouragement, a speck of praise. I longed to have someone be aware of the work I was accomplishing.

But my reading list wasn't enough to tempt the fated gods' curiosity, and I remained alone.

More months ticked by.

Though I had a voracious appetite, often eating till my stomach stretched painfully for the simple reason that I could, the larder never ran out. The ice chest was always full. Dresses and skirts were replaced as I filled out, putting a comfortable amount of meat on my bones for the first time in my life. Merrick somehow even knew when I had a growth spurt after residing in the Between for five months. There was never an article of clothing that didn't fit me exactly as it should.

In addition to tallying the days, I kept track of the books I'd consumed, arranging them in stacks throughout the cabin like tiny towers. Sometimes I'd pile them too high and they'd topple over in the middle of the night, jarring me from sleep with the excited hope that my godfather had, at long last, returned.

But it was never him.

As I made my way through the collection, other things showed up in the cottage, correlating with what I'd been reading. After finishing a book on home remedies found in common herb gardens, I suddenly discovered a patch of black earth outside my door, as if the glassy basalt had broken apart to reveal a hidden layer beneath.

Days after the soil arrived, tiny shoots of yellow and green began to poke through the dirt, stretching out to the pastel pink sky. I recognized some of the plants from our garden back home and was further pleased when I could identify others from my studies, but there were quite a few that stumped me.

I brought out Merrick's botany guides and spent many afternoons thumbing through the pages, watching the plants grow and doing my best to classify them.

As the garden grew, so did my collection of tools. Mortars and pestles of various sizes filled the kitchen shelves. Glass vials with cork stoppers crowded spare drawers. I woke one morning to discover a set of beakers and flasks along the worktable, ready for me to begin mixing tonics.

I studied recipes for salves and teas, and soon gained the confidence to tweak the measurements, inventing my own concoctions and writing my observations down in a giant ledger I discovered on a side table one day.

I read and I tended my garden. I made brews and lotions, elixirs and potions.

I talked with the plants, giving them personalities and funny voices.

I wondered if isolation could make someone go mad.

In moments of extreme loneliness, I even found myself missing my family and trying to guess what they might be doing.

As I began to read through surgical procedures, scalpels and knives showed up in the cottage, as did whole hams in the ice chest. I practiced slicing into pig flesh until my hands were as steady as any surgeon's, and when my mind was too full of words, I passed the evenings by working on embroidery samplers I discovered beneath my bed. My stitches went from gaping and uneven to fine and straight, so tiny they were almost impossible to see.

Three days before my thirteenth birthday, I picked up the final unread book.

It was nearly five inches thick, smelling of dust and mold, an impossibly large tome on little-known surgical practices and filled with spidery copperplate illustrations showing how to insert catheters to open blocked bladders, the best ways to cauterize wounds, and how to remove sections of the skull to reveal the mess of brains beneath. I'd avoided the book for months, ever since I'd opened it and seen a long, squiggly worm being carefully pulled free of a skin lesion and nearly lost my lunch.

But Merrick wouldn't return until I finished reading every one of the books he'd left for me, so, steeling my resolve and my stomach, I opened the behemoth and began to read.

I was surprised to find the text far less disturbing than I'd feared. After spending so many months engrossed in physiology, I didn't consider the surgeries so barbaric. These were practices designed to help, not hurt; to heal, not wound. If I ever had cause to perform anything described in this book, it would be in pursuit of saving a life, one in dire straits.

The thought humbled me. I caught myself sneaking glances at my hands throughout the day, wondering if they were up to the task.

Merrick had believed in me, even when I had not.

Merrick had said it was to be so, and after a year of living in the cottage he'd brought into existence through nothing but his own ferocious will, that seemed more important than anything else.

I read long into the night, turning in only when my eyelids began to flutter shut and I feared I'd miss learning something important in my drowsy state.

The next morning, over toast and jam, I read about the various ways one could trepan a patient. I learned how to drain weeping abscesses while sipping afternoon tea, and I practiced needling cataracts away from a clouded cornea on my hard-boiled eggs at dinner.

That night I dreamed of blood and bone matter but slept deep and well, and when I woke, I read some more.

The next day passed in a fog of incisions and instruments. I itched to recreate the surgeries I'd read of, to know what it was like to stretch open a wound, to feel the slippery heat of viscera, to set my tools down and know I had done a fine job. For the first time since Merrick had brought me here, I dreamed of becoming the healer he'd promised.

I woke on my birthday with only three chapters left and decided to venture outdoors with a breakfast picnic. Merrick's trees were in the process of shedding their blossoms and pink petals rained down throughout the morning. When I finished the book, closing it with a moment of wistful reverence, the blossoms were tousled about in my hair, like confetti on festival days back in Rouxbouillet.

I rolled over and stared into the pastel sky.

I felt good.

Better than good.

I'd done it.

It had taken an entire year, but I'd read every single book that Merrick had left for me, and I'd read each one as a scholar would, studying with intent, referencing ideas and concepts in previous chapters and tomes, and while I'd never once treated an actual patient, I felt as though I could now.

My stomach rumbled and I flipped back over, pushing myself to my feet. I stretched, marveling at the giant expanse of free time laid out before me. The afternoon sparkled with dizzying potential.

"I'll make lunch," I decided aloud, swiping up the book and heading down the hill to my cottage. "Then weed the garden, and perhaps take a walk, and I will not look at a single book."

As I swung open the door of the cottage, I hummed a little tune, not realizing what it was—the birthday song Bertie used to serenade me with every year—until I spotted the cake on the worktable.

It was a decadent tower of lavender frosting, colored sugar crystals, and edible violets. A tiny forest of golden candles—thirteen exactly—sprang from its top and lit magically as I stepped inside.

I approached the cake curiously; I didn't notice my godfather sitting in the armchair, warming himself by the fire, until he cleared his throat.

"Happy birthday, Hazel."

CHAPTER 12

"MERRICK," I SAID, STARTLED BY HIS PRESENCE. "You're back."

He smiled as if it had been only hours since he'd last seen me, as if an entire year had not passed. "I am. Just in time to celebrate."

"I finished the books," I said in a rush, eager to show him I'd done as he'd asked. "All of them. Just as you wanted me to."

"Excellent," he said, sweeping from the armchair. It was much too small for him, and his body creaked upon straightening. "Shall we have cake?"

"Cake?" I echoed with surprise. I assumed he had come back to talk about my studies, about all the things I'd learned and done.

He nodded, seemingly unaware of my confusion. "Yes. And then we'll be off."

"Off?"

He smiled with amusement, eyes crinkling at my befuddlement. "You're repeating everything I say, Hazel."

He pulled my plate from the shelf and, upon realizing there was only the one, snapped his fingers and another appeared, complete with utensils.

"I suppose I must be out of practice. I've been here for a whole year with only plants to talk to." I felt the edge in my voice, but Merrick didn't seem to notice.

"The garden, yes! I was very impressed by how large it's grown." He picked up a knife but paused before the first cut. "You'll want to blow out the candles, yes? I'm told that's the usual tradition."

Irritation flickering in my middle, I crossed to the worktable and extinguished all thirteen in one breath. "Where are we going?" I persisted, but was forced into accepting the plate he pushed my way. He'd made me a sponge cake, soaked in cherry compote.

"Eat," he insisted, taking a bite himself. "It's quite good, though the cherries seem a surprise with that lavender icing. Should it have been pink? It should be pink," he decided, and with another snap, the cake changed hue.

"You said we were going to be off," I said, my mouth half full. Like his cake the year before, it was too sweet. "Where are we going?"

He blinked, only now acknowledging my questions. "To your house, of course."

"My house?" I was beginning to feel like a parrot. "I'm going home?"

He nodded.

"You're sending me back?" I asked, the alarm spiking through me every bit as sharp as the scalpels I practiced with. I'd done everything he'd asked of me, hadn't I? I scrunched my face, wondering what I'd done wrong.

Merrick frowned. "Sending you back? No, no, no. Not there. I'm taking you home. To your home. Your new home," he clarified, most unhelpfully.

"I thought *this* was my home." I gestured about the cabin.

"For a time," he allowed. "I needed to make sure you had a place you could concentrate. Learn what you needed to. Study without distraction."

"And?"

"And you have," he said, as if it was the easiest thing in the world. "You've studied. You've grown. And now it's time for the work to begin. After cake, of course."

"After cake." I took another bite, hardly even tasting it now. "Where . . . where is this new home?"

He beamed. "It's a lovely little plot of land, just outside Alletois. It's a bit rustic, I suppose. Farmland, sheep. It will be the perfect place to perfect your techniques."

"I've never heard of Alletois." It wasn't what I wanted to say, but it was the first thing that fell from my lips.

It truly hadn't occurred to me that I would leave the Between, though I suppose it should have. Merrick planned to make me a great healer, and there wasn't a single patient to treat in this vast and empty liminal space.

"It's lovely," he assured me. "Only a few hours' ride from the capitol. A little rustic perhaps but . . ."

I stabbed at my slice again, cleaving the remains in half with petulance. "You said that already."

"I . . . I suppose I did." He pressed his fork against the plate, smashing crumbs together to make a more sizeable bite.

I studied his face, trying to spot any changes that might have occurred in the year since I'd seen him. There were none. Gods wouldn't age, I realized belatedly. "What have you been up to? Since I saw you last."

"Work." One slice down, he busied himself cutting another.

Merrick, I would learn in the years to come, had a prodigious sweet tooth.

"What sort of work do gods do?" I asked, hacking the last of my cake into more and more sections till the cherry juice ran everywhere, making my plate look like a small massacre had taken place.

He chuckled. "Work most godly, I suppose."

"It must take up a great deal of time," I pressed. "It's been an age since I've seen you."

"Yes, and look how you've grown!" he exclaimed, ignoring my censured tone as pride filled his red and silver eyes. "Why, you've shot up at least five inches! And your hair looks darker now, less auburn than it used to."

"There's no sun here to lighten it." I set my fork down, abandoning the pretense that I was going to finish my cake.

"That will be quite different in Alletois. Your cottage is in the center of a clearing. There are so many windows, sunlight streaming in everywhere. It will be enchanting come summer."

"My cottage," I said, picking up on his phrasing. "Not ours."

His brow creased as he tried sorting through my distress. "Of course not. It's yours. I made everything for you, exactly how you'll want it. Oh, I can't wait for you to see it. One slice more and then we'll go."

"How?" I asked, ignoring his offer for more cake. I shoved my plate toward him, and with a shrug, he began gobbling my remains.

"How what, Hazel?" His question was clipped, and there was a slight edge to his voice now, a current running through his words and charging them with warning.

"How do you know that everything will be exactly as I want? You don't know me. You've never been around me long enough *to* know me."

"You forget who you're speaking to, mortal." His voice boomed with omnipotent magnitude.

I faced his anger head-on. I would not cower before him. "I am speaking to my godfather. The one who promised my parents he'd raise me and take care of me. The one who I've not seen in a year because he left me in this realm of immortals all by myself."

The light in the cabin began to dim as forbidding black clouds rolled in, covering Félicité's starlight with their menace.

I squared my shoulders, steeling my spine. I knew I was right, and I was not going to be the one to back down.

Merrick's nostrils flared. "I didn't realize your time here has been so trying," he sneered. "Here, in this house, which is not a barn, where I've clothed and fed you with resources better than you could have ever dreamed of, given the time to expand your knowledge, learning the secrets and wonders of the mortal body. Yes. I could see what a time this must have been for you."

"You left me alone!" I exclaimed, and though I didn't want it to, my voice cracked as my heightened emotions made my throat swell. I angrily wiped at the tears welling in my eyes, threatening my vision. "For years I've been told that you would one day come for me and take me away to some grand manor, and I thought that meant that you'd be there too. That you would be there, with me, and that I'd finally have some sort of family. All those years ago, you told my parents you wanted me. And then you came, only to leave me here. For an entire year." The sobs rose then, breaking apart my words and making it impossible to speak. I collapsed upon the counter, burying my face in my arms, unable to look him in the eye, and cried.

Oh, how I cried.

Great, hot tears fell down my face, which was scrunched red and ugly. My shoulders trembled with the force of the sobs, and my chest felt as though it might cleave in two. I struggled to breathe through a runny nose and my cries turned to gasps, wretched heaving grabs for air.

And suddenly Merrick was beside me. His skeletal hand rubbed my back, attempting to soothe and assuage my anger and hurt.

"I . . . I don't know what to say," he said, sounding honestly perplexed. "I hadn't ever considered you'd want me here. You're all grown up."

"I'm a child!" I protested. "I *was* a child. I was . . ." I shook my head, unsure what category I fell into. I'd been relying on myself for years. *Did* that make me an adult? I didn't feel like one. I didn't feel like much of anything most days, and in this moment, I felt like even less. It hurt to speak, hurt to hold myself together. Without care, I threw myself at him, hiding away in the fullness of his robe. I felt his figure beneath the swell of fabric, but it was too gaunt, too wrong, too full of angles my mind couldn't wrap around, juts from bones my mortal frame did not possess. For a god so suffused with power beyond reason, his actual body did not take up very much space.

After a brief hesitation, Merrick folded his arms around me, holding on as I released my torrent of woe upon him. He patted my shoulders, then my head, eventually deciding to stroke my hair, saying nothing as I wept but making a soft, low noise of comfort.

I don't know how long we stayed like that, but eventually the tears trickled themselves out and I sat up, stretching my shoulder blades. I wiped the back of my hand over my face, shame burning across my cheeks. I couldn't guess what he thought of my outburst, what he was thinking of me.

Merrick watched on, the apprehension written across his face as obvious as a splatter of blood on surgical linens.

"I'm sorry," I said, struggling to put myself back together. "I didn't mean . . . I didn't mean to . . ." I stopped, unsure of exactly what I didn't mean to. I had needed that, but more importantly, *he'd* needed to see that, needed to hear my frustrations, needed to know how much his absence had undone me.

Merrick cleared his throat and it sounded like the wispy rasp of insect wings rubbing against each other. "I ought to be apologizing to you, Hazel. I didn't . . . I never would have dreamed you'd need me to stay, that you'd even want me here."

It would take me years to realize that for all his talk of remorse, he never actually did say the word *sorry.*

"You're my godfather," I protested. "You're my family—the closest thing I have to one now."

He tilted his head, pondering me. His eyes seemed more luminous than usual and glassy bright, as if he might be on the verge of tears too. "Family," he said, holding out his hand.

I placed mine in its center and when his long fingers folded closed, dwarfing mine, it felt oddly formal, as if we were concluding a business transaction. Impulsively, I threw my arms around him in a desperate embrace. I wasn't crying now, grasping at any comfort *I* could find. I wanted *him* to feel how earnestly I needed him, this odd father figure I'd been promised. I wanted him to need me as badly as I did him.

He hugged me back and my ears were filled with the rushing sound of a sudden wind. It roared all around us, a hurricane of motion, whipping my hair and animating Merrick's robes in a flurry of ripples.

He broke the embrace first, stepping back and giving me the space to find my sense of equilibrium. My ears ached, and for a second, I thought I wasn't in the right space. My cottage didn't look the way it should. The room skewed too long, too wide. All the furniture was in the wrong place.

I blinked against the vision and rubbed my eyes, certain the wind had kicked some grit into them. If I could just get it out, the cottage would return to normal.

But I did and it didn't.

I stepped away from Merrick, turning to look about with open wonder.

It wasn't that the furniture was in the wrong place . . . it was entirely different furniture. In an entirely different room.

"Where . . . where are we?" I asked, whirling around to Merrick.

His mouth rose in a smile. "Home."

CHAPTER 13

I RAN TO THE WINDOW AND LET OUT A NOISE OF surprise. The orchard with Merrick's soaring, fantastical trees was gone. In its place were other trees, beech and alder, cypress and yew. After a year spent in the Between, their ordinariness was almost shocking.

I turned back to the cottage, surprised to find doorways leading to other rooms. This house was much larger than my old one, with high rafters and beams. I could already picture how they'd look at harvest time, with bunches of drying flowers and herbs hanging from them. Everything was airy and light. Beams of sunshine danced through the many open windows. Eyelet curtains wafted back and forth, caught in the breeze. I took in a deep breath. The air was redolent with the scent of freshly turned earth, bursting blossoms, and a heady mix of so many green growing things. There had not been scents like this in the Between; there'd not been any scents at all. My senses tingled, as though this wealth of input was overwhelming them, like fireworks blasting through my bloodstream.

"What do you think?" Merrick asked, clasping his fingers

together. I could tell he was worried that he'd gotten it all wrong, that the cottage wasn't to my taste, that I hated everything in it and, by extension, him as well.

I wandered to the next room. One wall was lined with diamond-paned windows. Its opposite was all shelves, already full of books. My fingers trailed over their spines and I spotted many new titles among old friends. History and science, atlases and art, novels and poetry.

"Hazel?" he called again, wandering after me. I noticed he left a careful distance between us.

The kitchen came next. The cabinets were painted white and stenciled with tiny blue flowers. There were pots and pans of bright copper, a dark wooden ice chest, and a huge, hulking iron stove in the corner. There was a worktable and stools, a row of potted herbs lining the deep windowsill, and enough plates and cups to host a party of six.

I wandered through each open door, passing a mudroom and pantry, a cozy sitting room, and an indoor bathroom so beautiful I actually gasped, until I arrived at the bedroom.

It was so green.

Windows lined three walls, offering a dazzling view of the surrounding forest and fields of waving tall grasses.

He gave me trees.

I turned around. Merrick had hung back on the room's threshold, bending low to fit in the doorframe.

"You made this for me?" I whispered, overcome.

He nodded and I rushed to hug him, forgetting my earlier outburst. Somehow he *had* known everything that would delight me. He'd carefully filled the cottage, stocking it with luxurious practicalities. No detail was too small, no need overlooked.

I could feel every thought he'd put into this space, and my heart swelled, overwhelmed by it all.

This showed he cared for me, I reasoned. No one would go to such pains for a ward they only tolerated. He might have left me on my own for all that time, but he'd also done this. And if *that* wasn't proof of his affection, what was?

"And you'll stay here? With me?" I asked, pulling him back down the hall toward the kitchen, hope clattering painfully high in my chest. "There's more than one set of plates this time."

Merrick glanced toward the shelf, counting the plates and cups as though he doubted what I'd seen. "Yes. Often."

I could feel the rush of wind leave my sails. "But not always?"

He shook his great head, seemingly regretful.

"Your work," I guessed.

"And yours," he pointed out, evading my gentle prod. "Now that you've completed all your studies, you're ready for your next gift."

"You've already given me so much."

Merrick smiled widely. "Yes, Hazel. But this is the most important gift of all."

And then, for the second time, Merrick told me my birthday story. And on this sunny afternoon, he told me every bit of it.

When Merrick had finished, I collapsed back into one of the overstuffed chairs in my new sitting room, gazing off into the forest out the windows as I mulled over everything he'd said.

"I'll be able to cure anything?" I asked, feeling as if I were repeating him once again but needing absolute clarification.

In the periphery of my vision, I saw him nod. "Anything that can be cured."

"Just by . . ." I raised my hand and mimed touching someone's face.

Merrick nodded once more.

My head swam with dozens of questions demanding to be asked. "Why did you have me spend the last year reading all those books? I didn't need to learn any of it. Not with this . . . gift." It didn't feel like the right word, not exactly.

Merrick was still for a long moment, considering my words. "Do you remember our talk about magic and power?"

I thought back to that day in the orchard so many months before and nodded.

"The cure . . . your vision of it . . . is the magic. It's there, out in the world, waiting to be revealed. My gift to you, the seeing of it, is nothing but sleight of hand. It's pulling back a curtain, showing what was there all along. The power, the true power, comes from knowing *how* to use it. What good is knowing that someone needs stitches if you can't sew them? Knowing you need to set a fracture and being able to do it are two very different things. You can see the tonic needed, but if you don't know how to make it, your patient dies. You needed time to obtain your knowledge, to gather your powers. This gift is the confidence to know that what you're doing is right."

It made a degree of sense. I wanted to ask him more, but a great clatter of noise sounded from the front door. Someone was rapping frantically and calling for help. "Hello? Hello? Is the healer here?" The raps mellowed to thuds as the visitor switched to the palms of their hands, striking the door over and over. "Oh, please be home!"

"The healer?" I froze.

Merrick's eyes sparkled in amusement. "He means you."

"But how does he know I live here? We only just arrived."

"This has always been the cottage of Alletois's healer. When I came across its former resident"—he paused as if wishing to restructure the thought—"I knew that with a few changes here and there it would be the perfect place for you to begin practicing your new skills."

"You 'came across the former resident,'" I echoed, then blanched with realization. "They're dead?"

Merrick let out a sigh of annoyance. "It's not as though I left the body here." He gestured to the door. "*Your* first patient is waiting for you. Aren't you going to let them in?"

I stood, then looked back to my godfather, panic rising within me. "But what about you?"

"He won't see me," he promised quickly with a snap of his fingers. Merrick remained visible but there was a strange feeling to the cottage. The air flowed off me differently, as if I were the only one here.

"I still see you," I hissed.

"But he won't."

He.

There was a he somewhere who needed me.

The concept made my stomach quiver with nerves.

"Go on," Merrick nudged, sensing the hesitation.

I bumped my hip against a side table as I hurried to the front door. I'd only just arrived in Alletois. I wasn't familiar with the layout of my own house but already was being asked to leave it to tend to someone I wasn't sure I knew how to treat.

"Now or never," I muttered to myself, and opened the door.

The boy on the other side had his fist raised, ready to knock once more, and nearly struck me as the swinging door surprised him. He was flushed and out of breath, his collar damp and gaping.

He was the most beautiful boy I'd ever seen.

His skin was a rich chestnut and he had a head of thick, dark curls. His eyes were warm and brown and a faint scar traced across his cheek. I wanted to ask him how he'd gotten it. I wanted to ask him that and a dozen more questions.

After a year spent all alone in the Between, I was hungry for conversation. For companionship. For—

"Where's the healer?" he asked, between deep gulps of air.

"Here. Me. That is . . . I'm . . . I'm the healer," I stammered, feeling more incompetent with every syllable that fell from my lips.

"You are?" He peered at me dubiously.

I couldn't blame him. He looked about my age, and I couldn't imagine anyone allowing us to be trusted with anything of importance.

"I . . . I am," I said, deciding. I offered my hand, feigning confidence. "I'm Hazel."

"Kieron." He looked over my shoulder, as if searching for someone else.

"And you . . . you need help?" I looked him over. He didn't seem ill, but I wondered what I'd see if I cradled his face in my hands.

He shook his head. "Not me. My uncle. He's taken sick. You must know him. He lives just over the ridge, there," he said, pointing toward the tree line on the far side of the meadow.

"I . . . I am new to town."

"But you can help him?"

"I . . ." I faltered, unwilling to commit to something so unknown. "I'll need to gather some supplies first. Come inside and tell me what's ailing him."

"He's burning up with fever," Kieron said, stepping ahead of me to open the screen door with unconscious chivalry.

"Thank you," I murmured, ducking beneath his arm. Unreasonably, my cheeks flushed. He was so much taller than me, with the broad shoulders and lean muscles of a farmer's son. I idly wondered what things they grew, what crops they kept.

I wanted to know everything about him.

I opened my mouth, just about to ask about the scar, when clarity washed over me.

Now was not the time. Not with an uncle, sick and unwell. Not with that worry creasing the corners of his eyes.

I tossed aside my fanciful daydreams and headed into the workroom, certain I remembered seeing a leather valise and an arsenal of dried herbs and stoppered bottles. "Fever?"

"It started a few days ago," he said. "He says he's cold but sweats through any blanket I put on him. He's a widower—when we heard he was ill, my mother sent me to look after him."

"Body aches?" I guessed, finding the bag. *Focus, Hazel, focus.* I began checking the stock inside, listening to him as I worked.

"Terrible ones. I thought it was just a summer cold, but then . . . it's been getting worse. And today . . ." He swallowed, turning pale.

"Hazel," Merrick interrupted, suddenly filling the doorway. "I do believe you'll want to dispense with such niceties and get to this man. With haste."

I dared a glance back to Kieron, but he was only staring at me, watching me, completely unaware of the Dreaded End now peering down at him curiously.

Though I offered him my brightest smile, I could feel it quiver. "Take me to your uncle?"

CHAPTER 14

BY THE TIME WE ARRIVED AT THE FARMHOUSE, Reynard LeCompte was careening toward madness.

Kieron ushered us into the home but paused, lingering on the threshold as a volley of shouts rose from a bedroom deeper within. "He's in his room. . . ."

"Make it stop, make it stop, make it stop!" cried a voice stretched hoarse and painfully raw.

"Will you introduce me?" I asked uncertainly, glancing between him, Merrick, and the dark hallway leading to the back of the house.

"I don't . . ." Kieron cleared his throat. "If it's all the same to you . . . I'd rather not see him like that again." He frowned. "I suppose that makes me a coward, but I . . . I just can't . . ." He sighed.

The shouts morphed into a feral howl, ripping the house apart in its agony. Kieron winced.

"Send him away," Merrick advised. "You need to focus, and with that queasy constitution he'll be of no help at all."

My mind raced. "Camphor!" I blurted out.

Kieron raised his eyebrows.

"I just realized I don't have any camphor oil with me. Would the . . . perhaps the market in town might have some?"

Kieron paused and I began to worry my request was absurd. I wasn't even sure how far from town we were, wasn't sure there was a market large enough to have an apothecary shop. But then he nodded.

"I can take his horse," he volunteered. "I should be back in an hour or so. Two at the most."

"That would be so helpful, thank you," I said, my words nearly lost in the jumble of his uncle's babbling.

Kieron's gaze darted from mine to the room at the end of the house. "I'll be as quick as I can." Then he turned and fled.

Merrick watched him go, his gaze unreadable, before he gestured to the bedroom. "Shall we?"

Relief spread through my chest like a warm balm. "You're coming with me?"

"Of course," Merrick said, stooping to poke his head through the bedroom's doorframe. The farmer caught sight of him and howled.

"I thought you said no one could see you!" I fretted, whirling around.

Merrick waved his hand as if it was of no concern. "I said the boy wouldn't. But the farmer would, of course. He's close to death. If you do your work well, he won't remember anything about this moment." His skeletal fingers cupped the small of my back and guided me over the threshold. "In you go."

My leather valise was stuffed near to bursting with powders and elixirs, bandages and surgical tools. I'd nervously overpacked, not wanting to be underprepared. I set the bag on the bedside dresser with a loud *thunk* that made me wince, but Kieron's uncle didn't even notice.

He writhed across his pallet, bed linens soaked and stinking of sweat, urine, and loosened bowels. His skin had a dreadful pallor, somewhere between yellow and gray, and was covered with dark sores.

I immediately understood why Kieron did not want to return to this bedside. I didn't want to be here either. I did not want to be here, in this room that smelled of things worse than death, but Merrick prodded me forward.

"Sir?" I began, my voice breaking with a crack. "My name is Hazel." I twisted my fingers together, feeling stupid and small and wishing I could flee. "And I'm . . . I'm here to look after you."

He let out a deep groan, thrashing onto his other side. His breath was rank and reminded me of Papa's after a night of drinking. Sure enough, the floor was littered with empty bottles. I briefly wondered if he'd made the spirits himself—Kieron had led us through a field of rye on the way here—but I pushed the curiosity aside, knowing I was procrastinating.

"It burns." He gasped, digging his feet into the ticked mattress. I noticed with a sickening twist in my gut that his toes had a blackened hue. "Holy First help me, it burns."

"What does?" I asked, but he was too lost in his throes to answer me. "Reynard?"

He turned and vomited over the side of the bed. I had to jump back to avoid being splashed with the foul offering, and I felt my own stomach heave, longing to purge itself of every bit of Merrick's cake.

I whirled around to my godfather. "I can't do this." I knew I sounded panicked, lost in a rising hysteria, but I couldn't help it. This was bad. This was so much worse than I'd ever imagined.

I'd thought Merrick would ease me into life as a healer. I'd start out small—headaches, toothaches, stitching some wounds, maybe a few cases of summer colds.

Not . . . this.

Merrick stared down at me, appraising me with a placid expression that made me want to shriek. Didn't he understand what was going on?

"I can't . . . He's going to . . ." I sighed, none of my arguments forming into coherent thoughts. "He's going to get me sick."

Merrick shook his head. "He won't."

"The air in here is so tainted it'll be a wonder if *you* don't fall ill," I hissed.

"You won't get sick," he replied. "You've always had a strong constitution, have you not? In the whole of your life, can you recall a single bout of influenza?"

I thought back over my childhood. I recalled listening to my siblings as they coughed and sneezed, hearing them all the way from my little nest in the barn. I shook my head.

"An outbreak of spots?"

Another denial.

"Allergies?" he persisted.

I said nothing for a long moment. "Your doing, I suppose?"

He smiled pleasantly, as if we were having this conversation over afternoon tea. "It wouldn't do to have a healer who caught everything her patients suffered from, would it?" Merrick made a soft noise of sympathy. "I know this seems hard now, but I believe you are more than capable of helping this man. So . . . go on."

Behind me, the farmer let out a cry of pain, his arms flailing like a broken marionette. "Why did you bring this devil with you?" he screeched, using the last of his strength to fling a rancid pillow at my godfather. More vomit gurgled up his throat as he shrank back into the bedding, hiding under a quilt stiff with stains. "Oh Holy First, save me from this monster!"

"He's not a monster!" I snapped, striking the headboard with the heel of my palm. I just wanted to make the noise stop, to put an end to all those horrible sounds coming from him. "He's not!"

Despite the complete chaos of the moment, despite the screams and the stink and situation exploding past the point of my control, Merrick smiled down at me. He touched my cheek, making me look up at him, making me focus on his eyes alone. "You're doing fine, Hazel."

"I'm not! What is fine about any of this?"

Behind me, the farmer convulsed, shrieking about the fires of the afterworld come to singe him. He struck up a conversation with someone who was not in the room, and I looked back at my godfather with a pleading expression.

"Center yourself," he advised, his voice maddeningly calm. "Find your inner peace and try again."

I let out a sob. "I can't. I don't want to. Can't you just fix him? Please? We can go home and just . . ." I trailed off, hating myself, hating how much I sounded like a coward.

Merrick shook his head, not backing down. "There're clues here, Hazel. You need only look."

"I don't *want* to look," I admitted, tears welling up.

He paused for so long I started to believe he'd realized his mistake: I was not a healer. I never could be a healer. He'd call it all off and we could go home. Hope flared in my chest as I waited for him to admit he'd been wrong.

"Go on and touch him, then, if you're so keen on giving up."

My hope sputtered out, a flame doused with cold water. He wanted me to use the gift. The magic.

"I don't want to," I admitted, my voice small and weak and full of self-loathing.

Merrick sighed and crossed over to the corner of the room, giving me more space to work, giving himself a better angle to watch it unfold.

"We're not leaving until it's done," Merrick said, folding his long arms over one another. "Until he's treated or dead. It's your call."

A flurry of trembles shivered through my body at the impossibility of the situation.

I didn't want this man to die.

But I didn't want to be the one to save him either.

"Tell me what you see, at least," Merrick said, trying a new tactic. "You needn't touch him. Just tell me what you see."

I glanced about uneasily. I saw chaos. I saw despair. I saw the very worst things the mortal body was capable of doing, sprayed across every bit of the stinking room.

"It can help to focus on the small details," Merrick continued, seeing my stricken face.

The farmer thrashed again, ranting about a great creature of fire burning him whole. I tried to tune him out, tried to spot one small thing I could wrap my mind around.

"His sheets are soaked," I started, feeling foolish, a child playing at being a knowledgeable adult. "He's been throwing up and . . ." I stopped, struggling to find a phrase that didn't make me want to vomit too. "And . . . voiding his bowels."

Merrick nodded approvingly. "What else?"

"Peppermint could ease his stomach pains," I realized suddenly.

I'd read that in one of Merrick's books. I'd used the same treatment on myself when I'd eaten too much. "I have some in my bag. I could make up a tea."

"You could," Merrick said, and I could hear the touch of pride in his tone.

It was a small thing, a very small thing, but it was something I knew I could do. Something that would offer a bit of relief.

I opened the valise and rummaged through it until I found a packet of dried mint leaves.

"I'm going to make you some tea," I told the farmer. "And then . . . and then we'll try to clean up some of this mess."

It wouldn't be pleasant work, stripping the bed, scrubbing the filth from his skin, but it might stop the burning sensations he spoke of. The sores covering his body were likely infected. Infections could burn; I was almost sure of it.

I left the bedroom and made my way to the kitchen.

It too was a disaster. Bread and cheese had been left out for days and were now covered with dots of mold and drowsy flies. But I found a kettle and cleaned it thoroughly, using water from the hand pump in the side yard. I kept a watchful eye on the road as I worked, but it was too soon for Kieron's return.

I felt Merrick watching each of my moves, assessing every one of my decisions. He seemed pleased, and my confidence grew as I went through the familiar motions. I might not know the exact cause of this man's illness, but I knew I could treat an upset stomach. I knew how to make tea.

"I think the spots on his body might be sores from lying in all that filth," I told Merrick, coming back into the farmhouse. I set the kettle on the hook over the hearth and began lighting a fire. "I have some creams that will help, once he's bathed."

"And his toes?" he prodded gently. "Did you see them?"

I nodded. I'd avoided thinking of them, black and curling and looking so terribly wrong against the sallow pallor of the rest of him.

"I don't know what's causing that. They look withered somehow. As if . . ." I paused, recalling something I'd read in one of the books in the Between. "As if they're about to fall off. Wait. . . . I remember this. . . ." My fingers danced with impatience as I struggled to summon the word. "It's . . . it's . . . gangrene!" My triumph burst from me in a shout of excitement.

"Very good. Do you want to check your work?" Merrick asked.

I looked up at the Dreaded End, apprehension bubbling in my middle. "What will it be like?"

"I could tell you," Merrick said, his voice thoughtful and ponderous. "Or you could just see for yourself."

"Will it hurt?" I asked, peeking back into the bedroom. The man was quiet now, panting in an exhausted stupor. His eyes were so glazed over I didn't think he even knew I'd returned.

"You or him?" Merrick laughed at my expression. "Go on, Hazel." He nudged me gently back into the room.

Cringing, I knelt beside the bed.

The smell was so much worse up close. I could taste the foul air. It coated my mouth and left an unpleasant funk on my tongue. I looked to Merrick. "So I just . . ."

I fluttered my hands restlessly over Reynard's face, unsure of exactly where to touch, uncertain of how much pressure to use.

With care, Merrick put his fingers atop mine, guiding them to the man's cheeks. He held them in place for a moment before stepping aside to let me experience the full weight of his gift.

I couldn't help my gasp.

"What do you see?" he whispered, pleased.

"It . . . it's so beautiful," I murmured.

Sprouting out of the farmer's chest, there but not, were stalks of grain. They looked like the line drawings in my botany books, and the rendering shimmered and shone with an otherworldly sparkle, a holy glow that reminded me of Félicité's pink starlight. The stalks swayed back and forth, dancing in a flickering light that reminded me of a bonfire. This was the cure needed to heal this man—shining forth like a beacon in the night. I didn't understand it yet, how grain would help the farmer, but the answer would come, I was certain of it.

"Will it always look so wondrous?" I whispered.

I felt awestruck, weighted with a power most divine. I reached out to caress the image, but the moment I withdrew my fingers from the man's face, it faded away.

"It will," Merrick answered. "Exactly like that. On every patient who can be saved."

I turned toward him, tearing my eyes from the farmer as I heard the words he hadn't said. "What will happen when I come across someone who can't?"

Silence spread between us, filling the room.

Merrick shook his head. "Save who you need to save today, and worry about those walking with death tomorrow. Do you know what this man needs? Here and now?" I shook my head. "Then look again," he encouraged.

I cupped the farmer's face once more. "I see stalks of grain. They're waving in the breeze." I glanced to my godfather. "There's that field of rye we walked through. . . ."

Merrick said nothing but watched me closely.

I frowned. The answer was close, so close I should have been able to grab it, but it eluded me. I looked back at the shimmering stalks. "Something . . . something looks wrong with them," I realized.

Poking from the stalks' spikes were dark growths. They jutted out like the stamens of flowers, going against the orderly lay of the florets. The flickering light surrounded the wheat, consuming it until there was nothing left but a whisper of ash.

"What is it?" I murmured, asking myself more than Merrick. It felt familiar to me, something I'd once read or . . .

No.

The memory came to me in a rush. Back in Rouxbouillet there'd been a farmer's wife who'd come to market, trying to sell flour at a steep discount. Mama, always looking for a cheap way to feed her burgeoning household, had wanted to buy as much of it as she could, but Papa had stopped her.

"Haven't you heard, you idiot woman?" he'd hissed, slapping at her hands as she'd tried to pay. "The Duvals' fields were too damp this year. That flour is contaminated with mold. Are you trying to kill us all?"

Without a word to Merrick, I stood up and raced out of the room, following my hunch. I ran past the bottles of rye spirits, past the rye bread festering in the kitchen, and out to the field we'd seen earlier.

As I ran, I ticked through every one of the man's symptoms: Nausea. Convulsions. Stomach cramps and diarrhea. A prickling, burning sensation in the feet and hands, caused by a dying circulatory system. Gangrene. Hallucinations.

"Ergot poisoning," I whispered with triumph, stopping in the middle of the rye field. Purple tubular growths hung off nearly every bit of grain I could see. I could feel Merrick's approach, and I turned to him, my face bright with understanding and pride. "It's ergot poisoning! He's been ingesting contaminated rye."

I felt breathless and giddy as my godfather smiled at me, approval coloring his expression.

"It's too late to save his toes, but I know how to treat the other symptoms."

Merrick nodded. "And then?"

I let out a deep breath, remembering the flickering flames that had consumed my vision. The cure. "And then we burn the field."

CHAPTER 15

I SAVED KIERON'S UNCLE.

And the boy with the broken femur.

The mother who went into labor too soon.

The king's man who was thrown from his horse as he rode through our little village collecting taxes, his head split open like a melon grown too ripe.

I never did understand why my patients didn't question my lack of credentials, why they didn't wonder at my training. I couldn't begin to reason that they'd allow a thirteen-year-old girl to treat them, taking my suggestions as if they were words from the Holy First herself.

They could have balked. They could have called me a witch. They could have sought treatment in other towns, far from our valley.

But they came.

And I healed them.

Merrick remained with me in those first weeks in Alletois, only disappearing for his own work late at night, while I slept. Occasionally I would wake to frantic raps on the door, called away to another sickbed, and I'd realize Merrick was gone, his usual seat beside the hearth emptied.

He always left a white clover blossom in his absence, as promise of a swift return.

Weeks turned into a month.

Kieron visited, first bringing a bushel of apples in payment for helping his uncle.

Then a cache of carrots.

Then an invitation to join his family during the Holy First's feast day.

His parents' smiles were warm but uneasy. It was the same look many of the villagers gave me, the strange girl who had arrived without family, blessed with talents far beyond her age. I could only smile back and hope my skills would be enough to silence doubts.

A month turned to two.

Word of my miraculous talents began to spread, and patients came from farther and farther away, bringing coins or provisions to pay me with.

After four months of living in Alletois, I had to have a chicken coop built to house all the birds I'd been given. My larder was always filled, and I ate well, fortified by my neighbors' bounties.

It pleased me that I was able to provide for myself, that I didn't need to rely upon Merrick's graces to stay clothed and fed.

As summer turned to autumn, my workload doubled. There were more colds and cases of sickness as the weather fluctuated between frosty nights and steaming afternoons. There were more injuries too—farmers grown careless with their scythes at harvest, ranchers kicked in the gut as they tried to slaughter their sheep for winter provisions.

I treated them all, always finding the right plant, the right poultice. My salves soothed what was needed, my teas banished what they should.

My routine slowed in winter. So many of the townspeople hunkered away in their homes and wouldn't venture out until spring. Without my own garden to tend, I spent the short daylight hours looking after my chickens and guinea fowl and wandering about my property with a pair of snowshoes given to me by an ailing fur trapper.

Kieron would sometimes visit, bringing a deck of cards or a jacquet set. It was nice to have someone my own age to talk with, and we became fast friends. One winter night, I even confessed to him who my godfather truly was. Kieron was aware I had one and that he was often called away for business, but knew little more than that. The second the truth slipped from me, I regretted my impulsive confidence. I worried he'd laugh, or think I was crazy. Part of me thought he'd run from the house, screaming all the way to the village. But Kieron surprised me and said he'd love to one day meet him.

As the months passed, Merrick left for greater stretches of time, sometimes for two or three days. Once an entire week went by before he returned, and though I missed his company, I found I didn't mind as much as I once had. I was growing up. I had made a friend.

The days began to grow longer, the air warmer, and the ground softer. My birthday was fast approaching, and a tiny burr of worry grew in my middle as the day ticked closer.

Birthdays had never been a time of joyful anticipation for me, and I fretted over what might happen this year. I liked my life in Alletois and hoped Merrick had no plans to surprise me with a new cottage somewhere else or show me an unexpected facet of my gift to strengthen. I wanted things to remain as they'd been that year.

"Please let everything stay the same," I'd whisper before bed each night as the burr grew larger, shifting into a prickle, a spur, a spike.

On the morning of my birthday, I went into the kitchen and spotted one of Merrick's elaborately tiered cakes. It was pink—again—a vivid raspberry, with curlicues of frosting swooping around the edge of each layer. Shards of dark chocolate had been stabbed into the top, like a jagged crown worn by a barbaric king.

"Merrick?" I called, surprised to not find him in his armchair. I tilted my head, listening to the sounds of the cottage.

It felt empty.

Then I heard laughter coming from outside. Only my godfather's laugh could reach so low a bass.

I slipped my feet into a pair of leather clogs—payment from Alletois's cobbler after I helped ease the arthritic pain from his gnarled joints—and went out.

He was in the side yard, his silhouette a stark contrast to the sea of green shoots and leaves beginning to sprout. There was another black form beside him, smaller and lower to the ground, and as I watched, I realized it was chasing him.

"Down! Down, you beast!" he cried, but I could tell how happy he was.

It was a puppy, and it raced after my godfather with pure merriment, tail swishing back and forth like a furred fan. A bubble of laughter burst from me before I could stop it, intruding on their moment, and causing Merrick to look up, startled.

"Oh, Hazel, did we wake you?" he asked with concern, already across the yard in three long strides.

"Not at all."

"Happy birthday, darling girl," he greeted me, giving me a short but warm hug and a kiss on the top of my braided hair. "Many, many happy returns."

"Thank you," I said, reaching on tiptoe to press a kiss to his cheek. "Who is this?"

"A gift for you," he declared.

The puppy danced between us, as if begging to be introduced. Up close, he was far bigger than I'd realized, already coming up to my thighs. His paws were the size of teacups. He'd be a monster once fully grown.

"For me?" I squealed, and knelt down for a proper inspection. He was solid black save for a scattering of white freckles across his snout.

"They reminded me of yours," Merrick said, catching my observation.

"Does he have a name?" I asked, scratching behind the pup's floppy ears. He felt every bit as soft as my velvet quilt.

"I left that for you," he said, smiling. "He'll grow quite large—the perfect companion on a farmhouse so close to the forest." He nodded toward the tree line, and I was touched by his thoughtfulness. Through the winter, we'd heard the echoing cries of wolves, and there were many times, coming home late at night from visiting a sickbed, when I would catch sight of their green eyes as they stalked me.

"They look like stars," I said, rubbing his nose. "I think I'll call him . . ." I paused, considering his happy face. "Cosmos," I finally decided.

Above me, Merrick let out a sound of amusement.

"I'm so glad you returned today," I went on, allowing him to help me back to my feet. "The sweet irises are just about to open their petals. I hoped you wouldn't miss it."

Earlier in the spring, I'd filled my window boxes with medicinal flowers and herbs. Everything had begun to bloom, coloring the cottage with explosions of reds and purples, yellows and oranges, and so many shades of pink.

"I look forward to seeing them," Merrick said, but didn't follow me.

"Merrick?" I asked, turning back. He'd paused, suddenly motionless as stone even as Cosmos pranced about. Something had changed within him. "Do you want cake first?"

Merrick's eyes were suddenly huge and luminous and sad. "We can, if you like. After . . ."

"After?" I echoed.

"I . . ." He swallowed and looked over his shoulder, as if hearing things I could not. "I'm afraid there's somewhere I must take you first."

I glanced down the lane, hoping he only meant a stroll. "Right now?"

Merrick cocked his head, still listening to the silence, his expression pained. "Oh, Hazel. I'm so terribly sorry for this." He took my hand in his and without further explanation, he raised his free fingers and snapped.

CHAPTER 16

THE ENSUING FLASH OF LIGHT WAS BRIGHT AND BLINDing. Stars floated over my vision for a moment longer.

"Oh," I said once my eyes cleared.

"Yes," he agreed.

We stood in the middle of a small, overgrown lane deep in a forest, but I recognized the trees instantly. This was the road that would take us to my parents' house.

"What are we doing here?" I asked, panic seizing me.

Two years was not enough time to erase the memories of a childhood of neglect and scorn. Two years could not wipe away the last image I held of my mother, stooped in the dirt, grabbing at Merrick's coins.

I wondered if those coins had changed their lives.

I was certain they'd not.

But part of me hoped they had.

I pictured Mama in a new dress, one bright and fresh and not faded from years of being scrubbed on the washboard. Perhaps they'd finally fixed the roof, expanded the first level of the cabin, the way they'd always said they wanted to. Remy might have married the baker's daughter he'd been sweet on, and I pictured them all living together. Papa wouldn't have to hunt as much, and they could all spend their days chasing after the toddling triplets I invented for Remy and his imaginary wife.

"There are things here that need to be done," Merrick said, splitting my daydream open wide.

"What things?" I asked, stalling.

"Things you need to see." Merrick's lips rose. It would have looked like a smile if he hadn't been so terribly sad.

I shook my head. "They won't . . . they don't want to see me."

"It doesn't matter what they want. It's what you need."

I stared down the road, apprehension a tangible weight cloaking my shoulders. I peered up at my godfather. He looked as ill as I felt. "There's nothing in that house that I need to see," I insisted.

Merrick reached out and cupped my face, his long fingers icy on my skin. "I wish that were true. . . . Come along."

My feet, willful traitors, set themselves in motion.

The cabin looked nothing like I remembered.

They hadn't repaired the roof, and the back section of it had finally fallen in, collapsing under the weight of winter snows or a heavy rain.

They hadn't expanded either.

In fact, the cabin looked smaller now, somehow. It seemed impossible that the fifteen of us had ever lived together in such a confined space. Well . . . the fourteen of them, I corrected as my eyes drifted to the barn.

It too had aged poorly. Long swathes of paint peeled away from the weathered wood, unfurling down the sides like spools of fraying ribbons. I could sense it was empty, the cows and horses all long gone and never replaced.

The garden had gone to seed and now grew wherever it pleased, untended. Two chickens roamed the tangled jungle, pecking listlessly at the ground.

"They must have left," I said, glancing up at Merrick as I struggled to put together everything I saw. "After you gave them the coins . . . they must have moved. Maybe into town?"

Merrick's mouth was a thin, grim line. "They're still here, Hazel."

As if cued, a burst of noise came from somewhere in the cabin. It was an explosion of coughing, deep and wet and rattling and so very wrong.

A shiver ran through me. I'd never heard a cough like that.

I reached for Merrick's hand, suddenly feeling much younger than my fourteen years. I remembered the little girl who had scurried from that cabin to the barn each evening at sunset, terrified to be caught outdoors after dark. Something about the cough reminded me of that fear, that deep, unshakeable dread, that certainty that monsters lay just out of sight, waiting for you to make a mistake and devour you whole.

"Shall we go in?" Merrick asked and handed me my valise, plucking it from the air with a twist of his fingers. It felt heavier than usual. "I'm sure they're dying to see you."

Later on I would wonder at his choice of words, but in that moment, all I could do was open the door.

The smell inside was terrible, and it was impossible to determine what exactly was causing it. Rubbish and moldering food lay heaped on the table where our family had once gathered to share meals.

Flies buzzed in and out of the doorway. Their droning set my teeth on edge.

"Mama?" I called out uncertainly, caught on the threshold, half in, half out. I couldn't bring myself to go any farther. Deep in the pockets of my skirt, my hands balled into nervous fists. "Papa?"

From the shadows of their back bedroom came an answering moan.

I turned toward Merrick, silently begging him to intervene, but he only gestured for me to continue inside. A painfully long moment passed before I acquiesced.

I entered the cabin, stepping over bits of broken furniture, unidentifiable scraps and lumps of things. How had everything gone wrong so quickly? We'd never had the tidiest of homes, but it had never been like *this.* The house my siblings and I had grown up in was now nothing more than a hovel.

Windows were clouded over with grime and cobwebs, casting a false twilight and making it difficult to see where I stepped. The edge of my shoe struck a discarded wine bottle and it rolled under a table, clinking at others hiding there, and I immediately understood.

They'd spent the coins on drink.

Wine and ale and whiskey.

I spotted the evidence all throughout the cabin.

Casks and barrels and bottles, all empty.

Another volley of coughs drew my attention from the kitchen shelves toward my parents' bedroom. I pressed my lips together, wishing I'd brought a pomander with me, before wandering in to investigate.

"Mama?" I asked, lingering back from the bed. There were two forms lying in it, but it was too dark to determine who was who. The stink of them made my eyes water.

There was a low grunt, and I could make out a set of eyes peering from the soiled blankets, black as beetles.

"Who's there?" the other figure asked, struggling to sit up. "We've nothing to steal, leave us in peace."

"It's not a robber," the first said. Mama. That awful, emaciated crone was my mother. I blinked, trying to see her as she'd been.

Her cheeks had sunk into deep pits, and her skin was a mottled map of broken capillaries and spots. She was nearly as gaunt as Merrick, and the jut of her clavicles looked as sharp as a knife's edge.

"Hazel."

It wasn't a guess, it wasn't a grab. She knew who I was. My heart warmed a little, but I kept my distance.

Papa squinted from his mess of sheets, his eyes never quite focusing on mine. His mouth hung open, and I could see he was missing several teeth. "Don't be daft, you stupid woman. That's not Hazel. That's a fine lady."

Mama struck him with such force his spittle flew through the air, tainting the bedding with flecks of red. "I know my own daughter."

He scoffed. "She's not yours, she never was yours. She was always his."

I glanced back toward the open door, wondering how much of this Merrick heard.

"It's your birthday, isn't it?" Mama realized. "Is that why you've come back? You've come to celebrate your birthday? I should make you a cake. I never . . . I never made you a cake." She tried to push herself from the sodden mattress but fell backward into the dank mess with a cry of pain.

Her anguish spurred me to action, and I crossed the last few feet to kneel beside the bed. I set down my kit and grabbed her hands. Her skin was papery thin and clammy, with a feverish sheen. "No, Mama, don't worry about that. Don't worry about any of that. I came . . ." I paused. "I came to make you well again."

I was dimly aware of Merrick filling the doorframe, backlit and limned with the morning sun. He hadn't entered, and I wasn't sure if he was attempting to give me a moment of privacy as I reunited with my parents or if he simply couldn't fit into the room.

Mama's eyes drifted to him and she jerked back, pulling the sheet in front of her as a shield. With hooked fingers, she made a ward of protection against my godfather, then poked roughly at Papa. "He's here. He's returned," she hissed.

Merrick remained in the doorway, watching everything play out with hooded, worried eyes.

"Be gone, devil," Papa spat. "I'll not have you darken the door of my home again."

I suddenly remembered how Merrick described him in my birthday retellings.

The very foolish huntsman.

As I watched him flounder against my godfather's presence, I couldn't think of a better epithet for him, and it struck me as terribly funny. I'd been so scared of him as a child, but here he was, unable to even get out of his own bed.

"It's not you I'm here for," Merrick muttered, his voice low and dangerous. "My only concern is for Hazel."

"For years we waited for you to be concerned for Hazel." Papa laughed, and his eyes looked glassy and crazed and I could practically see the waves of heat radiating from him.

They were feverish, both of them, nearly deliriously so, and I wondered when they'd last had anything other than spirits in their systems.

"I'm going to get you some water," I decided aloud. "Water and soup. And good fresh bread."

Papa snorted out another little burst of mad laughter. "Good luck finding any of that here."

He wasn't wrong.

There was nothing in the larder save for a few potatoes that were more eyes than flesh, and the bread box held only the skeletons of unlucky mice.

My eyes darted around for anything I might have missed, but I kept coming up short. I couldn't understand how it had gotten like this. Where was Remy? Where were my other brothers and sisters? Didn't they visit? Why had they left our parents in such a state of rot and decay?

"I can at least get water."

I grabbed the little red pail hanging by the back door and headed outside to the creek. I was embarrassed to admit what a relief it was to be momentarily free of the house and all its smells.

Taking deep breaths of air, I cleaned and filled the pail, and wondered at the best way to begin treating my parents. I felt Merrick's approach but remained on my knees, facing the water. I didn't want to look at him. I wasn't sure how to process any one of my multitude of emotions, but if I met his gaze, I'd only start crying.

"Did you know it was going to be like this?"

Those people lying in that bed, in that house, they were not good. They were not kind. They'd never treated me the way parents ought to treat their children . . . but they were my parents all the same, and it shamed me to see them reduced to such a state.

"I did," Merrick said, and his admittance surprised me. I'd thought he would feign ignorance and pretend to be as surprised as I was. I'd thought he'd lie.

"Hazel—" Merrick began, but stopped.

"I'll heal them," I finally said.

I didn't understand why we were here, with them, today of all days, but I would pass this test. I'd pass it as I had every other test he'd given me. When I offered a smile, it felt thin and forced.

He helped me to my feet and trailed after me as I made my way to the cabin. Just before I ducked back inside, he called out, stopping me on the lip of the threshold.

"Hazel?"

I turned to meet his gaze.

"I'm here for you. For . . . whatever you might need."

It was an odd thing to say, an odd thing to offer, when he knew all I needed to do was find the cure. But I nodded as if his words reassured me.

After my reprieve in the fresh air, the smell was worse, a fetid, meaty funk, as though parts of my parents were already starting to spoil. It spurred me into action. I poured water into the cleanest glasses I could find and hurried them to the bed.

"Drink this," I instructed my parents, foisting the glasses into their hands.

Even that simple weight proved too much for Papa, and the glass slipped between his fingers, spilling the water all over the bedding. He didn't seem to notice and raised a phantom mug to his lips.

I helped bring Mama's glass to hers, making noises of encouragement as she took a small swallow, then two. She shook her head after that, unable to stomach more.

"I'm going to get you feeling much better," I promised her. "How did all this start? Was there a fever, or . . ."

She blinked, struggling to remember. "At first there was . . . my headaches. My head. Ache. Headache," she repeated. She blinked heavily before trying the sentence again.

I wanted to be patient; I wanted to listen and hear the details, but she stopped short as a burst of coughs seized her. They filled the room with a terrible odor, hinting at an infection somewhere deep within her.

Patience be damned, I needed to know how to help her now.

Without hesitation, I brought my hands up and cupped her face.

I gasped.

There was no flower. No shimmering, shiny plant beckoning me toward a treatment, toward a cure.

There was only . . .

I pulled my hands away, the image too dreadful to bear, but it lingered in my sight as if burned into my retinas.

A bone-white, gaping skull.

I felt as if the air had been knocked from my lungs. Did she have a tumor? An intracranial hemorrhage? Had a virus taken up residence somewhere within her brain matter?

With trembling fingers, I reached out again, searching for any indication of what I was meant to do.

The skull stared up at me without answer. It hung above my mother's face, motionless. Though there were no eyes within its deep sockets, I knew without a doubt it was staring at me.

As if the skull read my mind, its jaw shifted, opening, widening.

Was that a *smile*?

The lipless curve of it reminded me of my godfather: that was his smile, his grin.

"Merrick!"

He was beside me before I even registered he'd entered the cabin.

He stooped at a painfully contorted angle, reminding me of the gargoyles that lined the parapets of Rouxbouillet's temples.

"I don't understand what this is, what it's telling me to do."

"What do you see?" he asked, but I could tell by the wrinkle of concern marring his brow that he knew. He'd always known.

Without answering, I reached to cup my fingers around Papa's face. He squirmed away in protest, but not before the same glowing skull bloomed across his features.

"How am I supposed to treat them? Why am I seeing a skull? I don't know what it means."

My godfather blinked solemnly and a knife of fear stabbed at me, slicing deep into the quivering mess of my body, ripping and rending my soft insides.

"Merrick?" I whispered, and my voice sounded so small, so scared.

He cleared his throat, his voice like gravel. "Last year, you asked what would happen to the people who could not be saved."

I remembered.

I remembered him sitting in the chair at Kieron's uncle's house. I remembered the doubts swirling through me, the fears that I wouldn't be good enough, that I wouldn't be able to help the stricken man.

But I had.

I'd done it, and everything else my gift had required of me since.

And I'd been good.

Too good, perhaps.

My record was untarnished, perfect and whole. I'd started to believe that I could cure anything. A god had chosen me, of all the people populating our world, to carry his gift, to bestow his blessing upon. Didn't that make me as a god myself? Infallible? Unstoppable?

The skulls leering over my parents' faces suggested otherwise.

"They're going to die?"

"Everyone dies eventually," he murmured unhelpfully.

"But now. They're going to die now?"

He paused, choosing his response with care. "Soon."

"Then why did you bring me here? If I can't treat them, if I can't do anything to save them, then why—"

"You *can* save them," Merrick interrupted. "You're here *to* save them."

"But you just said—"

"Hazel," he interrupted. "There's more than one way to save a life."

I stared with bewildered confusion. He was speaking in circles, saying they were going to die but only a breath later telling me I was meant to save them. If I was going to save them, then they wouldn't die. If I was going to save them—

My breath caught as understanding detonated in my chest, as cruel as the skulls covering my parents' faces.

"No."

I think I spoke it out loud.

I knew my soul was screaming it.

"I'm not . . . I can't . . . You can't expect me to . . ." The words would not come. "I won't," I finally said, folding my arms over my chest to firmly dismiss the notion.

Merrick's silvery eyes drifted from me to the bed. "They're suffering," he reminded me needlessly.

"So I will help ease their pain," I said, searching through the valise. I rummaged through it, pulling out vials and sachets. "I can grind some—"

"It doesn't matter what you do," Merrick interrupted. "You'll only be prolonging their misery. There is no relief for them. Their pain will increase, they'll beg you to free them." His face darkened. "And before they do, they will infect others."

"Others?" I echoed, glancing around the abandoned cabin. "Who?"

Merrick cocked his head toward the door, listening to something I couldn't begin to hear. His eyes went distant, as if he were watching his words play out in real time. "Right now your oldest brother is making his way here. In his carriage is his new bride. They married in secret but want to tell your parents the happy news now. They plan to announce their marriage to her family in three days' time at a large country dance, where there will be plenty of people, so her family won't cause a scene. But Remy and his bride will have brought the sweats with them, caught from your parents. A hundred people at the dance will catch it. They'll bring it home to their loved ones. They'll spread it to more and more, and then—"

"You don't know that!" I shouted, trying to stop his horrid litany. "You don't know any of that!"

"You saw the deathshead," he said gently.

"I saw *a skull,*" I corrected him. "There could be fluid building up in their brains, an infection of some sort. If I can relieve the pressure, then—"

"They'll die no matter what you do, Hazel. It's not a reflection on you or your talents, it's a fact of mortal life. You're a healer, a great one, but no one can ever truly escape me. I come for all. And very soon, I will come for them."

Merrick's words were said without malice, without anger. They were quiet and matter-of-fact.

They infuriated me.

"If you're going to come for them, then why must I do anything? It sounds like all I need is to wait for you to do your job," I snapped. I was a cyclone of emotions burning too hot, fears running too cold.

"That's true," he admitted. "If you want them to suffer, go right ahead and wait. No one would blame you," he added quickly. "Your relationship is decidedly . . . complicated. Do you want to watch them in pain? Do you want to see how low one can stoop before the end?"

My nose wrinkled in horror. "No."

"Is it your brother, then? Do you want him to become ill? His bride? Her family? The minor nobles who will take it back to their estates, to their servants? They'll pass the sweats through them like money changing hands on market day. It might even travel as far as Châtellerault, can you imagine?"

"No!" I shouted, covering my ears to block out his wicked scenario.

He tipped his long fingers in a gallant sweep toward my bag. "Then perform your charge well, *Docteur.* Save them, end them. I'm certain your studies on poisonous plants will be most useful, wouldn't you agree?"

"I'm not poisoning them!" I protested.

"Have you a better idea? Will you bludgeon them to death? Strike them, as your father struck you? The kitchen is in shambles, but I'm certain a few of their knives are still sharp. You know which veins to open if you want them to go quickly."

"Merrick!"

He rolled his eyes. "Make up your mind, girl. Do you want their sickness plaguing the world, infecting everyone it touches? It matters very little to me. Their lives come to an end either way."

"Then *you* do it," I snapped. "You're the god of departures and the grave. You are the great and feared Dreaded End. If they're truly meant to die, then by all means, perform *your* charge well." I mimicked him, throwing my hands toward the bed in a mockery of his sweeping grace.

His eyes darkened and his mouth curled into a dangerous snarl. I knew I'd struck a chord within him, but I wasn't prepared for the full onslaught of his anger.

"How dare you presume to tell me my duties, mortal." His voice was smoke and sulfur. The red of his eyes flickered like banks of coals and bursting embers. I could feel the ground shake beneath the tremor of his bass. "You think yourself on par with me?"

"Of course not," I said, immediately bowing my head. It was too terrifying to look at him when he shed his usual affability. It was impossible to forget the true measure of his might when rage coiled so close to his skin's surface. "I don't understand what's happening. I'm seeking to understand." I reached out and placed my hand on his forearm, trying to form a connection with him, trying to remind him how small and weak and so very vulnerable I was. "Merrick . . . Godfather . . . Help me. Please."

He released a low growl and turned away, leaving the bedroom, leaving the house, leaving me. I was too scared to follow.

I glanced back to my parents, expecting to see twin expressions of horror on their faces, expecting them to cry and moan and beg for their lives. But they'd slipped into a dazed state of near sleep. Papa's eyes were half open, gazing listlessly out the window. Mama whimpered like a fox crying out in the night as something terrible plagued her dreams.

I put my hands on her face once more.

Now that I was prepared to see it, the skull wasn't as shocking.

It rested almost perfectly over her face, giving a ghastly glimpse of everything that lay beneath her skin. As I stared at the glowing ridges, the illuminated bones, it was easy to believe Merrick. This skull wasn't a suggested treatment, a cure waiting to be carried out. It was an omen of impending death.

Mama winced again, sucking in her breath, and I could hear a distinct rattle within her chest. I removed my hands, letting the skull fade away, and took in all the details I hadn't noticed before.

They were sick with the sweats, it was true, and I had no doubt that everything Merrick had predicted would come to pass. The plague would spread from them to my brother, from my brother to his bride, from her to her family, and so on and so on.

But there was more wrong here than just that.

The sickly pallor of her skin, the yellow cast that spoke of something gone dreadfully wrong. Bile was building up in her system, Papa's too, and I grimly thought back to the bottles strewn about the cabin.

I'd read of cirrhosis of the liver, knew that in its later stages it caused stomachs to distend as fluid built up, knew it brought on jaundice and confused drowsiness, knew it made it difficult for blood to clot.

Papa's gums were still bleeding from when Mama had struck him.

"It hurts, Hazel," Mama whispered, her lips barely moving. "It hurts so much." She clawed at the filthy sheet covering her, trying to free herself from its confining hold, and as I eased it away from her, I spotted what she was trying to show me.

Her nightdress—nothing more than a tattered collection of cotton threads frayed past the point of use—had ridden up, exposing her thighs. She raised the hem even higher, gesturing at the mass protruding from her abdomen. It looked obscene, as round as a baby but poking out from the wrong spot. Beneath the yellowed skin, I could see a network of veins pulsing.

"Help me, Hazel," she whispered.

I ran a tender finger over the bulge and she let out a shuddering groan. Her fingers curved into claws and she scratched at the mattress, trying to get away from my gentle pressure.

"I don't . . . I don't know how to treat this," I admitted, feeling helpless.

"You do," Merrick insisted from the doorway. I'd been so focused on the growth in Mama's stomach I hadn't heard him return. "Help us, please."

On the other side of the bed, Papa fought a wave of coughs that left his frame hunched and the bedding soaked in a bright swath of red. I looked away, unable to stomach the way it splashed out of him.

I looked instead to Merrick, my fingers already straying to my bag. His face was full of sorrow, but he nodded encouragingly.

Tears pricked at my eyes, sharp as needles. "When?"

No one answered, but they didn't really need to. I could feel the hoofbeats from Remy's carriage pulsing through my veins, drawing ever closer. It didn't matter if he was days away or only hours.

It needed to be done and over with.

Now.

I found vials of hemlock and nightshades. Used in small doses, they helped treat asthmatic patients struggling to draw breath. But if I were to brew them together, in a strong enough tea . . .

Their hearts would stop first, in theory.

I'd certainly never had cause to test it, but I was almost positive that the tea would make their pulse go slow and sluggish. They'd drift off, falling into a coma. It would be a quiet death, an easy death, one far more merciful than the horrors their own bodies intended for them. Than the horrors their bodies would pass along.

I picked at the cork stoppers with the tip of my fingernail, wondering if I could actually do it, if I could truly administer a lethal dose of poison to my own parents.

"You're not killing them," Merrick murmured softly from the doorway. He was so good at guessing my thoughts. "You're saving them. Saving them from the indignity of a death most brutal."

"But why am I the one who has to do it? Why can't you save them? Why can't you ease their suffering?" My voice quavered. I was still hopeful he'd intervene.

Merrick blinked curiously. "I *have* saved them. . . . I brought them you."

His words sank in deep, and I knew there was no way out of this. It was me or nothing.

We did not speak again as I set the kettle to boil.

CHAPTER 17

The Sixteenth Birthday

The morning of my sixteenth birthday, I woke to thunder and a chorus of dead faces pressed against my bedroom windows, staring in with hungry white eyes.

There were four of them, one for every deathshead I'd seen.

One for every murder I'd committed.

Papa.

Mama.

The baker three villages over, whose wicked case of consumption threatened to infect every customer unlucky enough to purchase his blood-flecked loaves.

A soldier who'd broken his ankle chasing after a maid who'd wanted no amount of his kisses.

Their mouths opened and shut again, wordlessly, like the great carp that surfaced in the pond behind my cottage, forever looking for a little something to fill their bellies with.

The first time I'd seen one of them—Papa, stumbling into my cottage the night after I'd poisoned him, with Mama not far behind—I'd been terrified out of my mind. For one long, horrible moment, I'd believed the poison had not worked. I'd feared them still alive, come to exact a horrid revenge.

I'd backed into my dining room table, blessedly knocking over the set of shakers and shattering one of the crystal baubles. A spray of salt scattered across the floor and my parents had recoiled, staggering back from the grains as their faces twisted in painful rictuses.

I'd spent the rest of the night pushing their foul specters back, inch by inch, tossing salt at them until they were out of the house, then had raced around the inner perimeter, dusting each doorway and window to keep them out.

I rolled over now, pulling my quilt to my chin, and lost sight of the soldier, my father, and the baker. Only one ghoul was at the window now.

Mama.

I studied her face, wondering if she remembered what today was, wondering if she remembered anything at all.

The ghosts recognized me, obviously, forever trailing after the person they'd spent their final moments of life with, but did she still know it was me, or was I simply a lantern, a beacon bringing in the moths of those I'd killed?

I pushed myself out of bed and joined her at the window, huddled safe and warm on my side of the salted glass. Somehow sensing me, she raised her hand to the pane in greeting. Her flesh had recently begun to fall away, and the tip of her finger bone tapped at the glass.

I raised my hand to hers, marveling at the difference between us.

My heart weighed heavily within me, full of so many things I wished I could tell her, things I wished she could understand.

It seemed an especially cruel irony that while she'd wanted

nothing to do with me in life, she found herself drawn to me in death.

"I'm sixteen today, Mama," I murmured, and outside she cocked her head. She could hear me speak, even if my words no longer made sense. I knew they didn't. I'd seen her brain liquefy and fall out of her nose and ears, months ago.

My ghosts were nothing like any of the stories my siblings had made up to spook one another on long winter nights. They weren't translucent, glowing forms, forever rattling chains or howling with off-pitch moans. They were like shadows to me, dark shapes seen from the corner of my eye until I willingly focused upon them, and only then could I see their terrible visages, the rot, the decay.

My fingertips trailed over the chilled glass, mirroring hers. There was no heat warming her side, and I wondered if she could feel mine.

I wasn't sure why I saw the ghosts of those I'd killed. I didn't know if it was meant to be a punishment for lives ended too soon or merely part of my responsibility, to hold on to the memories of those I'd snatched away as the world kept turning and the people they'd loved gradually forgot about them.

I hadn't found a way to ask Merrick.

I'd tried, nearly a dozen times, but the question always hung in my mouth, impossible to get out.

He'd never mentioned it, never indicated that he saw them. There was so much about my life that he already knew, that he'd foretold, it felt like a small victory to keep this one secret from him, however gruesome it might be.

I stayed with Mama for a moment grown too long, till the other ghouls noticed and made their way over, shuffling and stumbling slowly—they were always so slow—to press themselves closer to me.

I gave my mother one last uneasy look before turning to go.

"I suppose it's time to salt the fences again."

Merrick was sitting on a stool in the kitchen as I went in, still adjusting my hair. I'd never worn it up before and had had a bit of difficulty figuring out where to jab the combs and pins to get the chignon to stay in place. I missed my childish braids but wanted Merrick to see me as the grown-up I supposed I was. Especially today.

This year's cake was already set out. It was a grand, towering confection three tiers high, frosted pale pink and studded with sugar-dusted strawberries. The candles lit themselves as I entered, fizzing like tiny fireworks in bursts of rose-gold sparks.

"You've outdone yourself," I greeted him, leaning in to kiss his cheek and accept his warm squeeze.

"You only turn sixteen once," he said fondly.

"Is sixteen too grown-up for cake for breakfast?" I asked, already taking down two dessert plates from the shelf. I knew he'd never pass on the chance for sweets.

Merrick had changed out my servingware again, I noticed, spotting the raised flowers circling the plates. Their pink matched my cake, and the edges were ringed with what appeared to be real gold.

"What happened to my white plates?" I asked, turning the new ones over to study. They were impossibly thin and felt as though they'd shatter if I held them too tight.

"I thought these were far better suited for a young lady of sixteen," he said, pushing himself off the stool to look for forks and knives. They too were shining gold, every bit as ostentatious as a king's ransom, and I made a mental note to tread lightly.

Merrick had been after me for months to consider moving. He said my skills had grown past the point of Alletois and he wanted me to spread my wings in a larger city, often telling me how well I would take to Châtellerault, rubbing elbows with courtiers and nobles. I always sighed, remembering the one time I'd been in the presence of nobility, that dreadful day when I'd met Prince Leopold. I had no desire to move anywhere near him.

"Would you like some tea?" I asked, turning to light the stove with the flick of a match. "Assuming you haven't whisked away my kettle too?"

"I haven't whisked away anything," he protested grandly. "Nothing is missing, and everything I removed was replaced with something far nicer."

"Adeline Marquette gave me three lemons yesterday," I boasted, spotting the new pink kettle. I fumbled with the top for a moment before filling it with water. "Shall we cut one up for our celebration?"

Merrick had been rummaging in the ice chest and turned, holding a crystal pitcher. A dozen lemon slices bobbed in the pink fluid. "I already made us lemonade," he said, obviously pleased with the spread he'd created.

"Merrick!" I exclaimed, forgetting to temper my disappointment. "I was saving those lemons for something important!"

He frowned. "What could be more important than your birthday? Let's cut the cake and I will tell you the story of your birth."

I glanced in the sink, relieved to see he'd at least had the decency to save me the peels. Long curls of dimpled yellow lay in the basin like forgotten confetti, and I made a mental note to hang them up later, to dry. Powdered lemon peel helped with aching joints, and the butcher's wife would be pleased I'd thought of her come the next cold snap.

"Will you be staying long?" I asked, looking about the cottage for the best place to eat. There were windows everywhere, and I could already see Mama making her way across the back garden, her gait slow and unsteady.

"If you like," Merrick said. "But go on, make a wish, make a wish," he insisted, waving at the candles.

I took a deep breath and closed my eyes as I blew them out. I'd long ago stopped wishing for anything—I was more than capable of getting whatever I needed, and Merrick provided far too many extravagances in my life as it was. It seemed gluttonous to ask for more.

But it was one of his favorite mortal traditions, so I always played along.

"Kieron was planning on taking me for a birthday picnic," I said, watching him begin to cut into the top tier of cake. The inside was marbled pink and yellow. "Strawberry?" I guessed, accepting the plate.

He grinned wide, pleased to have fooled me. "With all the sugared berries, you'd think so, wouldn't you?"

"What is it, then?" I asked, poking at the sponge. I waited for him to serve himself before taking a bite.

"Dragon fruit," he intoned, his eyes fixed on me as he motioned for me to try it.

"Oh," I mused after swallowing a mouthful. Its sweetness lingered too long, and I wished there was something other than lemonade to wash it down with. "I thought it would be spiced, for some reason."

"Spiced?" Merrick asked, then took a large bite. He chewed with relish. "I have. I have outdone myself."

"Because of the dragon, I guess," I said, shoveling another piece onto my fork as though I were going to eat it. "Fire . . . spice . . ." I shrugged. "Would you want to join us?"

"You and Kieron?"

I nodded, watching dismay color his features. He didn't want to, but he also didn't want to tell me no. Not on my birthday.

There had been a recent change to my godfather and Kieron's relationship, one I wasn't sure the cause of or the solution for. No longer would Merrick join us in a game of cards after supper or a long stroll through my carefully salted acres. He always seemed to be rushing away whenever Kieron knocked on the door, snapping himself into the void after a harried remembrance of needing to be elsewhere.

"You said it was to be a picnic?"

A jagged bolt of lightning crackled down out of the sky as if on cue, and I absently wondered if he'd enlisted the help of the Divided Ones to turn my fortunes sour today.

"We could spread out a blanket in the parlor and pretend," I suggested. "It would mean a lot to me if you did."

"Because you miss me," he tried, already cutting a second piece.

"Of course. And because Kieron is so special to me as well," I answered carefully.

The edge of Merrick's fork dug into the plate with a decisive screech. "He's not good enough for you," he finally said, his voice quiet and subdued.

"You'd say that about anyone," I reasoned.

"And I'd mean it."

"That's not helping your cause," I teased him, and refilled his lemonade.

"I wasn't aware my cause needed assistance." Merrick frowned. "I don't like that you've gotten so serious about the boy. You're so young. You have so much of your life ahead of you. I don't want to see you hurt."

I set my fork down. "Kieron would never hurt me."

"You don't know that."

"But *you* do," I said playfully, nudging his side. "You see everything, and you know that it will all be well. You can see how happy he makes me."

"It . . . it's only going to make things harder."

"What do you mean?" I asked, a nasty, peevish worm twisting in my stomach. Any trace of lightheartedness had faded from his eyes.

"When he—" He bared his teeth as he ground to a halt, stopping the words that wanted to spill out. "When *you,*" he tried again, putting too much emphasis upon the new word. "When you leave."

I couldn't stop the sigh from escaping me. "I don't want to go. Alletois is my home. The home *you* picked out for me," I reminded him. I didn't want to fight, not on my birthday, not when I'd been hoping to make headway with him and Kieron.

"When you were a child," he said, his voice irritatingly patient and level. This was a god who could argue for millennia and not raise his tone even once—he didn't have to. He was the literal last word. "You're not one any longer. It's time you took the next step. It's time you left Alletois."

"Then Kieron can come with me," I said, brightening as the idea struck me for the first time. "So I'll have someone with me in the capitol."

It was absolutely the worst thing to say. I could see it the second the words left my lips, and in that moment I would have done anything to take them back.

"You'd have *me,*" Merrick said, sounding wounded.

It was a dangerous thing to hurt the feelings of a god.

"I only mean . . ." I pressed my lips together, trying to come up with the right set of words that would stop this from happening, that would keep him mollified. "I only mean that you have to travel so much, for all the important things you do. It would be nice to have a friend."

"A friend," he repeated skeptically.

I felt like a small beetle cornered by a scorpion. I could practically see the barbed tail thrashing back and forth, ready to strike with venomous speed.

"Don't assume my absences mean I don't know everything that goes on here. The two of you have been more than friends for quite some time now, and you'd have to be a fool to think I wouldn't notice." He leaned across the table, growing even taller as sudden anger swept through him. The red of his eyes sparked with fury. "And you know better than anyone that I will not abide a fool!"

Thunder rumbled outside, a long roll blanketing the land as he stalked out of the room, heading for the parlor. The windowpanes rattled in their lead casings, and my sternum ached from its force.

"We weren't trying to keep anything from you," I called out to him. "Truly, Merrick. We *are* friends . . . just . . . more now."

The *more* had begun last autumn.

Kieron had finished work for the day and had brought by a basket of apples to surprise me with. I'd taken them from him and, on impulse, leaned in to offer him a hug. It was meant to be nothing but a small squeeze of thanks, but it had somehow changed into something more, and when he'd pulled away, his face had held the loveliest look of wonder and astonishment.

And then I'd kissed him.

Or he'd kissed me.

It didn't matter who had begun it, because both of us had quickly surrendered to the magic of it, tracing shy fingertips across the other's face, the basket of apples forgotten.

It was my first kiss, and I hadn't known what I was doing, only that it felt wonderful and made me happy and that his lips had been a heady mix of crisp apple and a sweetness that was wholly Kieron.

I couldn't get enough of him, and later that winter, when he told me he loved me, that he'd always loved me, that he'd spend the rest of his life loving me, I knew I was his—and he was mine—forever.

I knew Kieron planned to propose today.

He'd been making noises about a grand surprise for weeks, and only days before, I'd caught him poking around in my jewelry box, looking at the sizes of rings Merrick had gifted me through the years.

I pressed the palms of my hands to my eyes. They felt hot with welling tears. This was not how I wanted the day to go. I wanted all of us together, happy and here. I wanted Merrick to smile as I accepted Kieron's hand and heart. I wanted us to eat the terribly sweet cake and plan for a dizzyingly bright future. Merrick and Kieron were my family now. Why couldn't we all be at peace with one another?

I sighed, turning to glance into the parlor.

It was quiet, and I could picture Merrick seated beside the fireplace, staring broodingly into its flames. I listened to the falling raindrops, counted the seconds, and wondered if enough time had passed. I'd go to my godfather and tell him how much I loved him, how he was right about leaving the village, how much I looked forward to being in Châtellerault. I'd tell him everything exactly as he wanted to hear it, coax him into a better mood, and then he'd see how he'd overreacted. He'd see how much Kieron cared for me and how we *both* could be right at the same time.

"Merrick?" I called softly.

He didn't answer.

Of course he was going to make this harder than it needed to be. There was nothing in the world worse than a god nursing a wound. Rolling my eyes, I cut him another slice of cake and carried it with me to the parlor, knowing he'd appreciate the gesture.

But when I surveyed the room, it was empty.

Merrick was gone.

CHAPTER 18

THE TRUNK SHUT WITH A DECISIVE CLICK BEFORE I hauled it from my bedroom, letting it join the other bags by the front door. I glanced out the windows, expecting to see Kieron's cart on its way across the field, but the lane was empty.

I sighed, twisting his ring on my finger over and over as I waited. It was still a novel oddity for me, making my hand look far more refined and grown-up than I felt.

Yesterday, just moments after I learned that Merrick had left, Kieron had rapped on the door with freshly picked wildflowers in one hand and his grandmother's ring in the other. I'd pushed down all my wounded feelings and pent-up frustrations, thrown caution—and Merrick's vague forebodings—to the wind, and said yes. We'd spent the afternoon on my quilt beside the fire, pretending it was the picnic we'd planned, kissing and dreaming of our future. When I'd asked if he'd wanted to begin that future then and there, starting right now, he'd laughed at my impetuosness but agreed.

Now my stomach was a ball of nerves, and every muscle in me jangled with barely suppressed anticipation.

We were actually doing this.

We were packing up and leaving Alletois for good.

I had no pretensions that Merrick would be unable to find us, to find *me,* wherever I went. But Kieron and I would be married by then, man and wife, and there wasn't a thing my godfather could do to break that vow.

My fingers tapped on the sill. Where was Kieron?

The clock on the mantel said it was half past eleven, and he'd promised to arrive by noon. There was still time left—so, so, so much time—but I felt annoyed with the wait. If our roles were reversed and it was me meeting him, I would have had the horse and cart waiting outside his farmhouse at daybreak.

I whirled away from the window, pushing aside the unhelpful thoughts.

Kieron had wanted to finish his chores, the last ones he'd do for his father, and see that everything at the farm was left just so. Following his lead, I stalked about my own house, making sure I'd not left anything important behind, scrawling out a list of instructions for the young boy I'd hired to look after the cottage until someone else would move in. Cosmos would come with us, but there were all my fowls and the gardens to tend to.

As I paced from room to room, feeling my anxiety and trying to understand its root, my pup skittered after me, his nails clicking on the wooden floors.

When the clock chimed twelve, I raced to the front window, but there was still no sign of Kieron.

Restless, I moved my belongings to the porch, certain he'd be here soon. He'd probably gotten caught up saying farewell to his parents.

The ghosts were in a line in their spot across the field, against the fence, nothing more than dark shapes on the horizon, but even from a distance, I could tell they were watching me. I'd driven them back there earlier that morning, then surrounded them with a circle of salt. I knew it wouldn't keep them there forever, knew eventually the circle would wear thin and break, but Kieron and I would be long gone by then. It could take them months to finally stumble their way to me again.

Unsure of what to do with myself, I went through the house one last time. I spotted my valise under the worktable in the study but left it where it was. I didn't know what the future held for me, for us, but I planned to never treat another person again. I would not add to my collection of ghosts. If I was cutting ties with Merrick and his dreams for me, I was going to sever them all.

A quarter of an hour went by.

Then another. And another.

And still no Kieron.

At one o'clock, I decided to go after him.

I loaded the cart with my bags and hitched up my dappled mare. I whistled for Cosmos to hop into the back and I left the cottage behind without a second glance. There was too much promise ahead to spend the day looking backward.

We took the land at a brisk trot, flying by the ghosts without acknowledgment. The sun was shining and the day smelled of warmed earth and flowering trees. I nearly laughed aloud as I pictured Kieron on his way to me now, how we'd run into each other on the narrow little lane and have to decide whose cart we'd take. But we didn't meet on the lane, and we didn't meet on the road, and I made it all the way to the LeCompte farm without seeing my beloved.

I hitched Zadie to a post, expecting Kieron to come out in a rush of apologies and explanations, but the farmhouse was still.

No one answered when I knocked, and I paused, wholly unsure of what I ought to do next. Were they still at work in the orchards? Had they gone into the village for supplies? It would be just like Kieron to want to help his father for as long as he could, putting in a full day's work before he snuck off to elope.

I was just about to go to the barn, to see if their cart was there, when I heard a swift *crack* from the back of the house.

Curiosity led me around the porch.

I found Kieron, still in his work clothes, splitting logs. I leaned against the railing to admire my almost-husband, watching the way the sunlight played across his long, lean form, the way the sleeves of his shirt strained over his biceps.

But something was wrong.

The swing of his axe was wide and unfocused, never striking its intended mark.

"Kieron?" I called, keeping my voice light. "Have you forgotten what time it is? What day it is?"

I tried to laugh, as if this would be a joke we'd tell many times throughout our lives, even when we were old and wrinkled and gray. *Do you remember the time you forgot you were eloping with me?* I smiled too widely, desperately trying to push down the sense of unease growing in my middle telling me that something wasn't right, that something was terribly, terribly wrong.

He turned on shaking legs, his eyes listing vaguely somewhere above my right shoulder, and all traces of my attempted laughter died away.

"Hazel!" he exclaimed, and his voice was wrong too, thick with consonants grown soft. A curtain of blood fell from his hairline.

I had to piece together the story on my own from the clues around him.

His parents had taken fruit to market and, because he was Kieron, he'd decided to do one last project before sneaking away, chopping a fallen tree for firewood. His axe had split a log badly, and a piece had ricocheted back and struck his temple.

There was so much blood.

His equilibrium was off. I saw evidence he'd thrown up. He trembled, flushed with fever, but his hands were like ice. He answered my questions in confusing circles interrupted by snorts of laughter that dissolved into tears.

"Do you hear that?" he asked, whipping around toward the house. He pawed at the air, as if trying to swat the cause away.

I heard a smattering of birdsong in the trees, but nothing that should have agitated him so. "Hear what?"

Kieron frowned, then cupped his hands over his ears. "It's so sharp. The ringing. It hurts! Make it stop! Make it stop!" He picked up a log and hurled it away from him, hard. It shattered a window along the side of the house, and I jumped at the sudden ferocity.

I'd treated patients with concussions before—there were dozens of ways a head could be struck during a workday—but this felt different, more dangerous.

His brain was swelling, I was certain of it, filling with fluid and pushing upon his skull. It would eventually restrict blood flow. His brain wouldn't get the oxygen it needed, and parts of it would begin to die. And when the brain began to die . . .

There was only one way to stop the pressure from building to such levels.

Trepanation.

I'd need to drill a small hole through his skull, giving the brain a way to let go of all the pressure. It was his only chance.

But I couldn't do it here.

Wrestling the axe from him, I guided Kieron to my cart. We'd have to go back to my farm, back to my cottage, back to where that damned valise waited. I'd send word to his family when I could and help clean up the mess of shattered glass later. Later, when Kieron was well.

Kieron didn't want to go.

His steps kicked out to the side like a newborn foal's. He nearly fell over trying to get up onto the wagon's seat, and Cosmos went mad, barking with excitement and fear.

"Stop!" Kieron ordered, slurring as he pointed a warning finger at Cosmos, hitting the side of the cart with a booming thud that finally silenced the pup. I'd never seen Kieron so aggressive before. I knew it was only the injury, knew that the swelling could cause him to react in surprising ways, but it still set my nerves on edge anticipating the next blow.

The ride back felt a million years long. We passed the ghosts, but I barely noticed, mentally preparing myself for the surgery to come.

Once back at the cottage, I struggled to get him inside and across the large worktable in my study. He didn't want to lie down, didn't want to be still. I held back tears as I tried to smile and reassure him.

As fast as quicksilver, his mood changed again. A dopey expression washed over his face as he grinned up at me. He reached out to hold my chin. It took him several attempts to catch it. "So pretty today Hazel. You. I'm today Hazel, you marrying today Hazel. You," he announced proudly, unaware his words were wrong, a jumble of noises and nonsensical sounds.

I wanted to howl. I wanted to fling myself over his heaving chest and burst into tears. I wanted to sit and wring my hands as someone else handled this, as someone else took care of him. But there was no one in town who could help, not like I could. Not like I would.

"It's going to be okay," I tried, the cords in my neck straining as I struggled for composure, and I wasn't sure if that promise was for him or me.

I needed to prepare, needed to grab at some sort of structure and plan to follow or I feared I'd lose my mind.

I opened my supply cupboard.

There were scalpels and braces and brushes, burrs of various sizes, and the drill.

I stared at the C-shaped piece of metal. It was thicker than my thumb. Its handle was made of polished mahogany, and it looked far too lovely to be used for such a gruesome service.

I'd practiced the surgery before—on the skulls of freshly slaughtered pigs bought at market—but I'd never done it on a live patient, and my hands trembled now.

"Today Hazel you," Kieron murmured again as his eyes fluttered, struggling to remain open.

There wasn't much time left.

As tenderly as I could, I probed at his head, feeling the wound.

"No," he protested, flinching at the pain. He wrapped his hands around my wrists, squeezing too tight.

"Kieron, that hurts," I said, trying not to flinch in pain, trying to keep the panic quelled. If he wanted to, he could cast me aside like a rag doll. I'd always loved how much taller he was than me, always admired how strong and capable he was, but now—though I knew he'd never hurt me on purpose—I feared just how much harm that powerful body might do. "Kieron, you're hurting me."

Instantly remorseful, he loosened his grip, lowering my hands to his cheeks, and I saw it.

A skull, gruesomely misshapen and black with poisoned blood.

The world around me stopped and shrank until all I could see was its dark form, its empty eye sockets, its bared teeth.

"No."

I wanted to scream, but instead that one tiny, small word escaped me. It was a puff of air, a breath on a cold morning, a wisp of vapor too fragile to last.

"No."

Not my Kieron.

Not today, when we were meant to be joined together. Our lives were supposed to be long, stretching out in front of us, rife with possibility and good fortune. We would be married. We would have children. We'd watch them grow and our house would be filled with love, with laughter, with comfort and care, and this was not happening. This could not be happening. The skull wasn't really there. The skull was wrong. The skull . . .

The skull snapped its teeth at me, demanding I pay attention to it.

I bit down hard on the inside of my cheek, swallowing the shriek that wanted to rip itself from my soul.

I had to think clearly.

I wasn't going to kill Kieron. That wasn't happening. There had to be another way. Another path.

So.

If I couldn't kill him, I'd have to save him, regardless of the consequences that would come.

If. *If* there were consequences to come.

My parents and the other ghosts had been sick. They'd been sick and would have gone on to harm others had they lived. Many, many others.

I didn't understand how the deathshead worked, what sense

of morality it operated under, how it decided how many potential victims were too many.

But Kieron wasn't sick. He wasn't a threat.

I narrowed my eyes as a thought crossed my mind.

It was a terrible thought.

Perhaps the worst one I'd ever had.

Kieron *was* a threat.

Not to me, not to his family or anyone in town.

But to Merrick . . .

To Merrick, he was the ultimate danger. The one who would take me away from my godfather, away from the plans he'd set out for me, the plans he expected me to follow without hesitation, the plans I always had followed . . . until I'd fallen in love with Kieron.

I cupped Kieron's face again, studying the skull with fresh eyes.

Had my godfather done this? Did this skull mean what the others had? Or was it simply doing my godfather's dirty work?

"Damn the deathshead," I muttered, then sprang into action. I laid out the instruments, pulled down bottles of antiseptics, and arranged everything I would need in neat rows on a tray, choking back sobs I couldn't afford to feel.

I didn't want to believe it. I didn't want to think Merrick would be behind something so dastardly.

But I also couldn't find it in me to say he wouldn't. . . .

Kieron's eyes flickered open and he tried to focus. "Where are we today, Hazel?"

I swallowed. "We're at home."

"Today Hazel home," he repeated, struggling to sit up. "Today Hazel's home. No. I need today Hazel my home . . ." His words were like apples left past harvest, wormy and softened to mush.

"It's all right. You're safe here. You were hurt, but I'll take care of you, I promise."

"Today Hazel promise," he repeated dully. "Prom . . . ise . . . prom . . ."

His eyes rolled back into his head as his body began to shudder, to shake. His muscles rippled beneath my fingertips as he bucked against me, and I fumbled for something to put in his mouth to keep him from biting off his own tongue.

After a moment, the seizure passed. His eyes fell open, gazing about the room, and when they found mine, he broke into a sloppy smile. "Not right today Hazel. Not . . . true." He blinked, struggling to find the right words in his addled mind. "Not right Hazel today. Today Hazel. Hazel."

I squeezed his arms. "Just rest now, Kieron. Rest."

I plucked the drill from its bath. The spiked bit gleamed inside the cylindrical blade, a gruesome flower ready for blood.

"Not right today Hazel," Kieron repeated behind me, pawing at my skirts, the pitch of his voice rising with panic. Was he trying to tell me he knew what I was about to do? Did some part of him know he was meant to die? Would he try to stop me?

The drill fell from my hands to the floor and I cursed. I'd need to clean it again and there was no time, there wasn't time, there wasn't—

"Not today Hazel," he insisted. A wounded noise of frustration escaped him. "I take care of today Hazel." His fingers shook as they wrapped around mine, tightening as if he was trying to impart the message his tongue could not convey.

With a final burst of strength, he pulled me down to him, kissing me with all the fervor I'd imagined for our wedding day.

But like everything about this afternoon, it was off.

The moment his fingers knotted through mine, I wanted to recoil. His soft lips had turned to bone, cold and unyielding. The ridge beneath his nose cavity pressed in painfully. Bared teeth clattered against my own.

"I . . . love today Hazel. Hazel. All . . . all . . . always."

Kieron's eyes rolled backward as he fell into unconsciousness, and I was ashamed to feel happy he'd slipped under. It would be easier to get through this without him breaking my heart each time he spoke, flailing and jostling the surgical table as I tried to work. It was for the best.

"I will see you soon," I promised his still form, pressing a quick kiss to his forehead.

And then I picked up the razor.

The surgery itself didn't take long.

When it was finished, a circlet of small holes had been drilled into the skull, revealing glimpses of slick white brain tissue. Before I bandaged the area with cotton gauze, I inspected the clean edges of my work.

My insides struggled between pride and utter revulsion.

Had it worked? Was it enough to break the deathshead and save him? A long moment of cowardice ticked by. I could not bring myself to check.

I was tying off the ends of the bandages when I sensed the change of pressure in the air and knew Merrick had come.

I turned with a smile but immediately stopped short.

Tangible waves of fury radiated off him. Still, I faltered forward, playing innocent.

"I did it," I said, pushing back a lock of hair. "My first trepanning. Do you want to see the holes? None of the skull splintered off at all—and on my first attempt! It was—"

"You stupid, stupid girl." He strode forward, peering down at the supine form spread across the table. "What were you thinking?"

I rubbed my hands together. I'd felt so triumphant only moments before but now trembled against my godfather's wrath.

"He was showing signs of edema. I . . . I had to operate if he was to live."

Merrick sliced through my nervous chatter with the swift whack of an executioner's blade. "He wasn't meant to live."

"But I—"

"Did you see the skull?" His fingers clenched the edge of the table, digging in so hard they left divots pressed into the wood. *"Did you see the skull?"*

"Well, yes, but it was—"

"Then what is this?" Merrick smacked the tray, scattering instruments across the room in a clatter of scarlet and steel.

A series of short, shaky gasps escaped my chest. Panic rose, choking me. "Merrick, please. I couldn't let him die. I just . . . I couldn't."

"I told you yesterday it was a mistake to let him into your life, and now this," he hissed. "What were you thinking, Hazel?"

"I couldn't lose him, I couldn't," I repeated, wanting to hide from the heat rolling off him.

"I'll never understand why mortals place such emphasis on the here and now. This boy will die and your life will go on. You can live without him. You *will* live without him. Why is that such a hard concept to grasp? Your heart won't stop if his does."

"It *will*!"

"It won't," he insisted.

I sank to my knees, small and broken, as tears raced down my cheeks. "It will feel as though it has. It will feel that way to me!"

For a long moment, the room was silent save for my gasps for air, wet and trembling.

Gradually, Merrick's shoulders fell and his fury faded. When he spoke again, his voice was softer, full of commiseration. "Leave him for a moment and come with me."

"I can't." I pushed away the tracks of tears, but more only followed. "I need to finish bandaging him and—"

"Hazel."

Merrick held out his hand, and for a moment, I was tempted to remain at Kieron's side, flexing the untested muscles of my newfound defiance. But before I could resist, Merrick's fingers wrapped around my wrist and with a snap of his fingers, we were gone.

CHAPTER 19

EVEN BEFORE I OPENED MY EYES, I KNEW WE WERE IN the Between.

I expected to see my little house, the copse of pink-flowered trees, but Merrick had brought us somewhere new. There was a vast body of water before us, its beach made up of icy green sea glass. Shallow waves lapped at the shore, making the glass sing like ringing crystal. At the far end of the lake, tall boulders rose like a mountain and roaring cascades of water ran off their edges.

Merrick headed toward those falls now. A narrow path wound through the rocks. The stones were slick with mist, and I slipped twice as I climbed after him. He ducked behind the rapids and I paused, eyeing the gap warily, unsure if I could make the leap. I landed clumsily on a wet ledge, and Merrick had to grab my waist to keep me from plunging to the rocks below.

"What is this place?" I yelled, shouting to be heard over the roaring water, but Merrick, hunched low against the cave's ceiling, didn't answer. He dodged stalactites as he headed toward a slit in the rocks, opening before us like a puckered wound. Something about its narrow darkness sent a cold stab of total dread down my chest, settling into my belly like a pickaxe. The darkness was alive somehow, watching us with an ancient interest.

If Merrick felt any of the malignant energy, it didn't affect him. "Come," he urged.

Stomach clenched, I shook my head. There were some secrets of the universe mortals were not meant to know, and whatever lay down that path was one of them. I felt the wrongness of being here. It pinged off my teeth like lightning crackling through a storm-lit sky, throbbed through my veins, and set my very blood on edge.

I was not meant to see this.

"Hazel."

He held out his hand, and against my better judgment, I took it. As his fingers closed around mine, I felt as though I'd just made a gravely important bargain but was uncertain of the exact terms. Glancing back at the falls, I longed for the breezes and light gray sky of the world beyond, the forests of my home, my little cottage. Even Kieron lying unconscious on my table, surrounded by bone chips and blood. Anything but this.

Without hesitation, he led us into the void.

Trickling water echoed off stones I could not see. The air around us was surprisingly clean, fresh, with a mineral bite strong enough to make my throat heave. I tightened my grip on Merrick's hand, terrified of losing him. If he were to leave me alone in this darkness so complete, I feared I'd go mad.

"Where are we going?" I dared to ask, and my whisper carried up and down the tunnel, returning to us over and over, until it broke apart into a barrage of words, out of order and without sense.

Merrick said nothing but quickened his pace. He never tripped, never faltered on a rise in the ground or a bit of rock poking into the path. I tightened my grip, grateful for his lead.

After a time, my eyes adjusted, picking up bits of light down corridors we didn't take. The ceiling rose to a steep point above us, like the nave of a great sanctuary. To our right, through arched windows, was a yawning cavern. Dim light filtered down, illuminating lengths of bridges that spanned the wicked chasm.

The air grew colder. Puffs of breath steamed from my mouth, clouding the passage.

"Every year I tell you the story of your birth," Merrick began, picking his words with care. His voice creaked, as if he was holding back a deluge of emotions, a crumbling dam about to collapse and ruin everything. "Every year I tell it to you, and there's a question I always expect you'll ask, but you never have."

The tunnel forked and he pulled us to the left. The air softened, scented with wafts of smoke and wax. We entered a chamber and I paused, wonder radiating from my core.

The room was full of candles.

Some were tall and fat, their flames steady and strong. There were skinny tapers, with trickles spilling down their sides. Some were small votives. Others were great pools of liquid, entirely melted, their lights about to sputter out. They were perched along rows of wooden tables, stacked plinths, and rocky outcrops. Above us, the chamber's ceiling vaulted to a wide curve. Polished by eons of rainwater, it reflected light from the hundreds of thousands of candles.

"What is this place?" I whispered. I didn't want to break the hypnotic beauty of the flames.

The fires highlighted the folds and sharp curves of Merrick's face, shrouding his eyes in deep shadow. He looked out over the vast cavern. "This is my home."

Home. The Dreaded End's home.

That could only mean . . .

"Are those lives?" I guessed, studying the candles.

"Mortal lives," he clarified. He pointed to hollow niches across the cave, near the swell of the ceiling. In each nook, a ball of light hovered, flames flicking over themselves, consuming the air with colorful light. "Up there are the gods."

There were hundreds of them, each burning their own unique shade.

"They have no wicks," I observed, squinting.

"We don't burn out. Not like them." He gazed back to the floor. "Each of these is one life. When the flame goes out, that life is over."

He glided down the shallow steps, walking deep into a row.

I trailed after him, lost in the sea of glimmering lights. "They're all so different."

"Some lives are long," he said, gesturing to a fat, round pillar. "Others are short. Some are over before they even have the chance to begin."

A series of tiny tea lights stabbed at my heart. They were small, so small, some just minutes from flickering out.

"Can't you do anything for them?" I asked, my gaze drawn to one writhing wick. The flame hissed and sputtered, meeting a swift death in the pool of wax. It was gone before I could offer it something to feed on. A wisp of smoke curled from the blackened filament, shimmering memories of a life burned out too quickly.

Merrick's eyes fell on me, heavy with sadness. "I do. I send their souls to an eternal rest."

"That's not what I meant."

He squeezed my shoulder as he passed me, going deeper into the chamber. "I know."

"Where is Kieron's candle? That's why you brought me here, isn't it? To show me his?"

He let out a short sigh darkened with resignation. "This way."

I followed him carefully, wary of creating a draft. I'd never forgive myself if I extinguished someone's flame with unchecked haste.

Merrick came to a stop in front of a bank of lights. I found I couldn't tell which one was Kieron's. I'd expected it to be a puddle of wax, entirely spent. But all the candles here burned tall and strong.

"Where is he?"

Merrick pointed to a taper, fat with wax.

I frowned. "Then . . . I was right to save him?"

He blinked at me.

"He has more life to live. So, so much more life." I leaned over, trying to somehow feel his essence, but it was just a candle. Nothing about it spoke of Kieron's being.

"Look closer," Merrick instructed, pointing.

There, at the base, was a slick of melted wax. It dripped from the sides of Kieron's candle and pooled across the table. It grew larger as I watched, spreading to its neighbors. I was horrified to see the hot wax begin to melt another candle, causing it to teeter precariously.

I grabbed the second candle before it could fall over and die out, but the wax spread, threatening more.

"What's going on?" I asked, swooping up another endangered flame. And another and another, until my hands were full of burning candles. The wax from Kieron's candle continued to pool. I couldn't save them all.

"Not all candles are made correctly."

The flames I held licked at my face, and I so desperately wanted to put these candles down. I didn't want to be responsible for their continued existence, but there was nowhere safe to store them. Kieron's candle was ruining the entire table.

"What does that mean?"

"Some candles must be extinguished before their time. For the good of others. For the good of those you hold now."

"Then why do you let them live?" I asked. My arms quivered under the weight of so much wax and fire. "You're the Dreaded End. Can't you stop the candle before it ruins the others?"

He shook his head. "There are limits to what even a god can do. I only collect the souls of those departed flames. I cannot blow them out myself. That's what you're meant to do. That's why you see the deathshead. You can act where I cannot. Your hands can carry out the work I wish I could do. But this is what happens when you don't."

His long fingers swept over the table.

"Couldn't we light another candle? For Kieron? One that's made right and will burn the way it's supposed to?" I asked, a stupid burst of hope rising in my chest.

"One candle for one flame. One life. That's how it's meant to work."

"You could change it, surely."

His shoulders dropped. "I can't."

"Then why did you bring me here?"

One of the candles I held sparked, singeing my arm with its embers, and I let out a cry of pain, almost dropping the dozen I held.

A noise of horror choked me as I realized what chaos that would cause.

"I wanted you to see and understand. I'm not doing this to punish him. Or you. The shape of his life was determined before he was born. It was written in the make of that candle. I can't change that. I thought you of all people would grasp this, Hazel. But you still see everything through mortal eyes, terrified of losing your tiny wisp of existence."

Merrick wiped his face. His voice creaked, and I realized he was close to tears.

"How else should I see it?" I demanded. "I *am* a mortal. I have mortal eyes. I don't . . . I don't understand what you want me to . . ." I froze, fear snaking into my belly and leaving me cold despite the thousands of flames surrounding me. "What question am I meant to ask? When you tell my birth story, Merrick . . . what question am I supposed to ask?"

He shook his head, disappointed. "We're going now. This was a mistake."

My mind raced through the birthday story, glancing up to the orbs of fire. One of them was the Holy First, and the others—the many, many others—must be the Divided Ones.

"Tell me, Merrick," I called after him, desperate to understand. "Tell me, *please*!"

He continued stalking away, his robes fluttering behind him like the wake behind a ship.

I thought through his story, the iteration he told year after year. He always said it the same way. I had it memorized word for word, practically tattooed on the back of my mind.

"'Give the babe to me,' the Dreaded End said," I recited aloud, nearly shouting at him, *"'and she will never know want or hunger. Let me godfather her and she will live lifetimes, learning the secrets and mysteries of the universe. She'll be a brilliant healer, the most powerful in the land, with the power to hold back sickness, disease, and even me with her hands.'"*

Merrick stopped walking and I knew I was on the right path. But what was I meant to ask?

"Lifetimes," I called out with sudden triumph. "You told them lifetimes. I always thought I'd just live a long life, but now, after seeing this . . ." I gulped, terror staking my middle. "Merrick, how many candles do I have?"

He remained still, his back to me. I was overwhelmed by the sudden and irrational fear that when he finally turned, it wouldn't be Merrick's face I'd see, but something else. Something sinister and profane. Not a human, not a god, but the terrible darkness that had been at the start of the caves. That ancient, evil void.

With the utmost care, I placed the rescued candles on other tables, far from Kieron's.

I swallowed the vision and placed a shaky hand on Merrick's shoulder. He turned, and when I spotted the familiar lines of his face, I released my breath.

"How many?"

"Three." His eyes shifted away, as if he was ashamed. "While your mother was pregnant, I had three candles dipped for you. Solid, strong tapers that would last many decades. I used the finest beeswax, the sweetest lavender for scent."

Three candles.

Three lives.

It was bewildering, too horrifying to wrap my mind around.

I would live out three lifetimes, long and full.

And alone.

I looked at the cavern of candles, every one of them a solitary taper. Each person was granted just one life. Except me. Every candle I saw now would be snuffed out and melt before my final one would. No person here now would be with me at the end of my life.

I felt numb with shock. It was too big a thought to take in. I'd go through life meeting people, making friends and connections, and none of them would matter in the long run. None of them would grow old with me. None of them would last.

Not my family. Not Kieron. Not anyone I'd meet in the future, twenty years from now, sixty, a hundred.

I wanted to throw up, wanted to give in to the rising terror that clouded my vision and sent tremors through my body. Instead, I met Merrick's mournful gaze and took a deep breath.

"Show me?"

He bowed his head and wandered down a path of flames. We turned along another lane, then another. Reaching the outskirts of the tapers, he stopped at a dark granite plinth.

A single candle, placed with care and encircled by a delicate silver wreath of flowers, burned brightly. At its base rested two identical tapers, unlit but ready to be called upon when needed.

They were so very, very tall.

I looked back at the thousands of other candles covering tables and stands. They were all so far away, a huddled mass of humanity that I would never be a part of. "I'm all by myself."

His bony fingers reached out toward the light with a tender affection before pointing to the god's flame above us. "You're with me."

I studied the slate-colored fire. Even Merrick's flame seemed to be in shadow. "That's you?"

He nodded. "I wanted . . . I wanted to always be able to watch over you." His back teeth clicked together, and he considered his next words with care. "Do you see now? I know this moment with the boy feels important to you, but in the whole of your life . . . this is just a brief breath. Oh, my darling Hazel. You'll go on and do more things. Bigger things. Without him. Let him die. Before he can hurt anyone."

"He would never!" I exclaimed. "I know Kieron. He'd never hurt anyone."

"He hurt you already," he pointed out, gently picking up my hand and examining the ring of bruises winding round my wrist.

"That doesn't . . . He didn't . . . he didn't mean to do that. He didn't know what he was doing. I fixed him. *You saw* I fixed him."

"I saw you stopped the swelling," Merrick allowed. "But there was damage done. Too much damage that you could not right."

"But I did the surgery," I insisted. "I did everything right."

"Oh, Hazel," Merrick said. I'd never heard him so sad before. "You were flawless. But some things cannot be fixed. You saw the changes in him already. The burst of anger, the surprising rage. Think of what that rage is capable of. Think of how many people he can hurt."

The shattered window echoed through my mind. Cosmos's yelp of fear. The memory of Kieron's hands wrapped painfully tight around my wrists.

"Isn't there something I could do to change it? If we retreat, if we go somewhere far from others? I can take care of him and keep him from hurting anyone else, and that will change everything, won't it?"

Merrick shook his head. "He'd burn through your candles without a second thought. He wouldn't mean to, but he'd hurt you, Hazel. And he'd go on to hurt so many others. More than you could ever treat, more than you could ever save."

"How do you know all this?" It was a foolish question. He was a god. He did not operate on linear time. He knew every possible future there was, could see them shift as we mortals wandered about in darkness, making dozens of decisions that altered every second of the yet-to-be.

Merrick only sighed.

I remembered the terrible thought that had come to me just moments before I began the surgery. An echo of it rang through me now, sneaking its treachery up my throat to wait on my tongue until I was stupid enough to speak it aloud. "And you . . . you're not behind all this?"

Merrick's eyes flashed. "How could you think that?"

"It's just . . . with this . . . with all of this . . . you get exactly what you want." I wanted to throw the accusation with anger and force, but it was too sad for me to speak it any louder than a whisper. "You get what you want and I get nothing."

Merrick took a step closer but stopped short of touching me. "This is not what I want. I don't want to see you in pain. I'd never want that." He reached out, and his fingers danced before me as if he were too scared to bridge the final gap. "Hazel, you are my daughter. My heart breaks when yours aches. If there were a way to spare you this pain, I would. But I can't. I'm so sorry."

"There are limits, even for gods," I muttered, echoing his earlier sentiment.

Miserably, he nodded.

I dared to glance back toward Kieron's candle. "I can't do this," I admitted. "I've killed so many others, just like the deathshead wanted. Please don't ask me to do this."

My plea broke his spell of stasis, and Merrick held out his arms.

I fell into them, letting myself be folded away in his embrace, and I cried. I cried great fat tears of grief and pain. For Kieron. For our future. For my future, which I was only now beginning to understand. I cried until I no longer had any tears within me and felt dry and miserable.

"Three lifetimes, Hazel," Merrick whispered into the top of my head. "Remember that. This moment hurts, and I'm sorry, but it's only a moment. Only one tiny moment."

I broke away from him, stumbling down the rows of candles to find Kieron's.

His wax had covered the entire table now, sinking other candles into its liquid heat. I tried to pick them up, tried to free them from being devoured, but it burned at my fingers, leaving angry red welts.

"Every choice we make alters the present and the future," Merrick said, coming up behind me. "By choosing to operate on him, by choosing to save him, you've put all these lives in jeopardy. Perhaps it won't be today, but they will eventually meet their ends far sooner than they should."

"I only thought I was helping," I murmured. "I didn't know."

With a twist of his fingers, he plucked a slender piece of silver from midair. "You do now," he said, offering the trinket to me. "And it's what you do now—in this moment—that matters."

When placed in my hands, the snuffer felt unnaturally warm, as though it had just come out of the forge, newly hammered and shining. Turning back to the bank of lights, I watched as Kieron's flame danced at the top of its wick, writhing and reaching out toward me. Begging for me to leave it be, to not listen to Merrick, to let it burn.

I thought back to Kieron, lying spread out across my worktable, sleeping and warm and whole.

Would he feel this?

I glanced at the other candles, weakened and wilting, their lives already altered because of me. I couldn't bear to hurt them any further.

"I'm so sorry," I whispered as I brought the little dome down upon the light, dousing it, Kieron's life, and all my earnest hopes in one fell swoop.

CHAPTER 20

PINK STARLIGHT FILTERED THROUGH THE LITTLE WINdow above my kitchen sink.

I scrunched my eyes closed and flipped over, snuggling deeper into my bedsheets, wishing I could slip back into my dream.

It had been a lovely dream. One of the best I'd had in months.

I'd been in Alletois. Kieron had been whole and healthy and alive.

We'd laughed and talked and kissed.

There'd been so many kisses, so many moments that made my broken heart shimmer with joy. I'd felt like myself again. I'd felt hope and happiness.

He'd opened his mouth, but before the words came, I'd stirred awake.

I tried to ground myself in the last wisps of the moment, holding on to the light in his eyes, the feeling of his hands around mine, but it was no use. Something in the room had caught my attention, and now my mind was too alert to go back and learn what Kieron was about to say. It cracked my grief open all over again, made me mourn another piece of him I'd never have.

Cosmos, awake too and ready to play, came padding over to the bed. His tail swung happily as he licked at my hand, knocking over a stack of books.

When Merrick had whisked me from the cavern of candles, he'd taken me home. Not to Alletois, where the memories—and body—of Kieron would be too painful to bear, but to my little cottage in the Between.

It was just as I'd left it so many years before, and being back in the home of my youth offered me a strange liminal space in which to grieve, in which to come to terms with Kieron's passing. It allowed me a safe place to work through everything I'd learned in the cavern and decide what I wanted from this small moment of my life.

Because no matter how big and overwhelming the present felt, no matter how my heart ached or rallied or sank again, no matter how I tried to wish myself out of the moment I was in, I knew that was all it was.

A moment.

One tiny moment in a life destined to have far too many.

I tried everything to push away thoughts of those two unlit candles, distracting myself by walking with Cosmos through the veritable forest of pink trees that had grown in my absence, resurrecting my abandoned garden, losing myself in all the new books Merrick had supplied—but I could not escape the memory of them.

They'd lain on that plinth so plain and unassuming. Just a pair of candles. But what they represented was completely mind-boggling.

Three lives.

Merrick had given me three lifetimes.

Three long lifetimes, if the length and width of the wax was any indication.

I felt prematurely exhausted imagining all I was meant to accomplish with such time. How did people fill their years?

Developing skills and a trade. That, I'd already done.

Falling in love, building a family. Impossible for me. Companionship, platonic or otherwise, was out of the question. My heart felt wholly shredded after Kieron. I couldn't go through that again. And again. And again and again.

It was terrifying to realize that everyone around me at this very moment, no matter how young or healthy or strong they might be, would not be alive at my deathbed. How many generations of people was I destined to see die? Why hadn't Merrick made another like me, someone to wander through this extraordinarily long life with?

"Why me?" I found myself whispering on those terrible dark nights when anxiety pounded at my temples, when my heartbeats thudded with horrible heft. "Why did Merrick choose me, why did he saddle me with all this? What purpose do I serve?"

These were the questions I yearned to ask him, but Merrick's visits to the Between were rare and always too short. He dodged any serious conversation, always keeping the tone light and shallow, as if bombarding me with merriment might somehow pull me from my funk.

My misery wore at him.

He flitted in for afternoon teas or alfresco dinners, for silly celebrations meant to distract me, and always for birthdays.

Two of mine passed in the Between, and the morning after my eighteenth, as I lay in bed, trying to grab hold of my dream of Kieron, I realized something.

I was tired of my misery too.

I was tired of living in the between—not just the Between itself, but the in-between I'd nestled myself into. Not quite in the past, but not wholly in the present. Unsure of how to move ahead, unwilling to let go.

I lay in bed, listening to Cosmos's huffs of breath, and suddenly knew.

I was ready to let go.

I didn't know what was to come, but I'd had enough of hiding here, with only my dog and my godfather for company. I wanted to be back in the world, back with people. I didn't know what my terribly long life was meant to accomplish, but puttering my days away in a hazy void wasn't it.

"Merrick?" I called, certain he was near, sure he'd lingered after last night's dinner, waiting for another slice of that gold-dusted cake.

The cottage door opened and my godfather poked his enormous frame beneath the lintel. "Is everything all right, Hazel?"

I stood up, tossing my quilt to the bed. For the first time in nearly two years, I felt alert. I felt sure-headed. I felt like myself.

"I think I'd like to go home now."

Merrick's smile was immediate and wide. "I'm glad to hear it."

CHAPTER 21

THE KNOCK AT MY FRONT DOOR SOUNDED BEFORE I was even aware that Merrick had snapped his fingers.

I was back in my kitchen in Alletois, and though everything seemed in order, laid out exactly as I had left it, I could feel the time that had passed. The air was too still, unstirred by the thousands of daily gestures and movements that were meant to fill the space, imbuing it with life.

It smelled funny too.

Not because Kieron's shell was still there—it was the first thing I checked, craning my neck around the corner with pained apprehension. I wondered how he'd been found, what his parents had thought when they'd discovered him laid out on my worktable, scalp shaved, skull drilled into. If they hadn't thought me a witch before, they certainly did now. How they must have cursed my name, ruing the day he ever came across me. It was a marvel the house had been allowed to remain at all. Surely someone tried to burn it to the ground.

The pounding came again, an impatient rapping that jarred me from my miserable musing.

"Open in the name of the king!" a voice bellowed.

Cosmos raced to the door, seemingly unperturbed by our abrupt change of location.

"Merrick?" I called, hoping my godfather had lingered.

The house remained still, my call unanswered.

With a sigh, I went to the front door and swung it open before the visitor could resume his shouting.

In the yard were four mounted riders clad in the black-and-gold livery of the king. Their black stallions danced nervously as Cosmos raced out to greet them, barking joyously.

The man at my door appeared to be the squadron's captain. Older than the other guards and boasting an impressive set of thick and unfashionable muttonchops, he towered over me. Rows of dazzling medallions were affixed to the left of his chest, blinding me with their brilliance.

"Are you the healer woman?"

I paused, wondering what would happen if I denied it.

"We were told this was the cottage of Alletois's healer." He glanced behind me, undoubtedly noting the signs of two years' worth of neglect. "It wasn't clear if anyone still lived here," he continued, sounding uncertain.

"I've been away for a bit," I admitted.

"So you *are* the healer," he challenged.

I longed to shut the door in his face. "I am."

"They say you perform miracles."

"Occasionally." I expected the men to smile, and when they did not, I shrugged helplessly. "I'm only a healer. Nothing more, nothing less."

"You're to come with us." The captain set his lips into a firm line.

I bristled at his presumption. "Am I? Is someone ill? Injured?"

"It doesn't matter. We'll have to set off within the hour if we're to return to Châtellerault by sunset."

My mouth fell open. "I'm sorry?" I said, on the verge of a laugh. "I'm not going to leave with you just because you say I need to. I don't know who you are, what you're asking."

The captain looked down at his uniform as though it should be obvious.

"You're clearly from the palace," I went on, and a flicker of irritation kindled against my sternum, the way it always did when I thought of the palace and the callous, horrible boy who lived within it. "Am I to presume someone there needs my help?"

The captain chewed on the inside of his cheek, as if reluctant to part with that information. "Well . . . yes."

I waited for him to divulge anything further. When he didn't, I did laugh, struck by his audaciousness. "I need to know more than that. Who is it? What's wrong with them? There are things I'll need to bring . . . balm, tonics, surgical equipment if necessary. . . . I can't pack up my supplies with nothing to go on."

The captain shifted from foot to foot. "You'll find everything you need at the palace."

"What I need is more information. Right now, otherwise I must bid you good day."

I knew I was being surly, taking out the anger I felt at my memories of the prince on this hapless captain, but I couldn't find it within me to care.

The captain let out a sigh, glancing toward his men. "May we . . . may we speak privately?"

I gestured to the side yard, where a low stone bench was situated beneath an arching mirabelle tree just on the cusp of blossoming. The captain stepped toward the bench but did not sit.

"You're a healer," he said without preamble. "I assume you have ears everywhere on such . . . sensitive matters."

"Sensitive matters," I repeated blankly, feeling every one of the days I'd been away in the Between with painful acuity. The royal family could have all sprouted horns and tails in my absence and I would be none the wiser.

He sniffed irritably. "What have you heard?"

I couldn't even guess at what I was meant to know. "About?"

"Don't be insolent with me, girl," he warned.

"I assure you, I know nothing. Truly."

The captain's eyes roamed over my house once more as he weighed the truth of my admittance. Now that I was outside, I could see that the roof was in desperate need of new thatching and a few windowpanes had cracked.

The captain took a step toward me, lowering his voice to a near whisper. "The healers at court have tried everything. Nothing has worked. They've sent for priests, holy men, oracles, and seers. They've all failed." His wiry eyebrows furrowed. "One of the oracles mentioned a healer, far away in the town of Alletois and blessed by the Dreaded End himself. A girl. You. She said you were the only one in the kingdom with a hope of fixing this."

"This?" I repeated, wishing he would just speak plainly. "Who? I don't understand what you're dancing around."

"It's . . ." He sighed. "It's the king."

My eyebrows rose. "He's sick?"

"Apparently," the captain answered unhelpfully.

"And what is he suffering from?"

"I don't know," he answered, his eyes darting cagily back toward his men.

"They sent you here. You must know something."

The captain squirmed, looking miserable. "Even so far out in the farmlands as you are, you must have heard of the great sickness from the north? The one causing so many in the capitol to . . ." He stopped short and I eyed all his badges and medals, skeptically wondering how so decorated an officer could be squeamish talking of death. "The Shivers?" he went on, then waited for me to confirm I had. I remained still. "They . . . they think it might be that."

"Tell me more about it?"

He sighed but began to fill me in, claiming the sickness felled nearly anyone who came into contact with it, saying whole villages were fine one day and dead the next. He made a sign of protection over himself.

"And there's no treatment for this yet?" I asked, already knowing the answer. This oracle, whoever she was, must have seen me because I was the only one who would be able to discern its cure. In the back of my mind, I was already putting together a list of what I'd need to pack.

The captain's dark eyes turned grim and he wordlessly shook his head.

"I'll ready my bags."

CHAPTER 22

THE TRIP TO THE CAPITOL WAS LONG AND ARDUOUS. Coming to find me, the king's men had traveled to Alletois as swiftly as possible, bringing only their stallions. They chafed when I suggested using my wagon to transport my trunks of medicines and supplies, certain it would slow the journey to a snail's pace. I told them I would not leave without my supplies, or without Cosmos, and now he rode in the back of the wagon, whining at each bump in the road.

Without a horse of my own, I had to ride with the mutton-chopped captain—I'd learned his name was Marc-André—and held on to his waist for dear life as we raced toward Châtellerault, scattering any villagers foolish enough to step out in front of the cavalcade.

"I've never been to the capitol," I'd admitted to Marc-André at the start of the ride. "What should I expect?"

He let out a huff of air that I guessed was meant to be a laugh. "It's a far sight grander than this." He gestured to the farm we were passing and I dared a glance at the orchards, wondering if I might catch sight of the LeComptes out working.

But it was not Kieron's family I spotted. . . .

Five figures stood in a clump between the rows of apple trees, their wraithlike figures marring the otherwise lovely landscape.

Mama's hair had turned into a curtain of filth hanging far longer down her back than it ever had in life. The last of Papa's face had finally fallen off, leaving only a greasy residue of gray tendons and muscle covering his skull.

My heart stopped as I noted the newest member of the gruesome brigade, the one with a flap of skin hanging loose at the back of his head. It blew back and forth in the breeze like the last leaf of autumn, too stubborn to let go of its tree.

Don't look, don't look, don't look, my thoughts raced, repeating in time with the stallion's galloping hooves.

But I couldn't help myself, and I saw the exact moment that he sensed me. A mild jolt surged through his body and he began to turn, turn, turn, slower than he ever would have while alive. One of his legs had already begun to decompose and he favored the spindly femur, leaning so heavily to the side, he teetered like an off-kilter top.

Before I had the chance to see Kieron's face, to see the milky white eyes winking in the light like cursed marbles, Marc-André followed the curve of the lane and I lost sight of my ghosts.

"Don't you think?" the captain asked, breaking into my thoughts, and I could tell by his tone it was not the first time he'd asked.

"Of course," I replied quickly, unsure of what I was agreeing to. I needed to push the image of my tormentors from my mind and focus on what was actually happening in the present. My years in the Between had been blessedly free of my ghosts' staggering, and I'd forgotten how draining their presence was, a constant weight and worry.

I wasn't certain how far the capitol was from Alletois, but it would take them days to creep toward it. No matter what was going on with the king and this new disease, I could be ready for them when they finally arrived.

"What about the rest of the royal family?" I asked, trying to center myself back in the conversation. "The children. The queen. How are they faring?"

Marc-André shot a curious glance at me over his shoulder. "The queen?" He snorted. "Just how long did you say you were gone for, girl?"

Try as I might, I could not get the image of the back of Kieron's head from my mind. He'd been just about to face me. What would have happened when he had?

"I . . ." I hesitated. "It was a rather long trip." I tried to offer a smile to smooth over whatever mess I'd unwittingly walked into.

"I daresay," he said, and clicked at his horse. "The queen has been dead for nearly a year."

"She's dead?" I exclaimed, so surprised that every trace of ghosts left my mind. "How? When?"

"Bad riding accident. One of her lady's maids found her, thrown from her mount. It was"—he paused, musing—"about ten months ago, I'd guess." He nodded to himself.

"How awful."

"The little princess took it the hardest," he went on, discussing the Marnaignes' great tragedy with all the casualness of pondering the weather. "She was only six when it happened. Didn't understand what was going on, didn't know why her mother didn't come home."

"Euphemia, isn't it?" Bursts of pink confetti had rained down in every village square in the kingdom as servants unloaded casks of wine gifted from the royal cellar to celebrate the girl's birth.

He grunted his assent. "I was on guard duty within the palace then." Marc-André shook his head and a shudder raced through him. "I still remember the howls coming from her chambers. Terrible, terrible thing."

I nodded. "Are any of them sick now?"

He shrugged. "Could be, for all I know. The king's valet holds on to every scrap of information tighter than a miser clings to his purse. I was only told to get you. So here we are."

"Here we are," I echoed, and sat back, mulling over everything he'd said.

Our ride continued. Farmland turned to villages, villages to towns.

I was surprised by how poor the roads were—muddy and torn ragged on edges stretched too wide, as if a marching parade had come through, flattening everything in its path. Marc-André studied the damage with dismay but didn't comment, and I wondered if he was somehow embarrassed that the king's highway had been allowed to fall into such a state.

Towns grew closer and closer together until eventually we were in the capitol itself and our path became paved with bricks. I'd never seen so many people milling about, nor buildings towering so high. There were more shops and storefronts than I'd ever have guessed possible or necessary, rows and rows of them, selling not fruits or vegetables or clothing but *things.* Tiny, sparkling things whose purposes I couldn't determine as we raced past the glittering windows.

Everything here glittered, and my head ached at the sheer amount of detail I was suddenly aware of: the scent of unfamiliar spices and smoked meats, the babble of languages I did not speak, dresses made up in shades I'd never imagined, cut in fashions that seemed over-the-top and ridiculous in their extremity, and a tang coating my tongue with the acrid sourness of too many bodies in too small a space.

Why anyone would regard this swath of overcrowded land as the epitome of civilization was beyond me.

Even the royal family seemed to want to be away from it. Though Châtellerault was the monarch's seat, the palace itself was not in the city proper. The grounds were set apart, hugging the northern border like a snug comma. A snug comma separated by a vast wall and a moat.

Black swans swam in lazy circles as we rode across the drawbridge spanning its dark waters. The horses' hooves clattered loudly over the lowered wooden planks, setting my nerves ajangle. The wall was at least three yards thick, and heavily guarded. Several dozen men jumped to attention, saluting the captain as we came through.

Only once we were past the gates did I realize how late in the day it had gotten. Twilight had fallen heavily, darkening the sky to the shade of bruised lilacs. There were too many clouds to see the stars, and I could feel the charge of an approaching storm.

The palace rose before us, wide and hulking. The main building was four stories high with wings spreading out on either side, like a bat unfurling to take flight. Built of dark gray stone with steeply pitched black gabled rooftops, the palace nearly blended into the evening mist. Tall oil lamps dotted the perimeter, creating halos of light as amber as gold bars.

We did not enter the palace from the front. Marc-André nudged the horse down a side road, taking us past stables and other outbuildings. I caught sight of fantastically landscaped gardens and a soaring greenhouse. My head spun at the opulence and luxury. Even in the moody gloom, everything *shimmered.* There was nothing left undecorated, dripping with detail and ostentatious adornments.

Statues of black marble were scattered across the grounds, like toys left behind by giant children. Intricate clusters of gilded roses spiraled down the post of each streetlamp we passed. Even the gravel we trotted upon seemed to be made of glittering quartz chips.

The air hung heavy, and I felt as if everything I saw was secretly sneering, proud and puffed with its own self-worth. It dredged up memories from my childhood: of the royal family's visit to Rouxbouillet; of the press of people in the streets aching to be near them—to be near such wealth; of the prince as he threw a handful of coins at me.

I wondered if Leopold remembered the little freckled girl he'd insulted, or if I'd made even the barest of impressions upon him at all.

We came to a stop at an entry along the back of one of the wings. A tall portico jutted out like a set of bared teeth. Though this entrance was clearly meant for servants and tradesmen, it was no less grand than any other door we'd passed.

Two footmen hurried down the black marble steps. They were dressed in matching suits of onyx with gold tassels, and they nodded curtly to Marc-André before one helped me from the horse. The other guards dismounted and began unloading my collection of bags and trunks. I'd packed three trunks near to bursting with my medicines and one bag with personal items, clothing and my toilette. I couldn't begin to guess how long the king's treatment would take, and I hadn't wanted to be caught without something I might need.

"I can help with those," I offered, but they waved my assistance aside.

"Follow us please, miss," one of the footmen said.

I offered a miserable smile of thanks to Marc-André but he'd already turned, issuing orders to a stable boy who'd hurried over to help with the horses.

"Cosmos, come," I called, and my pup jumped from the wagon, stretching with obvious pleasure as he sniffed at his new surroundings. I nearly smiled as I watched the footmen give him a wide berth. At least now I wasn't the only one filled with apprehension.

I hurried up the stone steps, then paused on the threshold, studying the golden coat of arms inlaid in the stone. The Marnaigne bull stared up at me with glowering eyes, and the weight of what I was about to do—meet the king, treat the king, save the king—descended over me like a stifling blanket.

I didn't want to be here, not truly.

I wanted to be back in my little cottage, readjusting to my life in Alletois.

If I was honest with myself, I wanted to be back in the Between, sitting beside the fireplace with Merrick and a book, whiling away the too-many years I knew I had.

But I wasn't.

I was here.

So here I'd be.

With Cosmos at my side, I took my first step into the palace.

"Good gods!" a voice exclaimed. "What is that *thing*?"

I glanced to Cosmos, who nearly blended into the black marble of the floor, making him look like a massive shadowy hellhound in a sea of darkness.

Just past the entry stood a man, tall and gaunt. His dark wool suit was impeccably tailored, accentuating his height. Everything from the shine of his shoes to the waxed ends of his silver mustache exuded a militant fastidiousness. He peered down at Cosmos, a delicate sneer marring the thin end of his nose.

"This is Cosmos," I offered. He let out a yip that might have been mistaken for a growl, and the tall man flinched.

"You brought your . . . dog." He said the word belatedly, as if unsure it was the accurate term. I didn't think the question needed answering and so remained silent. "Animals are not allowed in the palace," he continued. "I suppose he can bed down in the stables. Benj!" he called, raising his voice and summoning the young lad who'd been busy attending the stallions outside. "Take this . . . dog . . . with you as you leave, please."

The stable boy, all dark curls and dimples, nodded, then snuck a glance at me, smiling. "What's his name, miss?"

"Cosmos. He's very well trained. I shouldn't think him any trouble at all. In fact, I think he'd—"

"Be that as it may," the older man said, cutting me off, "there is much to be done. Any . . . distractions . . . could prove to have deadly consequences."

I sighed, then bent down to scratch at Cosmos's ears. "You go with Benj now and be a good boy. I'll come find you when I can." I kissed the top of his silky head, then straightened and watched the pair slip off into the night.

Slowly, I turned and offered the gaunt man a thin smile.

He cleared his throat. "Now then, I take you are Mademoiselle Trépas?"

"You can call me Hazel," I said, holding out my hand.

Pale eyes, neither blue nor gray, swept over my offer, and I could see him remembering how I'd just scratched Cosmos. I lowered my hand.

"I am Aloysius Clément, the king's valet. If you need anything during your stay with us, you must ask me and me alone. We needn't concern the whole of the palace with the king's . . . dilemma." Aloysius's gaze flitted away from me to the pair of footmen paused beside us. "What are you still standing here for? Take those things to Mademoiselle Trépas's room at once!"

The pair startled into motion, bringing in my trunks. Just before the door shut, I caught sight of five figures approaching the portico, and my mouth went dry.

They stumbled out of the darkness on legs too bony to support their weight, their grave clothes rustling like the husks of desiccated insect shells.

My ghosts.

I had no idea how they were already at the palace, how they'd managed to follow me so fast, but didn't have the time to wonder.

"Salt," I said, turning to the valet, sputtering out my nonsensical demand too loudly. "I will need to have the grounds of the palace salted before I can begin. Every doorway, every window. Any entrance will need to have a line of salt."

Aloysius raised a solitary eyebrow. "Salt?" he repeated.

I nodded. "The king is ill," I began, piecing together the first explanation that came to mind. "The salt will help to keep out bad spirits."

It was true enough.

The valet only blinked.

"It will need to be done immediately. Now, please, if you would." I tried to straighten my spine, drawing up to my full height, but still felt small and silly before him.

"Bad spirits." He licked his lips. "I must admit, when the oracle foretold that His Majesty's healer would be found in Alletois, I didn't realize just how provincial that would make you. Do you have any comprehension of how many doors and windows the palace commands?"

"I understand the magnitude of what I'm asking," I said, even though I didn't, not truly. "But I assure you, Monsieur Clément, my methods work."

After a painful pause, the moment stretched out like taffy pulled too long, he barked an order for the salt, and a trio of footmen I'd not even known were near us sprang into action, their footsteps echoing down the corridors.

"Thank you," I said in as dignified a manner as I could muster. "Now . . . this will be my first time dealing with the Shivers," I admitted. "Any details you can share, however big or small, would be most helpful."

Aloysius pressed his lips together before responding. "I am not a doctor, and I believe His Majesty would prefer an on-site examination of his personage. Better that you should see it with your own eyes than for me to describe it and accidentally speak out of turn."

I paused. I knew the words he'd spoken—they were said with a delicate simplicity that suggested he thought I might not understand anything bigger—but they were such a jumble of empty phrases and fillers, it was as though the valet was speaking another language entirely.

"Now, if you will follow me, I'll show you to your chamber. You may wish to freshen up before seeing His Majesty." His tone implied more a directive than a suggestion.

Aloysius turned on his heel and strode down the hall without checking to see if I followed. I lost sight of him after he took a swift turn to the left. He was surprisingly spry for his age, and I had to bolt after him to keep from getting lost.

We took another turn, going deeper into the palace. It seemed an endless maze of identical walls and closed doors. After six more turns, I wondered if he was purposely taking me down the same hall to confuse my sense of direction. But Aloysius hardly seemed the type for games or wasted effort. Just how many miles of corridors snaked through the palace?

I almost regretted making such a scene about the salt. Even if the ghosts made their way inside, it would be nearly impossible to find me.

At one junction, I stopped to stare at a set of closed double doors. At least ten feet tall, their lacquered white surface gleamed with flourishes of gold trim. Twin bulls served as door handles, with jewel-encrusted rings hanging from their nostrils.

"Do keep up," Aloysius prompted before heading up a set of stairs.

My footsteps fell too loudly on the treads, and it sounded as though there were a dozen of me racing behind the valet. We passed the first landing, then the second, and I tried to take deep breaths without sounding as though I was gasping for air.

When Aloysius opened a door on the fourth-floor landing and another long white hallway greeted us, I tried not to show my dismay. How on earth would I ever find my way around such a place?

"Your room," he said, outside one of a dozen identical doors.

I turned the hammered brass knob, pushing the door open. The room was stark and unassuming. An oil lamp burned on a side table, illuminating a narrow bed and one chair. An armoire far too grand and large to have been originally intended for the servants' wing took up the bulk of one side of the room. The window was covered by curtains of a serviceable twill.

My belongings lined one wall, the footmen already long gone.

"The washroom is three doors down," Aloysius prompted. "I'll return in half an hour's time. Will that suit you?"

The whirlwind of the afternoon had finally caught up with me, and I wanted nothing more than to face-plant on the uncomfortable-looking bed and go to sleep. But there was work to do. "Half an hour," I agreed.

The valet turned to leave.

"Monsieur Clément, wait!" He paused, his back still toward me. "I don't want to walk into this completely unaware. What can you tell me of the Shivers? Is it like pneumonia?"

"Do you think we would have summoned you over a simple cold?" His voice was not unkind, but his answer did flare my irritation.

"The sweats?" He offered no response, and I paused, biting my lip before daring to say the worst. "The plague?"

Aloysius faced me. His pale eyes flickered over me with a curious pity. "No. It's not like the plague."

A sigh of relief whistled through my teeth.

"I'm afraid it's far, far worse."

CHAPTER 23

THE MIRROR IN THE WASHROOM WAS ONLY BIG ENOUGH for me to see one aspect of myself at any moment.

But it didn't matter where I checked. I looked terrible from every angle, nervous and pale. I adjusted the mirror and caught sight of wayward hairs poking from my crown of braids. I caught them with my last pin, then brushed furiously at my skirts. The hem was dotted six inches deep with flecks of mud. I'd clearly been traveling for most of the day. The dozens of freckles that splashed across my cheeks stood out in stark contrast to my ashen skin, and my eyes looked too big and weary. The voice of the prince echoed in my mind across the years as I studied the hateful dots speckling my face. I pinched my cheeks, trying to bring them some color.

"It doesn't matter how many freckles you have," I said, scolding away the anxiety clutching my throat. "You're here because you can treat the king. You're here because you're the *only one* who can."

Once my sad attempt at a pep talk was over, I nodded to my reflection and left the washroom.

Aloysius was already in the hall, standing at attention, and I felt my heart race, wondering if I was running behind or if he was the type to forever be arriving early. There was another footman at his heels, waiting with a wheeled cart.

The valet's eyes swept over me as he counted every one of my faults. "I never expected a healer blessed by the gods to look so . . . rumpled," he finally said.

Shame burned my cheeks, but I straightened my spine. "I'm sure the court doctors and oracles all wear much flashier attire," I began, attempting to keep my tone flat. "If you'd prefer I dress in something else while attempting saving the king's life, I'd be happy to—"

Aloysius brushed off my rancor with an uninterested flash of his hand. "Gervais will bring any supplies you might need." He gestured to the cart.

I hurried back to my chamber and brought out the trunks of medicines and my leather valise. Gervais stacked them on the cart before whisking off with it, presumably taking it to the king's quarters.

"Follow me," Aloysius intoned.

I tried to keep track of the number of doors between mine and the end of the corridor but lost count somewhere around twelve or thirteen. The endless uniformity left my head throbbing.

We turned down a short hall before coming to another staircase. I peeked down the open middle, dizzy at the sight of so many steps, but mercifully, Aloysius stopped on the first landing. Sets of guards flanked another jeweled door, armed with halberds. Though archaic, the weapons still looked alarmingly serviceable.

"This is the new healer, Mademoiselle Trépas," the valet informed them, and I felt the weight of their eyes fall upon me. Some glanced away quickly, gazing back into the distance, as if readying for an attack, but one of them offered me a smile of encouragement. He moved to open the door for us, but Aloysius held up his finger, stalling him.

"This is the royal family's private wing," the valet began. He raised one waxed brow with a look of warning.

How poorly did he think of me? My clothes might be creased and well-traveled, but that didn't mean I planned to sprint through the palace like a feral child.

I held his gaze and dared to raise one of my own eyebrows at him. When it was clear neither of us was going to look away, he nodded to the guards, who pulled opened the doors, allowing us access.

I wanted to remain unaffected, but my mouth dropped open as we walked into the grandeur of the royal wing.

The hall alone was wide enough to serve as a ballroom, and three massive chandeliers hung spaced along its length. Crystal baubles bigger than my splayed hands cast shimmering rainbows across a ceiling of black and gold. Two walls were made entirely of mirrors, amplifying the candlelight and making the space as bright as noon.

Aloysius allowed me to take in the room's glory, hiding a twist of his lips as I turned in a circle to gape at the oil paintings, the marble columns, the gilding, and the sheer brilliance of this moment. My feet sank into the plush black carpet. I longed to run my fingers through its thick wefts but doubted the valet would appreciate my common gawking.

Aloysius beckoned me to a monumentally large portrait. I'd never felt so singularly small as I gazed up at the crowned figure. Forget-me-not-blue eyes stared out, surveying the room and somehow finding it wanting. There was a slight sneer along his nasal fold, drawing down one corner of his thin lips. A scepter rested across his lap. I wondered if he truly hadn't wanted to hold it while being painted or if the artist had hoped to imply something deeper by leaving it forgotten.

"King Marnaigne," Aloysius clarified unnecessarily. "Just months after he took the throne."

"He's very handsome," I murmured, studying the carefully rendered golden hair, his proud nose.

"He was a fine young man."

I turned back to the valet. "You've been with him long?"

He nodded. "Since he was a boy. It makes this . . . harder."

A dark seed of unease sprouted in my chest. What was I about to walk into?

"Shall we?" he asked.

His voice was softer now, almost gentle. How many healers had they gone through? How many had waltzed into the palace, claiming to have healing potions and cures, only to be cast out when their medicines failed? How many times had Aloysius performed this tour?

It was no wonder he was so clipped and abrupt.

I glanced back at the portrait for one last look, then nodded.

As Aloysius escorted me down the hall, I noticed he now walked at my side rather than five steps ahead. We stopped outside a set of ebony doors. An elaborate pastoral scene was carved so deeply within them, the villagers looked like three-dimensional dolls. There were trees, weeping willows with individual branches hanging down, tall pines with woodpeckers clinging to their trunks. There was a mill, with a waterwheel so intricately rendered, I had the urge to reach out and see if it spun. It was the only part of the door where the varnish was less than pristine. Clearly I wasn't the first to have such an idea.

Aloysius knocked once, drawing a muffled response from inside.

The doors swung open, revealing more guards, more livery, more halberds.

Before I could move to enter, Aloysius's fingers fell atop my forearm, stopping me. "If you would, Mademoiselle Trépas," he said, his voice tight, "remember him as he was in the painting."

I swallowed as dread bloomed within my gut. There was such naked pleading in the valet's eyes, such stark worry, it nearly took away my breath.

"I will," I said, wanting to wipe that horrible expression from his face, wanting to reassure him that I was talented and competent, wanting to promise that I would be able to save the king.

I stepped inside and promptly forgot every aspect of the portrait.

CHAPTER 24

King Marnaigne sat at the side of an oversized sleigh bed in a long damask robe, looking surprisingly small against the suite's sheer sumptuousness.

Like the rest of the palace, the king's chambers were done up in black and gold, with so much gilding along the walls and ceiling, I had to squint against its luster. A canopy draped over the bed and down the back wall. Heavy silk cords drew the dark satin up into decadent scallops. The Marnaigne emblem—a great bull—topped the frame, standing straight and proud, chest puffed against the world. Rubies the size of robins' eggs winked from its eyes, and it appeared to be made of solid gold.

I absently wondered if the king ever worried the weight of it might split the bed timbers and come crashing down on him in the middle of the night.

"Curtsy," Aloysius hissed, jerking my attention back to the present as he performed a deep bow himself. "Your Majesty."

Sweeping one leg behind me, I sank to one knee and lowered my head, feeling miserably uncoordinated. "Your Majesty," I repeated, then bobbed back up.

There was no response. He appeared to be studying his fingers, picking at a hangnail.

I hoped it was a hangnail.

"Your Majesty?"

He flicked aside a bit of something I'd rather forgot I saw and turned to us. "Is this the girl they said would cure me? The one who lives with Death?"

Aloysius nodded.

As King Marnaigne stood, his robe parted, revealing just how far the disease had spread. "So you've come to gape upon your fallen monarch. Well . . . what do you think?" He threw back his arms, showing more affected area.

I tilted my head, trying to make sense of what my eyes saw.

Was that . . . gold?

He started to laugh, a bitter, red sound, and shook his head. He turned to Aloysius. "She says nothing. Is she mute? A simpleton? Struck dumb by all of this?" The robe came off then, leaving him completely naked and exposing the full extent of his sickness.

I wanted to take a step back but held my ground.

"I'm told she's quite gifted, Your Majesty. Blessed by the Dreaded End." Aloysius nudged me forward, but my feet would not budge.

Marnaigne scoffed. "What a blessing. Go on and look, then, girl. Then run. They all run. The maids, the doctors, even that damned farce of a seer. Everyone runs."

If it was true, I certainly couldn't fault them. In all the books Merrick had plied me with, I'd never come across anything like this.

The king's body . . . shivered.

Series of muscles spasms twitched around the landscape of his flesh, causing fingers to twitch, shoulders to tic. As I watched, his side began to jerk, as if being tugged on a line.

The king rubbed at it irritably, softly at first, massaging the muscles, then with firmer fingers. He pushed into the skin harder and harder as the twitching continued, finally raking his fingernails over the spot until the skin broke open, releasing an oily fluid that was neither blood nor bile.

I wanted to step forward to better see it, but something continued to hold me back. This fluid looked *dangerous.*

Feeling the oil run down his rib cage, Marnaigne swore and swiped at it, smearing it across his torso, where it shimmered like gold luster. Another tic began, this time along the biceps of his left arm, and he began scratching there, repeating the process.

I felt the king watching me, gauging my reaction. Waiting for me to turn and run, like the other healers and charlatans promising cures.

After a long moment, I took a step forward.

"When did you first begin to feel as though something was off?" I asked, unpacking a satchel. I spread the tools over a credenza, keenly aware of how their surgical steel clashed against the opulent mother-of-pearl top.

We were in the king's private study.

Marnaigne lay stretched out across the large table at its center, completely naked save for a plush towel covering his groin.

Servants had rushed forward to drape a canvas cloth over the polished mahogany before the king had lain down. The fabric was now smeared with gold and scarlet as weeping fluids dripped down Marnaigne's body, creating a macabre painting.

"A month ago, perhaps a little more." He closed his eyes, breathing out a sigh.

I lifted one of his arms, watching as the muscles twitched, leaping to life of their own volition. Marnaigne had already scratched the skin raw, and more of the shimmering gold trickled out. It was a thin, viscous fluid—like diluted paint—and was uncomfortably warm beneath my gloved hands.

He winced as I pressed into his biceps, forcing more fluid to well up. I rubbed it between my fingertips, marveling at its iridescent hue. Nothing in the human body should ever be that color.

"I'd been in my council chambers, discussing the skirmishes in the north." He paused. "Have you . . . have you heard anything about my brother? It's been so long since I've left the palace. I never know what people around town are saying."

I shrugged helplessly.

I remembered Mama's stories of the bastard older brother, Baudouin, who had exiled himself deep in the northern territories after the old king had died. I remembered her snorting over rumors that the wrong brother had ascended the throne.

I remembered too the trampled roads I'd noticed on our journey here. The king had mentioned skirmishes. Had an army marched down those roads?

"With all due respect, Your Majesty, I'm more interested in hearing about you," I said carefully.

He sighed. "I'd just left the council when I felt a twitch at my eye. Here." He touched his face. "It grew worse throughout the day, and later that night, when I was reading a bedtime story to my youngest, it became quite painful. I went to one of her mirrors, blinking to dislodge the irritation, when a trickle of gold fell, like tears. More gold fell as both my eyes continued to twitch. It was actually quite lovely, like I was going to a masque. Euphemia suggested we ought to host a ball." His jaw clenched. "Then there were more twitches, more tics. Not just in my eyes, but in my fingers, along the sides of my hands. My arms and torso, my legs and feet. Even . . ." He gestured to the towel.

"And the twitches . . ." I paused, unsure of how to phrase the question. "Do they feel . . . like normal tics?"

"There's nothing normal about this!" King Marnaigne snapped, his anger sudden and booming.

"Of course not, Your Majesty." I hurried to appease him. His outburst reminded me of Merrick's bad moods, brought on sharp and swift and without warning. "I only meant . . . could you describe what they feel like? It's obvious that they're quite . . . severe." He stared up at the ceiling in stony silence. "Are you in any pain?"

"I look like a freak of nature, of course it pains me!" Marnaigne struck his hand against the table with enough force to splinter off a bit of gold decoration from the legs.

"Physical pain," I clarified, keeping a steady voice.

"The . . ." His hand suddenly jerked to life as he struggled to find the words. "The . . . twitches or tics or whatever you want to call them—the *shivers*—are uncomfortable, certainly. The tremors can be quite strong. But the worst of it . . ." He sighed. "When one of the . . . attacks begins . . . I can feel the oil moving beneath my skin."

"The oil," I repeated, wanting him to further explain without putting my words into his mouth.

"This gold . . . stuff," he said with frustration. "I can feel it moving in my body, like a living thing. I know it's not supposed to be inside of me, and I just want to . . . I just want to . . ."

As he spoke, his cheek began to tremble, caught in a spasm, and before I could stop him, the king slashed at his face, freeing the fluid beneath. It dripped down his chin, giving him an otherworldly leer.

"You shouldn't do that," I said, wrestling his hands away.

"I can't stop," he protested, his voice rising to a whine. "I don't want it in me. It just . . . it has to come out. I have to free it. I have to . . ." He swiped at his cheek again, releasing more of the gold.

"Have you tried to not scratch at it?" I asked, struggling to grasp his hands. They were slick and slippery with the fluid. "I know it must be uncomfortable, but what would happen if you try to make it through one of these . . . attacks . . . without hurting yourself, without freeing the gold?"

He shook his head, miserable. "It doesn't matter. It comes out all the same."

"How?"

"Through my pores, through my eyes, through my nose, through . . . anywhere it can." King Marnaigne winced, sitting upright, grabbing at his knee as it began to tremor.

"There was a footman who was sick," Aloysius spoke up. I'd had him remain in the far corner of the room, there to answer any questions I might have but a safe distance from the king and his mess. "They tied him to his bedposts to keep him from harming himself. The gold came anyway. Toward the end . . . he went mad with the pain, likening it to having metal filings shoved through his skin, excoriating the wounds raw with every breath he took. He struggled against the bindings with such wild force that his wrists snapped. He worked himself free and promptly slit his own throat."

I gasped at the sudden and swift end of the valet's tale.

Aloysius flexed his fingers, studiously avoiding my eyes, unfinished. "I'm told that the . . . material . . . closed up over the incision, keeping him alive for quite some time. . . . He had to perform the suicide three times before it took."

My stomach flipped over as I imagined the poor man's blood running together with the brilliant gold. "How ghastly."

"Don't forget that maid, before him. I caught this from her, I'm sure of it," King Marnaigne stated without ceremony.

"A maid?" I echoed. "I'll need to examine her as well."

Aloysius sucked in a deep breath. "I'm afraid that's impossible. She too is dead."

My chest deflated. "I'm sorry to hear that." I paused, weighing my words with care. "Did she . . . succumb to the disease or was there . . . an outside force?"

Aloysius ground his back teeth with a grimace. "Her mother, in an attempt to heal the wounds, wrapped her in wet leather dressings. She believed that as the leather dried, it would tighten the skin, closing off the pores and stopping the flow of . . . fluid."

"I assume it did not help?"

The king squirmed uncomfortably from the table. "With nowhere else to go, the gold began pouring out of the girl's mouth, dribbling out in clotted streaks. She suffocated."

"Drowned, to be more precise," Aloysius added, the words clipped. "There was another healer at court then." His pale eyes floated up to the ceiling, as if inspecting for cobwebs. "He asked permission to autopsy the body. The girl's lungs were filled with the gold, thoroughly saturated. She could draw no breath because there was simply no room for air."

I took a deep breath of my own, suddenly aware of the way my chest expanded so fully. I'd never thought to be grateful for that before.

"How curious," I muttered. "Could someone bring up a basin

of hot water and some towels?" Aloysius gestured toward one of the servants. "And you believe you caught this from the maid? Did she have occasion to come into close contact with you?"

His face turned stony before he shifted away, and I understood immediately just how close their contact had been.

"I'm not here to pass judgment on you, Your Majesty. I'm only trying to determine how this spreads. Is anyone else at court ill?"

Aloysius shook his head. "Not that we're aware of, but the tremors occur across the body at random. It's possible someone is hiding it."

I frowned, thinking this through. "If the maid had it first . . . is there reason to believe she might have also spread it to the footman?" I didn't dare to meet the king's eyes.

"It's very likely," Aloysius supplied after a long silence.

"I don't mean to pry, Your Majesty, but is there anyone else you might have passed it along to?"

"Of course not!" He struck the tabletop as another tremor shivered across his face like lightning.

I raised my hands in defense. "I meant nothing by it, sir, just—"

I was saved as the door opened and servants rolled in a cart full of towels, basins of hot water, and soap.

"What's this for?" he snapped as I dipped the cloths into the steaming water.

"I want to try washing you—"

A cry of indignation escaped from him. "You think this is all just dirt? You think I don't bathe?" He struggled to sit up, glaring daggers at Aloysius. "Who is this imbecile? Where did you drag her in from?"

I wanted to pinch the bridge of my nose to ward off my headache, but my hands were still gloved and covered in Marnaigne's fluids.

"I know it's not dirt, Your Majesty." I turned to my valise and pulled out a glass vial. "This is a mix I've made of yarrow and witch hazel." I removed the stopper and allowed him to smell it. His nose twitched, but I wasn't sure if it was from the smell or the Shivers. "They're very strong astringents."

King Marnaigne shrugged as if the word meant nothing to him.

"Astringents can help to draw water out of tissue. Your skin," I added helpfully. "We're going to try to draw out the . . ." I paused, feeling uncomfortable that there wasn't a proper term for the gold leaking out of the king's body.

From his corner, Aloysius made a soft noise. "I've heard the servants call it the Brilliance."

"The Brilliance," I repeated.

King Marnaigne fumed darkly. "Superstitious fools. You'll never guess what they claim all this is," he said, running his fingers over the gold dried across his body.

Wordlessly, I shook my head.

"Sins," he said, spitting the word as though it disgusted him. "They think the gods themselves have reached out and touched me. They think this is a purging of my sins. They think *me* capable of sin!" He struck the table again with a roar.

I kept my gaze studiously on the floor before me, letting him storm. Millennia ago, when the world was new, the Holy First had drawn up a list of one hundred sins, crimes against order and purity and her, that all mortals should seek to avoid. I tried not to tally up the number of sins I'd spotted since arriving within the king's chambers: excess, greed, vanity, and arrogance. Pretension and anger, wrath and rage. And there still was the matter of the maid. . . .

It didn't bother me. The king's morality was his to hold or cast aside as he chose, but if the servants believed the Shivers was an act of cleansing sent from the gods . . . I could see the logic of their superstitions.

But they were superstitions all the same.

"Why don't you lie back, Your Majesty, and I can begin," I instructed once his outburst had died away. Being around the king felt more and more like conversing with Merrick when he was in a bad mood. You had to tiptoe around their furies and find little ways to sweeten their tempers without drawing attention to the work you were doing.

Marnaigne sighed but didn't protest. He settled back onto the table and I got to work.

"We'll start with the hot water, washing away all the dried pigments, and then, once you're clean, I'll use the astringent to draw out more of the Brilliance. If we can get all of it out, it may stop the tremors from occurring."

The first pass of the towels revealed a map of scratches and welts that had been hidden beneath the Brilliance. Some of the wounds looked infected, raw and red. I washed his chest and arms, cleaning everything till pink skin showed once more.

Moving on to his face, I swabbed the ragged skin as gently as I could. Though he was older, with crow's feet and lines across his forehead, I could still see a glimpse of the haughty young man from the portrait outside.

Even Aloysius smiled, seeing the result. "It's very good to see you, Your Majesty."

I took off the gloves and discarded them, feeling inordinately proud of myself.

Marnaigne sat up, swinging his legs off the table before crossing to a large mirror. Standing before it, arms held slightly out from his body, he marveled at his features. He turned to look at his back, then around again to his front, preening. I wondered when he had last seen himself so free of the Brilliance.

"Aloysius," he whispered, joy coloring his tone. "I'm me again."

But as he spoke, a tic began at his forehead, twitching with sporadic jumps. Fluid welled up, pushed from his pores as he dabbed frantically at his hairline.

I took a sharp breath as I saw the shade.

"Sire?" Aloysius asked, stepping forward.

A single line of burnished bronze ran down Marnaigne's face, cleaving it in half with a long, ugly slash.

Wiping it aside, the king smeared its dark shadow across his cheeks. He studied the remains on the back of his hand, his eyes wide with horror.

"Aloysius?" he murmured. His voice was thick with panic. "It's darkening."

Their eyes met in the mirror, acknowledging some secret I wasn't privy to, before the king burst into tears.

In an instant, the room erupted into chaos.

"Out! Get out!" Aloysius shouted, waving at the guards.

Marnaigne sank to his knees, weeping. The more he sobbed, the more Brilliance gathered across his spasming face. It ran down his cheeks like painted tears.

I had assumed Aloysius meant the guards, but they turned to me, crossing their halberds and ushering me back from the king.

"What are you doing? I need to help him!" I shouted as they herded me from the room, the points of their weapons glittering dangerously.

Before I could protest again, the door shut in my face, and in the silence of the empty hall, I heard a lock click into place.

CHAPTER 25

"WHAT ARE YOU DOING OUT HERE?"

I startled awake with a gasp, nearly falling over.

After being removed from the king's chambers, I'd been unsure of what to do. A small part of me had wanted to remain on hand, in case I was needed. A much larger part wanted to take a nap. The only thing that kept me from abandoning the monarch was the certainty I'd never be able to find the way back to my rooms on my own.

I must have dozed off, leaning against a column, as I debated what to do.

How long had I been out? It felt like the middle of the night, but in this windowless hall, with its black marble and candlelight, it could have been any time of day. My neck had an uncomfortable twinge in it, and I felt impossibly grubby.

The voice belonged to a figure several columns away. He peered at me skeptically, giving me a wide berth.

My blood curdled as I realized who he was.

He was older now, obviously, but I would have recognized him anywhere.

Leopold.

Though he bore a strong resemblance to the young King Marnaigne in the portrait, his face was thinner, more pointed and angular, and his dark gold hair had been styled into a ridiculous set of curling waves. A flicker of irritation began to kindle in me.

"Well?" he said, testy with impatience. "I asked you a question. Aren't you going to answer?"

I paused, trying to remember exactly what he'd said to wake me.

"Are you deaf? My father has been into all sorts of oddities lately, but this is a first. Why aren't you in there, with him?" He overenunciated his last phrase, gesturing broadly to the closed doors.

"I'm not deaf," I snapped. "Your Majesty," I added feebly.

Was I supposed to curtsy? Or was that just for the king?

I ended up ducking into a short bob that could be a mark of reverence. I suspected it only looked as though I needed to relieve myself. Which I did, truth be told.

"Your Royal Highness," he corrected me, though he didn't seem bothered by my lack of accuracy.

He honestly didn't seem bothered by much of anything at all.

His pupils were dilated enough to render his irises completely black, and he squinted, as if the candlelight pained him. His skin looked damp and clammy, as if he were running a low-grade fever, but I had no doubt what was causing his heated flush.

After a surreptitious glance down the hall, the prince took out a gold-plated case of cigarettes. He offered one to me before lighting it for himself when I declined.

"My mother's favorite. I found myself missing her tonight," he admitted, taking a long drag. When he exhaled, the smoke was a strange shade of green and didn't smell of tobacco at all. "So if you're not my father's new whore, what *are* you doing outside his rooms?"

I flushed myself, feeling the same shock he'd given me that day in the marketplace. "I'm a healer. They summoned me to—"

"Oh yes." Leopold breathed out another puff of smoke. This time it was a deep shade of purple. "The Dreaded End's girl." His eyes wandered up and down my face, appraising. "Are you really any good? You look awfully young."

I stared at him, trying to decide the best way to answer.

He slid down the wall, sprawling his lanky legs at angles across the plush wool carpet. The cigarette ended in a puff of dark blue. "These are terrible, you know. You were right to turn it down."

"If they're so terrible, why do you smoke them?"

He shrugged. "I was feeling wistful, I suppose. Wistful and stupidly sentimental. I thought it might cheer me up."

"Has it?"

He chuckled, then patted the floor, indicating that I should join him. "Of course not."

I eased myself down, my body recalling every bump in the road it had ridden earlier. "I was sorry to hear of her passing."

He made a sound of deflecting acknowledgment. "Yes, yes. The whole of the kingdom is terribly sad. They're always going on and on about it, foisting their sadness upon us, the ones who actually knew her."

I studied him, unsure of what to make of this new version of Leopold. It was easy to assume that he was still the same dreadful boy, overindulged, forever getting his way in a palace that catered exclusively to just that. But the cigarettes—for all their foulness—gave me pause.

He was grieving, of that I had no doubt, and I knew better than anyone how strong a hold grief could have on a person.

"So, little healer," he went on, his head lolling toward me. "What do you think? Will I be taking on the crown anytime soon?"

"I . . . I honestly don't know." I hadn't had a moment alone with the king to see if this sickness was curable or if he was already too far gone.

Leopold took out another cigarette but didn't light it. "You will *try* to save him, though, won't you? All the others who've paraded in promised us the world—cures and full restoration and boundless health and wealth—but the second they saw what they were up against, they turned tail and ran. Every single one of them."

I swallowed, gathering my courage. "I can understand that. I've never seen anything like it. Not in books or stories, certainly not in person. But I will heal him, if there's a way. I won't run from this—from him. I promise."

His black eyes roamed over my face. "You don't look like very much . . . but you do look brave."

He reached out to touch my chin, and a long moment, slow and strange, passed between us before I tilted away.

"Where did you say you were from?"

"Alletois."

He sighed thoughtfully. "Never heard of it. It's strange, though. I feel as if I've seen you somewhere before."

I studied him, wondering if somewhere inside he did remember that little girl from Rouxbouillet. I nearly opened my mouth, ready to remind him exactly how our first meeting had played out, but something stopped me, holding me in check.

That had been just one moment in both our lives.

It had happened and time had moved on, and it suddenly felt wrong to hold this grieving young man accountable for the mistakes he'd made as a boy.

I wasn't that girl any longer. I'd changed and grown in ways that she'd never have dared to guess possible.

Perhaps the same could be said of Leopold.

With a shrug, he returned the unsmoked cigarette to his case and flicked his fingers, causing it to disappear in midair. I was certain he'd hidden it away in an inner pocket, a clever trick used to dazzle and delight pretty young courtiers, but smiled all the same.

"Surely the Shivers can't be so very rare. We've had four cases of it at the palace alone, in just a fortnight."

"Four?" I repeated. "Aloysius only mentioned three."

Leopold nodded, furrowing his brow as he dredged up the details. "It started with one of Father's holy men. A priest or a postulant, I think. For, you know . . ." He waved one hand in the air, gesturing toward the ceiling. "One of them."

I frowned at this turn of the story. "Do you know which god?"

Leopold shrugged. "Does it matter? When he grew sick, he went back to whatever temple he was from and we never saw him again."

"It could be helpful to talk with any of the other priests who took care of him."

"Took care of him?" He snorted. "They didn't nurse him back to health, they burned him at the stake."

My mouth fell open. "For what?"

"Breaking his vows, I imagine." He leaned in, dropping his voice warm and deep. "You know how mad about vows all those religious types are."

A laugh sputtered out of me before I could stop it. Surely he was joking. "That's absurd. What vows say you can't get sick?"

Leopold cocked his head, clearly amused. "You don't know yet, do you?"

"Know what?"

"What the Brilliance means. What the Brilliance *is.*"

"Your father said there are people who believe it's a person's sins coming out." I suddenly understood the priest's demise. "Oh."

Leopold nodded earnestly.

"Is that what you think?"

"It doesn't matter what I think. *You're* the healer."

"That's true. . . ." I sighed, beginning to formulate my next steps. I very much needed to see the king, to touch his face, but even with his door barred to me, there were other things I could do. "I need to examine others who've had it, see if I can—" The prince cut me off with a bark of laughter. "What?"

"There are no survivors to examine. Once you get the Shivers, you're done for."

I twisted my fingers together. "There must be *someone* there who's lived through it. No disease kills with that much efficiency. I heard it came from the north. Perhaps if we send out a search party, they'll find someone. . . ."

Leopold made a face I couldn't identify. "No one goes north these days. Not voluntarily, at least."

The king's inquiries on my knowledge of the skirmishes floated back to me, but before I could ask Leopold more about them, he went on.

"Have you heard they've made up a song about it?"

I shook my head, and my stomach recoiled. Only the truly terrible plagues had songs sung of them.

"Little Arnaud's head did ache, his eyes began to quiver. The gold rushed out, his mother cried, her boy had caught the Shivers," the prince sang in a mincing falsetto. *"His body danced, his body jerked, the Brilliance turned to black. His mother sobbed, his mother wailed, her boy would not come back."* The song blessedly over, Leopold pantomimed

a bow. "They say that the children of Châtellerault skip rope to it, can you believe that?"

I could. Children's games were often cruel, taking things of nightmares and setting them to music and dance.

"Wait," I said, stilling as the jaunty tune looped through my mind. It *was* appallingly catchy. "What does that mean—'the Brilliance turned to black'?"

Leopold shrugged. "They say that once the gold runs dry—once all your sins have been well and truly purged from you—then comes your atonement. The Brilliance darkens, running down first in streaks of bronze and rust—the Brilliance mixed with blood—until it's black as midnight. It's thicker then, tearing the body apart, ripping open flesh as it purges itself out. It's said to be quite painful. You know, there was a footman here who—"

I cut off the gruesome tale before it could be recounted again. "I heard."

He looked disappointed to not tell it. "Yes. Well. When your atonements are at an end, you fall into a shuddering fit and"—Leopold shook violently, miming a horrific seizure, before the movements came to an abrupt and horrific end—"and then that's it." He briskly wiped his hands. "It's all over."

"They're dead?" I asked, unsure if there was more performance to come.

"Obviously."

I thought through the timeline he'd laid out, grateful to have been given so much information, even if it had been theatrically presented. "So when the gold begins to darken, begins to bleed . . . how long until the seizures begin?" I asked.

Leopold shrugged. "I couldn't say. I've never seen anyone with it myself. Just . . ." A look of realization dawned on him and his brow furrowed, marring his otherwise beautiful patrician face. "Has Papa begun to bleed?"

"I think so."

Leopold sank back against the wall, wincing. "Then he doesn't have much time left after all." His head lolled my way but his eyes were distant, as if looking into a future I could not see. He looked as though he might throw up. "Tell me, little healer . . . ," he mused. "Do you think the crown will look good upon my head?"

I offered him a ghost of a smile. "I hope that's something we won't learn for a very long time to come, Your Royal Highness."

He sighed, seemingly content with the answer, and closed his eyes.

I noticed his lashes were thick with tears and I looked away, allowing him a moment to sit with his emotions. They'd laid his mother in her grave not even a year ago, and already he was having to deal with the notion his father might soon follow and the enormity of the changes that would ensue. The cruelty felt unspeakably heavy.

Leopold murmured something in a voice too hushed and too low to make out. I wanted to lean in to catch his words but remained where I was. He was probably praying to Félicité or the Holy First, begging them to intercede and spare his father's life, begging for good fortune, begging for strength and fortitude should the crown be thrust upon him.

Who knew what princes prayed for?

Stretching, Leopold shifted and leaned his face against the wall. He was nearly asleep but still his lips moved, forming words I couldn't help but overhear as he drifted off.

"His body danced, his body jerked, the Brilliance turned to black," he sang to himself. *"Then Leo sobbed and Leo wailed. The king would not come back."*

CHAPTER 26

THE GARDENS WERE BLACK.

No.

Not black.

Shades of midnight, navy, and deep eggplant, swirled together with obsidian and onyx. So much more than black.

It was like staring at the back of your eyelids as you tried to fall asleep.

But no one could sleep through this.

Music pulsed in the thick, humid air, setting it to life with cellos and basses. Their atonal notes felt like rolling waves against my sternum. They filled my body, setting it on edge until all I knew, all I could feel, was my consciousness and the black.

The not-black.

I could sense that the gardens were full of people. There was the feeling of being in a crowd, surrounded by others, even if I couldn't see them all.

Flashes of the party sparkled out of the dark like memories wrested across time, revealing glittering glimpses of masked courtiers gliding between sculpted trees. Gold wings and black lace. Caviar and crimson tulle. Champagne coupes and velvet beauty spots. I'd never been in the midst of such decadence.

It was glamorous.

It was intoxicating.

My mind spun, reveling. I felt drunk even though I'd not taken a sip of champagne. And I was dancing, swaying in the perfumed night like a postulant at one of Calamité's bacchanalias. I moved with a rippling grace I did not know I possessed.

And I couldn't stop.

It was irresistible and enticing. I wanted to throw my head back and surrender everything I had to that music.

So I did.

I spun and I twirled. I writhed and squirmed, contorting myself with outlandish movements as I strove to keep up with the dancers surrounding me. We moved in beautiful frenzy, a crowd gone collectively mad, all following the beat that pulsed through our bodies like a drum.

Hands moved over me, guiding me through intricate steps to dances I did not know. I couldn't see my partners' faces, could only feel their fingers and the brush of velvet lapels. When I finally caught a glimpse of myself trapped in the reflection of a grand mirror somehow hung between the bowed branches of an enormous oak, I paused.

I didn't look like myself at all. In a long gown, I was as sleek as a jungle cat. The gold satin clung to my body with a sensuous hold. The neckline was so daring, so plunging, you could see the trio of freckles between my breasts. A wicked slit in the dress's hem raced up to my thigh, showing flashes of the smooth, bare flesh beneath.

I wore no corset, no underthings at all.

I felt naked and on display, exposed for all the world to see.

In the mirror, my reflection grinned at me. Her lips gleamed with a bloody scarlet stain, and her eyes, lined in dark kohl, sparkled with heavy-lidded desire.

I was surprised to find I liked how I looked.

I loved how I felt.

Loosened and loose, a beautiful, dangerous creature freed from its cage, ready to run, ready to pounce.

I whirled into the arms of the nearest courtier, reveling as his hands roved over my exposed skin, squeezing my hips and molding my frame to his.

He spun me around and I caught my first glimpse of his face.

It was Leopold.

When he brought his hands to my face, caressing my cheeks with a familiarity that should have stunned me, I noticed they were dusted with a fine golden powder. In the shadowy light of our midnight garden fete, it looked like magic, strange and beautiful, luminous and otherworldly.

He was painted in it. Lines of the champagne-colored dust streaked across his forehead. Five of them, as though he'd wiped his brow after touching . . .

I frowned, studying the Brilliance with a clinical detail my body did not want to pause for. It wanted to dance and move, not stop and think.

It was my body that let the prince twirl me once more. My spine pressed against his chest as he folded me into his embrace. I allowed his lips to rove down the column of my throat, kissing me with a hunger that set my blood sizzling. I watched us in the mirror as he sucked at my skin and ran his fingers under the satin of my dress, teasing my breasts, toying with them until I cried out for more.

My body let all of this happen, let our hands slide down Leopold's chest to fumble at the length of his sudden hardness and stroke it till he groaned against our ears, crushing us against his ardor.

"Oh, Hazel," he murmured appreciatively, and his voice was low and dark and wanting. "What have you done?"

My body did this, but my mind watched.

It watched as the prince pressed his lips to where the Brilliance welled from us, raking the edge of his teeth through the gold. It watched as he smeared burnished handprints across our bodice, watched as those shimmering hands snaked lower, lower, lower still, clutching at our bare thighs as he searched for the hem. It watched as he found it and his fingers slipped beneath.

My mind railed against this brazen invasion, watching in horror as my body melted against him, melted into its desires, melted into the Brilliance itself. I was drowning in gold, unable to stop the sins that poured out of me.

The thought struck me like a wave of icy water.

The sins?

I shook my head. I didn't believe that. I believed in reason and logic. I believed the Shivers was an illness to be cured, not a penance to be endured.

"I have not sinned," I tried to whisper, even as a moan of ecstasy closed my throat. Leopold's hands roamed over me without restraint, finding parts of me I never even knew existed.

The world moved in strange lethargy as I watched this in the mirror. So much Brilliance had spilled out, and I couldn't stop it. This was a moment I couldn't undo. Some part of me had irrevocably broken. There was no fix for this, no going back.

In the mirror's reflection, I spotted a figure approaching me and wanted to cry. It was the king, dressed in russet velvet, a black domino obscuring half his face. I didn't want him to see me like this. Didn't want him to see me in the arms of his son, my lips swollen and cheeks flushed, and covered in gold, so much gold.

"What's this?" he asked, eyes darting from Leopold to the Brilliance. His nostrils flared. "What have you done?"

His sudden anger bewildered me. "I—nothing!"

"Something," he insisted. He cast the prince aside, wrapping his arms around to pull me into our own dance.

When our hands met, his were red, not gold.

Red and slick and slippery.

I looked back into the mirror and my shimmering dress had turned crimson as great blooms of blood spread across it, staining the fabric, staining the ground, staining me.

"Your Majesty?" I asked before the world spun sideways.

My mind was muddled. I was bleeding. I was bleeding a lot. Why was there so much blood? Dizzyingly light-headed, I fell into a swoon.

We were dying, my body and I. I felt my essence slipping from me, slipping away in the blood, in all that blood, and I knew this was the end. The end of me, the end of my body, the end of everything.

But the candles . . . , my body reminded me.

The candles!

I had the candles.

I rested my head against the king's chest, waiting for whatever was to come. Would it hurt? Would I feel Merrick transferring my flame? My mind felt weighted by too many questions and spinning with not enough blood.

I closed my eyes and danced with Marnaigne as the last of my life poured out of me.

He spun me with sudden force, and when I opened my eyes it was Merrick who held me, looming larger than I'd ever thought possible. He looked manic with distress. Tears filled his eyes, falling in black streaks down his dark face. They fell onto my dress, staining the now-red satin black.

My heart thudded, pumping in vain to circulate the remainder of my blood. Why didn't I have enough blood? There was something wrong. My next candle had not been lit. This wasn't a fresh start. This was . . .

This was the end.

I began to shake, chilled yet feverish. My limbs jerked and jumped. I was powerless to stop them. Black sludge welled from my pores, thick and viscous. More and more came out, ripping me open as it tried to escape. It was darker than the night, darker than my godfather, darker than even his tears.

It was absolute and unending and it was about to consume me, no matter how many candles my body and I had left.

I shut my eyes, for there was nothing left to do but welcome my certain death. Merrick's voice echoed after me as I fell down the darkened tunnel, a snarl of helpless rage.

"What have you done?!"

CHAPTER 27

I WOKE WITH A START, GASPING FOR BREATH AND FIGHTing against the sheets tangled around my limbs. It felt as if a terrible weight was holding me down, as if the nightmare had somehow followed me into waking life.

It was too dark to see the room around me, but I had a vague memory of returning from the Between, of being taken to the palace.

The palace, I thought, trying to sort through all the unfamiliar shadows of the room. I was in the palace. I struggled to roll over, remembering there'd been a candlestick on the little table beside the bed.

I struck a match, bringing a small glow to the room, and jumped, stifling a scream.

Kieron's face was just scant inches from my own.

His dead, unfocused eyes stared in my general direction with the terrible hollowness of no recognition. His nose had begun to rot away, leaving a tattered hole where fragments of gray cartilage poked out. And his mouth . . .

His mouth was too wide, too large, and without any lips. It hung open and slack, a perfect circle, like a lamprey's, and then suddenly it was on me, pressed against the hollow of my throat, not biting, not mauling, but sucking.

In vain, I swatted at him—I couldn't touch ghosts, but they could certainly touch me—extinguishing the match in the process, and the room fell dark once more. I heard the creak of the bed ropes as he followed me, as other figures I hadn't seen followed him, and I realized with a start that all my ghosts were here. They'd found a hole in the salt wards—Aloysius was right, there were too many doors here, too many feet walking over too many thresholds—and stumbled and staggered their way through the endless miles of halls, and now they'd found me.

I thrashed, feeling the pressure of their lips and the disgusting tugging sensation as they got what they wanted and pulled.

It didn't matter that I'd been acting upon the will of the deathshead, that it had been sanctioned by my godfather, that I'd been given a gift from an actual god—each of the ghosts had been victims of murder. Even as I'd tried to do my best, providing them with clean and easy deaths, their last moment of life had been one of confusion and fear and rebellion. There was nothing the dying wanted more than *more.*

One more minute of breath.

One more minute to remember the good parts of their life.

One more wish to magically fix what was happening.

One more, one more, one more.

And so, in death, the ghosts followed me, wanting more.

They went after my memories of them, pulling and sucking at me like leeches.

Some—the soldier, the baker—didn't have many to consume.

But Mama. Papa.

Now Kieron.

They drew my thoughts of them from me like a healer would excise a guinea worm, inch by inch, slow and winding. It felt like walking into a spider's web; I could feel the telltale sticky threads on me for hours after.

The ghosts had only caught me unaware a handful of times, but each attack had been brutal. I relived the memories as they fed, saw their deaths again and again, the horror, the pain.

Papa in particular had not gone down easy.

And Kieron . . . I had no idea what Kieron's last moments had been like. I'd been in the Between, killing him with the swift fall of a candle snuffer. What memories would he pull from me?

I had to get out of the bed.

I kept a vial of salt with me in my valise for moments like this, moments when I'd been distracted, moments when I'd thought myself safe.

I rolled through their grasping hands, wincing as their bony fingertips scratched at me, clawed at me. There would be no marks left behind, but it still hurt in the moment.

I fell out of bed and their disintegrating shapes paused, sensing their prey had departed. Papa tried to get around the bed first but stumbled and fell and began to drag himself over the mattress ticking, lumbering after me like a seal on dry land.

In the dark, I fumbled to find my bag, and once it was in my hands, I easily located and opened the vial. I threw a handful of salt at their approaching figures and they flinched, air rustling over throats that would never again make a sound.

Where to put them? Where to put them?

The armoire in the corner. It wasn't very big, but it would have to do for now.

There wasn't enough space in the room for a clear path to the piece of furniture. The only way to reach it was by going through the horde of spirits.

As I crossed by the soldier, he grabbed at my arm, and I felt something stretch from me, like taffy on a confectioner's pull. My head throbbed, my mind screaming in all the ways I wanted to but could not.

"Get in," I hissed, opening the door to the armoire and flinging more salt at the ghosts. I herded them past me, back and back, until they had nowhere else to go.

I had the presence of mind to pull my two dresses off their hangers and toss them aside before drawing a thick line of salt at the lip of the armoire. The ghosts flailed against one another, turning into a mass of putrefying arms and ragged clothes, milky eyes and protruding bones. They could no longer speak, but how they tried anyway, gnashing their gums, clicking teeth and bone in equal measure to form a ghastly symphony.

I slammed the door and salted the floorboards in front of it for good measure, then collapsed onto the edge of the bed, burying my head in my hands.

The day hadn't yet begun and I was already exhausted.

As if summoned by the unfortunate hand of Calamité himself, a knock sounded at the door. Without opening it, I knew from the crisp, efficient pattern it would be Aloysius.

"Good morning," I greeted him, feeling as though it was anything but.

"Yes," he said, his eyes flickering over my hastily donned robe. "I trust you slept well?" Before I could answer, he went on. "I wanted to apologize for your . . . removal last night. His Majesty is in much better spirits this morning and is eager to speak with you."

"Good. I'd like to start with—"

"But first, the royal family wishes you to join them for breakfast."

"Breakfast?" I repeated in disbelief. "No. I need to first see the king."

Aloysius blinked.

"To check on him . . . ," I began, feeling ridiculous for needing to further justify my request.

"I'm certain His Majesty appreciates your concern, but he believes that breakfast is a fine idea."

I could feel him silently urging me to simply go along with the plan, as absurd as it was. I had no time to share a leisurely meal with the king's children. I wasn't there to assuage them, I was there to treat their father. But I sensed that any argument would be quickly countered. "Of course," I finally said, smiling through gritted teeth.

At least there would be coffee.

"Breakfast will be with just the immediate family this morning," Aloysius explained later as he led me through the halls down to the dining room. "His Royal Highness requested a more intimate setting for your first meeting."

"Are all the king's children here now, at court?"

He nodded.

I twisted my fingers into my skirt. "Was there ever talk of perhaps sending them away? Since we're not sure how the Shivers spreads, it might be best to distance them from it."

"His Majesty had similar thoughts," Aloysius said, heading down another hall. "But given all the troubles with Baudouin, it seems safer for the children to remain here, protected from outside forces."

"I haven't heard much of . . . the troubles," I admitted. "Is it . . . bad?"

Aloysius sniffed. "I've known the boys since they were toddlers. There was never a moment when Baudouin did not yearn for his brother's things. He used to go through His Royal Highness's playroom, grabbing whatever struck his fancy, heedless of damage. All these years later, he's still after toys he can't have."

As a subject of the king, I chafed at being so summarily reduced to being a "toy," but I ignored the insult. "And yet there have been . . . battles?"

Aloysius scoffed. "Nothing more than skirmishes."

Coming to the end of a servants' wing, Aloysius rapped on a set of double doors. They swung open and we stepped through the pair of guards flanking them to enter a grand hallway. The high ceilings arched into sharp points above us, with golden stars painted upon the dark wood. The curtains and carpet runner were patterned in rich ambers, and the walnut paneling imparted a sophisticated gravitas.

"This way, please," Aloysius said.

The dining room was long and narrow, featuring a formal table with dozens of chairs positioned down its length. At the far end sat King Marnaigne's children.

The oldest, Princess Bellatrice, reclined against the tall back of her chair, utterly resplendent in layers of lemon chiffon. I'd never seen skin so luminously pale, like fine milk glass. Her hair was black as jet and just as glossy, swept into a low chignon. Her plate of food was untouched, but she sipped a cup of tea, leaving behind a perfect semicircle of lip stain along the porcelain rim. Her eyelids fluttered as Aloysius and I approached, her gaze flickering over me with unchecked curiosity.

Leopold appeared half dressed, in cream breeches and a lawn

shirt with impractically full sleeves. His vest, a dark green damask, was left unbuttoned, and his jacket was cast over the back of his chair in a thoughtless heap. He cut into a ham steak and dunked a piece in a puddle of syrup before biting into it with ravenous gusto.

Remembering how those lips had enraptured me in my dream, I looked away, feeling uncomfortably warm.

The youngest, Princess Euphemia, sat at the head of the table, presumably in the king's chair. She looked about seven years old, with wide eyes as blue as her father's and a halo of loose gold curls flowing down her back. Her dress was a pale blue silk, trimmed in white lace, with puffed sleeves and a full skirt. Her plate held mostly sugar-dusted berries, and one poached egg. Spotting us, she visibly brightened.

"Will we get to see Papa today, Aloysius?" she all but shouted from across the room.

"Perhaps," he answered without a trace of commitment in his voice.

Her eyes fixed upon me. "Are you the healer who is going to make Papa well again?"

The intensity of her hope unnerved me. "I certainly hope so." Aloysius needled me in the ribs and I remembered to drop into a curtsy. "Your Royal Highnesses."

Leopold took a long slurp from his mug. "Do come and join us. You must be famished."

Aloysius gestured to the place setting facing the two eldest, directly opposite the prince, with Euphemia on my left. I held Leopold's stare for a long, uncertain moment. He gave no indication he remembered meeting me the night before. Recalling his dilated pupils, I wasn't surprised.

His eyes were clear today, if a little bloodshot, shining the same light blue as the king's.

"This is the girl—the healer—the seer spoke of," Aloysius said, tilting his head toward the chair once more. "Mademoiselle Trépas."

"You can just call me Hazel."

"Sit down, then, Just Hazel," the prince said, and waved to a servant holding a silver kettle. "More coffee for me, Bingham, and whatever the healer would like. Cook is an absolute gem. I'm sure she can come up with an approximation of whatever rustic fare you're accustomed to."

His languid disdain shriveled any trace of hunger, and I waved aside the offer.

"Come, you must have something. Cook makes a delightful cinnamon croissant. Bingham, croissants all around. Aloysius will have one too," he ordered magnanimously, as if the host of a madcap tea party. "Tea or coffee?"

"None for me."

"Coffee, Bingham," Leopold decided with an upturned twist of his mouth.

Over the prince's shoulder, Bingham stared, silently pleading with me to not cause a scene. "Black, please." I offered the footman a smile. "Thank you."

From the corner of my eye, I watched Aloysius edge from the table. He remained at hand, there to help as needed, but blended himself into the surroundings to create a semblance of privacy.

Bellatrice rubbed her forehead, scowling at the windows. "It's too bright in here. Can't we close the curtains?"

Leopold's eyes danced with amusement. "This is what happens when you stay out all night doing"—he paused, glancing toward Euphemia—"well, you know."

"You're a fine one to talk." She set her teacup in its saucer with a petulance I'd never seen in someone older than three. "You were right there with me."

"I?" He chuckled. "I was in bed by midnight. Maybe not *my* bed, but bed all the same." He winked at me. "The curtains remain open."

"As His Majesty commands," Bellatrice said, sarcasm dripping from her words as she glowered at her younger brother.

"Too right. Besides, we're ignoring our guest."

The room's attention shifted back to me.

Leopold trailed a finger along the rim of his cup, sizing me up. "Tell us, Just Hazel, what trickery do you intend to peddle to our dear father?"

I was too surprised to answer, unused to defending myself. People who thought me a charlatan never called upon me when they fell ill. If Leopold had already made up his mind, I saw little chance of changing it. Speaking of past achievements felt like boasting, a language I wasn't fluent in.

Aloysius stepped forward. "We've looked into her background."

I stole a quick look his way. Had they? When?

"I assure you, she's quite celebrated in her region."

"Which is where?"

My eyes narrowed. We'd had this conversation just last night.

"Alletois, Your Royal Highness."

Leopold turned to Bellatrice, lowering his voice. "Is that the one to the east?"

She dropped the hand that had been shielding her inflamed eyes and squinted at him. "The south."

"No, I think east. With all the trees, yes?" His head swung back to me. "Trees, yes? You have trees in your region?"

"There are trees in Alletois," I replied flatly.

Leopold laughed as if my irritation delighted him, and every trace of sympathy he'd wrested from me last night went up in flames.

Before I could think through the ramifications of my anger, I stood, bumping into the table and causing the teacups to rattle in their saucers. "I don't need to be here, you know," I snapped. "I've plenty of other patients who need looking after. Ones who haven't dragged me into their homes and hurled insults my way for sport. If you think my skills so suspect, you certainly need not avail yourself of them."

I expected Aloysius to come running, stopping my outburst as he attempted to smooth everything over with his calm and careful wording, but he only waited for Leopold's reaction.

The prince studied me, his eyes unreadable. And then he smiled. "Oh, Just Hazel, I think I like you." He nodded enthusiastically, applauding as though he'd just witnessed a masque onstage. "Yes! I do! Brava, little healer. Show us your mettle, your stalwart backbone."

Bellatrice sighed, covering her eyes once more. "Must you be so loud in your praise? Of course we want her here. She's the one Margaux foretold, the one who lives with the Dreaded End. Who better to wrest Papa away from certain death?"

Euphemia gasped and Bellatrice blanched, realizing how cruel her cavalier words had been.

"Phemie, it's just an expression. Papa isn't really going to die. Is he?" she asked, turning her attention to me, arching one eyebrow to accentuate her point.

I looked down the table, wanting to say something to ease the princess's fears.

"The Dreaded End," Leopold scoffed, forestalling any false

assurances I might try to make. "What a useless god. Who in their right mind would worship a deity of death?"

"Do you really live with dead people?" Euphemia asked curiously, pushing berries around her plate.

"I don't actually live with him," I replied. "I have a very nice cottage that he visits. And he's not surrounded by the dead."

Not like me, I thought absently, wondering if my line of salt upstairs still held. I'd have to make my way to the kitchens later this morning for a larger container of salt.

Leopold let out a noise of disbelief. "A death god who doesn't live among the dead? It sounds as though your godfather is shirking his responsibilities. You know, I've never truly understood the purpose of half of these deities. What's the use of a goddess of fortune? A lord of anger? Next there will be a numen of potatoes, a mistress of silver polish." He smirked.

"You . . . you don't believe in the gods?" I asked, aghast.

"I suppose I must believe in them, but I think any power we ascribe them, any hope that they do things to benefit us, is utter rubbish. Their blessings—or curses—are just things the peasants make up to get through their days, to help them cope. Isn't it easier to blame an invisible all-powerful entity for your crop failure than to admit you're just a bad farmer?" He glanced around the table.

Euphemia looked stricken, while Bellatrice's expression suggested she agreed but found it distasteful to admit.

I'd never heard someone speak out against the gods like this, and witnessing such rancor from a prince so entitled, so clearly blessed by Félicité's favor, made my blood boil.

Bingham returned with a cup and saucer for me, temporarily waylaying my retort.

Leopold watched me bite my tongue, a lazy smile playing at his lips.

My anger amused him.

I narrowed my eyes, feeling the fury flicker up my spine. I'd wanted to give him the benefit of the doubt last night. I'd *pitied* him. It wasn't a mistake I'd make twice.

"You really shouldn't say things like that," chastised a voice from across the room. "They'll hear, you know."

A young woman, roughly my age, approached the table. She wore a long, oversized set of robes in layered navy chiffon. The silver bracelets encircling her wrists indicated she was a reverent of the Holy First. She stared at Leopold, openly challenging him with wide brown eyes.

"Just family today, Mademoiselle Toussaint," Aloysius warned, holding out a hand to stop her approach.

"Oh, please, can't Margaux stay?" Euphemia asked, her voice wavering. "I asked her to join us. She's family, yes? She's just like my sister."

Bellatrice's lips twisted, but she said nothing.

Aloysius paused, evidently weighing the consequences of his decision.

"Oh, let her," Leopold said, waving the valet back into his corner. "I don't mind. Bells? Healer? Do you?"

Margaux stepped forward, a soft smile lighting her face. "I'm so glad you've come!" She reached out without hesitation to embrace me, squeezing my shoulders before she pulled away. Her voice had a musical lilt, like a wind chime on a spring afternoon. "Welcome! Welcome! You look just as I imagined you would!"

I glanced about the table, hoping someone would help fill in the gaps for me.

Leopold sighed heavily. "Margaux is the seer who ordained your arrival."

"Oh." An oracle! I looked over the girl with fresh interest. I'd never met anyone else so intimately acquainted with the gods. "Thank you. I suppose."

"I'm sure you don't mean that at the moment," she said with a laugh, smiling beatifically at me, and I felt my icy disdain begin to thaw. For the first time since arriving at the palace, I felt as if I'd found someone I could relate to. "But you will be thankful. In time."

Her eyes went starry as she saw things the rest of us could not. She glanced at Leopold thoughtfully, then back at me, and I wondered if that was how I looked when I beheld my cures.

"Have you seen the king yet?"

"That's what we're trying to figure out, Margaux. Do sit down if you're staying." Leopold gestured to the chair on my right.

She slipped in and we waited as Bingham rushed into service once more, expertly putting together a place setting and pouring a cup of tea before fading to the walls near Aloysius.

"You mustn't take anything Leopold says seriously," Margaux said, leaning in to speak with a conspiratorial smile. She stirred a cube of sugar into her tea and tasted it. Quickly, as if hoping no one would notice, she added a second.

"I say what I mean and mean what I say." The prince fell back against his chair, ripping into a croissant. "Just because *you're* here on orders from the temple doesn't mean I'm obligated to listen to your drivel." He clasped his hands together. " 'I can see the future, this is what you're to do!' " He frowned. "How many of your prophecies have actually come true?"

"I didn't wake at the crack of dawn to listen to you two bicker,"

Bellatrice snapped. "I want to hear about Papa. You've seen him, yes?" she asked, fixing her hard eyes on me.

Something about this princess made me want to straighten my shoulders. "Briefly, last night."

"How is he?"

Aloysius cleared his throat. "As Mademoiselle Trépas said, it was a brief meeting. She arrived quite late, and—"

"I remember you!" Leopold exclaimed, striking the table with sudden triumph. "I saw you in the hallway! You and your freckles. I thought that was just a trick of the absinthe, but it was *you,* wasn't it?"

"What's absinthe?" Euphemia asked.

Leopold snorted into his coffee. "It's a glorious drink, Phemie. Green as a beetle and tastes like licorice. And when you drink it, you see the most beautiful worlds. Mermaids and fairies and—"

"Fairies! You see fairies? Why haven't you ever shared it with me?"

Margaux reached out, bracelets jangling, to derail the princess's thoughts. "Absinthe isn't for little girls like you, dear heart." Her eyes fell on Leopold. "It's not good for anyone."

"Truly? I find it just about the only thing that helps me tolerate the presence of some," Leopold quipped, a false smile painted on his lips.

"Have there been any improvements?" Bellatrice asked over the chaos. "In our father's health? You know, that very big and important reason we brought you here?"

I paused, certain someone would interrupt me before I had the chance to speak, but the table fell silent with expectation.

Bellatrice's eyebrows rose, exasperation radiating from her. "Well? We've established you've seen Papa, for however short a visit. How did he look?"

"I—I'll be doing a more thorough examination of him toda—"

She sighed. "So you know nothing. Just like the others. Thank you so much for all the trouble you took to find her, Aloysius. I can see it was well worth it." She slammed her teacup on the table and stormed off, leaving the broken bits of porcelain for someone else to clean up.

The room fell silent, and I longed to excuse myself.

Then Euphemia sniffed, and I saw her lower lip tremble.

"Oh, darling, no tears this morning," Margaux said. "I can't stand it."

Leopold pushed the tray of croissants down the table. "Phemie, chin up, love. Papa wouldn't want you sad today. Not with the healer here. She's come to fix him."

"Please, Mademoiselle Hazel, *please* heal him." Euphemia turned her large eyes to me, beseeching. "There have been so many who came, saying they could, but they all lied. You . . ." She paused, deep in thought. "I know you can."

"I'll try my best. Starting now." I set my unused napkin down beside the cup and saucer, readying to leave. "If there are no other questions for me here, I really ought to get to work."

The little girl's fingers twisted together. "Will you tell him that we love him and we miss him?" Euphemia looked at me with such wistful hope.

My heart ached for her, to be quarantined from her father so soon after losing her mother. I nodded, and she pulled a bit of folded paper from her pocket. Her eyes were bright with tears.

"Do you think . . . do you think if I drew him a picture, you could give it to him?"

"Of course," I promised quickly.

"When are you going to make me a picture, Phemie?" Leopold

asked, stealing her attention. "I want a painting on one of your biggest canvases."

"My biggest one is only this big," she said, approximating the size with her hands.

"Oh no, it'll need to be much bigger than that. You know the one of the fox hunt in the great hall? That awful one Great-Uncle Bartholomew did?" She nodded. "You can just paint over that!"

I excused myself from the table as she began to laugh.

Catching my eye, Aloysius indicated I should follow him, before disappearing through a side door.

I hurried after him.

"It would be best if you took Mademoiselle Toussaint's words to heart when dealing with His Royal Highness the prince. Very rarely does he say anything with complete seriousness."

"So I've noticed."

Aloysius bobbed his head, still looking fretful. "I would hate for certain words, most assuredly said in jest, to reach the ears of your godfather."

"You might be surprised to learn how little the opinions of mortals matter to him. To any of them, really. But tell me more about the seer—Margaux? How did she find her way to court?"

He indicated that we make a turn, guiding us toward a set of stairs that looked vaguely familiar.

"Ah. Mademoiselle Toussaint. Her mother was a distant relation of Queen Aurélie's. The queen wished for the girl to come serve as a companion for the princesses and act as spiritual counsel. I'm told she's quite respected within the Holy First's most inner circle." He leaned in, lowering his voice. "Some even say she has been particularly blessed, that her visions come straight from the Holy First herself."

I raised an eyebrow, fascinated. Though the temples all across Martissienes were filled every week with people praying for favor and good fortune, very few ever actually received a god's blessing.

"Do you know anything else about her family?" I prodded, curious.

We crossed under one chandelier, then two, then went by the king's portrait.

Aloysius frowned, thinking. "Lady Anne has quite a large brood. I believe Mademoiselle Toussaint once said she was her mother's thirteenth."

"Thirteenth?" I echoed with surprise. Her blessing made more sense now.

"Here we are," Aloysius said, stopping in front of the massive carved doors.

He tapped on the dark wood, and for a moment, it sounded like my ghosts, trapped inside of my closet and pleading to be let out. A chill rippled through me, and I had the terrible thought that Kieron would be the one to open the king's door, his skin flapping, white eyes roving over me as he took one staggering step toward—

"Mademoiselle Trépas?" Aloysius prompted, snapping me from the horrible daydream.

A footman stood at the open door, very much alive and very much not Kieron. Before he could usher me inside, I turned to the valet, keeping a light smile on my face. "I forgot to mention this earlier, but I'm going to need more salt."

Aloysius blinked, considering my request. "More . . . salt."

I nodded, unconcerned with how backward or foolish it might make me look. "Yes. Lots and lots more salt."

CHAPTER 28

King Marnaigne sat near the parlor's hearth in a canvas-covered chair, watching the flickering flames. He wore another robe, navy today, and must have recently bathed. He seemed mostly clear of Brilliance, and the ends of his hair curled wet around his neck.

"Good morning, Your Majesty," I greeted him.

He surprised me with a warm smile. "You're still here, I see." He gestured to the chair opposite him.

I'd decided it would be best to keep my tone as light as I could today. Laughter would help brighten his spirits and make the tasks at hand easier for me to carry out. "Did you expect me to dash away in the middle of the night?"

"No one would blame you if you did. I am just about to dine—join me?"

He gestured to a silver cart laden with plates of eggs and tartines, coffee and juice, along with a basket of croissants. After a moment's deliberation, I picked out a cinnamon one and nearly groaned as I took my first bite.

I hated that Leopold was right. I'd never tasted anything better.

"I'd like to know more about what treatments the other healers tried," I began.

"Treatments?" he repeated, letting out a snort. "Tortures!" Marnaigne took a bite of his own pastry, speaking around the crumbs. "The first doctor tried taking hot bits of metal to my skin, running the edges down my body, to cauterize the wounds."

My eyebrows rose with concern. "But there *are* no wounds."

He made a face of agreement. "It seemed to work for a day or so, and he was satisfied we were making progress. But after the third session, I couldn't endure the pain any longer. I sent him packing."

"And the next?"

He slurped his coffee, his movements mirroring Leopold's with an uncanny similarity. There was no denying they were father and son. "The second nearly killed me. Powders and potions and concoctions I'd never heard of. I was violently ill for a week, throwing up and—" He stopped himself, staring down at the food. "Well, you can imagine, I'm sure."

I could, and set aside the croissant.

"Did he happen to leave behind any notes? Lists of supplies, dosages given?"

He shrugged before looking to Aloysius.

"I believe there is a remainder of the powder," the valet supplied.

"I was supposed to take it three times a day, mixed with water." Marnaigne's mouth puckered.

"I'd love to look at it."

Aloysius nodded, jotting down the note.

"The next healer tried wraps. Slathered these long bandages with some sort of mud, then wound them all around my limbs and set me on the terrace in the sun. I was like a living brick when he returned. Took three footmen to chisel me out of the stinking mess."

"Did it help at all?"

"He made it worse, the stupid tête de noeud."

I nearly choked on my coffee, stifling a laugh at the king's choice of insults. "It's a wonder he didn't kill you. The minerals probably drew out the Brilliance with terrible speed."

The king snorted. " 'The Brilliance.' Don't you mean my sins?"

I set my cup down. "People think up all sorts of things to help them get through trials," I said tactfully. "I don't think it matters much what *they* say, only what *you* believe."

He wiped away a trickle of gold falling down his temple as his gaze drifted back to the fire. "I have no pretensions of being a perfect king. Or husband. Or father. I have my faults, just as anyone else. But it stings that my subjects believe this sickness was brought about because of them." He glanced up with a piercing intensity. "Tell me, little healer, what sins would fall out of you?"

My face warmed. I wasn't used to being the center of attention. Focus was always on the person being cared for, never on the healing hands behind them. His eyes were like shafts of light, angled directly on me. "I . . . I don't know, Your Majesty."

He took a long sip of coffee, squinting at me. "You don't seem the lazy type, and you're far too thin to be a glutton."

I smiled, hoping his little game would end there.

"You are quite a lovely girl, though," he continued, oblivious to my discomfort. "Perhaps vanity would come spilling out."

I tried to laugh. "It's hard to be vain with so many freckles across one's face."

He made a noise of agreement. "Something else, then? Your skills as a healer? To be so gifted at such a young age—that must cause your chest to puff, hmm?"

I'd never considered my expertise to be a source of pride or self-importance, but he was probably right. Merrick had given me too many talents for me to be entirely humble.

"I think you've guessed it, Your Majesty. Now, if you're done eating, we ought to start your examination."

"Lust."

The word fell heavy between us, the crack of a hatchet finding its tree, the blade biting sharp and irrevocably. It brought a stain of scarlet to my cheeks as I remembered my nightmare, the way I'd let Leopold take control of my desires, of my body, of my very self.

"Envy, perhaps," I responded with more honesty than I'd intended. "Coveting things that will never be mine."

Marnaigne clucked sympathetically. "It's a hard thing to admit, isn't it? Now, imagine how shameful it is, having evidence of those same weaknesses run down your body for all the world to see and judge."

I met his eyes again, compassion flooding my heart. "You'll receive no judgment from me. I promise you that, Your Majesty."

"René," he offered unexpectedly. "Please, call me René."

"René." I swallowed, gathering my nerves. "Do you think we could have a moment in private?"

"This *is* a private moment," he said, gesturing to the nearly empty chamber.

I tilted my head toward Aloysius and the two remaining footmen, the four guards standing watch at the chamber entrance. "Entirely private."

"Are you planning on murdering me, little healer?" The king paused, his small, nervous joke falling flat.

"Of course not, Your Maj—René," I said with a smile, trying to keep my words light and steady. There was a pang of worry creeping up my stomach and tightening my throat.

I might, I wanted to say. *I might have to.*

Studying me curiously, the king waved them out of the chambers.

Aloysius lingered on the threshold, his face burning with naked curiosity, but he eventually followed the other men.

Only once the door had clicked shut did Marnaigne dare to look at me, his lips set in a grim line. "I'm dying, aren't I? That's why you wanted them sent away." He took a carefully measured breath, flexing his fingers over the caps of his knees. "How long do I have left?"

"Oh," I began, startled. "Oh no. I didn't mean . . . That's not what I meant by . . ." I shook my head. "Let's start again, shall we?"

The king nodded, but his face remained dark with apprehension.

I licked my lips, unsure of how to begin.

I didn't usually have to use Merrick's gift on my patients. They came to me with familiar sicknesses needing familiar cures: broken bones required plaster casts, summer colds called for warm soup and herbal teas. I didn't have to double-check my work because I knew what was needed, I knew how those things could be fixed.

"A bath," I decided. I would wash the new Brilliance from his face and then cup his cheeks. "I'd like to draw you a bath."

"I've had one already this morning," he said, unmoving.

"Yes but . . ." I paused, my eyes flitting about the chamber. My leather valise was still on the side table where I'd left it the night before. "Not with my tonics. Where's your bath?"

"Through there," he said, indicating a room beyond the parlor.

The tub was massive and claw-footed. A curved golden spigot rose over its side, like the neck of a swan. I experimented with the handles, surprised to find both cold and hot running water pumped right into the porcelain basin.

As the tub filled with warm water, I added some of the witch hazel and yarrow I'd pulled out before, then grabbed a bottle of distilled geranium oil. It smelled as verdant as a greenhouse as I sprinkled it in.

"More astringents," I explained.

Marnaigne lingered on the room's threshold, watching me. "Should I . . . should I disrobe?" he asked, his voice uncertain.

"If you please." I shifted my gaze to the far corner of the room and studied the black marble tiles' pattern until I heard the king slip beneath the water.

"How sumptuous," he said, waving his fingers through the water. "I could almost believe I'm at a bathhouse, being waited upon by a harem of nubile young beauties."

"I'm terribly sorry to disappoint," I said, adding more of the tonics and testing the water temperature.

Marnaigne settled back against the tub's slope and closed his eyes.

"I'm going to let you soak in this for a few minutes, and then I want to try putting on something to draw out the Brilliance—slowly this time, gently. I'll start with your face."

He hummed an assent and relaxed farther down into the bath.

I dug through my valise until I found charcoal powder and several needed oils. I mixed them in a bowl, adding a bit of clay and a small dollop of honey.

"Will this hurt at all?" the king asked as I finished the mixture and brought it over for his inspection.

"Not at all," I said, kneeling. "Just lie back and pretend you're at that salacious spa of yours."

He laughed and shut his eyes once more.

I started with his forehead, covering it with a thick layer of the paste before drawing a line of it down his nose. I smudged more along his temples, and then, gently, so, so gently, I cupped his cheeks and peered down into the face of the king.

CHAPTER 29

THE SKULL COVERING RENÉ MARNAIGNE'S FACE WAS completely different from any I'd seen before.

It was as black and slick as tar, with an oily viscosity I wanted to cringe from. It looked grimy and foul, so terribly wrong against the severe austerity of the king's profile.

The skull's jaw fell into its usual leering, gleeful grin. Though there were no eyes in its deep sockets, I could feel it watching me with rapt interest, pleased to have been noticed, pleased to have so thoroughly disrupted everything.

My heart sank as I stared down at it.

A deathshead.

King Marnaigne was meant to die.

King Marnaigne was meant to die, and I was meant to kill him.

I felt sick as I imagined him following me around, another ghost added to my collection. I wanted to cry as I pictured his long, dark shadow, forever trailing behind me, stumbling nearer and nearer, until the day I slipped up and let him get too close. His bony, long-dead fingers would reach out and—

My horrible daydream stopped short as another, altogether more terrible thought flickered to life.

This was no ordinary man the deathshead wanted me to kill.

He was a king.

The king. My sovereign.

I would have royal blood on my hands. To even *think* of his demise was treason.

I'd heard tales of men who'd simply dared to disagree with the king. They were thrown in the stocks for weeks, and pelted with moldering food and spit and jeers. Marnaigne was swift to anger, swift to seek respect and revenge.

Should I be caught in the act of poisoning him, no matter how good my intentions were . . .

I shuddered.

I'd be sentenced to death, no questions asked, no chance to redeem myself. They executed people in Châtellerault's town square, setting up a gruesome platform and block, bringing out a temple reverent carrying a long, curved sword. People came to watch, came to cheer.

The grim hooded man would chop off my head, but it wouldn't take. I wouldn't die. Not at first.

I imagined my severed head coming to life yards away from my abandoned body as my second candle lit. I could hear the screams of the crowd, horror and elation mingling before panicked fear consumed them. Surely they'd see Merrick's gift as a sign of magic most foul and stomp me out of existence once more, burning through my second candle with swift vengeance. Then my third. My three lives would be over and done.

What purpose would my life have been for then? Would my ghosts follow me into the afterlife, forever haunting their murderer?

I didn't know what awaited beyond the veil—I'd always been too terrified to ask Merrick—but it was safe to assume I wouldn't have unlimited stores of salt with me.

The entire scenario was too terrible to bear.

"Hazel?" the king asked, and it jarred me from my reverie. There was a note of concern in his voice, an indication that this wasn't the first time he'd tried to get my attention.

"Sire?"

"You stopped applying the paste. Is everything all right?"

My hands flinched from his face, instantly erasing the wicked skull, but it was as if its image had burned across my retinas. A ghostly reverse imprint remained, white as bone and covering the king's features as effectively as a mask.

He opened his eyes and they stared up through the phantom skull's sockets, bright as sapphires.

"Everything's fine, Your Majesty," I said, turning back to the counter, back to my valise. I busied myself, poking through pockets for cures that were not there, that did not exist because *the king was supposed to die* and die soon, and die by my hand. "Just lost in my thoughts."

My fingers trembled, brushing vials of foxglove and hemlock, oleander and castor bean, and my heart thudded painfully in my chest, beating faster and faster until I could feel it in my throat, creeping higher and higher as the room spun about me. It was in this haze of distorted equilibrium that I realized I was having a fit of nerves. Panic was flooding my system, and my head felt too heavy to keep up. I wobbled on feet that seemed too small to hold me up.

"How long should I keep this on? It's beginning to tingle." He took in a sharp, hopeful breath, whispering with amazement, "Is it working already?"

I gripped the edge of the counter, clinging to the marble top as I fought to stay upright.

The king.

I was meant to kill the king.

I'd kill the king, then they'd kill me.

"Does it feel hot in here to you?"

I heard myself ask the question but couldn't remember when I'd decided to speak. I fumbled at my dress's neckline. It was too tight, making it hard to breathe. If I could just loosen it somehow, perhaps I could draw in some air and everything would be all right.

But I'd still have to kill the king.

"Hazel?" His words reverberated through my mind, bouncing back and forth like an echo caught in a chamber. My name splintered into nonsensical syllables before uniting, whole but still terribly wrong. "Hazel? Are you all right?"

I wanted to turn around and assure him that all was well, that all would be fine, but I couldn't because when I turned, I would see that ghastly skull over his face, hiding his expression, hiding everything but his eyes, and I wanted to scream but my words wouldn't form and my mouth wouldn't open, until it did, but only to release a soft hiss of air as my eyes rolled back into my head and the floor rushed up to meet me.

CHAPTER 30

I WAS NO LONGER IN THE KING'S CHAMBERS.

The air was cooler now, no longer humid with the steam from King Marnaigne's bath. It was softened by a resin incense and scented vapors so thick, I felt as if I were in a verdant forest. I took a deep breath and rolled to my side.

Slowly, carefully, I opened my eyes.

The room around me was spartan and functional. Rows of simple cots ran its length. I was the only occupant, positioned somewhere in the middle. The sheet covering me was rough and thin, the woven fibers coarse. I shivered, startled to find I no longer wore my own clothing. I'd been dressed in a cotton shift striped green and yellow.

Only when I sat up did I see the mural covering the wall.

The towering figure of the Divided Ones loomed over the room with potent energy. Calamité's and Félicité's painted eyes peered down with realistic flickers, watching with keen and discerning judgment.

I fought to free myself from the scratchy bedsheets, bewildered by the gods' presence.

"Oh, you shouldn't do that."

An older woman in yellow and green robes hurried over to my bed. Her eyes were a startling amber, full of radiant peace. Dozens of the Divided Ones' sigils clattered from the bracelets around her brown wrists.

"Where am I?" I felt embarrassed to ask it, ashamed to admit I couldn't remember coming to this place.

"You're in the Rift." She tried to get me to lie back down, her bony fingers digging into my arms. "I'm Amandine, one of the priestesses here."

There was a smattering of giggles behind her, and I leaned over to see a trio of small girls. They wore cotton dresses just like mine, and their pale blond hair was neatly plaited up and away from their little faces.

I stared at them in confusion, certain I knew them but unable to recall their names or where we would have crossed paths.

"That will be enough, girls," Amandine called to the three. "What do you remember?" she asked me. Her kind eyes flattened as I threw my legs over the side of the bed, winning the struggle.

"I was at the palace," I began, trying to pinpoint the last memory I had. I'd been with the king. He'd been in the bath. I stopped short as I recalled the deathshead. My heart thudded and I took a deep breath, trying to quell my rising anxiety.

"You fainted," she supplied when it was clear I wouldn't finish. "When they couldn't wake you, you were brought here so we might pray for a swift return to health."

"Oh."

The priestess made a face of understanding. "We know of your . . . godfather, of course, but he has no temples within Châtellerault.

Ours is closest to the palace. I hope the Dreaded End will show understanding and mercy. They were doing the best they could, under urgent circumstances."

I tried to smile at her, grateful for the care they'd shown me. A wide band across the back of my head ached, and I rubbed the spot tenderly. "I'm certain he will. Thank you for your kindness. Are the guards still here? I'm afraid I must get back." I tried to stand but quickly sank back onto the mattress as the room spun wildly.

"There'll be none of that," Amandine said, pushing me gently into the pillows. "Girls, water, please?"

The blond trio scurried out of the room, and their footsteps and whispers echoed down the corridor.

Woozy with vertigo, I allowed Amandine to tuck me back in. "How long have I been here?"

"A few hours, I've been told. Our high priest was with you at first. My charges and I took over after lunch."

"I appreciate your prayers," I said, pressing my fingertips at points along my forehead, desperate to relieve the building pressure. "But I truly must get back."

"Not until you can sit up without keeling over," she said firmly, and sat on the bed beside mine. "They said you struck your head on the tiled floors?"

I nodded, and it made me want to throw up. "There's marble everywhere at the palace," I confided.

"You've probably a concussion," she surmised. "You need observation and rest."

"You sound like a healer."

"We've all had to take on new roles," Amandine admitted. "Since the war began."

"The war?" I echoed, surprised at her ominous term. "It's only a few skirmishes, isn't it? With the militia?"

A burst of laughter barked out of her before she covered her mouth. "Militia? Is that what they're calling it?"

I nodded uneasily.

"Make no mistake, Mademoiselle Trépas. It's an army." She toyed with the charms on her bracelets. "I'm sure the palace doesn't want to admit it, but Baudouin is drawing ever closer to Châtellerault, gaining more followers by the day. They've been ransacking villages on their way in from the north. So many lives have been lost. So many children orphaned. We've been taking in as many as we can. The three you saw have only recently come to us. They're all that's left of their village."

I blinked, certain I'd misunderstood her. "What village?"

"Ansouisienne."

I'd heard of it. It was along the river, only a day or two's ride from the capitol. "Baudouin is that close?"

Why weren't more people in the palace concerned by this? Everyone was carrying on as if the fighting was nothing but a little annoyance that would soon peter out.

Amandine nodded, her face lined with sorrow. "He's been blazing a trail down from his duchy, recruiting soldiers to fight in his name. Those who do keep heading south. Those who don't . . ." She sucked in a breath, implying the worst, then waved her hand about the room. "This used to be one of our reflection vestibules. We've converted it into sleeping chambers for the littlest ones. Most of them are at services now, but come tonight, this will house dozens of children."

"Dozens." I looked around the room, wondering how they'd all fit.

Amandine nodded. "The Rift isn't the largest temple in Châtellerault, but we're doing our part. I've heard the Ivory Temple has over three hundred orphans now." She pursed her lips, her expression clouded. "The Holy First commands ever so many more offerings than the Divided Ones."

I wondered how often Margaux returned to the Ivory Temple, if she'd seen the number of children housed there. If she had, wouldn't she have said something to the king?

Even though the room was empty, the priestess dropped her voice, whispering to me. "I overheard that you're at court to take care of the king." I nodded, leaning in to make out her conspiratorial tones. "Not everyone knows, of course. But High Priest Théophane was asked to perform a special ceremony for the king, in private, to beseech Félicité's favor. We've heard . . ." She looked guiltily to the hall. "Théophane was told it's the Shivers."

I froze, unsure of what to say but certain I shouldn't reveal the extent of King Marnaigne's illness.

Amandine nodded, my silence evidently confirming her fears. "I hope you don't mind, but I've spent my time here praying for your successful treatment of His Majesty. He must heal, and heal quickly. The armies need to see their monarch strong and ready to fight with them. Only he can rally them to victory. Only he can stop this war."

I pushed aside memories of the grinning deathshead. It was hard to meet her open, fervent gaze. "I will certainly try my best."

Amandine grabbed my hands, encircling them with her warmth. "You must, Mademoiselle Trépas." Her smile deepened with embarrassed chagrin. "I don't mean to put pressure on you—I know you need rest and care yourself, but every hour the king is away, every day that he hides from his public, from his supporters, more are lost. If Baudouin should take the throne . . ." Tears grew in her eyes.

". . . it would be catastrophic. The country would be ruined, tens of thousands of lives lost. Maybe hundreds. Oh, Mademoiselle Trépas, we are putting every faith in you. I know Félicité will guide your hands."

I swallowed, unable to answer. The hopeful spark in her eyes pierced my heart.

There would be no saving the king. Not with the deathshead upon his face.

Leopold's voice echoed in my memory, asking how he'd look in the crown.

I shuddered.

The orphaned girls returned then, carrying a tray. Again I was struck by the uncanny sense that I knew them all from somewhere.

"Amandine has said that you are from Ansouisienne?" I asked, trying to make friendly conversation as the oldest busied herself at a side table, pouring the water and sprinkling herbs across it.

"We were," she said flatly. "Ansouisienne is no more."

"I'm sorry to hear that," I said, my eyes darting toward Amandine in apology. "Could I ask you girls for a favor?"

The middle girl, no older than seven, nodded before glancing at the high priestess for permission.

"I'm going to have to go back to the palace soon," I said, carefully pushing myself up from the mattress. "Do you think you could help me find my clothes?"

The youngest jumped into action. "I know where they are! I put them in the cupboard!" she exclaimed, happy to have a task.

"Not so loud, Hazel, please," Amandine reprimanded.

"I'm sorry," the little girl and I said in unison before I realized the priestess had not been talking to me.

I looked over at the little girl with fresh interest. "Is your name Hazel?" She nodded. "How funny! So is mine!"

She gasped before hurrying back, nearly tripping over my dress and petticoats.

"The gods must be at work here," Amandine mused. "Such coincidence."

"Mama named me after her sister," the little girl said proudly.

"Our aunt," the middle girl added.

I'd been about to slip out of the shift but paused. "You're cousins?"

Little Hazel nodded. "Their mama is my aunt Genevieve."

I took in their blond hair once more. It was as pale as corn silk, just like all of my siblings'. And their eyes . . . I wanted to laugh that I'd not noticed it before. Those were Mama's blue eyes shining brightly from their little faces.

"Your mother's name is Genevieve?"

Genevieve. My oldest sister.

Though I'd not seen her in years—*ten years,* a voice in my head acknowledged—my heart swelled as I heard her name. I turned to little Hazel. "And you, who is your mother?"

"Mathilde," she answered, handing me my petticoats, wholly unaware of the revelation unfolding within me.

"Mathilde," I echoed, feeling my blood sing with wonder.

These were my sisters' children.

These beautiful girls were my nieces!

"How are they?" I asked, hurrying to throw on my chemise. "Your mothers?"

I had a sudden urge to see them, to invite them to Alletois. They could bring their children and stay with me at the cottage. We could play in the wildflower fields with Cosmos and I would take my sisters out for afternoon tea at the village bakery. It wouldn't matter what our past had been; we could begin a new future, a new chapter. I nearly laughed imagining it all.

"Dead," the oldest girl said, staring at me as though I were incredibly stupid. "They're dead."

"Oh." My dizzying daydreams crashed as reality set in.

Amandine had said these girls were orphans, that they'd been brought to the Rift after their village had been overrun, its townspeople massacred.

Their mothers, my sisters, were dead.

"I'm so sorry, of course," I murmured, feeling flustered that I'd let myself be carried away in imagining all that would never be.

I wanted to tell these girls who I truly was to them. I wanted to promise that I'd take them from the Rift once my messy business with the king was at an end, take them back to the cottage and care for them, raise them, love them, but I stopped short.

I couldn't care for these children. I didn't know if I'd be able to return to Alletois. Not after killing the king.

No. I'd have to run, have to flee the palace, flee the capitol, perhaps even flee Martissienes itself.

A series of bells rang throughout the temple, and the priestess frowned. "That's the call to evening prayer," she explained. "I must leave you now, but someone else will come and sit with you."

Footsteps echoed in the hall just outside the room, and she brightened.

"Here he is now," Amandine announced, and I quickly slipped my dress over my head, letting the embroidered linen fall into place.

"Thank you for taking care of me," I began, memorizing each of the girls' faces. "I—"

"Let us leave Hazel to her rest now." The priestess reached out and smoothed a benediction over me, tracing her fingers over my brow, cleaving my face into segments, just like those of the gods she served. "Blessings on you, Mademoiselle Trépas, and may Félicité's fortune shine brightly upon His Majesty."

I thanked her once more and straightened out the sheet. I was unaccustomed to being the one in the sickbed and found I disliked having so much attention thrust upon me.

"Fortunes and blessings upon you," said the new postulant from the doorway. He carried with him a smudge stick that filled the air with a black agar–scented haze.

"And upon you as well," I said, turning to him.

Amandine placed a hand on the doorframe, barring the new arrival's entrance as she whispered instructions to him. I could see the top of his head bob with assurances before he pressed his fingertips together and offered the priestess a low bow as she turned to leave. He was much taller than her, with pale skin and sun-lightened hair.

Before entering the room, he flicked the smudge stick at each corner before setting it in a bronze bowl just inside the threshold.

He walked with a pronounced limp, heavily favoring his left side. When he reached the foot of the bed, I saw he was a member of the Fractured—one of the Divided Ones' sects so devout they carved themselves up into separate pieces, just like their gods. Long lines of scar tissue ran across his face, dividing it into five parts. One of the cuts had gone through his lips, tugging one corner of his mouth into a perpetual frown, leaving the other side in a smile.

But no amount of scarring could disguise him from me. I instantly knew who he was.

"Bertie?"

CHAPTER 31

He tilted his head, frowning with both sides of his mouth as he looked me over. "I'm sorry . . . do I know you?"

My smile began to falter. "It's me . . . Hazel."

For a long, dreadful moment, his eyes remained flat. "Hazel?"

"Your sister?" I couldn't help but ask it as a question. Had he forgotten about me?

"That's not possible." He squinted, searching my face for something to recognize. I saw the moment he realized it was true. "Hazel?" His words swelled with wonder. "I was told . . . I thought you were dead!"

Surprise flickered through me.

Bertie came around to carefully sit on the edge of the bed. He was so different than I remembered, but I could still see traces of the little boy he'd been, now stretched into shapes long and unfamiliar. His body folded into awkward angles as he perched on the mattress.

"It *is* you," he said, awestruck, before throwing his arms around me. "What blessings! What joys! I can't believe it!"

"Nor I," I admitted, tightening my hold on him. "How long have you been here?"

"Not terribly, perhaps a fortnight? I was one of the brothers charged with bringing the latest flood of children to the Rift. I was in Saint Genevasire before this."

"That's not far from Alletois—where I live now," I supplied.

"When was the last time you were at home?" he asked, his eyes wide, dancing over my face, my hair, drinking in the changes.

"I . . ." I didn't want to discuss my final visit. Not with Bertie. Not after all this time apart. "Not for a while . . . My godfather finally came for me. Just a few years after you . . ." I paused, unsure of how to phrase the turn his life had taken. "On my twelfth birthday."

He glanced toward the ceiling, struggling to do the math in his head. "You've been gone for so long. Did you hear . . ." His voice dropped a fraction. "Mama and Papa . . . they died."

I found myself unable to read his expression. "Yes," I said carefully.

He beamed. "But the blessed ones have brought us together once more. Such good fortune." He kissed the tips of his fingers and made a gesture of gratitude toward the air, then clutched at his necklace. A small set of bronze pipes dangled from it, riddled with etchings I couldn't make out and words I couldn't read.

"How . . . how are you?"

The question felt stilted falling from my lips. It was something that shouldn't have to be asked, something a sister should just intrinsically know. But I didn't. Not anymore.

I studied the lines of scars running across his face, down his arms. Even his fingers had been bisected and mended back together. He looked like a patchwork quilt, sewn by a child with stitches clumsy and too big, and my own body hurt as I took in the scars.

"My heart is overflowing," he said joyfully. There was a peaceful serenity to his countenance, a contentment I'd never felt within myself. He looked radiant, glowing with an inner happiness that the scars, no matter how severe, could not diminish. "I never thought I'd see your face again in this world, but here you are. Such blessings! Such fortunes!"

"Here *you* are," I echoed. There was something about his joy that made my innards squirm. Despite all the differences in our childhoods, we were surprisingly alike, each serving the gods in our own way. But I had never felt as happy about it as he seemed.

Bertie paused as if remembering why I was here in the temple. "But you're unwell. Amandine said you were unconscious when you arrived."

I nodded. "I'll be fine."

"Has anyone come in to examine you? Head wounds can be—"

I smiled. "No. I actually . . . I'm a healer now."

Bertie's face lit up again, as bright as a sunbeam. "How marvelous. I never would have guessed such a life for you. Mother Félicité has guided your path well. What blessings! What fortunes!"

My smile felt odd on my lips, too wide and trying too hard to mask my incredulity. I'd never heard anyone quite so . . . devout.

"It surprised me as well. Merrick . . . the Dreaded End . . . was the one who wanted me to study medicine. But I'm rather good at it. Do you have any troubles? I could mend them in minutes," I offered playfully. Reaching out, I traced one of the especially wicked-looking lines across his cheek. "I could even lighten those if you want. I have a salve that—"

He shook his head, panic striking his face. "I'd never want those to go away," he assured me. "I'm proud of each and every one of them." He rolled up a sleeve of his robe, showing me his inner forearm. Jagged lines exploded from his wrist like lightning.

"Did . . . did you choose to do this?" I asked carefully. "Mama said that . . ." I paused, wondering if she was still trapped within the confines of the palace armoire.

"It was my choice, by my hand," he said softly, as if this statement was meant to reassure me. It did anything but.

"It must have hurt terribly." I gestured toward the ones crisscrossing the bridge of his nose.

"It's an honor to be in service to them."

I wondered what Calamité and his brethren thought of the Fractured, how they felt about mortals trying to replicate their disjointed appearance. I couldn't believe Félicité would condone such a practice. I could almost hear her motherly clucks of dismay.

"Are you happy here?" I scrunched my face, trying to rephrase my words. "Not just here, in Châtellerault, but . . . *here.*" I waved my hand in the air, gesturing toward a higher, more meaningful plane.

"Exceptionally," he promised. "I know the last time you saw me . . ." He sighed. "Like you, I would not have chosen this path for myself, but it makes me feel all the more content, knowing that the path chose *me* instead. The day that High Priestess Ines picked me from our lineup of siblings . . . that was the best day of my life, Hazel. Truly. This is my life's calling, my life's work. And . . ." He glanced about the dormitory, his eyes drifting toward the beds. "There is so much work to be done. Especially now, with the turmoil in the north."

Some of the beatific light died away from his eyes.

"You helped bring the orphans here," I prompted, gently nudging him for more information. "The little girls who were with Amandine, did you know—"

He nodded sadly. "Genevieve's and Mathilde's girls, my nieces. Our nieces," he corrected himself quickly. "They . . . they don't know who I am." He glanced up in alarm. "Did you tell them about yourself?"

I shook my head. "It didn't seem right . . . at least, not now."

He nodded.

"There's not been much news of the skirmishes at the palace."

His face darkened. "They're not skirmishes. They're massacres. Baudouin's armies are slaughtering whole towns overnight. They leave the bodies out to rot and bloat in the fields, in the rivers where they fall. It's poisoning the earth, the water. There's no one to tend the plants, no one to feed the livestock. Come winter, so many will starve. And the children . . ." He sighed. "It sounds callous, but King Marnaigne needs to leave his grieving chambers and do something. There are small bands of men trying to form, trying to fight against Baudouin, but there's no organization. They're acting without a leader. Marnaigne is a good king. He can put an end to all this."

I smoothed my skirts as I weighed my response.

"What aren't you telling me?" he asked, instantly guessing something was troubling me. Bertie had always been able to read my quiet moods like a book.

"You mustn't say anything to anyone, but . . . the king isn't just grieving," I confided quietly to my brother. "He's ill."

Bertie's face brightened. "Is that why you're at court? You're taking care of him? Oh Hazel. Fortune has smiled upon the king! What blessings! What joy!"

His fingers tangled up with mine, squeezing tight, and I found myself wanting to shrink from his touch. His reverence bordered on mania. It was impossible to see Bertie's younger self anywhere in this man.

"Help him see how much he's needed. Tell him how his people ache for his return. Spur him back to his duties, and then—"

"It's not that simple."

His smile deepened with chagrin. "Of course, I'm glossing over your work, but—"

"The king has the Shivers," I whispered, cutting off whatever fervent call to action my brother was about to deliver. "There's no cure for it."

"Yet," he persisted. "There's not a cure *yet.* But you're working on it, aren't you?"

I glanced down at my hands. My hands, which had killed so many. My hands, which were meant to go on and kill the king. "I am . . . but he's very sick. . . ."

The room fell into silence. It bloomed across the stone walls, filling the space like ink in a basin of water, tainting it, twisting it, making it impossible to ever return to what it once had been.

"You've given up?" he asked, and his tone bordered on accusation.

"It's hard to explain."

"Try," he said, narrowing his eyes. "Try to explain why you'd rather see a barbarian seize the throne, dripping with the blood of his subjects. Good men and women. *Children.* Try to explain that."

"I don't wish Baudouin to take the throne," I protested, bristling against his growing anger.

"He certainly will, if you allow the king to die."

"I'm not *allowing* anyone to die. There's no cure, no way to stop it. And Baudouin wouldn't get the throne anyhow. It would fall to Leopold."

Bertie scoffed. "Another fine choice. He doesn't know the first thing about leading a country. He should be out there now, fighting his uncle, fighting to hold the front, but where is he?"

My brother wasn't wrong, but he wasn't wholly right either.

"His mother died less than a year ago. His father is grievously ill."

"Then fix him!" Bertie all but screamed. His words echoed in the chamber, ringing sharp and hateful. "You need to find a cure, Hazel," he said after a long pause. "Our world will fall into chaos if he dies."

When he dies, I silently corrected him. *When I kill him.*

My eyes drifted up to the painted figure of the Divided Ones.

"I should go," I said, suddenly wanting to be away, wanting to be as far from my brother as I could get.

"Back to the palace?" he asked, sounding distant, and from the corner of my eye, I could see he was staring at the mural too. "To find the cure, to save the king?"

I shrugged, suddenly too exhausted to even bother trying to explain.

He licked his bisected lips, his body tense with unspent energy. He looked like a large cat, caged and aching to pounce. "You should ask for a blessing before you do. It would be good to have every bit of the gods' favor upon your work."

"It would," I agreed, sounding hollow.

Bertie toyed with the little bronze bauble I'd seen on his necklace before, and I wondered if he was about to press it to my forehead, offering a Fractured's prayer.

Instead, he put it to his lips. "Félicité favors the bold," he murmured, then blew.

CHAPTER 32

I WANTED TO BARE MY TEETH AGAINST THE SOUND. IT was louder than anything in the natural world had a right to be. Only the gods could create such cacophony. The pitch was so wrong it hurt my ears, and though I covered them, I could still hear its echo through my body. It made my very blood feel uncomfortable in its veins.

When it mercifully faded, I dared to lower my hands. "What was that?"

"You need a blessing," Bertie said simply.

He'd turned to me, his eyes round and luminous. He looked intoxicated, possessed by something bigger and stronger than he'd ever be.

He looked crazed.

"Who better than Félicité to give it?"

"You summoned the Divided Ones?" I hissed, horrified. "You can do that?"

Bertie held out his scarred arms as if that was all the response I needed.

"Oh, little mortal, we meet again." The unified voices of the gods curled out from a corner of the dormitory that suddenly seemed too dark, impossibly shadowed on such a sunny afternoon.

Then, a shift in the darkness and the Divided Ones moved into the light.

I frowned. "Hello, Félicité. Calamité."

I'd not seen them since I was twelve years old, and could almost trick myself into believing they'd not changed. Why should they? They were immortals, ageless and eternal. But there was a hint of difference in their shared face. Their eyes, devoid of both iris and pupil, looked fuller somehow, heavy with the impossible weight of their collected knowledge.

Bertie plummeted to the ground in abject devotion, pressing his forehead to the stone floor, spreading his fingers wide, palms up, as if hoping to catch any bits of favor the Divided Ones might offer. "My lords, welcome! Thank you for answering my call, thank you for the blessings of your presence, thank you for—"

The giant gods stepped over his prostrate form as if he were nothing more than a decorative tile, without sparing even a single glance toward him.

"What in all the mortal realms could bring the Dreaded End's daughter to our house of worship?" Calamité wondered. He swept their body in a circle, inspecting the room. "It looks different in here."

"I was . . . injured . . . while working at the palace," I said carefully. "They brought me here for convalescence."

"Who heals the healer?" Félicité mused, as though thinking through a particularly tricky riddle.

"Apparently our devotees," Calamité quipped. "Something *is* different. I don't remember all these beds in here."

"We had to bring them in, my lords . . . for the children," Bertie said, still pressing his forehead to the floor with contrite reverence.

The Divided Ones glanced at the floor, only now noticing him.

"I take it you've met my brother Bertie?"

He dared to peek up, if only to offer a deferential bob of his head.

Calamité ran his eye across Bertie's scars. "Of course. Bertrand is one of our most faithful Fractured. Don't you find his devotion most . . . impressive?" He smirked at me, somehow knowing I did not.

"What's this about children?" Félicité asked, turning their head as she too noticed the rows of beds.

"The Rift has been taking in children orphaned in the bastard prince's uprising," Bertie explained, far more succinctly than I would have.

"Baudouin's trying to go to war?" Félicité turned her shoulder, initiating a private conversation with her twin. "What have you to do with this?"

Calamité made a face of disgust. "Why am I always blamed for things going wrong? If the king so badly wants to stay in power, perhaps he ought to put a stop to the madness himself."

Bertie spoke up. "He can't, my lords. He's sick. That's why I summoned you."

"Marnaigne is ill?" Félicité frowned, casting her eye first to her brother and then toward me.

I nodded.

Calamité tilted their head curiously, looking far too pleased. "What is it?"

"The Shivers," I responded. Neither god reacted. "His case is . . . most severe."

"So heal him," Calamité instructed, as if it were the easiest thing in the world. "That's what you're meant to do, isn't it? Heal?"

"I . . . I can't. Not this time."

Understanding flashed across their eyes.

They knew. Of course they did.

Calamité flicked his wrist at Bertie. "Théophane keeps the most delightful plum brandy in his study. There's a bottle hidden behind the Book of Schisms. Would you mind fetching us a glass? We're parched."

Bertie tensed, wanting to stay and listen but always ready to serve. "Certainly, my lords. Is there anything else I can bring you? Any of you?"

Félicité's smile was tight and thin, but she kept her voice melodious as ever. "You might as well bring the entire bottle. My brother's thirst is legendary."

Bertie nodded and rushed from the room, nearly tripping over himself as he went backward, bowing every other step.

"That should buy us some time," Calamité said.

"You could have just ordered him out of the room," I pointed out. "He is one of your postulants."

"And let our stomach go wanting?" He shuddered before returning to the conversation at hand. "So you've seen a deathshead."

I nodded miserably.

"Then what are you doing here in our temple?" Calamité asked. "Shouldn't you be swathed in black? Mourning your king's end?"

"I'm going to kill him," I protested. "I just haven't had the chance."

"Obviously," he said with a smirk.

"Something seems to be troubling you," Félicité observed.

"Well . . . yes. He's the king. If I am caught . . . if someone should even suspect me . . . they won't understand my calling. It would be seen as an assassination."

"It *is* an assassination." Calamité blinked, studying me. "You're a clever girl, I suppose," he admitted, most begrudgingly. "There is any number of ways to ensure your act of treason goes unseen."

My stomach flipped. Why must he call it that? "There's also the matter of the oracle."

"Whose oracle?" Félicité asked. "Surely not one of ours."

I shook my head. "She's from the Ivory Temple, one of the Holy First's reverents. She told the palace to bring me to court." I sighed, unsure how to articulate my concerns about Margaux. "She sees the Holy First's visions, yes? Isn't that how oracles work?" The gods shrugged, neither confirming nor denying. "Won't she see my intention? Won't she try to stop me? She has been shown that *I* am the one who will save the king. If I return to the palace with a different goal, I feel like she'll . . ." I trailed off as another thought occurred to me. "She saw the vision of me saving the king. That is what brought me to court. So . . . doesn't that mean that I'm supposed to save the king? If that's what the Holy First showed her, then . . ." My head ached, jumbled by all the possibilities. I felt like I was speaking in circles. "Who is right in this—the deathshead or the Holy First?"

Calamité tapped one of his fingers against their chin. "You're thinking too much like a mortal. The Holy First knows all, she sees all—not just in this moment but in *all* moments—so she already knew you would see the deathshead, and that by sending her vision to this oracle, she was actually bringing you to court precisely to kill the king."

I sighed, feeling hopelessly deflated.

Félicité squinted at me. "There are so many worries behind

your eyes, little one. What makes this kill so much harder than the others?"

I shrugged. "I . . . I understand the purpose of the deathshead—I'm meant to take one life to prevent many others from being ruined. But the king . . ." I released a shaky breath. "His is such a big life."

Calamité rolled his eye at my sentiment. "No one life is greater or lesser than any other. In the end, all mortals are dust."

"In the end, yes," I admitted. "My godfather comes for all. But before that . . . there are so many lives that the king has the power to affect. To protect. And with this war . . ." I trailed off, everything I wanted to express too large to be articulated. "I met my nieces today. Here, at the temple. I didn't even know I had nieces, but they're here. Orphaned. Their mothers—my sisters—are dead."

"I suppose you want me to apologize for that?" Calamité said, looking exceptionally put out.

"No, but it got me thinking . . . if the king weren't sick, how many of these orphans would be here? If I could find a cure for the Shivers, a cure for him, he could stop this war, keep his subjects safe. He could prevent so many other children from ending up like my nieces."

Félicité frowned. "It's a noble thought, I suppose. But a pointless one. You've been given a task—just like reading all those books so many years ago. Carry it out."

I pushed my hair back, tucking the loose strands behind my ears. "But . . . what if that task is wrong? Who determines that it's right?"

"Your godfather, I'd suspect," Calamité deadpanned, as if it were obvious.

I hadn't wanted him to say that. "But what if Merrick is wrong?"

"A god is never wrong." Even Félicité was beginning to sound annoyed.

"But more people will die if the king does than if he lives. Right? It seems so logical, don't you think?"

"We don't think," came the gods' reply, dozens of voices speaking in unison, as loud as a droning beehive. "We only know."

"Then you ought to know if I'm right," I snapped.

Félicité wrested herself away from her holy collective. "What is it you want from us, Hazel? What can we do to make this easier?"

I wasn't sure how to answer. When all was said and done, what *did* I want?

I didn't want to kill the king, but I didn't want to let the deathshead down. I didn't want people to die because he had, but I couldn't bear the thought that I'd endanger more people if he lived. I didn't want any of this blood on my hands.

Each of my wishes felt impossible, even for the gods of fortune.

"Bertie called you here to give me a blessing," I finally said. "He wants me to save the king and stop the war. But . . ." I pressed my lips together. I wasn't sure if I was holding back tears or a scream. ". . . apparently that's not what the Holy First wants. It's not what the deathshead or my godfather or any of the thousands of gods trapped inside you want. So . . . I guess I want a bit of a blessing too. When it comes time to . . ." I couldn't say the words, couldn't voice my treachery here in this room that housed so many unfortunate innocents. "When I'm about to deal with King Marnaigne, I would like everything to go right. To go well." I felt my eyes prick with tears. "I don't know what lives I save by taking the king's, so I suppose I'm asking you to help ensure that my own is safe. Let me get out of this disaster with my own skin intact."

There was a long moment of silence; then Calamité patted my back. "It takes a great amount of courage to show such cowardice," he said proudly, as if his commendation wasn't also an insult. "I quite like you, mortal." He reached into his side of their robe and withdrew a long necklace, a perfect match to Bertie's little set of bronze pipes. "When the time comes, blow on this and we will bless the endeavor."

He lowered the chain over my head and I slipped the bauble into my bodice, feeling sick.

"I suppose our work here is done, then," Félicité said, not sounding sure of it at all. "Shall we?"

"And miss the brandy?" Calamité pouted, but his sister was already raising her hand to whisk themselves away.

"Wait!" I shouted before they vanished. "Could I . . . could I ask for one other thing?"

The goddess stopped short, hope flickering in her eye. "Yes?"

"I can't save the king and I can't stop the war, but I should be able to do something about this plague, the Shivers. I'm a healer. I should be able to stop it, right?"

She waited, sensing I had more to say.

I swallowed, already pained by the admission to come. "I haven't seen the cure. I only see the deathshead on the king. And it's already killed so many, whole villages and towns, and I just . . . I need to know. Is there one? A cure?"

Félicité considered this. "All sicknesses come to an eventual end."

I wanted to stamp my foot with frustration. Did she truly believe that was an acceptable answer?

"But if I can't find someone alive to—"

Shouts rang out down the hall and we all startled, heads snapping toward the open doorway. For a horrible moment I feared the rebellion had reached the capitol, that forces had already descended upon the Rift.

"Just tell me. Plainly," I demanded, whipping back toward the gods. "Is there a cure?"

More shouts. One of the raised voices sounded like Bertie's. There was a great crash, followed by the sound of glass shattering.

Calamité sighed. "That would be the brandy. I suppose there's no point in staying now."

"Tell me!" I exclaimed, reaching out toward them.

The god rolled his eye. "So dramatic. Of course there is."

"And I'll find it?"

He raised his shoulder in a one-sided shrug. "You know how to find *us.* That's what matters, mortal."

Before I could ask anything more, Calamité bopped my forehead with all the irreverence of a bothersome uncle, and the gods were gone.

The patter of footsteps grew closer. I could hear laughter too.

My eyes darted about the dormitory, looking for a spot to hide, a weapon to use, anything so that when the soldiers arrived I wouldn't be standing in the middle of the room, empty-handed. I grabbed the first thing I saw—a brass figurine of the Divided Ones—and hefted it over my shoulder, poised like a warrior ready to strike.

A figure raced in, panting and out of breath. Bertie trailed behind, close at its heels.

I nearly dropped the statue in surprise. "Leopold?"

He smirked at my choice of weapon. "Come on, little healer. We're getting you out of here."

CHAPTER 33

"WHAT ARE YOU DOING?" I ASKED FOR WHAT FELT like the thousandth time as I settled into the royal coach.

Leopold only grinned as he pulled the narrow door shut.

The driver set the horses into action and the Rift began to recede into the distance. Bertie stood on the stairs before the temple's entrance, scarred arms folded over his scarred chest, looking exceptionally displeased. I waved goodbye to him. He did not wave back.

When we rounded a corner and my brother was well and truly out of sight, Leopold leaned back against the velvet cushions. "I do believe most damsels reward their heroes with effusive gestures of gratitude, not an inquisition."

"Thank you," I said perfunctorily. "Now, why were you at the Rift?"

He had the audacity to look offended. "I was rescuing you, of course! Dear Aloysius mentioned you'd had a bit of a scare and were a little unconscious and had been sent off to be prayed over."

He pressed his lips into a firm line, trying to cover his smirk as he let me know exactly what he thought of the valet's plan.

"The priestess told me all that. It doesn't explain what *you* were doing in the Rift."

"I . . ." Leopold blew out a breath of annoyance and pushed back his curls, mussing their pomaded perfection. "I thought it wouldn't sit very well with you—or your godfather—being in a temple that was not his. I don't pretend to know how the relationships between deities and their . . . their . . . manservants' work, but I thought you'd be uncomfortable when you woke—if you woke—and I wanted to bring you back. I suspected the powers that be might try to keep you there longer than you wished. I assumed the only one who might overrule their say was me."

The sincerity of his admission surprised me. It was such a thoughtful gesture. Such a thoughtful, lovely, so-very-unlike-Leopold thing to do. I couldn't help but be touched by it.

"Well, thank you," I said after a moment. This new gratitude didn't sit well with the offensive irritation he'd kindled in me earlier, and now I didn't quite know what to think of this prince. How could such an arrogant and entitled, spoiled boy think to do something so attentive, so considerate?

"You're welcome," he responded, and the words sounded like marbles falling from his mouth. It was a phrase he'd obviously not had much practice in exercising.

Outside the coach, the buildings of Châtellerault whizzed by, exacerbating the way my head ached, and I found the simplest thing I could do to hold my impending migraine at bay was to keep my focus squarely on the young man before me.

"And . . ." There were so many things I could segue into: his father's health; any news I'd missed in the hours I'd been gone; more stories he'd heard of the Shivers, however salacious, however untrue. There were so many things I needed to learn, so many things I needed to plan and execute and . . . "I'm not a manservant."

He laughed and my heart warmed. I was glad I'd taken a more frivolous, easy approach.

"You and Margaux go about running whatever errands your gods require—what else am I meant to call you? A retainer? A lackey? A drudge?" He paused, searching for more words, clearly enjoying himself. "Ooh! A beatifically blessed handmaiden!"

I laughed, surprising us both. "I can't speak for Margaux, but I prefer *goddaughter*."

He made a face. "No one can speak for Margaux exactly the way she can."

"You seem to dislike her most acutely," I observed, feeling as if my words were not wholly my own. There was something about Leopold's undeniable charisma that rubbed off on whoever he was near. I felt wittier and more sophisticated after mere minutes with him than I had in the whole of my life. I wasn't sure it was my best self he drew out—such snark did come with a touch of feeling slightly superior to Margaux as well—but it was awfully fun in the moment.

"I don't trust anyone who claims to not speak for themselves," he said simply. "She spends her days passing along messages from this gloriously holy mother figure that none of us poor louts are deemed worthy of even being permitted to see. Have you?" he asked suddenly.

"What?"

"Seen the First. Basked in the radiance of her magnitude. Fallen to your knees in reverence and awe."

"I have not," I admitted.

"See—even the Dreaded End's goddaughter hasn't seen her. But Margaux has. Margaux *claims* to have. So who is holding *her* in check? She could say the Holy First has declared the moon is made of pumpernickel and we all would have to believe it because no one can say otherwise."

"Oh, Your Royal Highness," I began earnestly, "the moon is clearly a brioche."

The corners of his eyes crinkled. "But you see what I'm getting at, yes? And the way she fills my father's head with all these pronouncements, with all these so-called prophecies. She has so much more power than anyone realizes. She presents herself as this dowdy little reverent, covered chin to toe in all those heavy layers, but whatever she whispers to my father is taken as gospel. He could pass a law tomorrow confirming the lunar pumpernickel and all the best sandwiches would be gone forever."

Even though he gave his argument as a carefree example, I could see the seriousness of it and wondered if there was any way to check her claims, to confirm Margaux's messages from the other realm.

In the back of my mind, I saw the blackened skull covering the king's face. I could feel the tug of a connection between the two—Margaux's visions, my callings. Were we truly just pawns on a playing board of the gods' design? Or was there a way to take our gifts and twist them for personal gains, for ulterior benefits? Merrick knew the instant I dared to defy my orders; wouldn't it be the same for Margaux with the Holy First?

"She brought me to court," I offered, feeling guilty for thinking badly of the oracle, who wasn't here to defend herself. "She was right there. Unless you're lumping me in with all her blessed handmaiden schemes."

Leopold shrugged. "At least you carry out your work. It's your skills that guide your hands, your head that holds all that boring and complicated knowledge. I personally don't see how you do it."

"At breakfast you called me a charlatan," I reminded him unkindly.

He had the decency to look ashamed. "I'm never my best self after a night with those cigarettes."

"Perhaps you should stop smoking them, then."

"Perhaps I should," he agreed with more ease than I'd anticipated. "I did recognize you, you know. Not this morning, but last night. All those freckles."

He fell quiet for a moment, leaving me to grasp at what he'd meant.

Leopold sighed, shifting around on the coach seat. "I'm sorry I threw those coins at you. That day in the marketplace."

I was stunned, shocked into silence.

He waved aside his words, a red stain of embarrassment creeping up the sides of his neck. "You probably don't remember. It's fine."

"Do you really think my life so exciting that I wouldn't have occasion to remember a crown prince making fun of my freckles and then hurling a fistful of money at me while an entire village descended on us, grabbing and fighting over it?"

He picked at his fingernail, a fidgety gesture I'd never have guessed him capable of. Fidgeting meant you were uncomfortable. You were uncomfortable when you were in the wrong. I wondered if Leopold had ever thought himself in the wrong before.

"I am . . . ," he began, and a flash of doubt washed over him. "I am deeply sorry for that. For the coins and for the insult. I actually . . ." Leopold sighed. "I rather like your freckles," he admitted.

"You like my . . . freckles?" I wanted to laugh.

"They suit you. They give you character, make you stand out as your authentic self."

"I'm glad you enjoy them so," I said. "I've always wished they'd disappear."

The coach clattered over the moat, then slowed to a halt as the iron gates were opened.

"I had a . . . something once," Leopold confided once we were off again, heading up the winding drive to the palace. He gestured to the spot below his earlobe. "A birthmark, not very big, but such a rosy shade that my parents knew it needed to go."

"Go?" I echoed in disbelief. "It's a birthmark. Where exactly would a birthmark go?"

"Away," he laughed. "Far, far, far enough away that it would never dare to come back and visit my royal personage again. I don't remember all the treatments, all the ways the healers tried to remove it, but Bellatrice does. She's told me all about the horrid pastes and lotions, acids and cleansers."

"There's nothing there now," I noted, feeling flustered as I studied the sharp line of his jaw, the curve of his ear. It was a strangely intimate spot on the body, out for all the world to see but a curious place to fix your focus on. I wanted to reach out and feel the skin there but kept my hands in my lap, unsure if the impulse was professional or personal.

The dream I'd had the night before still danced in my memory.

He nodded. "When they couldn't lighten it, they had a surgeon take a hot knife and just—" He swished his fingers through the air, a quick flick of the wrist.

"That's barbaric!" I exclaimed, my anger bursting from me before I could stop it. "And it worked?"

"See for yourself," he said, angling his head back to better show me. There wasn't a trace of a birthmark, and the scar was tidy enough to be nearly invisible.

The coach stopped outside the front entrance, all sculpted colonnades and gilt tracing, but even its ostentatious grandeur could not pull my attention away from the crown prince.

"They did good work," I finally admitted. "But I'm sorry you were put through it, even as a baby."

He shrugged good-naturedly. "It was a lesson, I suppose. One that needed to be learned. Anything less than perfect, anything less than the idolized ideal, has no place at court, no place in our home, no place in our family." He shook his head, and I couldn't tell if this truth made him sad or merely resigned. "So yes, Just Hazel, despite what my brattish younger self may have implied, I rather like your freckles."

The carriage door opened and Leopold hopped out, seemingly unaffected by the private confidence he'd just shared with me. He went straight inside without looking back to see if I followed, not even once.

CHAPTER 34

I STARED AFTER LEOPOLD'S RETREATING FIGURE AND FELT a strange restlessness. I knew I ought to go inside to check on the king, but I'd been stuck behind walls all day, a feeling I was wholly unaccustomed to. The thought of wandering through the maze of identical halls, feeling the weight of the bricks and marble and the eyes of every golden bull, made me want to scream. I needed fresh air and open spaces, room to stretch and walk through all the problems weaving in my mind.

If I'd been at home, I would have set out with Cosmos for a long ramble along the creek that wound round my property. Our walks always helped me gain clarity and see whatever troubled me with fresh eyes, in a new light.

A walk was just what I needed now.

I turned to the coach's driver. "By chance are you returning to the stables?"

"Benj?" I called, poking my head into an empty tack room. "Cosmos?"

The stables were enormous, long and narrow and housing dozens of horses. They poked their heads from their stalls, stallions and mares and even a few ponies perfectly sized for Euphemia. Each was a flawless specimen, well-toned and lustrous, with bright, intelligent eyes that peered at me curiously as I passed. Every one of the beasts was the same dazzling shade of black. There wasn't a white star or fetlock among the entire lot of them.

I heard the familiar click of claws against the brick aisle and turned to see my pup sprinting my way. Benj, the stable boy, followed him, running to catch up.

"Couldn't go a day without seeing this brute, eh, miss?" he greeted me.

"Has he been any trouble?" I asked, kneeling to scratch at Cosmos's belly and tickle his ears. He rolled and snuffed and made such a delighted fuss one of the nearby mares let out a whinny of dismay.

"Not at all. He seems so big and scary, but it's all just for show, isn't it, you giant lapdog?"

"Thank you for looking after him. It's been . . ." I paused, remembering the events of the day. It seemed like a week had passed since I'd woken with Kieron kneeling over me. ". . . busy."

"So I've heard," the boy said. He looked to be about twelve and reminded me of a younger, human version of Cosmos, with paws and ears too big for his puppy frame. "Are you feeling better now?"

"You knew I fell?" I asked with surprise.

Benj nodded. "My aunt Sylvie is a maid on the family's floor. She fills me in on the best gossip during lunch. Besides," he added with a cheeky grin, "who do you think harnessed the horses that took you to the temple?"

I laughed. "I doubt there's a secret in the whole of the palace you don't know."

"True enough." He puffed out his chest, beaming with pride.

"Benj . . . ," I began as an idea came to me, "have you heard why I was brought here?"

"No," he admitted. "But it's not hard to guess. You're a healer, aren't you? I figure someone in the family must be sick."

"Someone in the family," I echoed.

"Well, it's not as though they'd bring in a special healer for one of us, would they? Delia's whole family had the Shivers and they didn't do anything but lock them in their rooms."

My eyebrows rose. "There's a family sick? Here at court?"

I nearly grinned at this twist of good fortune. I could pay this family a visit and discover the cure tonight. By tomorrow morning, we could begin spreading word of how to treat the Shivers. The king could send out his fastest riders and town criers and people could begin to get better. The plague would be over, thousands would be saved, and then I could kill the king with a clear conscience.

I stood up and Cosmos whined, pleading for more scratches. "I'm so sorry, boy. I'll be back as soon as I can. I need to go meet some new friends."

Benj's eyes widened, and he looked horribly stricken. "Oh no, miss. I didn't mean to suggest . . . The Cloutiers are gone. Dead and buried." He made a face. "Well. Dead and burned. No one really knows what to do with the bodies once they turn lumpy with the black bits."

It was as though the ground had dropped from under me. All

the whirling, giddy thoughts I'd been entertaining pitched forward, toppling like a house of cards. "All of them?"

"Save for Delia. But she's not at court now. After she got better, they sent her to stay with an aunt."

"In town?" I asked hopefully, already knowing luck would not be on my side. I could practically hear Calamité's cackle.

Benj frowned, thinking. "Somewhere south, I think. She was awfully happy to leave."

I sighed, feeling well and wholly deflated. "After such a loss, it's no wonder."

He bobbed his head back and forth, neither agreeing nor disputing. "And it got her away from the princess."

"What do you mean?"

"Delia was a maid for Princess Bellatrice. When she first was getting sick, with the twitches and the, you know . . ." He pantomimed the spasms I'd witnessed King Marnaigne go through. ". . . she was getting the princess ready for the day and I guess she dropped a bottle of perfume or . . . what's that stuff called? The fancy stuff girls clean themselves with?"

"Eau de toilette?" I guessed.

The young boy made a helpless gesture. "She had a bad spell and the bottle fell and broke, and the princess was so mad. Said she was docking five weeks of Delia's pay. But then all the Cloutiers got locked in their rooms, so it wasn't as if they were working anyway, and now . . ." He shrugged as though the lost wages were a sorrow on par with an entire family stricken down.

Something about his tale poked at me, prodding me into paying closer inspection. "You're certain Delia was sick?"

"She was shivering bad that morning at breakfast."

"But she's not now. She survived."

Benj nodded and I bit my lip, feeling as though I was on the verge of a breakthrough.

"She got well again . . . after she was doused by that perfume. . . ." My fingers jangled, itching to be put into action. "I think I need to pay the princess a visit."

CHAPTER 35

AFTER A HASTY STOP BY MY ROOM TO ENSURE THE ghosts were still warded away in the closet—they were, but I added a generous handful to the line of salt from the serving dish Aloysius must have left me—I arrived at Bellatrice's suite.

The door was slightly ajar but I tapped at it anyway, waiting to be admitted. There was a soft, distracted call and I went in, marveling at the room's high ceilings, the swags of satin rosettes, and the veritable treasure of gilt furniture and objets d'art.

An irritable sigh came from the far side of the room, where the princess was seated, facing her vanity. Its surface was littered with pots of lip stain, powders, brushes, discarded hairpins and ribbons, and more perfume atomizers than I could count.

She was dressed in a ball gown, a shimmering, spangled confection with skirts so full they showered over her chair's arms, piles of fabric pooling on the floor. She reminded me of a bouquet of alliums, spiky bursts of lilac and raspberry hues.

"Phemie, I've already read you seven stories tonight. I need to get ready for the— Oh," Bellatrice said, catching sight of me in the mirror. "It's you."

"Princess," I greeted her, bobbing into a brief curtsy.

"What do you want?"

"I was hoping to ask you a few questions." I took a tentative step toward a set of cream-colored bergère chairs situated near a marble fireplace. I noted curiously that no one had come to light an evening blaze for the princess.

Bellatrice caught me staring and sighed once more. "If you must. But don't make yourself too comfortable. I'm leaving soon."

She turned back to the mirror and I noticed that the back of her dress was entirely see-through—nothing but a skim of flesh-toned tulle, save for a row of silk-covered buttons going down her spine like candy-colored vertebrae.

"So late?"

My eyes darted to the set of tall windows lining one wall. The sky had deepened from twilight's lavender to the dark bruise of evening.

Bellatrice, who had returned to her primping, paused on the verge of wiping a smear of color across her mouth. The stain made her fingertip look as though it were bleeding. "Is *that* the question you wanted to ask me?"

"No! No, I came to see about . . . I wanted to know more about . . ."

She dabbed the red on her lips, looking amused. "Do I really make you so nervous?"

"A bit," I admitted, folding my hands in my lap.

Her laughter was as delicate as blown glass. "Would it help to set your mind at ease if you knew I admire that honesty?" One corner of Bellatrice's lips rose in a wry smile. "You'll find it's an unusual trait to possess at court."

I almost laughed myself. "So I'm beginning to gather. . . . I wanted to ask you about one of your maids—Delia?"

Her expression soured. "What of her? She's not back at court now, is she? I won't have her waiting on me, not again, and if Aloysius and I must have words over the matter, then so be—"

"She's not," I hurried to explain. "Was there . . . is there something wrong with her?"

Bellatrice picked up a jar of kohl and began smudging the dark powder over her already-dark eyebrows. "Where should we begin? She's lazy," she started, ticking off the offense on a blackened finger. "And incompetent. And worst of all—a thief." She dropped the pot back to the vanity, case made.

I looked around the chamber. Trinkets lay on most surfaces, glittering and beguiling, and though stealing wasn't right, I could understand a young girl's temptation.

"Things were forever going missing when that urchin was around. On her last day, I caught her pocketing a bottle of perfume. One of the other maids tried to deny Delia had done it, so I wrested it away from her as proof. It was awful. She went into some sort of fit, screaming and jerking, and the vial shattered. The perfume went everywhere. It splashed across my best dress, and the scent . . . you can't even imagine." Bellatrice shuddered, then slipped a small rose-colored flask from a hidden drawer and took a long swig. "I can smell it even now. Can't you?"

I took a deep breath. There *was* a delicate sweetness in the air.

"Do you want any?" she went on, offering the spirits.

"No, thank you. When the bottle broke, do you remember if any of the perfume fell on Delia?"

"Of course. We were drenched in it. Adelaide was too."

"Who?"

"My very dear friend Adelaide." She made a face. "Well. *Friend* is a strong word. Acquaintance, I suppose. She's a courtier, and they're all such sycophants you never really get to know the true side of any of them. And so you, in turn, never show them yourself either," she mused. "Anyway. She's the one throwing the soiree tonight. The one I'm terribly late to," she added pointedly.

"Have you replaced the perfume yet?" I glanced at the vanity's glass trinkets and atomizers.

"Of course not. Mother gave it to me on my sixteenth birthday. . . . They probably haven't made it in years." She looked wistfully at her collection of scents. "I don't even remember its name now. And she's not here to tell me." She took another sip from the flask. Then another.

"I'm so sorry, Bella—" Her eyes flashed sharply; evidently she was irritated by my slip into casual familiarity. "Your Highness. Do you at least remember what it looked like? The bottle, I mean."

Bellatrice slouched against the back of her chair, her eyes growing glassy and distant, and I wondered what exactly it was she'd been drinking. "It was a heart. Cut from crystal and faceted. Mother told me it was made of diamond, and for a time, I stupidly believed her. She said I was her little diamond, her special jewel. Prized above my brother and sister because I was hers and hers alone." She threw out this sentiment with a mincing tone, but underneath her brittle irreverence, I could see how much her mother's words had meant to her.

"That's such peculiar phrasing," I said gently, wondering if any of the Marnaigne children had ever had the space to openly discuss their loss. "What does it mean?"

"I've never been my father's daughter, not truly. I was always only hers."

My eyebrows jumped; I couldn't help it. "You're not King Marnaigne's daughter?"

She blinked the hazy fog from her green eyes, looking confused. "What an absurd comment. Of course I am! I only meant . . ." She flitted her hand as though I'd been entirely to blame for the misunderstanding. "Are you done with this ridiculous interrogation? I'm already late for Adelaide's party."

"I just have one more question. Do you remember anything else about the perfume? What notes it had? I smell vanilla . . . and something floral, maybe?"

I took a deep breath, then choked as Bellatrice hit me with a well-aimed squirt from a sparkling, tasseled atomizer. My eyes stung and she tittered.

"All of my perfumes have peony in them. Every girl needs a signature scent. Why?"

"Delia was sick with the Shivers that day. Her whole family was, but she was the only one to recover, to survive. I think there was something in the perfume that helped her get well. I need to know what was in it."

"You think if you sprayed Papa with this miracle perfume, he would get well?"

I thought of the black skull resting over his face. "I . . . I don't want to make any promises, but possibly."

Bellatrice was quiet for a very long moment, considering my request. "The dress I wore that day is in my armoire."

I sat up straighter. "And you haven't washed it?"

She shook her head. "No, it was already ruined—good silk can't get wet—but I didn't want to get rid of it. It was a present from

Mother on my last birthday." Bellatrice licked her lips, her eyes welling bright. "It was the last gift I'd ever get from her. I couldn't bear to throw it out. You should still be able to smell the perfume on it. Perhaps that will help."

"Would you mind if I borrowed it—just for a little while? I need to try to figure out what went into that perfume and—"

She shrugged. "Go on. Do whatever it is healers do. But I want it back when you're done."

"Of course," I promised. "Thank you, Princess. Your generosity is most appreciated."

Bellatrice raised a sharp eyebrow at me. "Don't go around telling anyone about this. I've a reputation to uphold."

CHAPTER 36

IT WAS FAR TOO LATE AND MUCH TOO DARK TO BE WORKing in the greenhouse.

Amber light from the gas lamps outside filtered through the leaves of oversized palms and other hothouse trees, but it wasn't enough to truly see by. I walked up and down the landscaped paths, holding my lantern low to cast back shadows from the neatly labeled stakes identifying each of the plants.

Armed with the perfumed dress, I wandered through the greenhouse, searching for anything with a similar scent. I had already picked out the notes of peony, water lily, and vanilla, but there was a darker, woodsy undertone that eluded me. I knew I knew it, I knew I'd smelled it before, but couldn't identify when or where.

The walkways seemed to wind for miles. This greenhouse was the largest I'd ever been in, home to a gloriously curated collection of plants. Fruit trees lined the perimeter, their produce ranging from simple red-cheeked apples and peaches to exotic berries and citrus. A pond lay in the center, full of lily pads and lotus blossoms. In the dim light, painted turtles bobbed in and out of the reeds, popping their striped necks up for a quick breath before darting back into the water.

Even without the heat of the sun, a warm humidity lingered in the air, so thick the surrounding greenery's heady sweetness swirled across my tongue, coating my lungs.

The scent I sought was too dark to have come from violets or pansies. Perhaps some type of rose?

I stepped into a lane of roses, bending to sniff at the first bush. The sterling-colored petals were breaking into bloom, and felt like velvet to the touch, but they weren't the source. Nor were the next roses, red as wine and as large as saucers. I soon lost count of how many flowers I'd smelled. Yellow heirlooms with extravagantly frilled edges, cabbages roses as soft and sweet as a young girl's first blush, white tea roses that needed to be deadheaded, their petals withered and dry. None was quite right.

"What are you?" I muttered to the perfume, bringing the dress to my nose once more. My eyes watered, I felt a touch lightheaded, and my sinuses ached. I was in desperate need of fresh air and a cool breeze.

I turned down a row of palms, certain it was the quickest way out of the greenhouse, but the path ended at a patio overlooking the pond. The full moon had come out, casting blue beams down through the tempered glass, highlighting the wicker furniture and cushioned seats.

"Oh!" I exclaimed, spotting a dark form perched on a lounge chair, hands held out before her, fingers laced tightly together as if in prayer. "Margaux."

At the sound of my voice, she startled, jumping to her feet. When she saw me, she sank back into the chaise.

"Hazel," she greeted me warmly. "You weren't at dinner tonight. Were you with the king?"

"For a bit. He was sleeping when I checked in earlier. I've been . . ." A sigh escaped me. "I feel as though I've been everywhere today."

"Join me," she said, gesturing to the empty seat across from her. "You look as though you need a rest."

I sat on the edge of the lounge chair, wishing I could lie back in the plush cushions, but decorum held me in check. "What are you doing up so late? I would have guessed the whole palace asleep by now."

"Or out at Adelaide Moncrieff's grand fete," she said with wry observance. "I spotted Leopold and Bellatrice getting into a carriage earlier." She rolled her eyes with a flippancy that I was surprised to see in someone reported to be so very pious. "You'd never guess they just came out of mourning and that their father was in his sickbed, would you?"

I shrugged. "It does seem indelicate, but we don't know—"

Margaux made a face at me. "Don't we, though?" Her lips began to form another accusation but then she shook her head, apparently thinking better of it. "I'm sorry. It *has* been quite a day. My tongue is getting the better of me. But I'm glad you're here now."

She leaned against the angled back of the chaise and rubbed her eyes. When she looked at me again, she smiled. I couldn't remember the last time someone had looked at me like that, like they were genuinely glad of being in my presence. It was a lovely sensation, one I'd acutely missed in the years after Kieron's death.

"I can't imagine all the things you've been through in the last day. Sit back, kick up your feet. As you said, the palace is asleep. No one is going to check to see that you're still working away."

Following her lead, I allowed myself to relax into the chair and let out an appreciative sigh as my muscles released the tension they'd been carrying since I'd woken up with Kieron atop me.

A mischievous twinkle sparkled in her eyes. "Better?"

"Much," I agreed.

"Tell me everything that has happened to you today."

"Everything is . . . a lot," I began. "But I do think I've made good steps toward finding a treatment for the king."

Her face seemed to freeze for a moment, as if she was concerned. But it must have been a trick of moonlight, because a radiant grin spread across her lips just seconds later. "You have? That's wonderful!" Margaux practically beamed. "I knew the Holy First sent me your image for a reason! What is it? The treatment?"

I told her the story of the broken perfume bottle and the maid who had survived the Shivers even as the rest of her family had not.

"You think something in the perfume helped her to heal," Margaux all but shouted, putting the ideas together. "Do you know what it is?"

"No. I've a sample of it. . . ." I raised the dress. "But I can't seem to pick out all of the notes."

The oracle sat up excitedly. "Can I help? Ohhhh, please, Hazel, let me help!" She clasped her hands together in earnest pleading.

I felt on the verge of laughter. "I thought you said we were done with work for the day."

"I've changed my mind. I want to work. All I do is sit in my reverie chamber day after day, waiting for the Holy First to use me. Let me do something real. Let me use my hands!"

Her sentiment so perfectly echoed the very thing Leopold had accused her of earlier that day in the carriage that I couldn't find it in my heart to say no.

"If you insist," I said, handing over the silk dress. "What do you smell?"

She took a short whiff, then blinked with surprise. "Bellatrice does love her florals, doesn't she?" She smelled the dress again. "Vanilla, certainly. Maybe a peony?"

I nodded, waiting for more.

Margaux thought for a long moment. "There's . . . there's a very green scent to it, isn't there? Almost like a forest." She paused, chewing at her bottom lip. "I know I've smelled it a dozen times before, but . . ." She brightened. "Geranium!"

"Geranium?" I echoed, taking the dress back to smell it once more. I did smell the woodsy note that she'd mentioned, but it didn't seem as though geraniums could be its source.

She nodded adamantly. "They're my mother's favorite flower. She always has giant bushes of them planted around her windows so she can see their cheery red blooms all summer long. I'm certain that's what it is."

"They *can* help to treat pain," I mused.

Margaux let out a little shiver of excitement. "Then that proves it!" She immediately faltered, her face darkening. "But how do you turn geraniums into medicine?"

"That's not hard. Making tonics is a lot like cooking. We'll need to distill it down into an oil. That way it can be spread as a paste or added to tea. We'd just need to get the geraniums themselves. A lot of them," I added, thinking of how much of the king's body had been secreting the Brilliance.

I brought Bellatrice's dress to my nose again, still uncertain if the blend contained the essence of the squiggled leaves.

"Come on," Margaux said, tired of waiting for my response. She grabbed my hand and pulled me to my feet. "They're this way!"

CHAPTER 37

SHORTLY AFTER SUNRISE, AFTER A NIGHT SPENT OVER burning fires and sweltering steam baths, the oil was ready.

Margaux had stayed with me through the entire process, cheerfully fetching water and tools, bringing us carafes of coffee during the thin hours before dawn when giddy exhaustion threatened to overtake us.

We'd worked all through the night, but it was finally done.

I filled a cart, packing it with gauze strips, my medicine chests, and a heavy iron skillet, still sizzling with the green elixir. Rather than straining it out into a fine oil, I'd left in the wilted leaves and stalks, stewing as much potency from them as I could.

Margaux made a gesture over me as I wheeled it out, ready to bring it to Marnaigne.

"The Holy First sees your work," she said with a beatific, if somewhat tired, smile. "She will watch over you and the king. She will watch it all. But I . . ." Her expression twisted with chagrin. "I shall watch nothing, for I will be asleep. Go do great things, Hazel."

"Thank you, Margaux. I couldn't have done this without you."

She gave me a short bow and trudged off to her chambers.

When I turned the corner, pushing my cart into the great hall, I was surprised to see Euphemia, already up and dressed and lying on her stomach in front of the king's door. She had a stack of paper and some oil pastels in front of her, and was so hard at work on her picture, she didn't look up until I was nearly on top of her.

"Good morning, Hazel!" she cried with a wide smile, pushing herself to her knees. "I'm decorating a note for Papa!"

I knelt beside her, ready to look at her work and offer praise, but she snatched it away before I could get even one glimpse.

"It's just for Papa," she explained. "Are you going in to see him now?"

I nodded, gesturing to the cart. "I've got some things that I think are going to make him feel much better very soon."

Her little face lit up. "Really?"

It was hard to meet her eyes.

She folded up her missive, staining the creamy paper with colorful fingerprints, then offered it to me. "Can you give this to him? When you go in?"

I stuck the letter in my skirt's pocket and promised I would.

"And tell him how much I love him," she insisted.

"I will."

"And that I miss him."

I laughed, even as my stomach flipped. "I'll do that too."

The little princess threw her arms around me in an impulsive hug and kissed my cheek before scooping up her art supplies and skipping off down the hall.

"Good morning, Your Majesty. I've such good news!" I sang, pushing my cart into the king's chambers.

I had to stop short, allowing my eyes to adjust. The drapes were pulled shut and the fire had burned low, casting the room in lurid orange flickers and deep shadows.

"Your Majesty?" I called curiously.

"Ah, my healer has returned."

My head snapped to the left as I tried to place where the voice had come from.

"Would you like me to draw back some of the curtains?" I asked, already crossing to the nearest window.

"No!" I thought the cry came from one of the armchairs, but it was too dark to tell. "Leave them!"

"I will need *some* light to work," I murmured, peering at the hulking shape of the canopied bed. Was he ensconced in its satin folds like a fat black spider lurking in its funneled web?

He sighed. "I suppose you must."

I glanced over to the corner, where I knew there was a desk. It was too dim to see paper and pen. What was he doing over there all alone? "May I light some candles?"

There came a series of rattled clinks, as if the king was struggling to set down a glass on a marble tabletop. "If you insist."

I fumbled at a side table and lit a filigreed candelabra before rounding toward him. "Sir?"

I tried not to jerk in surprise as the jumping flames highlighted the new shape of his visage.

The Brilliance was no longer gold, and it clumped on his face like wax melting down a taper. It was almost entirely black, with red rivulets of blood swirling within the sodden mess. The dark sludge had ripped apart pores as it flowed out, leaving his skin pocked and puckered.

He looked like a demon summoned from the deepest pits of hell. He already looked like one of my ghosts.

"Oh, Your Majesty," I breathed, unable to hide my horror.

The grim line of his lips said more than words ever could.

"I don't know what to do," he whispered, holding up his hands. The thick tar fused his fingers together into leaden stumps.

"A . . . a bath first," I stammered. "We'll clear all that away and get you into the wraps."

The king shook his head. "It's valiant of you to try, Hazel, but I don't . . . I'm afraid I no longer see the point."

Professionally, I agreed with him. It was a wonder he was still standing. He looked like an eldritch horror, an ancient being of wood and stone, a monster. It would be an act of kindness to let the deathshead have its way and end him now. But I needed him alive for just a bit longer to test the effectiveness of this new tonic.

"Into the bath," I insisted, brushing the callous thoughts from my mind. "We're getting this off you. And then a new treatment." I gestured to the cart. "Geranium oil."

Marnaigne let out a bark of laughter. "That's your cure?"

"That and other things. We're testing the potency of this blend, but I am certain it will help."

"At this point, nothing can possibly hurt," he allowed, his voice as rough as gravel.

I drew the bath as hot as the king could stand, adding the wilted geranium stalks. They sank into the steaming water, turning it slick and verdant. Next came a sprinkling of witch hazel and comfrey.

"Please take off your robe," I requested.

Without shame, the king dropped it to the floor, showing the full extent of damage. Heavy strips of Brilliance peeled from his body, taking thick ribbons of flesh with them, and I fought the urge to gag. This sickness was flaying him alive.

I put on my gloves and offered my hand to help him into the steaming tub.

The king let out a sharp curse as the water washed over him, breaking away more of the buildup, more of his skin. Everything beneath the hardened sludge was wrinkled and sodden, corroding into pale curds. His flesh smelled dank, like milk gone sour.

Marnaigne looked up at me, mournful and silently crying out for an end to his suffering, but I busied myself with a washrag, gently massaging away the last of the sludge so that my tinctures could soak in.

"I've made a paste as well," I said, turning to my cart of supplies as if I were simply showing him my work and not needing a moment's respite from his pained stare. "Once we're done with the bath, I'll get you covered in that and let you rest. Rest will help. The paste will help."

The king shook his head. "There are things I need to do. Before . . ." He took a laboring breath. "Before the end. If I can't . . . if I can't see my children, I need to write to them. There are things they need to know. So many, many things." He blinked at me, and his eyes were so round. "Will you write for me? I can't hold anything."

"Of course I will. Oh!" I turned back toward him, happy I could offer at least one thing I knew was sure to make him happy. "I've a letter for you, from Euphemia. She was outside your rooms earlier." I reached in to grab it from my pocket before I realized I was still wearing the gloves. "I'll read it to you after the bath."

The corners of his mouth rose, and I supposed he was smiling, but his lips split with half a dozen deep cracks and blood streamed from his chin to the bathwater. "Yes, she'd tucked herself beside the door and was singing me a song she'd learned. She has the sweetest little voice, my Phemie. A songbird, like her mother." He let out a shaky breath and I could hear the Brilliance rattling in his lungs. "I'm never going to see her again, am I?"

"Oh no, Your Majesty. You will. These wraps are going to do wonders, you'll see, and then we'll—"

I never got to finish because a flurry of shivers spread across the king, starting at his shoulder blades, then racing outward as his arms and legs jumped. He thrashed like a marionette on uneven strings. A froth spilled from his mouth and his eyes wept black tears, but through it all, Marnaigne didn't make a sound. It was the eeriest thing I'd ever borne witness to.

There was a great shudder, a collective spasm of every muscle within him contracting in one horrible united motion. Then he crashed back into the bath, spilling water across the floor, and lay completely still.

"Your Majesty?" I dared to whisper.

It was so quiet, as if the very air around us were waiting with bated breath.

"René?"

Had he—

Was he—

Dead?

In a flash, I was kneeling beside the tub, soaking my skirts in a foul mixture of geranium parts, bloodied bathwater, and blackened Brilliance. I pressed my fingers to the king's neck, searching for a pulse. I couldn't feel anything at first, the Brilliance was too thick, so I peeled back sections of it, horrified when he didn't move, didn't stir, because *there was so much skin and muscle ripping off of him and why wasn't he moving?* But then . . .

It was there. Faint and thready, but there all the same.

I watched the shallow rise and fall of his chest with a careful eye, feeling a wave of relief crash over me.

Marnaigne was alive.

Just barely.

I sat back on my heels, wondering what I ought to do next, when I heard the crunch of paper in my skirt pocket.

Euphemia.

I thought of what the king had been saying just before the seizure had come over him, how Euphemia had been at the door that morning, to sing him a song. He couldn't watch her, she couldn't see him, but still she wanted to sing; she wanted one part of her, however small, however tenuous, with him.

I couldn't imagine a love like that, so pure and earnest and insistent on existing in a world where things that were pure and earnest were so often crushed. I wondered what it would be like to feel such a love so wholeheartedly. Had I ever cared for anyone with even a fraction of Euphemia's devotion?

I wanted to believe I had with Kieron, but when Merrick had laid out the consequences of letting him live, I'd destroyed him.

Not with my own father, certainly. But if things had been different—if *I* had been different, if I'd been born first instead of thirteenth—would our relationship have been different as well?

I'd never know.

The deathshead had demanded I kill him, erasing any chance we might have had for reconciliation, however slim.

And now it was demanding I kill another father.

Tears welled as I thought of Euphemia being given the news that her father was gone. I could imagine the way her blue eyes would widen in disbelief, in denial. They'd widen and then they'd shatter.

"I can't," I whispered into the too-quiet bathroom. "I can't do that to her."

The words were easy to say, but the next steps were treacherous.

If I wasn't going to kill the king, I needed to save him, and my best effort, the geranium oil, had nearly ended him.

Calamité's voice singsonged in my head: *You know how to find us.*

Slowly, methodically, I peeled the sodden gloves from my hands and dropped them into the muck.

The Divided Ones' pipes still hung around my neck, the metal charm always a few degrees cooler than my skin. Even as I'd toiled over the hearth, distilling all that oil, it had felt chilled against me, a constant reminder that the gods who'd given it were only a breath away.

I marveled at how easy it would be to call them.

Merrick had never given me anything so helpful. Merrick had only ever foisted books and cakes at me, blessed me with a gift that felt more like a curse, and saddled me with a job I did not want.

If I did this, if I used the Divided Ones' offer, I would be severing something deep with Merrick. I wasn't a fool. I knew he'd be enraged. I knew it might not end well at all. But nothing in my life ever had, and this act, this one act of defiance, ensured that one little girl got to keep her father and her childhood and her innocence. It felt like a fair trade.

I put the charm to my lips and, bracing myself, blew.

The blast was just as loud and horrible as it had been in the temple. I winced as the notes echoed in the marble room, and waited for the palace guards to break in, running to see why the end of the world had begun in the king's chambers.

But somehow, they didn't, and I was left wondering if only I could hear it.

I waited, flinching at every sound: a drop of water, the king's labored breathing, and then, the splitting of the air as a host of gods entered our world.

"What a mess you've made in here, little mortal," Calamité chastised me, looking around the room with a curl of disgust wrinkling his side of their nose. "And you're just sitting in it?"

"I need your help," I began without preamble, keeping my voice calm and my cadence measured. This wasn't the time to let emotions reign. I needed to say my piece and let the chips fall where they may. "I don't believe the deathshead is right in telling me to kill the king."

Félicité's eyebrow arched. Calamité's side of their lips grinned.

"I want to save him," I went on, my words feeling strong and right and true. "But I need your help, your . . . blessing."

Both the gods' eyes flickered with interest.

"The Dreaded End's daughter comes to us for a blessing," they intoned in a unified voice, hundreds of gods strong.

"I need to know how to treat the Shivers," I said. "I thought what I was doing would work, but it didn't, and now . . . now I don't know what to do. I feel very lost."

"We're not in the habit of giving even a single blessing to most mortals, and you ask us for many," Calamité mused.

"Just one," I protested.

"You want to save the king *and* you want to end the Shivers."

"I have to end the Shivers *to* save the king," I argued.

The gods shook their massive head.

"Wresting the king away from his sickness will not erase the deathshead covering his face," Félicité explained.

My heart fell as her words sank in.

"There is, of course, another way." Calamité's grin was vicious. "We know about the candles, Hazel."

I froze. Merrick had made it seem like they were a terribly hushed secret, one to be kept at all costs. But Calamité knew. Which meant Félicité knew. Which meant all the other gods trapped within their crowded body knew.

"You take Marnaigne's flame onto one of your unused candles and he's good as new," Calamité went on, speaking slyly from his corner of their mouth, as if that would keep his words from Félicité. "Cured. No more sickness. No more deathshead."

"But . . . but then I lose a candle."

"You've got another. What's one little life compared to the tens of thousands, the hundreds of thousands, that Marnaigne touches? That Marnaigne protects? You were so concerned about the war and the orphans and the . . . whatever, before. This one little act could save them all."

Félicité *tsk*ed. "You're both treading on dangerous ground."

"What do you say?" he went on, unconcerned. "One life for countless multitudes? It seems an easy decision, don't you think?"

When he put it that way, it did, of course.

And there was still the third candle. Two lifetimes were enough, so much more than enough.

But when I tried to agree with the god of chaos, the words stuck in my throat.

It was tempting. It was so terribly tempting. But I shook my head.

"It doesn't matter. I can't get to the candles without Merrick. And he'll never agree to any of this."

Calamité looked offended. "Do you really consider your kindly uncle so toothless? I could have you there with a snap of my fingers."

Many years before, I'd traveled to a small seaside town to help with an outbreak of the pox. After nearly a month spent at sickbeds, I finally made my way to the shoreline and stood in awe of the water before me. I'd kicked off my boots and waded into its cooling depths, letting the waves rush over my bare feet. With each sweep of water, the sand beneath me was tugged back, and I'd felt it pulling at me too. Half delirious with exhaustion, I'd nearly allowed the water to take me deeper, dragging me into depths and currents I could not swim in.

I felt like that now. Calamité had set a plan in motion, and I was helpless to do anything but go along with it.

"The candles all look the same," I pointed out, playing my final card of resistance. "There's no way I could pick out the king's from any of the others."

"No," Calamité agreed. "Not with those mortal eyes."

Félicité made a sound of disappointment I knew she did not feel. "So unfortunate we aren't able to traverse the grounds of his domain." She shrugged her shoulder, the matter closed. "Oh well."

Calamité scoffed. "As if I'd allow such a minor snag in logistics to derail this master plan of mine. Of Hazel's," he corrected himself quickly.

I could hear the goddess of good fortune grind her teeth. "Brother, I swear if you—"

"I don't want to save the king like this," I started. I didn't know how I'd fix this, but it didn't feel right. It felt very, very wrong. "I'll find another way. I'll—"

"Of course you do and of course you won't. Close your eyes now, healer," he interrupted, reaching out to press his thumb against my forehead.

A sudden wave of motion swept over me and I scrunched my

eyes closed, trying to squirm away from him. I'd never been struck by lightning, but this was what I imagined it felt like. Bolts of power sizzled from my head down through my veins, electrifying my senses and burning the ends of my nerves. I fell to my knees, a meteor striking Earth, and curled in on myself, hunching over in a shell of protection.

"What did you do to me?" I shrieked.

"The Dreaded End isn't the only one who can bestow gifts," Calamité said.

Félicité sighed. "He's going to be so mad at you."

"Take it away, Félicité, please!" I howled, pawing at my face. "I don't want to do this, I don't want this, I don't—"

"I can't," she admitted softly. "But this gift won't last forever, mortal, I promise you. Only an hour or so, at most."

My head pounded in agony. "What *is* it?"

"I've blessed you with the godsight. For a time, you'll see as we do," Calamité explained. "It will let you find the king's candle. You might try saying thank you, at the very least."

I clawed at my scalp, wanting to rip my head open and free the pressure building within it. "You don't know what you're talking about. I'll never be able to find him. There are thousands, hundreds of thousands of candles."

"*You* don't know what you're talking about," Calamité snapped. "He keeps them organized, families and friends next to those they know and love. Study the flames. You'll see." He laughed darkly. "You'll see everything."

"Don't!" I started to cry, but before I could protest any further, I heard the snap of fingers.

CHAPTER 38

THE AIR SUDDENLY TASTED OF MINERALS AND WET stone. I was back in the Between.

I could hear the rush of the waterfall to my left. Calamité had brought me right to the rocky opening leading into Merrick's domain.

I took a deep breath, mustering my courage, then opened my eyes.

Instantly I shut them, balling my fists into their sockets.

The godsight showed me *everything.*

Each droplet of water hung suspended in the air; lacy patterns of lichens on the stone were magnified, impossibly large. I could see each ray of light as it shot through the gaps in the waterfall's spill. Just one second of sight stretched into millennia as I noticed the detail of everything around me.

It was too much.

Mortals weren't meant to see this much.

My stomach recoiled, and I felt as though I was going to be sick.

How would I make it to the cavern? How would I be able to look at the hundreds of thousands of candles, the multitudes of flames? I wanted to retch imagining it.

Sightless and unseeing, I tried to move toward the back wall to find the opening, aiming myself where I remembered it had been. I only made it three steps before stumbling over the uneven ground. I pitched forward and landed on my knees with a terrible *crack*.

Eyes scrunched tight, I reached out with trembling fingers, feeling the ground before me, noting the dips and rises in it, and began to crawl. I prayed I was going in the right direction, prayed I wasn't about to go right over the edge.

I ran straight into the wall, bumping my head. Stars flashed behind my eyelids as I searched for the entrance. I'd have to open my eyes once inside. There were too many chasms, too many bridges. I'd have to be able to see where I was going, see where exactly my feet needed to step.

"Maybe it won't be as bad inside," I whispered, coaching myself. "There's not as much light, not as much to see."

Tentatively, I opened my eyes, squinting through the fringe of lashes.

It was so much worse.

There were *things* in this darkness better left unknown, ancient living things that regarded me with too many eyes, that salivated over my flesh with too many tongues. I remembered when Merrick had first brought me here. I'd felt so uneasy in this darkness. Now I knew why.

"Focus on the path," I said aloud. "They're not there if you're not looking at them."

Even with my eyes fixed on the ground, I saw too much. Every speck of dirt, the shape and texture of each tiny pebble. It all seemed vitally important, demanding to be registered. Squinting didn't help.

I was able to see each and every one of my eyelashes, noting the angle of their curves, the slight variation of their colors.

Catching my foot on another dip in the terrain, I stumbled on the hem of my dress and saw the way each individual thread had been woven to make the cloth.

"Stop taking in the details and just *walk,*" I hissed to myself. An impossible order.

My eyes felt the size of dinner plates. My mind was stuffed too full, holding on to each detail and giving it equal weight and importance. How did the gods live like this?

With my new sight, I could easily see the path I needed to take before me. I could see the candles' glow, see the way they lit the darkness, even around corners and turns in the labyrinthine puzzle. I could see the heat they threw, watching the temperature rise around me in colors I'd never seen before, colors I wasn't sure any mortal was meant to see, ever.

It took me ages to make my way to the cavern.

At its entrance, I braced myself for the agonies to come.

Each candle burned my eyes like a fiery poker, white-hot and blazing, leaving pinpoints of light lingering on my eyelids every time I blinked.

I threw my hands over my eyes, shielding myself from the worst of it. I careened down the stone steps, caught in a dizzy stupor, drunk on details, the way the flames leapt and danced, the way every dust mote was limned by their light.

Above me, the gods' orbs burned with impossible luster, luminous as a lilac morning sky, riddled with swirls of gold, flecks of silver. They were so beautiful, so pure and dazzling, I wanted to cry. I wanted to watch them forever, hypnotized by their power, beguiled by their radiance.

Time stopped as I drank in their wonder. I didn't want to move. I didn't even want to blink lest I miss a millisecond of their splendor.

"Just a minute more," I promised myself. "Just a minute . . ."

I paused, suddenly aware that it no longer hurt to look at the lights. The candles were not burning across my mind, blinding my vision.

My dose of the godsight was already beginning to soften and fade, and I'd not yet found Marnaigne's candle.

With a curse, I pulled my gaze from the gods' orbs and wandered the cavern until I found the plinth holding my candles.

My flame looked just as strong and cheery as before. The taper was tall and proud. It didn't look as though any of the wax had melted in the years since I'd last seen it. My other two tapers lay beside it, waiting to be called into service, their wicks pristine and white. I reached out for one but my stomach lurched, reeling against what I was about to do.

"This is a bad idea," I murmured. "This is a very, very bad idea." I dropped my hand and sank to the ground, feeling despair claw at my throat.

I wasn't going to do it. I would close my eyes against this horrible gift and wait until the Divided Ones pulled me back.

If they pulled me back.

I dreaded the thought of going back.

Back to the palace, back to the king's chambers, back to where I was expected to kill him.

I opened my mind, and a new idea suddenly occurred to me: I didn't have to return to the palace to kill the king. I could kill him here, with one errant breath, and no one could ever think it had been my fault.

The king would have passed away while I was working in the greenhouse. No one would blame me. Countless other physicians and soothsayers hadn't been able to save him. No one had yet found a cure for the Shivers. I could return to my cottage without fear of punishment. My life, my stupidly long life, could go on as it always had.

"I need to find the king's candle," I whispered, jumping into action. "I need to blow it out."

I stood up, brushing off my skirts, and felt something inside one of my pockets crunch.

Euphemia's note.

I pulled it out, guilt needling me in my middle. I thought of her tiny little face, so bright and hopeful. This was the last note she'd ever write to her father, and I'd not delivered it.

Curious, I unfolded the parchment. I would read it once, then set it to burn upon my candle's flame. I'd kill the king, and in time, I would forget this moment. I would forget the guilt.

I smoothed out the paper. It was a picture, drawn in a talented but childish hand, showing the king and Euphemia out in the court gardens, a blanket spread beneath them as they picnicked. *You're my everything, Papa,* she'd scrawled at the top of the page, beneath a showering rainbow. *All my love, Euphemia.*

My fingers traced her words. Inside me, the guilt grew.

Without a mother and with her older siblings drinking and dancing themselves into stupors, the king *was* her everything, I realized. Killing him would be orphaning her. She'd be left without either parent, just like my nieces.

Not just like, the voice in my head argued. *She's a princess. She has resources beyond comprehension.*

But the little girl who'd made this picture hadn't drawn her wealthy trappings, her privilege and resources. She hadn't drawn their crowns. She'd simply drawn her father.

Marnaigne's death would sentence her to a future full of heartache. I held her happiness in my hands now. I held . . .

I blinked in surprise.

My hands did hold something.

Without thinking, I'd picked up one of my spare tapers. Without reasoning and fretting, I'd known what I was supposed to do.

This was the right answer. This was the only answer.

I only needed to find the king's candle.

I roamed the aisles, my eyes darting over each flame. There was enough godsight left to let me see the life each one represented, see the world each person was a part of. I saw wedding days and first kisses, smiles given and hands shook. I saw arguments and deep conversations, tears and embraces, laughter and music, and so many moments of inconsequential ordinariness. I saw how thousands of lives were playing out at that exact moment and wanted to cry, struck dumb by how beautiful these perfectly normal lives were.

Calamité had said Merrick arranged the candles by the circles mortals kept in their real lives, so when I spotted a glimpse of Aloysius chastising an errant footman, I knew I was close.

Marnaigne's candle was in the center of his table, surrounded by tapers that looked identical to his. Without the godsight I never would have known who he was, what power he held. His was just a simple white taper, nothing more and nothing less than any of the other millions of candles in the cavern.

In his flame, I watched him as he sat slumped over in the bathtub, utterly motionless. It was a wonder he'd not yet drowned.

I plucked up his candle, then knelt, placing it upon the most level patch of ground I could find.

"Bless me with good fortune, Félicité," I prayed before raising my taper. I kept my free hand ready, poised to snuff out the king's old wick just as the new flame caught. It danced and writhed in the still air of the cavern, looking very much like a living thing.

Suddenly the risk of everything felt too great, impossible to take on. Could I really do this? I would be going against Merrick's orders, against the deathshead, against everything I'd ever been taught. My hand trembled so badly I dropped my candle, and the taper rolled beneath the nearest table.

"You're doing the right thing," I whispered. "You're doing this for Châtellerault, for peace, for the whole country, for even the world, maybe. You're doing this for Euphemia."

I let out a quick breath and retrieved the fallen candle before my guilty conscience could stop me.

The new wick caught.

The old wick twisted out.

I had just enough of the godsight left to watch Marnaigne's new candle, to see him give a strange little shudder, as if a sudden chill had crept over him while in the bath. The water around him jostled and I saw his chest rise and fall.

I breathed a sigh of relief and placed the new taper in the center of the table, leaving the old one behind.

From the far side of the cavern came a terrible clattering crash, like the crack of thunder on a muggy summer afternoon, heralding the storm that would rip the sky apart.

The black smudge of Merrick loomed tall, unfurling in the cavern like a bat spreading its wings. He was bigger than I'd ever seen him, a dark, smoldering shadow vibrating with rage and retribution.

He crossed the cavern with single-minded fury, faster than my eyes could take in, skittering directly toward me.

When he spoke, it was in the voice of my worst nightmares, the voice of hot embers, of brimstone and sulfur, molten tar and venom. *"What have you done?"*

CHAPTER 39

"MERRICK, I CAN EXPLAIN, I CAN—"

I never did get to say what I could do because he lashed out and I was suddenly flying backward, through the candles, through the length of the cavern itself, until I struck a stone pillar on the far wall. I hit it with enough force to shatter every bone in my body and crack my skull, but I miraculously, horribly, did neither.

"What have you done?" he demanded again, before me in a flash, picking up my crumpled form from the floor and holding me aloft by my neck.

I felt the Divided Ones' necklace snap and fall to the floor, lost to the darkness of the cavern as I squirmed and kicked and gasped for air. I searched for the right words, the words that would somehow get me out of this, the words that would not come. Black stars danced before my eyes and I could feel my muscles grow weak and limp, but before the blessed darkness could take me, Merrick cast me aside with a snarl of disgust.

"I'm sorry," I cried, trying to break an opening in the wall of fury he'd built around himself. "Merrick, I—"

"You saw the deathshead," he snapped, cutting off my pleading, and I shrank back into the ground, wary of being struck once more.

Mutely, I nodded.

"You saw the deathshead and yet you went and did *that.*" His arm flew back toward the king's new candle, once again lost in a sea of flickering flames. "Do you have any idea what you've done?"

Knees pressed into the rocky ground, I shook my head, tightening every muscle in my body as I tried to make myself as small and inconsequential as I could.

"That was your candle, Hazel. That was *you*! Do you have any idea what I had to do to get those candles?"

I kept my spine curved low, my forehead pressed against the cold ground. "No."

Merrick released a cry of frustration, striking out and hitting the pillar. It shattered, raining shards of stone down upon us. I felt one slice my cheek, but it was only my godfather I thought of as I saw him pull back his fist, wincing.

"Merrick!" I cried in alarm.

He shook off the blow and stalked away from me, his breath hot with muttered curses. "You stupid girl," he growled. "You stupid, stupid girl."

"I had to," I whispered, my lips brushing the rocks beneath me.

His laugh was thunderous with disbelief, making my sternum ache.

"I did, I . . ." I was at a loss to explain it. "There's a war going on, and . . . all the orphans . . . His daughter wrote him a letter, and . . ." Everything I said sounded small and wrong, excuses too minuscule to cover the full expanse of what I'd done.

"There will always be wars. There will always be orphans."

"Yes, but . . ." I faltered again. I wasn't going to persuade him to my side with the scope of the good I'd wanted to do. He didn't care about that. He cared about me, his goddaughter, the one mortal in all the world he held in his heart. "If I did what the deathshead wanted me to do, I'd have the blood of thousands on my hands. Not just the king's, but that of everyone else who died because he was not there to protect them." My voice broke. "I know I disobeyed you. You have every right to be upset with me, but I couldn't have so many souls haunting me through eternity, Merrick. I just couldn't."

His eyes narrowed to ruby slits as he considered my words. He was unquestionably still mad at me, but I could see a change stirring, softened with curiosity. "Do you feel remorseful for the lives you've taken?"

"Of course."

He frowned. "How strange."

"It's not."

"I've always been so proud of you, knowing how many lives were saved by your hands in those moments of mercy. Yet you only remember the scant number you've taken?"

I shrugged. "I don't know any of those saved, not definitively, not for sure. But the people who I . . ." It was so very hard to say the word.

Merrick thought for a moment. "Freed."

"Killed," I corrected him unhappily. "They were people I knew, family members and neighbors and people I was acquainted with." I thought of the dark Kieron-shaped ghost who trailed after me now like a dog on a leash. "People I loved. *Those* are the ones I remember, the ones I can't forget, ever."

The ones who were forever following me, always there, always wanting to be closer.

"I still see them," I confided in a hushed whisper, finally admitting my darkest secret to Merrick years after he'd saddled me with its curse.

Merrick's eyes flickered behind me, staring at the wall of tiny flames. "I . . . I suppose it's natural to feel that way, to want to remember them," he finally allowed. "But I'm sure with time—"

"No," I said, stopping him short. I couldn't remember ever daring to interrupt my godfather, but this was an important moment that I could not afford to let him get wrong. "I *see* them. All the time. They're always with me, always following me."

"Memories," he guessed.

"Ghosts."

Merrick straightened, studying me with fresh eyes. "That's not possible."

I kept my gaze steadily upon him, using silence to make my point understood.

"Hazel, I . . ."

Never before had I seen my godfather at a loss for words.

"They're with me all the time. My father and my mother. Kieron," I added, feeling my eyes prickle. "I have to keep them at bay with lines of salt, but it doesn't stop them forever. They're always pressing in, always seeking me out, and when my guard slips, when I forget or the wards get too weak, then they're upon me. . . ."

A pitiful sob welled up, breaking my argument apart as I remembered their touch on me, that sticky spiderweb sensation as they pulled at my memories, pilfering the good ones and leaving me a hollowed-out shell of misery.

"I couldn't have the king join their ranks. I couldn't bear the thought of Baudouin's victims being there too. There's not enough salt in the world for that many spirits. They would have broken through. They would have smothered me. I would have drowned in them. Merrick—" My voice caught again as tears began to flow. "I'm sorry. I'm so sorry. I didn't want to go against you, I didn't want to go against the deathshead. But I also couldn't . . . I just couldn't."

Merrick sighed, and I could feel the heat of his anger begin to retreat. He paced down a row of candles and I knew he was headed toward my plinth, toward my remaining candle.

After a moment of wary hesitation, I followed him.

As I approached, I saw he'd reached out, tracing the length of the last unlit candle. He kept his touch impossibly gentle, stroking the taper as if it were the full, round cheek of a newborn babe.

"Never again."

His words were low and deeply growled.

This was not something he was asking me to promise to, a request, a wish to be carried out. This was a command, plain and simple. One that would not be broken, no matter what my reasons might be. No matter how right and righteous I might think my cause.

When he turned toward me, his eyes were all rubies, flashing with dangerous warning. "I will see what I can do about the ghosts. I will. . . ." He swallowed the promise. "But never again."

All I could do was bow my head and nod.

I kept my eyes down, studying the wafting edges of his robes, the way they disappeared into the floor. I wanted to cry beneath the full weight of his anger and expectations but knew it was my penance to bear them as stoically as I could.

"Thank you for your understanding, Merrick," I whispered, flinching as his hands balled into fists. I dared to look up and meet his eyes. "For your mercy. I do not deserve it."

"No," he agreed. "You don't. And it will not be given a second time."

"Of course," I agreed hastily. "I promise you, Merrick. Never again."

The Dreaded End turned away from me with a disappointed shake of his head, and before I could make any other attempt to soothe or assuage him, he snapped his fingers and sent me back to Châtellerault.

CHAPTER 40

"I'VE BEEN THINKING ABOUT SOMETHING," MARNAIGNE began, and my muscles tensed at the gravity of his tone.

I'd returned from Merrick's cavern a week ago to find the king still in the bath. He'd come back to consciousness but didn't remember the seizure. He wasn't aware that any time had passed, and he certainly didn't know his life had hung so precariously in the balance.

I'd helped him from the stinking water and rubbed him with a light mix of witch hazel and comfrey, and we'd watched for more of the dark Brilliance to weep out of him.

It hadn't.

He'd laughed in amazement, poking and prodding and trying to push out more of the blackness as I feigned astonishment.

We kept watching.

His skin had remained clear.

It remained clear that afternoon and again the next day.

I'd cautioned him to take everything slowly, carefully, to do nothing that might provoke a relapse. I was worried a miraculous recovery would look somehow suspicious, so I applied rose hips and the oil of sea buckthorn seeds and covered him in gauze wraps, helping to heal the damage caused by the Brilliance while also hiding just how quickly I'd managed to heal him. I checked in on him throughout the day, tending his dressings, giving him restorative teas and baths heavily laden with soothing tonics.

Marnaigne had been so delighted with my progress, he'd never stopped to ask how exactly the cure had worked, simply taking it at face value.

But now . . .

"Yes, Your Majesty?" I dared to prompt. I was in the middle of examining his back, dabbing at one of the nastier wounds he'd suffered as the sludge had pushed its way through. It was healing well but would undoubtedly leave a scar.

"I've had lots of time to sit and mull, these past few days."

"It's good that you're resting so much," I said cheerfully, trying to delay the inevitable.

He made a sound of consideration. "Yes, well, I've been thinking of you, of your work with me . . ."

I tensed, scrambling to come up with a valid-sounding excuse.

". . . and I keep returning to the matter of payment."

My ribs relaxed. If he was thinking about payment, then he didn't believe he'd need me much longer. I could return to my cottage and work on finding an actual cure for the Shivers.

"I'm told you're usually paid on some sort of barter system, with food or livestock—"

"Or coins," I interjected hopefully. I had no desire to wrangle one of the royal stallions all the way back to Alletois, and I had a far better idea on how to use any money he saw fit to give me.

He smiled. "My preferred method as well. But when I began to contemplate what a fair amount would be, I was rather stumped. Without doubt, I would have died without your care. How do I put a price on that? How many chickens or horses—or coins—equal a life? And is my life worth more, as a father? As a king? It's quite an exercise in self-examination."

I could feel the conversation going off track. "Actually, I've been thinking too, and there is a favor I'd like to ask of you. . . ."

He raised an eyebrow and I had the distinct sense he was annoyed I'd interrupted his reflection.

Hurriedly, I raced through my request. "When I was in the Rift last week, I met a trio of girls. Orphans from one of the villages the militia raided. They're my sisters' daughters." I swallowed, feeling heated and out of breath. "I didn't even know I had nieces, and they certainly didn't know me, but . . . they have no one now, and the temple was so crowded with other children in similar plights . . . I was thinking of trying to adopt them. Taking them back with me to Alletois to raise and care for. But I'm not sure how to go about that. A word from you would help."

I bit the corner of my lip, waiting for his verdict.

"No."

There was no attempt to soften the blow. Just the refusal, as weighted as an iron block.

"Oh." I wasn't sure what to say after that. His answer had been too absolute to attempt a negotiation.

Marnaigne glanced back at me, reading my expression. "Oh, don't look so downcast, Hazel. Of course I will see to the children. We'll find homes for them, ones where they'll be well taken care of, loved and wanted. But I'm afraid it won't be with you."

"I . . . I know I'm young, but I really think—"

"Age has nothing to do with it, and I'm certain you'll be an excellent mother one day, but you're going to be much too busy for all that."

"I am?"

He smiled, looking pleased. "That's what I was trying to tell you before. Rather than let you slip away, back to tending farmers' scrapes and head colds, I'd like to offer you a position here, in Châtellerault."

I froze. "You want me to stay in town?"

The king laughed. "Closer than that. I'd like to appoint you court healer."

"Me?" It sounded like a squeak.

"Of course! You're the only one who saw the situation and didn't run. You're the only who has determined the Shivers' cure."

I smiled uneasily at the praise I had not earned.

"Your Majesty—"

"René," he corrected me.

"René," I agreed. "I'm flattered you think so well of me, but—"

"I've already seen to everything. Aloysius is moving your belongings to a fine suite as we speak, here in the family's wing. I want to make sure you're close by should anything ever befall me again."

I tried to arrange my face into an expression of gratitude while racing through ways to gently decline the king's offer. "I appreciate that most fervently, sir, but my gardens are in Alletois. My study and plants and everything I need to do my work are back at my cottage."

He made a face of easy dismissal. "I'll send men to gather whatever you need, or we can purchase things here in town. As for plants—surely nothing of yours could top our greenhouse or gardens. We have more herbs and flowers and trees than anywhere else in the whole of the country. And I'll personally ensure that your workroom here has the finest supplies."

"Yes, but—"

"You'll have your choice of assistants, apprentices, however many you need."

I frowned. "I usually work alone. . . ."

"And you'll continue to, with me, with the children—though Holy First please, never let them get ill—but you'll want to train others in how to administer your cure."

"My cure?" I repeated. My head felt like a kaleidoscope spun out of control.

The king nodded. "For the Shivers. Now that you've solved its mystery, we'll need to spread word throughout the capitol, throughout the country." His smile was painfully bright, cutting into me like a knife. "You're going to save thousands, Hazel. What more could a healer ask for?"

It *was* the very thing I'd wanted to do, the thing I'd used to justify so many of my recent actions. I'd ignored the deathshead and kept the king alive to be used as a glorified test subject, telling myself the cure would save so many.

And now he was giving me the opportunity, the platform and reach, to do all that and more. What more *could* I ask for?

But there wasn't a cure. Not one I could replicate. I'd cheated and used one of my candles, giving Marnaigne a new, illness-free life. I couldn't do that again and again, with every stricken person in Martissienes.

No.

A cure, a real cure, would need to be discovered.

And soon.

CHAPTER 41

THE WORKROOM WAS HOT, THE AIR THICK WITH STEAM and humidity.

I pushed aside a loose lock of hair, feeling as wilted as the leaves I fed into the boiling pots.

My back ached. My arms ached. My head throbbed.

I couldn't remember the last time I'd gotten a full night's rest.

Since moving over to the family's wing of the palace, I'd been given an arsenal of supplies, the finest that Marnaigne's money could buy. My workroom was lined with medical texts and treatises. Brand-new pots and pans, vials and stoppers, mortars and pestles. A whole articulated skeleton stood in the corner, its bones having been forcibly donated by some poor soul who'd met their end on the executioner's block.

It had been a month since I'd saved the king.

A month since he'd appointed me court healer and promised the country I'd soon be saving them all.

An entire month had gone by, and I still hadn't come up with the cure.

The Shivers had spread through Châtellerault with devastating momentum. Whole households fell ill overnight. Servants woke to find their lords and ladies fallen into contorted messes of golden, twitching limbs. Marquises came down for breakfast only to discover their entire staff had died, leaving behind pools of blackened fluids no one dared touch.

I suddenly had my pick of patients to examine, but every time I brought my hands to their faces and cupped their cheeks, I saw nothing. No cure, no sparkling beacon showing me the way toward salvation, nothing.

My gift was gone.

Merrick had done as he'd promised and taken care of my ghosts. I no longer had to worry about coming across their staggering forms in unguarded moments. I no longer heard their scratching pleas for admittance. I no longer had to worry about my memories being stolen.

But something inside me had changed with their removal.

Merrick had taken my ghosts, but also, it seemed, my gift.

I tried everything I could think of to summon my godfather but was only met with stony silence. I understood: he was mad; he needed time to cool off.

But time was something I didn't have.

Every day for nearly a month, the king asked for updates on my progress, asked when I expected to have the cure ready to send out.

And every day I lied to him.

There were dozens of excuses: we'd stripped the greenhouse bare to make his cure, the new seeds hadn't sprouted as quickly as they should have, the wrong oil had been delivered and my batch had been contaminated. I used every pretense I could muster, buying myself time as I scrambled for the true cure.

I could feel the king growing impatient with me, hear his sentences turn terse and sharp. But—for now—his attention was divided, because while Châtellerault writhed and shuddered, Baudouin and his army continued their march toward the capitol.

Upon resuming his daily duties, Marnaigne had quickly instituted a draft, calling every healthy young man into service. Tented campsites began to bloom outside the capitol walls as squadrons were formed and the king's armies began to take shape.

The recruits trained at all hours of the day, running drills and exercises in splendid black-and-gold uniforms. They made such a sweeping, heroic picture, young women would often line the parapets to watch them, setting up chairs and blankets on which to picnic and gawk.

But even the threat of war couldn't completely overshadow the Shivers.

One afternoon, a cluster of spectators began to twitch, setting off a terrible reaction. Many present tried to herd them back to their houses. One girl refused to go, saying she wasn't sick, saying it was a joke, but the frightened crowd surged around them, throwing the most ardent protesters from the wall before guards could intervene.

Mobs began to form, set on barricading the sick in their homes. Some bolder members outright killed anyone they suspected of being ill, claiming it was the only way to keep the disease from spreading.

I felt the horror of every story in the marrow of my bones.

These deaths were because of me, because I'd not found the cure.

Each day I woke before the sun and worked well past midnight, until my muscles screamed and wanted to give out, quivering so badly that a footman once thought I'd contracted the Shivers myself. He'd raced down the halls, shouting the terrible news to all who could hear.

Still, my effort wasn't enough.

I tried countless combinations of medicines and herbs, testing the tonics on samples of the Brilliance secretly delivered to the palace. Glass plates lined nearly every inch of flat surface in my workspace. I'd filled half a dozen notebooks with observations of each trial.

One day I was studying a round of samples, trying to will at least one of them into responding to a new tonic, when Bellatrice's laughter rang out brightly, catching my attention. I rubbed my pained eyes, my concentration shot, and peeked out into the corridor.

A group of courtiers and the princess, all bedecked in gowns and garments so dazzling it hurt my eyes to look upon them, were coming down the hall. I couldn't tell if they were on their way out or in. Several of the young men wobbled as they walked, and every one of the girls was in a fit of giggles or tears. They smelled of pomanders—citrus, clove, and other spices—the only indication that a plague had besieged the country and that the streets were overflowing with the bodies of the dead.

I watched in disbelief as they tottered by, laughing uproariously and waltzing past me without a single glance. I rolled my eyes and began to turn back to the workroom but stopped short.

This was all so pointless. Without my gift I felt as though I was stumbling in the dark, slamming my head over and over again into a wall I could not see. Nothing I'd done had worked. Nothing I'd done had given even a hint at the cure. There was nothing I'd do tonight that couldn't be done tomorrow. I'd strip out of my damp dress, pat my poor, neglected dog on the head, and then get whatever sleep I could before waking with a panic attack and starting it all over again.

I closed the door, feeling impossibly low. I hated this time of night. Of morning. Of whatever liminal hell this was.

"Is that you, healer?"

Leopold's voice stopped me in my tracks, and before I turned around to face him, I took a deep, centering breath.

"Your Royal Highness."

He was neatly camouflaged against a marble column, all black velvet and gold buttons. His cravat was left casually untied, giving him a careless air I didn't doubt he'd spent half an hour mastering.

Since our carriage ride back from the Rift, I'd not seen much of Leopold, and while I wanted to remember that moment of intimacy—his confession to liking my freckles, to admiring my whole authentic self—his public behavior didn't do much to assist in that memory.

"What in the name of the gods are you wearing?"

I glanced down. I'd been covered up in a linen apron all day, but my shirt was still stained with streaks of green, and the starch of its collar had steamed away hours before. My skirt was a serviceable gabardine, thick enough to keep any wayward fluids from my skin. Compared to the shimmering nymphs who had just passed by with lithe, exposed limbs and painted lips, I felt impossibly dowdy. Their cheeks had been flushed with high spirits and anticipation, not a roaring hearth and the weight of an entire country's expectations.

I wondered what it would be like to be so careless and carefree, to dance past the dead and the dying and not feel compelled to do a single thing to stop it.

"One might ask the same of you," I threw back.

I was frustrated; I was so frustrated. With the painted courtiers, with the king who'd trapped me in this nightmare, with my godfather and his untouchable silence, but mostly with myself. I'd been the one to stumble into this mess. I was the one who couldn't forge her way out of it.

I could tell by the dilation of Leopold's pupils that I could say whatever I wanted to him tonight, say it in whatever tone I wished, and he wouldn't recall a bit of it come dawn, and I lashed out with an angry spitefulness I didn't know I was capable of unleashing.

"You are aware there's a war going on? And a plague? I know you spend most of your days in a drunken stupor, but you have heard whispers of these rather important events, yes?"

Leopold tilted his head, receiving my scorn with an infuriatingly placid smile. "You're upset with me."

His tone was as warm and inviting as the bath I so desperately wanted to get to, and I balled my hands, grinding my teeth. He peeled himself from the column, crossing to me for a closer examination. The prince dipped his head, trying to catch my eye as his smile grew to a grin.

"You are! I've angered the healer!" He raised his voice in triumph, as if calling out to his companions, but they'd left him behind, doubtlessly unaware their prince was gone. His gaze flickered back to me when he realized it was just the two of us. "You don't like me very much, do you, Just Hazel?"

I started to deny it, but he went on, rolling over my words, and any desire I felt to assuage him withered.

"I can't understand it. They like me," he said, pointing down the hall where his friends had vanished. He patted at his jacket, searching for something. Finding his gold case, he slipped one of his mother's cigarettes between his lips. "They adore me. Everyone does. Everyone except for you." His match lit, flaring too high before catching the paper wrap. He inhaled deeply. "It bothers me that you don't. I know it shouldn't, but it does."

"There are many things about you that bother me too. We're even."

He brightened. "Do I really take up so much space in your thoughts, then, healer?" His words came out in a rush of crimson smoke.

"That's not what I said."

He looked delighted. "But it's what you meant. Isn't it?"

"I thought you were going to quit smoking those."

He held up the cigarette, studying it thoughtfully. "I had. Mostly. Did you know today would have been my mother's birthday?"

I hadn't.

"I suppose this is my way of celebrating. Birthdays are important times, don't you think?" he went on, musing.

"I've never thought so."

Leopold made a face. "They are, and anyone who says otherwise had something terribly traumatizing happen to them as a child."

He wasn't wrong.

"You should come out with us tonight. Come out with me, I suppose," he corrected himself. "If they want to go on without me, damn the lot of them. We'll find somewhere else and have a far grander time."

"I think I'd rather go to bed," I admitted.

His eyebrows shot up. "So forward, Just Hazel, but I wholeheartedly approve. Why should the men always be the ones doing the chasing? Women have every bit as much right to go out and take what they want, when they want." He stamped out the cigarette, then held up his arms. "Go on, then. Take me."

I sighed and took a step to the right, ducking past him, then paused.

He'd put so much effort into preparing for his evening, pomading his hair into perfectly disheveled waves and dousing himself with cologne. It wafted from him, an intriguing blend of musk and greenery designed to entice and enchant.

I knew that smell.

"What are you wearing?" I asked, whirling to him.

He tilted his head, grinning. "Are you mimicking me, healer?"

"Not your clothes, your cologne. What is that?"

He shrugged. "Just a little spritz of something."

"But what? What's it called? Where did you get it?" I dared to step closer to him, pressing my nose near the hollow of his throat and inhaling deeply. The cologne was obviously not the same as Bellatrice's perfume, but there was a note in the blend that seemed a perfect match.

"Hazel!" Leopold stepped back with surprise, dropping his rakish façade just a sliver, alarmed by my advance.

"Hold still." I grabbed his shoulders and pulled him to me. We were close enough that I could feel his breath at my temple, and I was sure he felt mine as I sniffed again. "This isn't what you normally wear," I observed.

He raised an eyebrow. "You've noted what I smell like?"

"No!" I protested, jerking my hands back. "Only . . . I've been trying to track down that scent for a month. I would have recognized it on you before now."

"I don't wear it often anymore."

"Why not?"

He ran his fingers over his jacket, smoothing nonexistent

wrinkles. "Mother gave it to me," he admitted. "I'm not certain where she got it from, and . . ." He glanced over my shoulder as if looking for his entourage to come back and save him. He sighed. "I don't want to use it up too quickly, you know? She always gave us bottles for our birthdays, saying that all one needed to make an impression on this world was a great deal of confidence and a signature scent."

It was an absurd sentiment, but I was willing to overlook that if it helped me. "And what's yours?"

"Black agar."

"That's a tree resin, isn't it?" I mused.

Leopold shrugged helplessly. "Mother liked it for me because it's what they burn at some of the temples, for incense. She said she wanted everyone who came across me to remember"—he let out a pained noise of chagrin—"that I was like a god on earth."

A thought occurred to me even as I resisted the urge to roll my eyes. "Do you remember when you came to get me, in the Rift?" He nodded. "Were they burning black agar that day?"

"I wouldn't be surprised. The Divided Ones were always Mother's favorites of the gods."

"I need to go," I decided, switching directions and heading for the greenhouse. Sleep could wait until this mystery was solved.

I was nearly to the end of the corridor when he called after me. "Why *don't* you like me, healer?"

There was something in his tone that made me turn around.

He made such a forlorn, solitary figure standing there. It was a rare thing, catching the prince alone, without his cluster of courtiers and the pretty girls that always seemed to trail them.

"I never said I didn't," I stalled, hoping it would appease him enough to let him trot after his friends and leave me to my work. If I could find a sample of the agar, my night was not coming to an end; it was just beginning.

He laughed. "I may spend my days in a drunken stupor," he began, using my words against me, "but even through all that haze, I can tell you don't think well of me."

"In truth . . ." I frowned, torn between the desires to placate him and to lay out each and every one of his many shortcomings. He blinked, waiting. ". . . you give me very little to think upon at all."

He clutched one hand to his heart. "Healer! Do you slice all your patients with such savage skill?"

My shoulder blades tightened, a fight bristling within me. "I find myself thinking with far greater frequency of the young men marching up and down the battlements outside, preparing to risk their lives to protect your family. I find myself thinking on the dozens, the hundreds, the thousands of people across the capitol, across the province, across the *whole country,* who are depending on me to show up and do my job. That is where my thoughts lie, Your Royal Highness, not with you and your revelries."

We stared at each other in silence, only a dozen paces apart, but the distance felt far greater.

Leopold opened his mouth but couldn't seem to find the words he wanted to say. He frowned, his dark brows lowered.

My feet itched to inch forward, to make sure he was all right. Had I actually hurt him? Wounded his feelings?

At last he closed his mouth, swallowing. "Well."

"Leopold—"

He held up his hand, stopping me with a shake of his head.

"Don't go back on all your noble convictions now." He paused. "I'd imagine with such heavy thoughts you must be quite tired. I hope . . . I'll leave you to your slumbers."

"Leo." It fell from me before I could stop it, short and familiar and achingly intimate. But I didn't know how to go on, what to say to ease the sting of the truth. "I . . . I hope you enjoy your evening."

His smile was small and lopsided and sad. "Sweet dreams, healer."

Sunlight streamed in through my curtains. It was amber and golden, the light of late afternoon. I groaned and flopped over, hiding beneath a mountain of pillows, before remembering the night before and sitting up with an excited cry.

After a month of trying, after a thousand attempts gone wrong, I had found the cure.

It was black agar, a resin found in certain trees infected by a specific strain of fungus. It was used in holy ceremonies, in cleansing rituals, in perfumes and colognes, and now . . . now it would be used to save Martissienes from the Shivers.

On the first floor of the palace was a series of niches, each a small shrine to the gods. I'd raided the Divided Ones', stealing their smudge of incense and bringing it back to my workroom. I'd mixed it into a paste, into an oil, and into salve, and every version of it had an immediate effect on my samples. The Brilliance writhed and swirled, ultimately shrinking until there was nothing left on any of the glass plates.

Overjoyed at the breakthrough, I'd collapsed into bed just after sunrise and fallen into the best sleep I'd had in a month.

But now there was more work to be done.

I stood, stretching, before I spotted a dark square of marbled black on the floor of my parlor. It looked like an envelope, pushed beneath my door sometime while I'd slept.

Someone had left me a note.

The exterior of the envelope had been left bare, and its paper was thick and impossibly fine, the nicest I'd ever felt. I broke the wax seal at its back and slid out three sheets of black parchment. Swirls of golden ink popped out in surprising relief from the dark background, shimmering across the pages.

Just Hazel, it began.

Leopold had written me a note.

A novella, I amended, scanning the long missive. His words filled nearly every inch of each page.

I brought the letter with me to my favorite armchair and settled in for its reading.

Just Hazel,

I've begun this letter half a dozen times so far, but couldn't quite find the proper opening or nail the exact tone I wished to convey. My primary goal was to rant at you and take you to task for ruining what should have been a most enjoyable evening. Vincent-Eduard Gothchaigne's soiree was full of all the very best things—beautiful women, good food, and even better drink—but I spent an hour in the most uncomfortable misery before deciding to quit it entirely.

Your words, healer, have burned their way into my skin, sinking in deep, deeper than you surely believe possible.

I know you think me nothing more than a shallow,

entitled little waste of a human, but I am human all the same, and your assessment of me was most grievous.

I want you to know that.

And I want to respond in equal measure with some scathing and witty retort that would absolutely eviscerate you and make you rue your callous and hurtful words.

But I can't.

I can't, because I find myself agreeing with you.

This is the first letter tonight that I've been able to admit that, to put pen to page and write it out.

I agree with you.

I'm not surprised to find I take up so little space in your thoughts. There truly is little about me to think upon. Nothing I do makes me particularly memorable. Nor words I say. Certainly no actions. I am a prince without purpose. A handsome figurehead.

I can hear your sigh, reading those last lines, but—for the first time in perhaps the whole of my life—I'm being exceptionally honest with you . . . and myself.

If I didn't have my looks or charms, I would be wholly unremarkable, completely and miserably forgettable.

It's true.

You know it.

I now know it too.

And . . .

I find myself questioning whether that's what I want my legacy to be.

. . . It's not, if you were wondering.

It's not. It's not. It's not.

I thought that by writing out the truth so many times,

inspiration would come to me and I'd suddenly know what to do, what course of action to take to change everything. But there is no one right answer, I suppose. There are only many, many small choices that will (hopefully) make up the whole of one good, long life. A life worth remembering, I hope.

If all that life boils down to is our choices, obviously I need to start making better ones.

And so . . . I'm leaving, healer. You've been right on so many fronts tonight. There is a war brewing, and—apart from my debonair looks and standing at court—I am no different from any of the other young men who have come to the capitol to train, to protect, to do something good with their lives. Perhaps they will rub off on me.

Until we meet again, Just Hazel.

(I pray we meet again.)

—Leopold

CHAPTER 42

The Nineteenth Birthday

"HAPPY BIRTHDAY, HAZEL!"

As I entered the dining hall, Euphemia burst from behind a tall potted fern and threw a handful of sparkling confetti on me. She flung her arms around my waist and spun me in a hug so exuberant I nearly lost my balance.

"How did you know?" I asked, brushing off the stiff brocade of my gown. Flakes of golden tinsel fluttered to the ground, a cheerful mess that made me feel guilty knowing someone else would have to clean it up.

Euphemia tugged me into the hall without giving the debris a backward glance. "What do you think?"

The table's usual austerity had been replaced with festive banners and rosettes swagged along a tablecloth of garish pink lace. Riotous blooms sprouted from a dozen vases set between platters of sweets. There were trays of pain au chocolat, towering stacks of kouign-amann and mille-feuille, and madeleines in every shade of the rainbow.

The king's youngest beamed up at me, obviously pleased to have so surprised me.

I didn't know how she'd found out today was my birthday. I hadn't told a soul.

"You didn't have to do all this for me," I said, sinking into my usual spot. Bingham set a cup and saucer before me as I placed a napkin in my lap. I offered him a smile of gratitude before taking a large swallow of the coffee.

It wasn't in fashion at court to drink coffee black anymore—in a fit of tipsy glee Bellatrice had one day declared that the year had already given us too much bitterness—but Bingham had used only the sparest amount of cream and cinnamon in mine.

"*We* didn't," Bellatrice said with a careless laugh.

She sat across the table from me, swathed in a gown of citron silk, her sharp gaze softened by the haze of steam wafting from her raised teacup. There were dark smudges beneath her eyes, and she looked paler than usual. We'd both been out the night before, attending a symphony performance followed by a soiree, and hadn't returned to the palace until well after midnight.

Since Marnaigne's triumph over his brother's militia just a fortnight before, Châtellerault had been given over to an endless series of parties and parades, balls and bacchanals, joyfully celebrating the War That Never Was, and Bellatrice, deciding my company was preferable over "that holy oracle," had dragged me to each and every event.

The biggest celebration of all was scheduled for tomorrow night in the palace ballroom. Baudouin was set to be executed in the citadel's courtyard at noon, launching a three-day party. Anyone with the right amount of cachet and allure had been invited, and Aloysius had confided to me that the palace was expecting over a thousand courtiers, dignitaries, artists, and other bons vivants to attend.

It seemed impossible to me that my name was on such a list.

My appointment as court healer had thrust me into a dizzyingly high echelon of society. I could walk into any salon in Châtellerault and be waited upon with doting servitude and extravagant deference. My armoires and chests were bursting with dresses and jewelry appropriate for every possible court function, from high teas with the princesses and other noble ladies to council meetings and state dinners.

I'd never felt so far away from the little girl growing up in the heart of the Gravia Forest. There wasn't a single person from my past who would recognize me. Even my freckles had begun to fade, lightened by exorbitant face creams and Bellatrice's dogged persistence.

"Of course we did," Euphemia said, drawing me back to the sugary feast before us. "Papa said tonight's dinner is all for Leopold." She made a face. "We couldn't ignore your birthday."

My heart skipped out of rhythm, the way it always seemed to when the prince's name was brought up.

Bellatrice let out a melodramatic sigh. "We absolutely must celebrate the golden son's return with pomp and fanfare. I wouldn't be surprised if Papa commissioned a float to carry the decorated hero throughout the halls."

Leopold's decision to run away to enlist had shocked the entire palace. He'd opted to serve not as an officer decorated with multitudes of shiny and meaningless medals but as a new recruit. He slept in a tent with other cadets, ate the same rations as everyone else, and carried out his commanding officer's orders, however lowly.

To everyone's amazement, Leopold had thrived in the trenches, quickly rising through the ranks, and when the skirmishes ended, he'd stayed with one of the colonels to continue his studies. While

I knew that Marnaigne kept close tabs on his progress, no one had received word from Leopold himself since he'd left court.

"Does anyone know when he's meant to make his grand entrance?" Bellatrice asked, squinting down the table, looking for something suitable to eat. "You must have overheard some tidbit while looking after Papa."

I shook my head. "Only sometime today."

"I had Cook make chocolate crepes." Euphemia pointed, clearly eager to begin the feast. "They're your favorite!"

"Hazel doesn't like chocolate," a voice pronounced with great authority.

I froze.

It was Leopold.

I wanted to turn and greet him but suddenly couldn't make up my mind what to do with my face, my hands.

In the months he'd been gone—*eleven months! how had it been eleven months?*—I'd read his letter again and again, unfolding the black parchment so many times the edges had begun to tatter and the golden ink had lost some of its shimmer.

But that would never diminish the weight of his words, impressed on my heart.

I pray we meet again.

I'd lost myself in so many daydreams of what the man who'd written that line would be like, for he clearly wasn't the Leopold I had known. Would he return home from battle triumphant and sure, full of action and determination? Would he be more thoughtful and perceptive, radiating seriousness and deep stoicism? Who was this new Leopold?

I'd imagined our reunion dozens of different ways—crossing paths in a deserted hall; spotting each other on either side of a crowded ballroom only to be drawn together like magnet and steel, our eyes saying all the things our lips could not—but none of them had involved meeting him with his sisters present.

It was better this way, I supposed. It wasn't as though Leopold was going to return from the front, stride into breakfast, and throw me back into a kiss most passionate, ravishing me in appreciation for all the things I'd opened his eyes to.

Was it?

Just because you made him change does not mean he changed for you.

I'd told myself that so many times.

But still, a foolish hope burned.

"Leopold!" Euphemia's face lit up and she pushed her chair back from the table to race across the room, skirts flying.

I turned and saw him scoop her into a twirled embrace.

Leopold had changed dramatically while away from court. He was longer, and leanly muscled. Gone was his head of elaborately pomaded curls, shaved to the close crop of a soldier. I wasn't sure what the medals and sash decorating his uniform signified, but he no longer wore the standard black issued to every new recruit. His suit jacket was a fine amber wool, showing off his elevated rank.

"Oof, you're getting too big for this, Phemie," he said, and they tumbled to the ground in a mess of petticoats, epaulets, and giggles. "Stand up, stand up," he ordered. "Let me take a proper look at you."

Euphemia hopped to her feet, standing tall, her back straight, playing at military precision.

"My, how you've grown," he admired.

"I haven't!"

"Oh yes, I believe you have. You're quite the little woman. I fear Papa will have you married off any day now."

Euphemia let out an elaborate cry of alarm. "I shan't ever marry. All the boys at court are horrid!"

Leopold nodded with theatrical solemnity. "I daresay they are. That's why I brought so many friends home with me." He nodded to the cluster of young men standing behind him in the doorway. Like Leopold, they all wore military suits, though none had nearly the number of medals and badges he did.

"These are my sisters, Bellatrice and Euphemia," Leopold told them, and they quickly bowed, several of them sneaking surreptitious glances at Bellatrice. "This is Mathéo, Gabriel, Maël, and Jean-Luc. We were all in the same battalion and have continued on at the academy."

Euphemia waved hello.

Bellatrice shifted back in her chair to study the young officers with catlike interest. "Welcome to court."

"Did you really fight in the war?" Euphemia asked breathlessly, amazement making her eyes seem even bluer than usual.

"Wouldn't call it much of a fight," the tallest of the group said, his eyes darting to Bellatrice, making sure she was taking notice.

I glanced back at my unlikely friend.

She had noticed.

"I take it my uncle's men didn't prove much of a challenge?" she asked, leaning forward on her seat to push forth her very best assets. Her smile curved with calculated seduction.

"Look at these strapping lads," Leopold said, slapping one across the back. "Is it any wonder Baudouin's militia up and turned tail?"

"We heard stories of life on the front," Bellatrice allowed. "What a frightful business. You all must be incredibly brave. And have quite the stamina," she added, a wicked glint sparkling her eyes.

"We're hungry too, after the morning's ride," Leopold said, commandeering the conversation once more. "Is there enough to go around?"

Bellatrice gestured to the table. "We've plenty. Join us."

At his watchful perch near the hidden servants' door, Bingham snapped for assistance, and within a moment, more settings were laid.

Leopold took his usual seat and I kept my eyes fixed on him, waiting for him to look up and notice me, but he played with his coffee and made finicky, minute adjustments to the servingware. The soldiers filled the other seats, and I noticed the tallest hustle to secure the chair to Bellatrice's left. He slid in with a wide grin.

"What a spread!" Leopold said, surveying the table. "The instructors at the academy are brilliantly skilled, but I must admit, the kitchen staff leaves quite a bit to be desired."

"It's Hazel's birthday," Euphemia announced, and I felt the gaze of every one of the men fall upon me.

"Is it?" Leopold asked, startling as though he'd only just noticed I was there.

I sat up straighter, ready to salvage the moment we'd finally greet each other.

He opened his mouth and closed it quickly as a look of indecision flickered over his features.

Just because you made him change does not mean he changed for you.

"Good fortune to you on your birthday," the tallest soldier quickly supplied. "And many happy returns."

"Thank you . . . ?" I said, drawing out the last word so that Bellatrice might learn his name.

"Mathéo," he supplied.

"Mathéo," Bellatrice echoed, a coy smile playing at her lips. "Tell me of all the noble deeds you have carried out."

Leopold set his coffee cup down with more clatter than was necessary. "Why, Hazel, you've not said a word to me since we arrived. One might think you were unhappy that your future monarch has returned."

"Certainly not, Your Royal Highness," I said, struggling to keep my voice even. "It's good to have you back."

"Just Hazel," he announced to the table, gesturing to me. "My father's healer."

Bellatrice snorted. "The way you say that makes her sound like she's one of Papa's prostitutes."

"Bells—" I began, wanting to laugh off her irreverence, but the prince interrupted, shocking me.

"Isn't she a bit of one, though?"

My mouth fell open, but Leopold held his hand up to stop my protest.

"I only mean that she provides services for Papa," he explained, as if the comparison was impossibly easy to draw. "Services for things he could not do on his own," he continued, eliciting snickers from his companions. "And she is paid quite handsomely for it."

The snickers turned into guffaws, filling the dining hall with the echoes of brute laughter.

Just because he said he'd change does not mean he's changed at all.

"You've just laid out the definition of any skilled tradesman." I kept my tone as sweet as I could as I mentally set a torch to every version of the prince's return I'd ever played out. What a fool I'd been. "Is this truly the best conversation to have in present company?" I added, tilting my head toward Euphemia.

For the briefest moment, Leopold looked pained, as if ashamed of his words, but the expression was gone in a flash, replaced by his usual look of imperious boredom. "I suppose you're right, healer. Go on, everyone; eat, and find a more suitable topic to discuss." He waved his hands benevolently over the feast as if he'd been the one to spend all morning preparing it.

I grabbed the first thing in front of me, not bothering to notice what it was. I forked a stack of chocolate crepes onto my plate, keeping my fevered stare upon Leopold. He popped a madeleine into his mouth and chewed around a lazy grin, relishing both it and my discomfort.

"Will you all be attending tomorrow's . . . festivities?" Bellatrice asked, stirring her cup of tea.

"Uncle's execution?" Leopold clarified, mincing no words. "They wouldn't miss it. Mathéo was actually one of the guards who escorted him into the citadel."

"Oh yes?" Bellatrice turned to the soldier with interest. "Did he put up much of a struggle?"

"Nothing we couldn't handle, Your Grace," Mathéo replied, unable to mask the swagger of his smile, knowing he'd gained an edge over his friends by earning Bellatrice's admiration.

"How did he look?"

Mathéo cocked his head, as if trying to determine what answer Bellatrice was hoping to hear. "Very . . . uh . . . very defeated, Your Grace."

Her eyes narrowed as she considered the response, and I noticed a tightening in the corners of her mouth. "I'm glad to hear it," she said carefully.

Curiously, I tried to catch her gaze, but she wouldn't look my way.

"And the ball tomorrow night?" Euphemia asked, adding a small collection of petit fours to her plate. "Will you be there?"

"The entire country has been abuzz with news of the king's ball," one of the other officers said, smiling. "We wouldn't miss it."

Euphemia sank her teeth into a cake. It was filled with a raspberry compote, and for one horrible moment, she looked as though her mouth were filled with blood. I looked down at my plate, glumly realizing I would have to eat some portion of the crepes.

Picking up my fork, I dug in.

CHAPTER 43

"THIS WAY! THIS WAY!" EUPHEMIA CALLED, SPRINTING through the maze of rosebushes an hour later. After breakfast she'd begged to show Leopold the changes she'd done to her playhouse in his absence, asking far too earnestly for him to decline.

We made our way into the gardens, tipping our faces up to the warm light. We'd had a particularly wet spring, with more rain than sunshine, and it now felt like a blessing to soak up so many rays.

It was misleading to call Euphemia's chalet a playhouse. Centered in the rose garden, it was a structure larger than my cottage in the Between had been. The rooms were filled with all the furniture and trappings a real house would have, scaled down to perfectly fit Euphemia's stature.

She redecorated it every season, painting and wallpapering over whatever had struck her fancy only months before. At present her favorite color was teal, and every surface had been bedecked with various shades of robin's-egg blue. Just the day before, I'd helped her hang floral chintz curtains in the sitting room.

Her playhouse had a sitting room.

"You ate the chocolate crepes," Leopold said, falling into step beside me.

"What?" I'd been trailing after the group and hadn't realized he'd stayed behind as well.

"The crepes, at breakfast. You ate them."

"Yes?" I responded, unsure of what he was getting at.

"You don't like chocolate."

Only now did I recall what he'd said upon his arrival. "I don't . . . I don't dislike chocolate," I began.

"But you don't particularly care for it either. Why would you eat something you don't like? And on your birthday, no less."

"Euphemia made them for me. I didn't want to be rude."

He snorted a laugh. "Euphemia's never set foot in a kitchen a day in her life. She sent word to Cook via her maid, and you know it."

"But she thought to make an effort, and I didn't want to hurt her feelings, and—I'm sorry, why do you think I don't like chocolate?"

Leopold's eyes flickered from the path before us up to mine. "You never take dessert."

"I take dessert," I protested, a strange fluttering starting in my chest.

"You poke at it. You also never add sugar to your coffee. I don't think I've so much as seen you take a sweetened mint to cleanse your palate between courses."

I stopped in my tracks, floored that the prince had not only noticed this about me but had also filed it away. An entire war had been waged since I'd last seen him, but he remembered that?

"I . . ." I felt as though I ought to deny it, not because it was anything particularly important, but just for the sake of disagreeing with him. Instead, I found my shoulders relaxing, and I dropped the rigid pretense I'd armored myself with since moving to court. "I actually don't like most sweets," I heard myself say.

Leopold raised his eyebrows as if the honesty surprised him as much as it did me. "Not even on your birthday?"

I laughed. "Especially then."

"What's funny?" Leopold asked, starting down the path again.

"My godfather . . ." I stopped, wondering why I was about to tell him any of this, wondering why he cared. "He loves to celebrate my birthday. I think he's trying to make up for missing so many of them."

Before I could continue, Leopold held up a finger. "He missed your birthday?"

"A few of them," I allowed, feeling as if the admission was a betrayal of Merrick. "He's the Dreaded End. He's quite busy."

I wondered if I would see him today. Since that terrible day in the cavern, he'd remained away, and the silence between us felt charged and ominous.

"Doing what?"

"You know, I'm not actually sure," I admitted, feeling the need to laugh. "He's my godfather and I don't have the slightest idea what he spends his time doing."

Leopold looked amused. "You've never asked him?"

I shrugged. "I honestly was never sure I could."

"He must be terrifying," he offered, giving me a gentle allowance.

"Sometimes, but not usually. He always makes these overly elaborate cakes. There's filling and sweetened cream and colored sugar or candied fruits or . . . whatever. One year he used five different kinds of chocolate."

"Sounds delicious," Leopold said, swatting at a stalk of oleander growing into the path.

"Merrick always gobbles them down with relish."

He blinked in surprise. "Is that what you call him? Merrick?"

I nodded.

"It makes him sound so . . . normal."

"He *is* normal, most of the time. To me, at least," I added hastily.

He paused, reflecting. "I suppose it would be odd calling him the Great Darkness, the Dreaded End. So why don't you tell *Merrick* you don't like all the fuss?"

I shrugged. "He enjoys making them, and it feels easier to just let him do it." Leopold snorted. "A slice of cake is not a hardship."

"No," he agreed. "But going through life allowing others to impose their will upon you, simply because it gives them pleasure to do so, could be. Not could be," he corrected himself. "It is."

Leopold's observation struck me more deeply than I wanted to admit. No one, not even Kieron, had ever seen me so thoroughly. It galled me that of all the people in the world, it was Leopold who'd bothered to look.

But it also was a bit flattering.

"Who are you and what have you done with the crown prince?" I demanded, causing him to smile. "The one who, only an hour ago, compared me to a prostitute?"

He winced, rubbing at his head. "I'm sorry for that. It's . . . it's easy to get caught in that pattern of talk when I'm around the other officers."

"That talk didn't surprise me," I pointed out. "But this . . . talking about cake and sweetened mints. I never would have thought you would notice—"

"Of course I notice," he cut in, quicker, perhaps, than he'd meant to. "Didn't you . . . did you get my letter?"

His tone had grown softer, hushed, as if he was holding back some feeling he wasn't yet ready to give away.

Just because you made him change does not mean he changed for you.

"I did."

"You never wrote me."

Did he sound . . . hurt?

"I didn't know I could," I admitted. "I didn't know you'd want to hear from me."

Leopold dared to look my way, meeting my eyes with a stare so blue my heart began to rekindle some of those ridiculous daydreams.

"For a girl who's so terribly smart and skilled, there's a surprising amount you don't know."

I didn't know how to respond.

"I thought about you quite often, there, at the front," Leopold mentioned.

"Why?" I asked, my eyes narrowed with distrust.

He paused, choosing his words with care. "I'd never been close to death before. The nearest I'd ever come was when Mother . . . but even then, I hadn't seen the process of it, the moment it happened. She just went out for a ride and never came back. And then . . . servants took care of the body. The embalmers took care of it after that. I'd never had to deal with the aftermath . . . the after."

I nodded, understanding. Since the Shivers had passed, I'd noticed how unpleasant an intruder death was here, a distant relation you couldn't bear to spend time with. People didn't know what to do with it. They did not sit with their dead. They did not prepare the bodies of their departed themselves, the way people would in smaller towns and villages. They sent their loved ones to a place where someone else would clean them and dress them and make them appear as though they were every bit alive as the living, who would mourn them too quickly, eager to return to their own lives.

"But on the front," Leopold went on, "there was only us to deal with it. There were no servants, no gravediggers." He let out a small laugh that held no trace of humor. "There weren't even enough men to take away the bodies. They were just left there, with us. So there was no choice but to deal with the after. There they were, taking up space and reminding us of everything that would come for us, no matter how hard we fought, no matter how brave we pretended to be. And I found myself thinking of all the afters you must have seen. I know . . . I know you're good at your job, that you're very, very good at it . . . but even very good healers must eventually deal with afters."

"Yes." It came out softly, less than a whisper, as my mind dredged up every after, every terrible moment before the after.

"It helped me, in a way, thinking of you." He smiled and the corners of his eyes crinkled, giving him a gravitas I had not seen in him before. "Sometimes I'd even talk to you, in my head."

"You'd talk to me?"

Leopold blew out a breath, as if hardly believing he was admitting such thoughts. "You became this kind of daydream to help me through everything. I'd imagine what you'd do, how you'd treat the boys dying all around me. Elevate the wounds, apply pressure to staunch the blood flow and all that, but also . . . more, you know?" His smile deepened. "So now you know my little secret and I can die of shame in these box hedges here."

I studied him, trying to see if it was a trick, trying to see where the punch line might lie. He returned my stare with an open guilelessness that undid me. "You don't need to be embarrassed."

"I just told the pretty girl who I've been thinking of for months that I've been thinking of her for months. I truly think I should, Hazel."

Pretty? My heart glowed, but I pushed the word away, certain he didn't truly mean it. No matter how introspective he might become, Leopold would forever be a flirt. "You never need to feel ashamed of striving to become a better you." I tucked a lock of hair behind my ear. "I think the changes suit you."

"Not everyone does. I can feel people expecting me to go back to my old ways now that the war is over. And being home . . . it feels far easier to watch the world through gilded glasses, but . . . it's also tiring to *not* care about things, you know?"

I raised an eyebrow. "So now you care about . . . cake?"

I was happy to hear him laugh.

"I am trying to care," he began, deliberately emphasizing each syllable, "about those around me. Which includes you now too, healer—in case you don't know. I'm sorry for what I said earlier. I feel as though I'm trying to please so many people, to be everything to everyone. But I find that costume no longer fits so well." He pressed his lips together. "You'd be surprised at how it now chafes."

I wanted to respond with some airy remark—a talent I'd found came so easily in conversation with Bellatrice—but those words would not come.

"My mother used to make my brothers and sisters a spiced nut cake for their birthdays," I finally said, feeling as though I'd handed him something precious.

"But not you?" he asked, hearing the words I hadn't said.

"I . . . I wasn't ever really hers to care about. Not after Merrick claimed me."

"Was it very good, this spiced cake?"

I smiled. "I didn't think so at the time, but now I'd love to have it again."

Slowly, as though worried any sudden movement might jar this delicate moment growing between us, he reached out and brushed his fingers over mine. It wasn't an attempt to hold my hand. It felt as if he wanted to touch me, just to know he could.

"Perhaps—"

"Leopold! Look! Look! See all the changes?" Euphemia said, running back toward us. She grabbed her brother's hand and whisked him off, chattering in an excited rush.

Leopold glanced over his shoulder, just once, but I felt his expression linger with me for the rest of the morning.

CHAPTER 44

"TAKE A DEEP BREATH IN AND HOLD IT," I INSTRUCTED when, hours later, I pressed my ear to the bare curve of King Marnaigne's shoulder blade. I listened to the soft swoosh of his lungs—clear—and the pounding pulse of his heart—strong and steady—then straightened.

"Everything sounds fine to me, Your Majesty," I said, warming my voice with all the reassurance I could muster.

The king turned his head to scrutinize me. "Are you absolutely certain? Listen again. Please. I'm sure I felt something rattling within me," he fussed.

I listened to the other lung, then from the front and the back once more.

"There's nothing."

Marnaigne released a short sigh of impatience. "You're sure?"

"You're in perfect health, sire."

Physically, this was true.

Mentally . . . I was unsure.

Since his recovery from the Shivers, Marnaigne fretted over everything. Each headache, every aching joint, was proof he'd fallen ill. His worries ranged from sicknesses as simple as a head cold to delusions of more exotic woe: skin lesions and festering ulcers, hematuria and myiasis.

My biggest responsibility as court healer was to examine the king each time he felt the stirring of something wrong within him. Aloysius made sure to keep one hour of Marnaigne's afternoons free for these appointments. Since the war's end, they'd increased in frequency and were now a daily habit.

Though I no longer could automatically see the cure any patient needed, I still had my knowledge of medical treatments and procedures and often found myself feeling incredibly grateful that Merrick had insisted on taking my training so seriously.

"Do you think I'll be well enough to attend tonight's dinner?" he worried, pulling on his brocade robe and tying the sash.

I straightened the collar for him, using the activity to hide my smile. "I absolutely do, Your Majesty."

"René," he tutted, sounding miserable with my clean bill of health.

"René," I repeated. Despite how close Bellatrice, Euphemia, and I had become in my time at court, it still felt strange and informal to call the king by his given name. "If you do feel as though you might need a bit of a boost for tonight or for tomorrow's . . . events," I said, trying hard to choose a neutral turn of phrase, "you can add a few drops of this to your tea." I turned to rummage through my valise before offering him a small brown bottle. "It's a tonic of concentrated eleuthero root and schisandra berries. It will help keep your energy level up."

"Do I seem fatigued to you?" he asked, grabbing fast at a

meaning I'd not intended. He rubbed at the spot above his heart as if feeling for a sluggish pulse.

"Not at all, Your—René. I plan on taking some myself tomorrow. There are so many events. It will be good to have the extra vigor."

The king frowned. "I suppose that's true. . . ."

"Is something else bothering you?" I asked carefully.

The king looked distant, lost in thought. "Nothing that you could provide a tonic for, I'm afraid." His laugh rang sad. "I only wish it were so simple."

I shrugged. "I'm an excellent listener. Sometimes the best thing you can do for your body is to unload your mind."

Marnaigne chewed on the corner of his lip, as if reluctant to proceed. "It's about tomorrow. The . . . execution." He looked down, examining his fingernails. "I'm having second thoughts about it."

My brows rose and a sound of surprise startled from me.

He looked up guiltily, his eyes finally finding mine. "I know it's mad. I know all the treacherous crimes he committed. I know the horrors he caused. But . . ."

"He's your brother," I supplied, sensing the words that would not come.

"Half brother," he corrected me hastily.

"Still."

"There's a dream I keep having, two, three times a night. I'm on the citadel's platform. There's a crowd below, watching and cheering. There are pennants and banners waving. There's a beautiful blue sky overhead. But then the executioner comes out and recites the sentencing, lists all the crimes, and out comes his sword. And then the sky changes. . . . The angle of it goes wrong, terribly wrong, and I realize that I'm not watching the execution at all. It's *my* head that's been lopped off. I'm seeing the sky from the basket below the block." His nose wrinkled. "You can't imagine how terrible the realization is. The last thing I see is Baudouin's face peering down at me. And then I wake up screaming."

"That's horrible. I . . . I could prepare a sleeping tonic for you. Something to help ease you into deeper slumber. It sounds as though you need rest."

He shook his head, looking disappointed that I missed the purpose of his story. "Each time I see Baudouin, I want to ask him why. Why he would do such a thing to me. Why he wouldn't offer mercy, forgiveness. But I can't say that. I have no voice, no throat through which to speak. I want to scream it. Why? Why? Why not?"

With a sigh, Marnaigne ran his fingers through his hair, scratching at his scalp.

"And here I am," he continued, his eyes flickering to the window, to his view of the citadel. "Here I am, able to offer that mercy, offer that kindness, but have I? Will I? I feel so trapped, Hazel. Bound by duty, tormented by loyalty. But he was not loyal to me. He sought my throne. He waged war upon my kingdom. Thousands of my people are dead because of him. Why should I show mercy to such a tyrant? I shouldn't. I know that. But still . . . I think I want to save him. I think I want to try." He glanced back to me, his eyes so terribly blue. "Does that make me a weak king?"

"Of course not, Your Majesty. It makes you a compassionate king, a forgiving ruler. There are ways Baudouin can be punished without death. There are ways to show your people that mercy can be a strength."

He clicked his tongue, musing. "Do you truly think it could be done?"

Mutely, I nodded.

"We would still have to carry on as if the execution was going to happen. The public is expecting some sort of spectacle to take place."

I reflected on this. "You could offer him clemency on the stage, in front of everyone."

"He would have to be imprisoned after, of course."

"But he would be alive. You would still have the chance for reconciliation. One day."

Marnaigne nodded, considering my words. "You're right. It does feel good to let go of built-up thoughts."

"I'm glad to hear it, sire."

We shared a smile before he cleared his throat, looking embarrassed by the depths of his admissions. "Are you looking forward to the ball, at least?"

"Of course," I lied.

In truth, I was already exhausted. We'd been to so many balls already. They'd merged into one monotonous montage of decadence and music, dresses too tight, food too rich, and conversations too shallow.

My world-weary thoughts made me remember Leopold's musing on court life, and I smiled.

The king immediately fixed upon my reaction. "Aha! I knew it! There must be a young man who's caught your attention, is that right?"

I shook my head, smiling as bashfully as I knew he wanted me to. "Oh, no. I was just thinking of something the prince said earlier."

Marnaigne continued to study me, his expression grown curiously hard. He seemed more alert, sharper somehow, a dog cocking its head to listen to whistles unheard by humans.

"You've seen him already?"

I nodded. "At morning meal, with several of the soldiers."

He brusquely pushed himself away from the table, leaving me feeling as though I'd angered him somehow. "And how does he seem to you? My son?"

There was a strange charge to the air, the feeling of a summer storm about to break.

"Much changed, I think," I began carefully. "Though you would know that far better than I." I turned to my valise, wanting to quickly pack up and hurry from the room before the king's temper had the chance to flare.

He made a noise of agreement. "He has changed. He seems . . . matured, grown in ways I'd always hoped for yet wasn't quite sure he'd ever master. For the first time in his life, I can envision him as a king." He swallowed. "It's a relief, I must admit."

"I can only imagine," I murmured. "But I don't see him taking on that role for many, many years to come."

Marnaigne busied himself at a side table laden with bottles and decanters. My feet itched to move closer to the door. The ground beneath me felt unsteady, as if one word might cause it to all fall apart. Despite the afternoon sun streaming in through the open windows, a chill had settled over me, impossible to shake.

"I don't want him falling into old habits now that he's returned." He pulled the cork from a bottle of wine before turning to me. "Do you understand what I mean?"

I nodded.

"It's time he stepped up his responsibilities. His duties. It's time he followed his path."

"Of course."

"And he can't do those things if his head is turned. There are so many temptations to lure a young man off his path, don't you agree?

Trees to climb, flowers to . . ." He waved his hand with an irritable swish, as if fighting to remember the right word. "Pluck."

"Game to hunt," I continued for him, as if I understood exactly what his muddled metaphor alluded to.

He snapped his fingers. "Exactly." He let out a sigh. "It's a comfort knowing I can always count on you, Hazel. You are one of the very few bright points in a very bleak year."

I startled as the king offered me a goblet. "What's this for?"

"Euphemia mentioned it's your birthday," he said. "With all the excitement going on, I don't want it to go unmarked."

"Oh, Your Majesty, thank you."

He raised his glass in the air. "May the First watch over you with smiling eyes. May the Divided Ones bring only good fortune and blessings to you. And may the"—he caught himself, laughing nervously—"and may your godfather keep away for many years to come."

The crystal rang with a bell-like *ding* as we touched our glasses together.

The clock on the mantel—a tiny replica of one of the fountains in Châtellerault, made of gold and covered by a dome glass—whirred to life. Little figurines zipped along the promenade, growing more frenzied as the clock prepared to chime out the hour.

"Damn," Marnaigne said, his brow furrowed. "Is that truly the time? I'm meant to be meeting with—"

A cheerful knock sounded, and before he could grant admittance, the door opened wide and Margaux entered. She wore her usual robes of blue and silver, every inch of her covered, from neck to toes. I felt overheated just looking at her.

"Are you ready to see me now, Your Majesty?" she asked. "Oh,

Hazel," she said warmly, noting my presence. "I feel as if it's been an age since I've seen you!"

"You've been busy," I allowed.

In truth, it had been weeks since I'd seen her. Between Bellatrice pulling me to every event of the season, Margaux's increased visions from the Holy First, and all the necessary meetings and conferences with the king those brought about, I felt much removed from my friend.

Marnaigne took a great swallow of the wine, trying to finish it quickly, and gestured that I should do the same. It tasted of bitter cherries and was much stronger than the table wine served at meals.

"Margaux, yes, yes. Come in. Hazel and I were only finishing up."

"The Holy First sends her blessings to you both," she said too brightly, as if struggling to find a topic of conversation as I went for my valise.

"Does she?" The words were out of my mouth before I could think. A quick hiccup followed, and I covered my mouth, aghast. "I'm so sorry!"

Marnaigne let out a boisterous laugh, amused by my skepticism.

"Of course," Margaux said, looking wounded. "She cares for us all. She loves us all." She turned to the king, suddenly rapturous. "And, sire, she has the most amazing message for you! I was having tea this morning when a vision overtook me. She wants you to know—"

"Is that all, Hazel?" the king asked, cutting her off with a surgeon's precision.

"Oh—yes, sire," I stammered. I snatched up my bag and was halfway across the room before the king called after me.

"Hazel?"

I turned, my eyebrows raised, ready to do whatever he bid me. "You'll remember our little talk today, won't you?"

My mind picked that exact moment to remind me that Leopold had said he thought I was pretty.

I smiled as brightly as I could. "Of course, Your Majesty."

CHAPTER 45

THE MOMENT I OPENED MY SUITE'S DOOR, I KNEW Merrick was inside, waiting for me. The air was charged by his presence and filled with the light, sugary scent of a cake too sweet.

I paused for a moment on the threshold, feeling the absurd and pointless urge to flee. Where could I possibly go that my godfather could not? With a deep breath, I entered and shut the door behind me.

"Hazel," he greeted me from somewhere in the parlor, and for a moment, I couldn't make him out on the plump black divan. When he stood to greet me, it seemed as if the chair itself had sprung to life, a horrifically large shadow of jumbled angles and moving parts. "Happy birthday."

"You came."

I knew I should go and embrace him, let him dote upon me, but my feet were stuck, unable to move, as if I'd wandered into a patch of tar.

"Of course I did."

I noticed that Merrick made no motion to move closer either.

It stung, but I'd brought this distance upon myself. I'd burned something sacred between us the moment I'd dared to go down a path different from the one he'd wanted. Whatever familial bonds we'd forged, however tenuous, however unlikely, they'd been severed, and I wasn't sure they'd ever be repaired, no matter how many years I had before me to try.

"Your pup seems bigger than ever," he noted, gesturing to Cosmos, who was padding happily about the room, wagging his tail like a fool. He had always preferred my godfather to me. Merrick gave better belly scratches.

"He's gotten fat." I smiled, not feeling it. "The cook here dotes on him."

"And you . . . you look so—" He stopped short, tilting his head as he studied me, taking in every change the year had brought.

"Tired?" I supplied.

"Stylish," Merrick finished. "So very grown up and lovely. Life at court suits you, Hazel. Far more than the cottage ever did."

"It's what you always wanted, isn't it?"

He cocked his head, his eyes winking curiously.

"When you first gave me the gift, you said I'd become so great that kings would ask for me by name."

The edges of his mouth rose in a bittersweet smile. "I did."

"Now they do."

"That's good."

I pressed my lips together. He wanted my contrition, wanted me to keep begging for his forgiveness, a little girl scared of punishments that might be meted out against her. All I had to do was take up that role again and play my part with every bit of the earnestness required.

The trouble was, I wasn't that little girl any longer.

I glanced down at my hands. They felt ungainly without a task to occupy them. "I smell cake," I finally said, desperate to find a neutral subject. "What kind did you make this year?"

Merrick frowned as if knowing he was being cajoled. "Chantilly cake with berry compote. Mascarpone frosting," he added reluctantly.

"It sounds delicious," I lied. It seemed the easiest kindness I could offer. "Would you like me to cut it?" I wandered over to the credenza where the towering confection rested, keenly aware of how Merrick stayed behind, swaying from foot to foot.

"Are we truly not going to talk about it?" he called, making no move to come closer. "This past year. The . . . incident that led to this estrangement?"

"Estrangement," I repeated as my fingers danced over the knife and serving wedge.

"I haven't seen you in an entire year, Hazel."

And whose fault is that?

The words balanced on the tip of my tongue, but I kept them back. It wouldn't serve either of us to have them said aloud.

"I didn't know you wanted to see me."

"Of course I did." He wrung his hands in an anxious gesture so ill-befitting the Dreaded End that I nearly smiled. "I've missed you, Hazel," he admitted. "You're the only one I . . . It's been a very long time to go without seeing my goddaughter."

"Then why did you stay away? It's not as though I can go after you."

"I didn't think you'd want to see me," he pointed out in a near echo of my excuse.

I wanted to laugh. Merrick had never once taken my desires into account. He'd whisked me here and there on whims he never bothered to explain. He decided when to visit, never wondering if it would be convenient for me. He'd laid out the entire course of my life before I was born, even ensuring that that life would go on for as many extra years as he wanted.

I wanted to scream all this at him, wanted to let the accusations burst from my chest with thunderous force. I was right, I knew I was, and I just wanted him to see that. To admit that.

But I could feel his mood darkening, setting my blood on edge, and I swallowed every trace of righteous indignation.

"Cake?" I asked, taking up the utensils. "It looks like your best yet."

He made a grunt of acknowledgment and finally stepped closer.

"No candles this year," I observed, then winced at my stupidity.

"I couldn't watch you blow them out. Not after . . ." Merrick sighed.

His honest admission was painful to witness.

We couldn't go on like this, slicing each other with daggered confessions so sharp the cuts weren't felt until the blood began to fall.

Merrick wouldn't be the one to change. He'd spent countless millennia being exactly who he was, uncontested, undisputed.

It would have to be me.

I pressed the tip of the knife into the table's surface, marring the wood. It hurt too much to continue with the sham of a celebration, but I also couldn't forfeit the pretense altogether. "Merrick." I swallowed. "I owe you an apology."

He sniffed.

"I never truly thought about how my actions affected you. I

never considered everything you went through to get those candles. My rejection of one must have seemed like such an insult."

He licked his lips but said nothing, letting me flounder in my misery.

"What . . . what *did* you have to do for those candles?" I dared to ask.

He looked away from me, out the window, and the afternoon light played off his two-toned eyes, causing them to refract light like those of a predator slinking in the dark. "There was a trade," he said after a long moment. "With the Holy First." He allowed himself a very small smile. "After your father's refusal of her, she almost didn't grant my request, but I was quite persistent."

"What did you trade?"

Merrick let out a very long hiss of air. "What I deal in best."

"Death?" I guessed.

"Lives," he corrected me flatly. "The point at which lives end." When I frowned with confusion, he sighed and continued. "We see things very differently from mortals. You perceive everything around you in a linear fashion. This happened, so this happens, which will cause that to happen. But the gods . . ." Merrick waved his long fingers in a giant cyclical gesture. "We see every version of every choice, every effect every cause can trigger."

I remembered my small taste of the godsight with a queasy stomach, then felt a sense of déjà vu wash over me. I was certain we'd had this exact conversation before.

But not about the Holy First.

It was about . . .

"The First wanted me to save lives," I said, putting it together. "Not just as a healer, but . . ."

"She is the reason you see the deathshead," Merrick confirmed. "It's her will you're meant to carry out. It's never been mine."

"Oh." I stared at my fingers, still clutching the knife. I didn't know what this meant, what it meant for me, what it meant for him, but my chest ached. "Was it her choice or yours that I become a healer?"

He shrugged, the body of his robes hefting up before wafting down into rippling shadows. "At the time, it didn't matter to me what you did. You'd not even been born yet. I only knew that I loved you, that I'd want all those extra years for you. I didn't care much what needed to be done to get them. I never considered the toll it would take on you."

"Was she . . . was she very upset about Marnaigne?"

He nodded.

It was difficult to imagine an angry Holy First. In all the stories of her, she was made out to be a benevolent, motherly figure who was far more likely to leave you smothered in guilt over all the ways you disappointed her than to ever raise her voice. But . . .

"I think she took my gift away," I admitted.

Merrick frowned.

"I can't see cures any longer. Not since . . . not since that day in the cavern. It doesn't feel like it's ever going to return."

He made a pained noise. "Probably not. I suppose it's a good thing I made you read all those books, then."

I smiled, as if he'd made a joke.

He grabbed the knife from my hand and I flinched. "Give me that," he said. "You shouldn't have to cut your own cake."

Part of me wanted to sit back and let him serve. We'd eat it in stilted silence and it would be horrible, but it would be the first small step to getting back to the usual rhythm of us. I just needed to keep my mouth shut and let him celebrate my birthday.

"Merrick?"

I wanted to pinch myself. All I had to do was stay quiet and this disaster of an afternoon could soon be at an end. But it was like an aching tooth. I couldn't not poke at it. I had to keep testing the pain, seeing if I could handle it.

He grunted.

Don't do it, Hazel. Don't do it, Hazel. Don't—

"Do you ever regret making me your goddaughter?"

The knife fell through the cake as easily as a guillotine. "What?" he asked.

I winced. "Sometimes it feels like all I do is disappoint you, and I just . . . I've always wondered."

"Always?" he echoed, sounding hurt.

"When I was little . . . when you didn't come for all those years, I thought it was because you realized you'd made a mistake."

"All those years . . . Did it truly feel so long?"

"Merrick, I'd been waiting my whole life for you."

He stared at me with shock and sadness, looking impossibly ancient, looking every bit the god he was. "I never thought of it that way." Merrick shook his head. "I've never regretted that moment. Not once. And I never will."

He set the knife aside, leaving the slice of cake untouched.

"Gods don't want for anything. Not truly. But before you . . . there had been an agitation building inside. This burr that poked at me, this sense that something wasn't whole, wasn't complete. I didn't know what would fill it. I didn't know how to stop its ache. But when I heard your very foolish parents making those very foolish plans, I realized I'd found what I'd been searching for. I'd found you. I felt you. I could feel who you were. Who you'd become . . . You captivated me, Hazel."

My chest felt too heavy to breathe. "You've never told me this part of my birthday story."

"I suppose I should have. . . . Once I found you, I was selfish. I made the trade with the Holy First and she granted me three candles. Three lives with you."

He made a pained noise and crossed from me to the fireplace. He ran a finger over the mantel, tracing memories.

"It was agony waiting for you to arrive. I didn't know what to do with such an interminable length of time. So I waited and I planned. I planned *everything*. I knew you'd have blond hair and deep blue eyes. Your mouth would pucker into a little rose. I imagined your smile, your laughter, the sound of your voice. I pictured our lives together, all the things I'd teach you, the things you'd show me."

As he spoke, I pictured how his words might have played out. I saw myself take my first steps holding tightly to the Dreaded End's fingers, watched as we whiled away childhood afternoons in a sun-drenched meadow, playing at tea, then checkers, then chess.

Regretfully, Merrick shook his head. "I was wrong, though, about so many things. About everything, I suppose," he reflected.

Merrick's admission stung. "What a disappointment this freckled, dark-haired creature must have been."

He turned back to me, his eyes bright with emotion. "Never a disappointment. Always a wonder." He reached out and touched my cheek. "Today I look at you and wonder what you might have become if I'd not saddled you with dreams of only my own making."

It was the closest thing to an apology I'd ever heard from my godfather, and I wasn't sure how to respond. I felt as if I should say something to absolve him, but I couldn't find it in me to ease his guilt.

"I don't know what I would have been. I suppose I never will," I admitted honestly. I offered him a smile, but he didn't return it. "Let's eat," I said, holding out my hand to draw him back.

One hug. One embrace would erase the hurt and frustration and disappointment, and we could go back to muddling along together, an unlikely pair that somehow worked.

"I'm not hungry," Merrick said. I'd never heard him so sad before. "I . . . I think it's best if I leave you to your celebrations, here, in your new home. At court."

"Just like you wanted," I pointed out, my voice light, hopeful he'd find enough pleasure in that to smooth over the moment.

"Just like I wanted," he agreed. He crossed to me then and pressed his papery, dry lips to my forehead. "Happy birthday, Hazel."

He was gone before I could answer, slipping through a void of his own making. I sank down in the nearest chair, feeling a strange pain across my chest. I felt as though I was about to cry, though I couldn't see the point in it.

Merrick was unhappy—with me, with himself, with the situation we were in—and there was nothing to be done about it. I couldn't soften his pain, I couldn't find a way to make him smile and forget about it. After years of tiptoeing around his changeable moods, doing everything I could to keep him light and happy, I felt a complete failure to be so helpless now.

I wondered when I would see him again, if another year would go by before he returned to me. Or two, or three, or an entire decade. How long did it take for a god to make peace with their shortcomings? How long would he stew upon this? And what was I meant to do with my time while I waited?

There was a knock at my door and I rushed to answer it, foolishly thinking it might be Merrick come back. But when I threw it open, breathless, as I anticipated seeing my godfather there smiling, shy and contrite, I was only disappointed. The hall was empty save for a serving cart.

On its top tier, perfectly situated in the center of a golden charger, was a white plate bearing a square of dark cake studded with slivers of walnuts. It warmed the air with cloves, cinnamon, and nutmeg and smelled like my childhood.

A single lit candle had been stabbed into the cake, wholly unassuming, plain and white, and reminding me uncomfortably of the one I'd given away.

Curious, I brought the cart into my suite.

I picked up the fork resting alongside the plate, marveling at how Leopold must have persuaded the kitchen staff. I was certain it wouldn't be right, sure that Cook had added fistfuls of brown sugar or candied ginger to punch up the flavor, to create something intriguing and playful for the palate.

He hadn't.

It was simple and nutty, a recipe far too rustic to ever be served to this court.

It was the most perfect cake I'd ever eaten.

And Leopold had been the one to give it to me.

I pictured him as he'd been in the garden, more serious and thoughtful than I'd ever guessed possible, and remembered how the sunlight had played across his features, warm and radiant, and my heart jumped within my chest, feeling almost like a wish.

With a wistful smile, I blew out the candle.

CHAPTER 46

THE MORNING OF BAUDOUIN'S SUPPOSED EXECUTION dawned unseasonably hot.

As the royal family and their guests assembled beneath the tented dais in anticipation of the ghastly event, everyone was flushed, their skin damp with sweat, their eyes heavy-lidded.

The servants were doing their best to keep everyone comfortable, passing out folded fans and flavored ices, but the air held too much tension and the desserts were left abandoned, melting into colorful messes that dotted the table linens and drew flies.

"This is barbaric," Bellatrice muttered, flapping her fan near her face with irritation, both to stir a breeze and keep the buzzing insects at bay. "Picnicking while a man is put to death. Look at those people over there. . . ." She snapped her fan shut and jabbed its end toward a cluster of people farther down the hill from us, gathered on spread blankets. "Are they feeding each other roasted chicken?"

Margaux leaned back, silver bracelets clinking against one another as she fluttered her fan. "I feel as though I'm the one roasting."

She looked miserable. The neckline of her dress went all the way up to her chin. Her robes covered every inch of her arms and were long enough to skim her heavy boots. I wondered if such costuming was her own choice or something meant to mark her as the oracle. Several priestesses from the Ivory Temple were in attendance, each wearing diaphanous gowns of lightweight fabric that showed off their sleek limbs and bare feet.

Beside Margaux, Euphemia swayed listlessly. The little princess was hidden away in layers of heavy brocaded satin as dazzling a blue as the sky overhead. Her round cheeks were apple red, and I instructed one of the servants to bring her a fresh goblet, fearing heatstroke. "Why can't we go home?" she whined, taking great gulps of the water when it arrived.

"They can't begin until Papa arrives," Leopold answered, continuing to scan the crowds, searching for any sign of the king.

"Where is he?" she snapped. "My head hurts."

"Drink more water," I instructed, struggling to speak up. The heat had lulled me into a foggy haze, and I longed to unclasp my bodice and fan my chest. "We all ought to be drinking more water."

I wanted to tell them the secret of the day, that all this pomp and ceremony was nothing but a distraction from the real event: The king was going to forgive his brother. He was going to allow Baudouin to live, albeit it far from Martissienes, exiled in a monastery to the south. He'd be confined to a life with the reverents of the Holy First, taking vows of silence, poverty, and servitude. But Marnaigne had made me swear I would not say a word. The element of surprise would be his most powerful asset in helping the public accept this decision. I'd seen him that morning for a quick examination, and he'd paced his chambers, palpable waves of angst and elation rolling off him in equal measure.

When all this was said and done, I was going to prescribe him a very long rest.

"Good fortune and favor be blessed upon you all!" called a great booming voice at the back of the tent.

We all turned to see a new delegation of reverents arriving. Each temple in Châtellerault had sent members of their highest circles to watch the execution from the royal box. They were meant to offer us their spiritual counsel and add a touch of needed gravitas to the event.

"Amandine," I said, rising to welcome the high priestess from the Rift. "It's good to see you once more."

I visited the Rift often, checking in on the orphans and other refugees, offering what services I could while wishing I could mend broken hearts as easily as other wounds. Amandine was always with the children, giving out blankets and meals as freely as she offered hugs and blessings upon their tiny foreheads.

"Oh, Hazel," she greeted me. "What a joyous day, is it not? Triomphe and Victoire rain their blessings upon us. Félicité smiles brightly today." Before she could exclaim another platitude, a figure approached, interrupting the moment.

"Hazel!" exclaimed my brother, pulling me into an embrace. "I didn't expect to see you here today. Such fortunes! Such blessings!"

Over his shoulder, I caught sight of Leopold noticing Bertie's arrival and wondered if he remembered my brother chasing him through the Rift the day he'd come to rescue me.

"I didn't realize the Fractured would be in attendance," I said, pulling back to look at him. It was a struggle to not wince. No amount of time would ever make me accustomed to the scars running across his body. A fresh cut bisected his temple, giving his face the appearance of a shattered mirror.

He smiled broadly. "Oh. Yes. High Priest Théophane wanted me to stop by the royal tent before . . . well, before it all begins." He nodded toward an older man trying to begin a conversation with Bellatrice. "I've begun my training to take a spot on the high council in the Rift."

"Bertie, that's wonderful," I said, unsure of what it meant.

"Bertrand," he corrected me quickly, his eyes darting toward Théophane. "I'm twenty years old now. A man. The high priest says it's time I gave up my childish nickname. It's taking a bit of time to adjust, but it truly is such a blessing, such a joy."

"That's right," I said, feeling foolish I'd forgotten. "Happy belated birthday." I stood on my toes to press a swift kiss to his scarred cheek. "Many, many happy returns."

"To you as well, little sister." He reached up and pressed two of his fingers to my forehead, offering a blessing I wanted to squirm from. "May Félicité and Gaieté bring you great favor in the coming year."

Ritual done, he looked around the tent, taking in the pageantry and spectacle. As he caught sight of Margaux—refilling Euphemia's water goblet while also trying to fan the heat-dazed princess—he frowned. Her face was beet red and dripping with sweat.

"Ices," she declared to no one in particular. "I think the princess needs more ices." She hurried from the box.

"Aren't you glad your gods allow you to wear linen?" I asked with a small laugh.

"It does seem Misère is out in force today," Bertie allowed thoughtfully, wiping his own brow before allowing his attention to wander once more. "The prince has returned home."

Leopold quickly looked away as Bertie's gaze met his stare.

"Yes. Yesterday. Just in time for the . . . ceremony."

"Celebration," Bertie supplied quickly. "It *is* a celebration, Hazel. Peace has returned to the land. Félicité is well pleased, and Revanche shall have his due. What a day! Such blessings! Such joy!"

I wanted to nod, but it was too hot to make the effort.

Far above, along the walls surrounding Châtellerault, a cannon fired, signaling that something was about to begin.

Bertie nodded toward the older priest before looking at me. His thick, segmented eyebrows were drawn with a look of contrition. "I'm so sorry to run. Our visits are always too short."

"You're not watching from the box?"

He shook his head, his smile twisting with pride. "No. Théophane has given me a different task for the day." He beamed, his eyes bright with a zealous gleam. "A great honor, actually. Such favors! Such good fortunes! I'm to be Revanche's hand of—"

The high priest cleared his throat and my brother flushed.

"I must go, Hazel. But I'll see you later on. After," he promised.

"After," I echoed, feeling confused. "Will you be at the ball tonight?"

Though it seemed an unlikely excursion for a member of the Fractured, he nodded, then hurried off, disappearing into the crowd. I turned my attention back to the stage, more than ready for the whole dreadful affair to be over and done with.

"I can't recall it ever feeling this hot in spring before," Leopold said, suddenly at my side. "Such blessings. Such joys."

I laughed at his monotone delivery, a flicker of flirtation rising in my chest. It was a feeling I'd never expected to experience again, not after Kieron, and certainly not for Leopold. But it shimmered through me anyway, like the furtive darting of a butterfly.

I knew I ought to ignore such feelings, knew Marnaigne wouldn't approve, but they felt too good to push aside so easily.

And besides, the king appeared to be in a most forgiving mood.

"It's terribly crowded here, don't you think? Perhaps there will be better breezes over here," Leopold suggested louder than necessary before taking my elbow to lead me to a quieter corner of the box. "How was Papa, when you saw him this morning? Truly?"

"Very . . . agitated," I admitted. "His emotions were swaying from one high to another, like a pendulum. He needs to rest after all this is over. His nerves are . . . frayed."

He nodded.

"And you?" I prodded. "How are you today? Truly?"

If he noticed my echo of his question, he didn't show it.

"I'm . . . also agitated, I think. Part of me—the one who was on the front for all those months, the one who was in the trenches, in the rain and the muck and the cannon fire—is pleased, knowing a very real and dangerous threat will be put to an end today. The other part of me is sad. Sad for so many reasons."

I wanted to tell him. I wanted to tip King Marnaigne's hand and let Leopold know that his father would be choosing mercy. I wanted to say anything to take that terrible look of remorse from his face.

But I'd promised the king.

"Were you two particularly close?"

"No," he reflected. "And now I'm losing the chance to ever get to know him, to have anything to do with him. Papa has so many stories of him before . . . before he left court. Baudouin is the older of the two, did you know that?"

I shook my head.

"By many years. He was born my grandfather's bastard, but for a time it seemed as though he would someday take the throne. My grandmother . . . she had quite a lot of trouble conceiving.

Baudouin lived at court then. He'd been given a strong education and the finest horses. Grandfather brought in the very best instructors to teach him how to fight and ride, how to strategize and dance. He'd been raised as if he was a prince in his own right. But then Papa came along."

"And that's why Baudouin claimed to have more right to the throne," I realized slowly. "He was first. He'd grown up believing he'd become king." I frowned, thinking of how many innocent people had lost their homes, their families, their very lives, over a slighted brother's wounded rage.

Leopold chewed on the side of his lip thoughtfully. "For a time, they were close. It wasn't until my mother had Bellatrice that the cracks began to show. Grandfather was still alive then, but unwell. I suppose seeing how close Papa was to inheriting the throne, seeing him start a family, seeing the next generation of heirs that would push him farther down the line of succession . . . it was just too much. He and Papa quarreled, and then he was . . . gone. Till now."

"I think . . . I think today will surprise you," I said, allowing myself to hint at the turn to come. "Perhaps Miséricorde will have a chance to shine."

He smiled faintly. "I think you've been among the Fractured for too long. Or perhaps all this heat has finally gotten to you. Should I get you one of Phemie's ices?"

I offered him a shy smile. "I think I'd prefer a spiced cake."

I was pleased to see his eyes twinkle and his dimples wink as he grinned. "Was it everything you imagined it would be?"

A roll of drums broke our conversation and drew everyone's attention to the citadel.

Baudouin emerged from the gated portico, flanked by a stronghold of guards. His wrists were in heavy iron shackles. He wore a shift of ivory linen, the mark of a condemned man, the mark of one destined to meet the executioner.

The soldiers marched him across the cobblestones and up the stairs to a platform dominating the middle of the courtyard. It was such an innocuously plain structure, like a stage hastily built for a group of traveling players.

Baudouin had been sentenced to death by beheading, and he shook visibly when he spotted the dark walnut block at the center of the platform.

Beside me, Leopold took a deep breath. He flinched and our knuckles brushed. I waited for him to jerk his hand away and fumble for an apology.

He didn't.

Neither did I.

Slowly, as if pulled by the gentle but persistent current of a stream, our eyes met.

He took a deep breath.

I took another.

All around us, the crowd began to cheer as Marnaigne and the executioner stepped into the courtyard.

The king looked resplendent, dressed in full imperial regalia, including an ermine-lined cloak, despite the oppressive heat broiling the afternoon. He stood tall and straight. He made his way through the crowd, nodding to several merchants and pausing as a line of little girls curtsied before him. It was the first time I'd ever seen him wear his crown, and I was struck by how well it suited him. It boasted countless rubies, emeralds, and diamonds along a lustrous gold circle. In direct sunlight, the crown was enough to almost blind me.

Dots of color danced over my eyes as the king spoke, reciting the long list of Baudouin's crimes and reading the formal statement of sentencing.

I shifted from one foot to the other, only partially listening to the proceedings. I understood that the king wished to drum up the moment of forgiveness, to turn it into the day's production, but Leopold was right: the heat was getting to me. I longed to be out of the heavy costuming, away from the crowds and back in the blessed coolness of my chambers.

Down on the stage, Marnaigne asked for his brother's repentance, and I breathed a sigh of relief. The moment had come. This would all be over soon.

Despite the fear holding claim on Baudouin's body, tensing his muscles into ripples of trepidation, he shook his head and spat at his brother. The king went rigid, nostrils flaring, and I could feel the crackle of his rising temper all the way from the royal box.

My heart hammered an odd cadence in my chest.

That wasn't supposed to happen.

That wasn't going to—

"I had hoped you would come to see reason," Marnaigne began, his voice booming over the crowd, a seasoned actor performing before the largest audience of his life.

I cringed, sensing the impending explosion.

"I had hoped you would repent and we could end this in reconciliation."

I could not make out Baudouin's response, but the twin dots of anger burning across Marnaigne's cheeks indicated it was not what he wished to hear.

"I know now it is not meant to be. It will never be, as long as you and your line are allowed to traverse the earth. Guards!" He snapped, and a cadre of uniformed soldiers marched from the citadel. They brought out other prisoners, a middle-aged woman and a young boy, flanking them as if the captives might run. It seemed an unnecessary precaution.

I'd never before seen a set of more pitiful people. They'd not been treated well during their confinement. Iron shackles had left welts ringing their wrists and ankles. The wounds had broken open and were festering with pus and bits of hay, and I couldn't begin to guess at the last time they'd been allowed to bathe.

When the woman spotted Baudouin on the stage, she all but collapsed and had to be carried up the steps, howling her despair.

"No!" Baudouin shouted, bucking at his guards as he tried to break free. "Unhand her, René. She had no part in this. My son had no part in this!"

A strangled gasp escaped me as I put the scene together. The prisoners—wearing a matching set of ivory shifts—were Baudouin's wife and child.

My mind couldn't take in what I was seeing. Baudouin's family had been here for months. They'd been dressed for execution all along.

Marnaigne hadn't ever been ready to offer his brother clemency.

He had always intended to put him to death.

And the family . . .

With a terrible nod, Marnaigne ordered the ceremony to begin, and the crowd jeered, tossing clods of earth and the remains of their lunches at the disgraced duke and his family.

The soldiers manhandled Baudouin to the block, positioning his head in the curved recess and locking his shackles to the hooks bolted to the platform. The duke thrashed, squirming against any amount of slack he could manage, an animal caged in confines far too small. "Stop this madness! Show them mercy! Brother, *please*!"

Marnaigne froze and a flicker of hesitation wavered on his face. "Wait!" he called, struggling to be heard over the shouts of the crowd. "Stop this now!"

The guards froze, listening for their king's orders. Baudouin stopped his struggles, brightening with painful hope.

"Unlock the shackles. Unlock the chains."

A murmur of confusion swept over the gathered, stilling the courtyard to a hush.

Marnaigne studied his brother, and I could see the range of emotions ripple over his face: compassion and sorrow, pity and forgiveness. He looked down, as if about to cry, and swallowed hard. When he straightened, his eyes were full of fury and scorn.

"The boy should go first," he decided, raising his voice so that all might hear his horrible decree. "Let his father see the fruits of his labors."

"No," Leopold murmured, so softly I wasn't even certain he'd spoken. "Don't do this, Papa!"

Before anyone could protest, before anyone could think to stop him, to stop them, to stop this horror from unfolding, the executioner sprang into action, and I gasped.

Certain he would not be needed, I'd not noticed him until this very moment. Now he dominated the platform. His two-toned tunic fluttered in the breeze, and bronze bracelets laden with holy charms tinkled against one another as his scarred arms flexed, picking up the large curved axe.

Without a thought, I grabbed Leopold's hand as Bertie took that weapon and swung it high over his head, aiming it directly at Baudouin's son.

CHAPTER 47

LEOPOLD'S GRASP DID NOT FALTER.

Not when the axe descended with such a rush we could hear the whir of it, slicing the air before hitting its intended mark, square across the nape of the boy's neck.

Not when Bellatrice let out a strangled scream, the color draining from her face.

Not when the wife's blood spurted forth, spraying my brother's face and anointing him in a baptism most foul.

Not even as the crowd leapt to its feet, rejoicing, dancing, screaming their delight to the heavens. Throughout it all, Leopold's hand was warm and tight around mine.

Loud peals rang out as temples all around the city began their celebrations, cheering the demise of a family who had once threatened so much of Châtellerault's way of life.

Baudouin's head rolled off the edge of the platform, joining those of his family on the stones below. I knew they could no longer see, I knew they were no longer truly there, but in that moment, I swore his wife's eyes met mine, sharp and accusing.

Somehow she knew this was my fault.

I had chosen to save the king, and now all three of them were dead.

I let go of Leopold then.

I shook my hand free, bringing it to cover my mouth as my stomach lurched. I turned from the bloodied stage, turned from Leopold, turned away from the hateful glares of so many bodiless faces, and hurried from the royal box.

I made it down the steps before throwing up into a swag of curtains. The sweat beading at my temples chilled, and despite the heat, I shivered. Footsteps raced after me, and I somehow knew it was Leopold. I curled into a ball, rubbing my arms and bracing against the wave of utter misery that threatened to overtake me.

It didn't matter how small I tried to make myself. Leopold found me almost instantly. "Hazel," he said, his voice breaking through the white noise filling my head, his fingers tracing against my shoulder blades with concern. His touch was as light as a hummingbird and just as restless.

"I'm sorry, I'm sorry, I'm so sorry," I repeated as my stomach twisted again. I struggled to swallow the biting bile. It burned as it went back down my throat, but I would not allow myself to be sick in front of the prince. "I'm sorry."

I wasn't sure if I was apologizing to him or his uncle.

"Hazel," Leopold said again, kneeling now. I turned my shoulders, trying to hide the evidence of my weak stomach. "Hazel, it's all right. You don't have to— Are you shaking?"

I shook my head even as I trembled.

He ran his hand across my back, harder now, as if trying to drum up warmth for me, as if the air wasn't already as thick as sludge, sweltering and humid. It was tainted now with the coppery tang of blood.

I felt as if I couldn't draw enough breath. I felt as if the ground had somehow flipped, somersaulting my axis and skewing my sense of equilibrium. How could the king have done this?

Baudouin I could understand. He'd incited a rebellion and waged a bloody civil war in his attempt to unseat the king.

But his wife had not.

Their young son had not.

And King Marnaigne had carried out their murders cheerfully, with all the spectacle of an operatic villain.

The memory of his deathshead washed over me, roiling my belly with more bile hot and foul.

I wanted to ground myself in the earth, wanted to rest my too-heavy, too-muddled head upon Leopold's chest and let the waiting darkness rush up and claim me. I wanted . . . I wanted . . .

I caught myself just before I swooned against the crown prince. Flashes of lights danced across my vision, and the only thing I could make out around their blinding brilliance was my brother.

Bertie strode off the stage like a hero coming home from war. He tilted his face back and forth, basking in the golden radiance of his moment, then stooped to snatch up Baudouin's severed head. As he held it aloft in triumphant jubilation, the crowd screamed King Marnaigne's name, and my world faded to black.

"There you are," a voice said sometime later.

I assumed it was later.

I assumed it was later and we were elsewhere, but I didn't know for certain because my eyelids were too heavy to open. Too heavy with the last traces of groping, grasping oblivion. Too heavy and far too tender to open and see any more of the world's horrors.

"Drink this," the voice said, and I felt the press of a glass against my mouth.

I parted my lips, swallowing the blessed water in greedy sips. It was cool and had been sweetened with cucumber and mint, and I knew then that I must be at the palace, because where else would anyone sweeten water with cucumber and mint?

The person holding the glass let out a dry husk of a sound that I supposed was meant to be laughter. "Look at me, healing the healer."

Leopold was beside me, gently offering me sips of water.

Leopold.

I felt the touch of his fingers on my forehead. "A fever," he murmured too softly to be speaking to anyone but himself.

Against my better judgment, I opened my eyes and squinted at him in the chamber's dim light. I was in my room, in my bed, and my curtains had been drawn. Leopold perched on the side of my bed, a look of grave concern darkening his face.

I blinked at the unlikely scene, certain I was hallucinating. "You can't actually feel a fever using your fingers. Not accurately." I struggled to arrange the pillows behind me so that I could sit up without feeling as if I were about to keel over once more.

"No?"

His irises were wide and dark, reminding me of the first time we'd met. He'd caught me sleeping then too.

"You were just holding the water. I could feel how it cooled your fingers when you touched me. Anything would feel hot to you," I said, nodding to the pitcher at the bedside table. "Could I have some more, please?" My limbs felt like weighted clay, incapable of movement.

Leopold obliged, even bringing it to my lips for me.

"Thank you," I said, falling back into the nest of pillows.

"So what *is* the best way to check for a fever?" he asked, keeping hold of the glass, waiting for me to need it again. "In case my skills in the medical arts should ever be called into service. I think I may have a promising career before me."

I studied him, unable to reconcile my initial memories of Leopold with the prince who sat before me now. He was a puzzle piece worn too out of shape to ever slide back into his intended position. "The best way for *you,*" I teased, "would be to call in a healer and have them take it for you."

He smiled but waited.

"The inside of your wrist," I finally said, relenting. "Its own temperature is more stable, letting you actually feel the changes in others."

Wordlessly, he reached out and laid his wrist over my forehead. His touch was far more tender than I would have ever given him credit for. "You still feel warm to me," he said after a long and charged moment had passed.

"Heatstroke," I diagnosed. "I can't believe I fainted."

"It was quite a shock. The executions," he said, gently. "It's not surprising you swooned."

I shook my head and instantly regretted it. "I'm made of far tougher stuff than that."

"You don't have to be," he pointed out. "I've no doubt you've seen more than your fair share of things, terrible things. But"—he gestured around my suite of rooms—"there's no one else here now. No one else ever need know."

I shifted uneasily, glad to realize I was still in my formal gown and hadn't been undressed in my unconscious state. Even so, I pulled the coverlet up over my chest, feeling far too exposed.

"Thank you for taking care of me in my . . . absence," I said before adding, "and for your discretion."

"It's a very hard thing to see."

"Watching someone die?"

"Watching lives be taken against their will," he corrected me.

The memory of my father's face flickered through my mind, and all I could see was his expression of shocked horror as the end came rushing over him. His was the first life I'd ever taken. He had not gone down easily.

"When I first saw it happen on the front—a soldier right beside me was struck across the throat with shrapnel—I couldn't stop screaming." Leopold licked his lips, and his voice was strained and drawn too thin. "Sometimes I think I'm screaming still."

"I'm sorry," I heard myself murmur, but was too caught up in a haze of remembrance. Mama had asked to be released, had smiled as she drank the potion I'd mixed, but the others . . .

Yes, those had been very hard things to see.

"You apologize too much," Leopold noted. "You didn't dress me in a uniform. You didn't send me into battle."

"I'm sorry all the same," I said, realizing that he was wrong and that my actions inadvertently had done exactly that. If I'd not saved Marnaigne, if I'd let Baudouin storm his way to the throne . . . how many lives would still be here?

But how many lives did your actions save?

There was no good answer to either question.

"Did today really happen?" I asked, feeling impossibly small. "Did the king actually . . . ?"

Leopold nodded.

"He'd told me he was going to offer clemency. Yesterday. He said he wanted to show mercy. To offer forgiveness. When I left him with Margaux, he was ready to . . ." I paused.

Margaux had come in after our talk.

Margaux had kept him behind closed doors, discussing something so late into the afternoon that the king had nearly missed the grand dinner he'd arranged for Leopold's return. I'd thought it odd at the time but had chalked up his tardiness to all the many dignitaries visiting, the many things I'm sure he was busy with.

What if . . .

"Margaux. She said she'd had a vision from the Holy First. Do you think she said something to your father to make him change his mind?"

"My father is a mercurial man," Leopold said carefully. "He's easily swayed by those around him. Those who whisper loudest. And everyone is whispering at him."

"But to execute that little boy? His own nephew? Why would the Holy First want that?"

Leopold winced, remembering. "I don't think she would. But Margaux might."

"You've said similar things before, questioning her motives. Why would she want . . . why would she want any of what happened today to play out?"

Leopold shrugged. "I don't know. You'd have to ask her. But Papa . . . Papa always wants to look strong. And he'd want word of such strength to reach far and wide, to stop anyone who might think of taking up my uncle's cause. It's an effective strategy."

"You agree with him?" I asked, horrified.

He shook his head with vehemence. "No! Not at all. Not ever.

But . . ." He swallowed. "He *is* the king. And the one man who tried to stand against him just wound up with his head in a basket. So . . ." He drifted off, and I knew that the sentence would never be finished.

"Could I have some more water?" The words tumbled out perfunctorily. I felt too numb to think. The deaths that afternoon had been the worst I'd ever witnessed, and I couldn't stop seeing them. The executions played on an endless loop in my mind. I watched over and over again as Bertie slaughtered Baudouin's family.

Bertie.

My Bertie.

I tried to remember him as he'd been before, when we were young, before he'd been conscripted into a god's service, before he'd sliced up his body in the name of his newfound faith, but I couldn't do it. All I saw was the man who'd stood before the executioner's block, carrying out the orders of a vengeful king gone mad.

Marnaigne *was* mad. Of that I had no doubt.

The deathshead had been right.

He was volatile, dangerous. The Shivers had changed something in him, breaking parts of his mind, altering him in ways no one could have foreseen.

And I could have prevented it all. Today's deaths were on my hands. Whether their rotting spirits followed me or not, those ghosts would haunt me for the rest of my too-long life.

"How are you feeling now?" Leopold asked. He shifted his weight on the bed, as if making a move to rise and leave me, but stayed instead.

There was no way to truthfully answer that. Not at this court. Not with King Marnaigne as he was now, so jumbled in his emotions and paranoia that it was as though he was at war with himself.

No. The only way to make it out intact was to go along with him, appease his better side, then run at the first chance. There was nothing for me here any longer, and I already felt I was on borrowed time. Marnaigne would think up some sickness to worry over and demand that I fix him, but without my gift, without being able to see the cure, I'd fail time and time again. There would be no sympathy from this new version of the king.

I now feared his disappointment more than I worried about pleasing my godfather.

I reached for the silver compact mirror on my nightstand and studied my reflection. My face was pale and my eyes dark with worry. "At least tonight's ball is a masquerade."

Leopold looked horrified. "You're not going to that, are you?"

I drew my legs out of the bedsheets before swinging them to the ground. "Your father expects it."

"There will be hundreds of courtiers packing the hall. He couldn't possibly notice your absence. And as you said, it's a masquerade."

"He'll expect me there," I said. "And the last thing I want is for him to find offense with me."

"I suppose all of us are dancing to the music of someone else's making here," he murmured. I'd never heard him sound so bitter. "Do you always do what's expected of you?"

Leopold's words were spoken in a voice so low I strained to make them out and then spent too long wondering if I'd actually heard them at all.

With a sigh, he put his hands down to push himself from the bed, and our fingers brushed against one another. It was just a light touch, a whisper of skin against skin, but it sent a shiver down my spine.

"I don't," I admitted, daring to look up and meet his gaze. "I used to. Always. But then . . ." I trailed off, unable to continue.

But then I gave up one of my lives for your father.

But then I sentenced your uncle and his family to death.

But then I broke my godfather's heart.

"Why are you here?" It wasn't what I meant to say, but it fell out and I couldn't take it back.

"What do you mean?"

"There are any number of people who could be here right now, who could have brought me back and watched over me. But . . . you're here. And they're not."

"They're not," he agreed. "I was worried. About you, yes," he added before I could pry for clarification. "And no, I don't know why. I don't know why I notice the way you eat or the colors of the ribbons in your hair. I don't know why my eyes search for you at every function and why my heart feels lighter once you're found. But they do and I do and, Hazel, I . . . it was frightening to watch you faint this afternoon, to see you so vulnerable and helpless. Especially when I know that you help everyone around you. And so . . . so I wanted to be the one to help you." He let out a rushed breath. "And it felt good to do that. And I want to go on feeling good. Especially today. Especially after Papa . . ." He swallowed. "There's so much of my life I *haven't* felt good about, that I *don't* feel good about. But none of that seems important when I'm helping you."

His honesty undid me, erasing any breezy comment I might make to defuse the rising tension. It felt as though every molecule of air was stacked around us, building an impenetrable wall, trapping us in too tight a space, in too close a confine.

"I don't . . . I didn't mean to make you uncomfortable," he

continued. "I just . . . you're the only one in the world I feel like I can share my honest thoughts with. But perhaps I was too brash in speaking them all."

Before I could think better of it, before reason could dissuade me, I leaned forward and kissed him.

My daring caught us both by surprise. A startled noise choked deep in Leopold's throat, but I couldn't retreat and apologize—again—because his hands were suddenly tangled in my hair, bringing me closer. He held me with remarkable tenderness, cupping the curve of my face like a long-treasured prize, a thing hoped for and happily gained. I let out a sigh as his lips left mine, pressing themselves to my forehead and eyelids, my temples, even the tip of my nose.

"You've no idea how much I adore these freckles," he murmured, whispering his words across their scattered dots, his voice warm and low and so full of desire.

There are so many temptations to lure a young man off his path, don't you agree?

Marnaigne's voice echoed through my mind, but I pushed it back into the dark recesses with a reckless shove, longing to forget both the king and whatever plan he had for the boy I was kissing.

With brazen fingers, I ran my hands up Leopold's chest, feeling his heart race beneath the fine wool uniform, under the medals and insignia, and then grabbed hold of his collar and pulled him back to me.

With a dark chuckle, he moved his mouth over mine. I answered with unchecked hunger, opening my lips so that I could taste him.

"Hazel," he whispered around kisses.

I didn't respond but shifted positions, tracing my lips along the sharp curve of his jaw, pressing a reverent kiss on the small scar just below his earlobe, before working my way down the length of his throat. I smiled as I felt him swallow.

Kissing Kieron had never felt like this.

Kieron had been sweet and light. His kisses promised we'd have a lifetime together. They were fervent but gentle. Respectful.

I didn't want Leopold's respect. I didn't want him promising our lives entwined.

That was impossible.

But I also wanted more of his mouth against mine. More of those little strangled noises rising from deep in his chest. I wanted to push him back onto the bed and crawl on top of him until he somehow stopped this aching need blossoming in my middle.

I couldn't have a lifetime, but I could have this moment.

I wanted his now.

"Hazel," he repeated once more, firmly this time, cupping my jaw and holding me back so that our eyes met. "I'm delighted by this turn of events, truly I am."

"But?" I asked, and the flames flickering in me dampened, leaving me cored and hollow.

"You've had a hard day. You need rest," he added quickly, talking over the protest rising in me. "Especially if . . ."

"If?"

"If you obstinately plan on attending the masquerade tonight. I don't want my dance partner swooning in the middle of the farandole." Leopold leaned in, touching his forehead to mine as he whispered, "Of course, if she did, I'd have to carry her back to her rooms to make sure she got a proper night's sleep."

His lips roamed over mine once more, with a maddening softness that made my toes curl.

"Is anything with you ever proper?" I asked.

"You tell me," he murmured, deepening the kiss.

I felt lightheaded and giddy, close to another swoon as my words fell into his mouth. "Is this really happening?"

His finger grazed my cheek, setting my blood to sizzle. "I truly hope so."

As much as I wanted to push away worries of King Marnaigne and the instructions he'd explicitly bid me follow, they wouldn't retreat. "But your father . . ." I gasped as Leopold pressed his lips to my throat. "He won't like this. He won't—"

With a sigh, Leopold sat back, creating an expanse of air between us that felt as wide as a canyon. "After everything we saw today, I can honestly say I don't give a damn what my father likes. I want you on my arm tonight. I want you on my arm every night. Will you save me your first dance?"

I knew I shouldn't say yes. I knew I shouldn't do anything to encourage this heated yearning building between us. Ignoring Marnaigne was playing with fire, a dangerous one that could blaze out of control, scorching the earth and everything it touched until there was nothing left but ash.

Still, I could not find it within myself to tell Leopold no.

"I wouldn't share it with anyone but you," I promised, smiling at the twinkle in his eye, feeling suddenly shy. "My mask and dress are in the armoire. If you need help finding me tonight."

"Oh, Hazel." He grinned, pressing a trio of kisses across my cheek and then crossing to the door. "I'll always know it's you."

CHAPTER 48

Bellatrice had picked out our gowns for the masquerade, spending a full week dragging us from one atelier to another, all across the city. She'd examined hundreds of renderings and fabric swatches, determined to find the most exquisite masterpieces for us to wear, ensuring our names would be on the lips of every society matron and our appearance at the forefront of the minds of their handsome, eligible sons.

Unlike the parties we'd attended earlier in the season—each vying to have the most over-the-top and spectacular theme—the only thing to pay homage to tonight was the Marnaigne name itself. Everyone was to don their best black-and-gold finery, showing support for and allegiance to their most triumphant monarch.

Wanting herself to shine brightest, Bellatrice had selected the more daring of the designs—a gown with a sheer fitted bodice and a full skirt made of layers and layers of flesh-colored tulle. Dozens of black flocked-velvet snakes were carefully stitched into the netting, twisting artfully through the skirts and across her bodice, barely covering her nipples. One serpent wound about her neck before plunging into the deep V of her cleavage with a bold flick of its threaded tongue. Bellatrice's maid, Cherise, had let out a gasp of dismayed delight after spotting the wicked creature.

Bellatrice's smile had been noticeably subdued.

I watched her carefully in her giant dressing mirror as Cherise stabbed hairpins into the sweep of my updo, attempting to keep my halo tiara in place. Bellatrice had insisted I borrow one of hers to complete my look, choosing a delicate headdress with golden rays radiating from its arch, each topped with dazzling celestial spangles. I couldn't fathom the number of jewels currently atop my head, each winking with far too much luster to ever be mistaken for paste.

My dress hung off me like liquid gold, giving me a far more festive appearance than my mood prescribed. The sparkling lamé wrapped around my torso with an asymmetric sunburst of pleats that left my shoulders and back bare and luminous, thanks to a dusting of pearlescent powder.

Though my black agar tonic had put an end to the Shivers, glittering skin was now macabrely vogue throughout Châtellerault, prompting dressmakers to dip their bodices lower and lower to show off greater swaths of sparkles.

Bellatrice had opted for a flashy smear of gold over her collarbones, lips, and eyelids and was now absentmindedly dipping her hands into a pot of paint. The shimmering cosmetic gave the impression of gloves and imbued her with an otherworldly glamour.

"I should have put my mask on first," she realized, waving her hands back and forth to dry them. Her sigh was heavy.

"I'll handle that for you, milady," Cherise promised, jabbing one last pin in my hair. "How does that feel, Mademoiselle Trépas?"

I tilted my head from side to side. "If it should fall off, the fault will be entirely my own."

"Or your dance companion's," Bellatrice predicted. Her words were witty but her tone sounded hollow. "They're all perfectly dashing, but I can't imagine any of our esteemed soldiers will make for graceful partners."

"Not even Mathéo?" I asked, trying to nudge her into a cheerier mood. I picked up my mask—a shimmering domino of hammered gold with black painted stars—and tied it in place.

"Especially Mathéo."

Cherise laughed, fitting a thin strip of black tulle over the princess's eyes. Bellatrice fussed at the mirror for a moment before nodding to the maid and dismissing her from the room.

I waited until I heard the door click shut before speaking, keeping my words hushed. "Are you all right?"

For the barest moment, I saw her freeze, her spine growing rigid, but she immediately shook it off and leaned back against the elegant slope of her chair, peering at me thoughtfully. "You should have gone with the gold dust instead of that opalescent shimmer."

"Bells . . . ," I began worriedly.

She sighed, annoyed at my persistence. "I need to find a husband, Hazel. Tonight."

It was such an unexpected turn of topic, I could only raise my eyebrows in response.

"I'm twenty-three," she went on. "I'm tired of being kept at court with no word of when that may change, if ever. First we were in mourning, and then there was the war and I thought perhaps Papa was keeping me here should something happen to Leo, you know, at the front."

She paused, arranging her face into a look of expected contrition.

"It's a terrible thing to contemplate, of course, but if Papa no longer had a male heir, he would be forced to pass the crown to his eldest child . . . me," she added unnecessarily. "But now the war is over, and the threat to Leo is gone, and I . . . I just need to get out."

Marnaigne had made it clear he knew exactly what was meant to happen in Leopold's life. It seemed impossible he hadn't laid out Bellatrice's with as much foresight.

"Why the sudden rush? The war has only just ended. There's sure to be dozens of parties all season long. You want to find the right man, not just any man."

Bellatrice looked back to the dressing table mirror, her expression impossibly sad. She touched the corner of her lips with her knuckle. "If only I'd been born a boy . . . ," she whispered.

I knelt beside her feet, yards of shining fabric piling up between us like a cloud. I reached out, taking her gold-flecked hand in mine. "You know you can tell me anything. What's bothering you?"

Her eyes fell on me, and even with the obscuring bit of tulle, I could see they were round and glassy. The princess was close to tears.

"I need to get out of here, Hazel," she whispered in a quick rush. "This afternoon showed me that we're not safe here. None of us are, but especially . . ." She stopped short, weighing out her next words. "Me. I'm not safe. Not anymore."

I frowned. "What do you mean?"

Bellatrice blew out a long breath, looking queasy. "There was a rumor, years ago, that I . . ." She leaned close to me, whispering her next words. ". . . that I might not actually be Papa's daughter."

I couldn't help my gasp of surprise. "What?"

She nodded, her eyes darting toward the door as if she'd heard Cherise return. Silent seconds ticked by before she continued. "There was talk that Mama and Uncle Baudouin had been . . . particularly close friends. That's why he left court after I was born . . . when my eyes changed."

"Your eyes?"

Her knees jangled with uncharacteristic nerves, bumping her vanity. "They say all babies are born with blue eyes, you know? And mine were, at first. Mama said they were every bit as blue as Papa's, that I was a Marnaigne through and through. But when I was about a year old, they started to change, lightening to green."

"Does Baudouin have green eyes?" I asked, then blanched. "Did."

"He did, yes," she agreed. "It took Papa some time to notice, but when he did . . ." She blinked and a tear fell on the net of her mask. "Mama tried to smooth it over. She swore to every single one of the gods that her grandfather had had eyes as green as jade, but the damage was done. Baudouin left court and Papa never spoke to him again. Not until this morning. Not until Papa vowed to kill off every member of his lineage. A lineage that probably includes me, no matter what Mama said."

"Your perfume bottle," I murmured, recalling the odd comment Bellatrice had made here in this room, so many months ago. "Your mother used to call you her little diamond because you were hers and hers alone."

She nodded reluctantly. "You have no idea how much I wish she were here now. She could make everything better. She could help divert his moods. But it's just us." She blinked several times, trying to clear the tears from her eyes before more fell. "You can't breathe a word of this to anyone. Ever. But especially now." She shook my hands in hers and squeezed tight. The gold paint between us dug into my palms like shards of glass. "Please, Hazel."

"Never. You have my word," I swore.

She licked her lips. "Good. Just let me dance tonight, Hazel. Let me be as carefree and foolish as any other girl there. Let me find a man who thinks me witty and charming and will get me out of this palace alive. Please."

"But if we could only—"

I stopped short as Cherise bustled back in, carrying with her Bellatrice's tiara on a tufted pillow. Immediately, Bellatrice turned to her vanity and began dabbing at her cheeks.

"Is everything all right, milady?" the maid asked, catching sight of the princess's red eyes.

"Of course," she snapped with a testy façade. "Only you tied my mask on too tight and now I've got this shimmering mess in my eyes."

Cherise scurried to the bathing chamber for water, murmuring a dozen apologies.

"Tell me, Hazel," Bellatrice went on, her voice bright and inviting and giving away nothing of her true state of mind. It also sounded too loud, raised so that Cherise could hear her in the other room. "Is there anyone you're hoping to dance with tonight?"

In the mirror, our eyes met, open and honest for one painfully brief moment, before an aggressively pleasant expression settled over her face. It radiated lighthearted gaiety and would be the most impenetrable mask she'd don that night.

CHAPTER 49

THE GRAND CHAMBERLAIN ANNOUNCED THE NAME OF every guest as they entered the hall, and his voice boomed proudly over the din of the revelers who had already made their way into the ballroom. I hadn't been announced myself yet—as an esteemed member of the king's circle, I would follow with other nobles and council members—but I wandered about the hall anyway, admiring its transformation.

Long tapestries depicting a triumphant Marnaigne bull hung between black marble pillars, and there were heavy bowers of gilt flowers swagged everywhere the eye could see. Hundreds of golden candelabras held thousands of lit tapers, each made of onyx-colored wax. The air shimmered with their heat, giving a hazy, dreamy atmosphere to the night, filling it with the promise of provocative things to come.

Though the hall was just half full, there was a palpable buzz building as couples strolled through the crowds, searching for friends to see and be seen with. Women in enormous gowns of taffeta and satin brocade preened and made last-minute adjustments to their companions' masks. Heads tossed elaborate feathered fascinators this way and that, and the candles caught the sparkle of so many jewels, both real and paste, that I felt as if I'd stared directly into the sun.

You'd never guess that only hours ago, these well-dressed party-goers had cheered, watching as a family was publicly executed.

"It all looks so lovely!" cried a small voice, and I looked down to see Princess Euphemia standing beside me. She wore a dress of deep charcoal with an old-fashioned black tulle ruff, full of extravagant pleats and embellished with onyx paillettes along its edges. Her mask was little more than a piece of black lace covering her entire face, its ends artfully pinned to her shining curls.

"Phemie! What are you doing here? I thought everyone was to enter later on, with your father."

"You're not supposed to know who I am!" she protested, pointing to the mask. She sighed. "Papa said I'm too little to stay for the whole party, but he let me come look at everything before it's too crowded." Beneath the lace, I could see a pout beginning to form. "I always miss the fun!"

"Don't be silly," I said, and knelt down so we were eye to eye. "I think you're the lucky one tonight. Balls and parties are never as fun as you imagine they'll be. Feel how warm it is in here already?"

She nodded suspiciously.

"Now imagine how it will be later tonight when there're hundreds more people, dancing and sweating and stinking the whole room up! And look at all that champagne," I went on, pointing to one of the banquet tables, where a stacked arrangement of crystal coupes towered. "All the grown-ups will have too many of those and laugh too loudly and step on everyone's toes. Oh, how my poor feet will ache tomorrow!"

Despite her best efforts to keep her frown, Euphemia giggled.

"And you, you get to go upstairs and put on a comfortable nightgown and eat macarons while Margaux tells you bedtime stories. That sounds like a perfect night to me."

"But I'll miss all the dancing," she murmured sadly, her eyes fixed on the handful of couples already waltzing about the room as the orchestra played softly underneath the grand chamberlain's announcements. "Papa said I could dance once with him but then I have to go to bed."

I mulled this over, looking as thoughtful as I could beneath my own mask. "Oh, that's really too bad. . . . You see, I'm actually in need of a dance partner myself." I fumbled for the little booklet hanging from my wrist on a black ribbon and opened it, revealing the rows of empty lines. "See? My second dance is wide open."

"I could dance with you!" Euphemia suggested, brightening. "If Papa says yes!" Without waiting, she took the dangling pencil stub in her hand and scrawled her name across the second line. She opened up her own dance card and proceeded to fill in my name, beaming.

"Papa is sure to say yes," a voice said behind us. "Especially when I explain that I've already claimed you for the third." Leopold stepped out of the crowd and bent to write his initials with a theatrical flourish.

"Thank you, Leopold!" she exclaimed, leaping up to hug him.

"Leopold?" he asked, playfully aghast. "I'm not Leopold. I'm a handsome lothario, come from afar with the intention of dancing with every pretty girl I see. Can't you tell by my mask?"

He'd certainly done his best to look the part. Leopold was delightfully undressed, wearing only a fitted striped vest over his shirt, allowing the fine lawn of its sleeves to billow like a romantic notion of a bygone era. His mask was black velvet, shot through with golden threads, like lightning during a summer storm.

My face warmed just looking at him. Only hours before, I'd been kissing this rakish devil—*He kissed me!* my mind sang out—as we tussled in the tangle of my bedsheets. I wanted to laugh at the unexpectedness of it all. I wanted to shout my befuddlement to the heavens. I wanted to kiss him again, right then and there, consequences be damned.

Euphemia giggled, bringing me back to the moment, and Leopold glanced my way, eyes sparkling beneath his domino. With a hum of appreciation, his eyes roved over me, taking in the crown and the cut of my dress before spotting the dance card swinging from my right arm.

"And you, pretty miss? Might you be in need of a dance partner?"

He took my hand, bringing my fingers to his lips before flipping through the booklet. My breath caught as his thumb traced an absentminded circle on the soft skin of my inner wrist. Could he feel how my heart raced as I imagined where his hands might roam while we were on the dance floor?

"Oh dear," he murmured, keeping his voice playful for Euphemia. "Your card is nearly empty. This won't do at all." He took up the little golden pencil and proceeded to fill in every line with his initials. "Much better," he announced once he was done.

"Are you certain I want to spend so much of my evening dancing with you?" I teased. "Some might say your zeal borders on presumption."

"Are there other ways we might spend the evening instead?" he asked with a wicked smile.

"Oh, but you have to dance!" Euphemia said seriously, blessedly oblivious to her older brother's inference. "Leopold is the best dancer! He won't step on your feet no matter how much champagne he has. Dance with Leopold and then you'll have fun tonight too. Even without the macarons and bedtime stories."

"Bedtime stories?" he echoed, raising his eyebrows as his grin widened.

"Do you really think so, Euphemia?" I asked, ignoring both Leopold and the nervous flutters he inspired.

The little princess stamped her foot with theatrical discontent. "You're not supposed to know who I am!"

Aloysius suddenly appeared at Leopold's shoulder. "Your Royal Highness. Your Royal Highness," he added, spotting Euphemia. "And . . . Mademoiselle Trépas," he said, squinting to ascertain my identity under the mask. "We're beginning to line up for the king's entrance."

With efficiency, Aloysius led us through the crowd, guiding us out a side door I'd never before noticed and leading us through a maze of halls until we arrived at an intimate parlor just off the ballroom, steps from the grand staircase.

Marnaigne was already there, dressed in a fine suit of amber wool. A cape, black velvet with ermine trim, hung from his shoulders, suspended by a massive chain of gold medallions. Bright tourmalines, as pale as freshly churned butter, winked from their centers, and he was again wearing the Imperial Crown. His face glowed with a wide smile, and I could hardly believe he was the same man who'd put a family to death hours before.

"Your Majesty," I murmured, and dipped into a low curtsy.

"Hazel! How well you look this evening. Lovely, lovely," he praised me approvingly.

"What about me, Papa?" Euphemia asked, racing into his arms.

"You?" he asked, hoisting her into the air and spinning her

around so that her full skirts flew out in a flurry of ruffles. "I'm afraid to admit I don't know who you are!"

Euphemia tore away her mask, mussing her coiled hair and laughing with delight. "It's me!" Her cheeks were red and her eyes burned bright with the evening's excitement.

"So it is!" he exclaimed. "You look so wonderfully grown-up and sophisticated, I hardly recognized you."

"If I'm so very grown-up now, may I stay at the party longer? For three dances? Please? Look!" She held up her wrist, allowing her father to skim over Leopold's and my initials.

"Two dances claimed already!" he marveled. "I suppose I need to secure my spot before someone else tries to take it, hmm?" With bold strokes, he scrawled his name upon her first dance before setting her down. "Hazel, I do want to make sure to have a moment with you as well. Which dance would you prefer?"

Before I could stop him, the king took up my wrist and opened the booklet.

"Why, it's nearly full already!" he exclaimed, laughter booming from his chest. "Though I'm not surprised in the least. Actually . . . it seems your whole night has been claimed. . . ." He paused, scanning the list. I could tell the exact moment he noticed that the dances had been claimed by the same set of initials. His gaze snapped to Leopold, standing in the corner, chatting with Aloysius. "I see."

Marnaigne turned his attention back to me, his eyes running over my gown and up to Bellatrice's headdress of stars pinned in my hair, and I knew exactly what he saw: a girl playing at dress-up, a little nothing plucked from the depths of the Gravia, suddenly elevated to heights beyond all expectation. It didn't matter that I'd saved him; it didn't matter that he continued to rely on me.

I wasn't who he wanted for his son.

And in the end, that was all that mattered.

"His Royal Highness was far too kind and terribly exuberant," I said with a light smile, trying to mend the damage I saw playing out over Marnaigne's face. It wasn't anger, not yet, but it was coming. I needed to divert the rage before it broke. I needed to smooth everything over, show him it was a simple misunderstanding, assure him there was nothing to worry over. "My . . . my third dance is open. I would be most honored to share it with you, René."

I used his given name on purpose, hoping to remind him that he liked me, that he trusted me. I wanted him to remember all the time we'd spent together, all the ways I'd helped him. But he dropped my hand, letting the dance card sway between us, treacherous as a snake.

"This will not happen," he hissed, leaning in so that only I was shocked by the sudden vitriol in his tone. His words burned like acid. "Do you understand me, healer? He is not for you. If you don't put a stop to this"—he swiped at the dance card, tearing it from its ribbon, and it landed open upon the carpet, revealing the long line of Leopold's initials—"I'll put a stop to you."

"Your Majesty . . . ," I beseeched, tongue-tied and fumbling, but his attention snapped to Bellatrice as she entered the room, wafting in on her cloud of perfume. Her eyes had a far-off, dreamy look, and I worried she'd already begun sampling the champagne. Or something even stronger.

"You're late," he snapped.

She started to laugh and then hiccupped. "It's impossible for me to be late. We're the hosts of this grand affair."

"I wanted you here ten minutes ago, and instead Aloysius had to track you down like a bloodhound, like you were nothing more than a common criminal— *What* are you wearing?"

Leopold's eyes darted to mine. *What is going on?* he mouthed.

I couldn't do anything but frown.

Bellatrice glanced at her dress, lingering at the forked tongue of the snake between her breasts. "Oh, this?" She spun in a circle. "Do you like it?"

Before King Marnaigne could start in on his eldest, Euphemia grabbed his hand and gently swung their arms back and forth.

"Is it almost time for the dancing, Papa?" she asked, looking up at him, her expression hopeful and guileless.

The entire room seemed to freeze, waiting for the king's response.

Finally, a smile returned to his lips, and I wanted to hug the princess.

"Yes," he announced, all traces of his temper vanishing in an instant. "Yes. Let us greet our public, and the dancing can then begin!"

CHAPTER 50

IN THE END, I WAS NOT ON LEOPOLD'S ARM FOR THE first dance.

We left the parlor in an orderly line, arranged and nervously fretted over by Aloysius.

First were a number of pages, young sons of the oldest families of Martissienes. Next came a chorus of small girls in gowns far too large for them to comfortably manage. They tossed yellow rose petals along the path the king would take, carpeting his steps with fragrant decadence.

A bright fanfare of trumpets indicated that the true procession was about to begin, and the crowd fell to a hush, waiting for their king's arrival.

Marnaigne went down the grand staircase ahead of us all, with Leopold only a step behind him. Bellatrice was next, then Euphemia, hand in hand with Margaux.

I admit, I studied the back of the oracle's robes with wounded scorn. *Her* spot near the royal family was secure, granted without a second thought, while mine felt suddenly precarious, about to be snatched away.

I'll put a stop to you.

What had Marnaigne meant by that? Would he have me sent from the palace? Exiled from Martissienes? Hoisted onto the same platform as Baudouin, my neck laid on the block as Bertie brought an axe down?

I shuddered, wanting to turn and run, but Aloysius pushed me forward into a group of dukes and duchesses. The king's ministers of finance and foreign affairs followed closely behind, making escape impossible.

By the time I'd made my way down the staircase, the royal family was deep in the ballroom, greeting guests with smiles and nods as Marnaigne led them ever closer to the throne. As he ascended the steps of the raised dais, the orchestra gracefully brought their song to an end and the room fell into complete silence.

"Friends," the king greeted his guests, holding out his arms. All traces of his earlier ire were erased, and his smile was warm and paternal. "It gives me great pleasure to welcome you here tonight, to commemorate—to celebrate—the end of the uprising, the end of our struggles, the end of the war itself!"

A wave of applause broke out, and the king paused appreciatively. Shrill whistles came from a group of soldiers in the far corner of the room, eliciting titters of laughter and echoed attempts.

The crowd was uproarious, and I found the jubilation grating; it rubbed my wounds raw and spurred on the sense that I needed to leave, needed to run. Their smiles were so wide, their exhilaration completely over-the-top. There was a current running through the ballroom, a hunger to please the king at all costs, a righteous fervor that felt strong enough to tip the mood from revelry to mania.

"This past year has been hard, unimaginably hard, on us all. There was uncertainty and strife, sickness and discord, but time and time again we have triumphed. We put an end to the Shivers, and today, with my treacherous brother's death, we have put the last of this year's difficulty and fear into the past. Martissienes looks forward to a bright future, one blessed by the gods with fortune good and prosperous. And so, my dear friends, let us celebrate! Let us feast and laugh, let us rejoice and raise toasts for those who cannot. Let us honor their sacrifices, let us drink to their memories. But let us also remember that we are alive and we are the victors, and we should be reveling. Merrymaking! Dancing! Let the masquerade commence!"

The room burst into another round of applause, and the orchestra hastily shuffled through their pages.

Leopold made a motion to step off the platform, to head toward me, but Marnaigne stopped him. Scanning the crowd, the king pointed to an ambassador newly come to court. Beside the man was his very pretty daughter. With a flick of his wrist, the king beckoned her over, then all but pushed her and Leopold onto the dance floor.

Mathéo swept up the steps and gave the king a gallant bow before asking if he could have Bellatrice's first dance. Seemingly content with the soldier's show of deference, Marnaigne consented, and the pair hurried off.

Euphemia grabbed her father's hand and tugged him out as the song began, lest they miss a moment of the dance.

This was my chance. I could leave now without anyone noting my absence. I could go up and lock myself in my chambers and have a good cry before deciding what I was going to do next. I could pack. I could scream. I could take off this ridiculous tiara and dress and feel like myself once more.

But my feet stayed in place, my attention fixed upon the dancing couples and how much my pride hurt.

I knew I was not the sort of girl the king would select for Leopold. I could not offer alliances or dowries, easy charms or the promise of beautiful children. But I'd thought Marnaigne liked me well enough to treat me better than this, casting me to the shadows with such severe derision.

It stung, how wrong I'd been.

I was nothing more than a particularly gifted servant, called upon when her services were needed. A healer and nothing else.

I thought of the candle I'd given him—*the candle I wasted on him*—and wanted to cry. Merrick had been right. I should have listened to him, listened to the deathshead.

I felt miserable and flushed, my blood boiling. My dress felt too tight, and I had the urge to pick up the shiny skirts and run, run from the court, run from the city, run to a new life in a little town where no one knew me, no one knew my past, no one knew all the horrible things I had done.

Do it, a tiny voice within me said. *You could do all that and more. There is no shame in turning on those who turn from you.*

Leopold and the ambassador's daughter danced by me. I felt his eyes search for mine, but I couldn't bear to meet them, couldn't bear to tear my gaze from her, from her perfect heart-shaped face, her dimpled cheeks, and her demurely lowered lashes. She radiated a grace and confidence I would never possess. She looked at home on Leopold's arm, as if she'd been born to be there, and in a way, I suppose she had.

Not like me.

My lashes grew wet as tears welled in my eyes. My vision blurred, warning me they were about to fall. I turned from the dance floor, searching for the closest exit, the fastest way to flee. I would not give King Marnaigne the satisfaction of seeing me cry.

Before I could make my escape, I felt a small hand close over mine.

The first dance had already come to an end, and Euphemia had found me, ready for ours.

"Where are you going, Hazel?" she asked, her blue eyes filled with concern. "Don't you want to dance?"

I blinked hard, hoping my mask would catch any falling tears. My smile felt shaky, and I was certain she'd see through its false brightness. "Of course I do! I was just on my way to find you!"

"I was out there!" she laughed, pointing. "With Papa. Come."

I tried to keep an eye out for the king as she pulled me to the center of the dance floor, stopping beneath one of the chandeliers, but he'd been swallowed by a crowd hungry to hear his take on Baudouin's final moments.

"Are you feeling all right, Euphemia?" I asked as she positioned herself in front of me. Even through her lace covering, I could see that her cheeks were flushed, and her eyes seemed glassy.

"You were right!" she exclaimed, fanning her hands at her face. "It's too warm in here!"

"I told you!" I tried to laugh.

My heart panged as I watched her skip around me. I knew with utter clarity that this was the last time I would see Euphemia. Once our dance was over, I was going to escape to my rooms, pack a bag, and slip into the night. I didn't know where I was going, but it didn't matter. Any place was better than here, with a king's temper swaying from exuberant highs to dangerous lows, close to a boy I'd come to care for but could never be with.

I wasn't concerned with the details of my flight. I had money, more than enough to get me out of Martissienes. It didn't matter after that. Healers were needed the whole world over. No matter where I went, I would be able to work, even without the added assurance of my gift. I could make a life for myself.

I distantly wondered when Merrick would find out, when he'd find me, and where I'd be when he did. I knew other countries had other gods, revering them for other reasons, but I'd always supposed they were just different iterations of the ones I already knew. Death was death, regardless of how one characterized him.

"Are *you* all right?" Euphemia asked, breaking into my dark thoughts. "Your eyes are all watery, Hazel."

I shoved away my plans and vowed to be present in the here and now, grounding myself in this dance, in these last moments with this little girl I'd come to think of as a sister.

The best sister I'd ever had.

"I'm fine," I promised, and impetuously picked her up, twirling her around and around in a close embrace. My exuberant gesture knocked both our masks off but allowed me to press a quick kiss to her temple. "I was just thinking how much I shall miss you once you've gone to bed."

She laughed, delighted, and threw her arms around my neck, prolonging our hug. I held her close as long as my arms could stand it, performing all the frenzied footwork of the dance while keeping her aloft. I could feel her chin resting on my collarbone as she watched the other dancers over my shoulder.

Eventually, her little body grew too hot and heavy. As the final notes of the song blessedly faded, I set her back on the floor, my spine aching.

"Thank you for such a marvelous dance," I said, wanting to give her a proper farewell without showing my intentions. "I will remember it always."

Euphemia had stooped to search the ground for our missing masks. Finding hers first, she pinned it back in place. "I don't see yours!" she worried. Glancing up, she brightened. "But, Hazel! You look so lovely tonight! You shouldn't hide under a mask anyway!"

I wiped my brow and cheeks, feeling the sheen of sweat from carrying her about the dance floor for so long. Beautiful was the last thing I felt in this moment.

"Oh, you mussed it," she fretted, grabbing my hand to show me a smear of gold powder across my palm.

"I'll go freshen up," I promised, glad to have an excuse to leave the ballroom. "And you need to go find Leopold before . . ." The shimmer of paint sparkled strangely in the light of the chandelier, and I frowned. "Before . . ."

Something twinged inside me, screaming to be noticed, and my words trailed off as I started to piece it together.

Gold.

There was gold on my hands. A burnished gold, fine and slippery.

But I hadn't been wearing gold.

Cherise had doused me in a pearlescent powder, gleaming like an opal. Bellatrice had said it clashed with my gown, but I'd thought it beautiful.

So where had the gold come from?

I looked down at my dress, wondering if the metallic threads could have somehow caused this. Or the inside of my mask. Or . . .

My eyes fell on Euphemia.

Little Euphemia, who had only moments before had her cheek pressed to mine.

Little Euphemia, all in black, without a speck of gold upon her.

Heart thudding with dread, I snatched the lace mask from her. She let out a cry of dismay and tried to grab her covering. As she struggled, three new streaks of Brilliance ran down her heated face.

CHAPTER 51

"I DON'T UNDERSTAND," THE KING SAID, REPEATING HIMself as he paced Euphemia's chambers. "I don't understand, *I don't understand!*" His muttered recitation grew to a roar as I bent over the little princess, rearranging a cooling compress on her forehead.

After seeing the streaks of Brilliance, I'd quickly ushered Euphemia from the ballroom, all but hauling her over my shoulder to her suite, and sent word to King Marnaigne.

By the time he arrived, I'd gotten her out of the heavy ball gown and into a nightdress. I hoped she'd be able to breathe easier in the thin lawn shift, but still she gasped for air, eventually falling into a hazy stupor of grumbled protests.

Even in her daze, her fingers twitched at angles strange and taut, tapping out a relentless rhythm against her sparkling duvet. There was a tic along her left cheekbone, and her toes quivered restlessly.

Safe along the edges of the room, two of her lady's maids fretted, wanting to help but terrified of catching the illness themselves. I longed to send them away, but the king held all authority.

"I've done everything right," he went on, striking at the backs of chairs, grabbing throw pillows and flinging them across the room. "I won the war. I destroyed every threat to our realm. I've done everything the gods have asked of me, and this is how I'm repaid?"

He growled, striking out at a little side table and sending its potted fern flying through the air. The vase shattered against the marble tiles.

One of the maids jumped into action, trying to clear the debris before King Marnaigne could pace through it. One of the shards sank into her fingertip, and she winced as droplets of blood dotted the floor.

I pushed myself from the bed, but Marnaigne blocked my path, a finger stabbing at my chest. "Not till you fix my daughter!"

"She needs stitches," I said, gesturing to the slick of blood.

"Then she can find assistance elsewhere!" He whirled on the maid. "Get out! Both of you, get out, and find somewhere else to be incompetent! You shan't darken my house any more with your idiocy."

The maid burst into tears as she fled the room, clutching her wounded hand to her chest. The second maid hurried after her, and I wanted to call after them, beg them to come back, because I was suddenly, horribly alone with the king.

He stood in the middle of the chaos he'd created, surveying the torn-apart room. His grim eyes fell upon Euphemia.

"It's the Shivers, isn't it?"

I swallowed, trying to find my voice. "I honestly don't know. At first glance, it would seem so . . . but there are things in Euphemia's case that I can't explain, that don't make sense. The Shivers starts off slowly—the muscle spasms, a dusting of Brilliance. But see how much is already coming out of her? She's nearly coated in it."

Marnaigne made a small pained noise of agreement.

"And she's burning up," I continued. "I've never seen patients with the Shivers have a fever. It could be a good sign . . . her body is fighting hard and strong . . . but her breathing . . ." As if on cue, Euphemia let out a harsh wheeze. "It *looks* like the Shivers, but it's acting like something else entirely."

Marnaigne sank into the nearest chair, like a marionette cut from its strings. The fury had left him, and he now seemed hollowed out, exhausted and grieved. "I'm being punished. Again."

"Oh no, Your Majesty. The gods didn't do this," I said, instinctively reaching out to reassure him. Just before I touched his back, I noticed my hands were covered in Brilliance, and I quickly pulled away.

"They did," he insisted. "They're punishing me for something I've done. For my faults. For my sins. For . . ." He trailed off, his eyes distant as he searched for a reason. He scratched his scalp, tugging at the ends of his hair. His fingers were trembling, not with an onslaught of the Shivers but with building frustration. "What did I do to deserve this? What did *she* do? She is an innocent. She couldn't have . . . No. It must be something else. It's a message for someone else." He muttered something under his breath too hurried to catch, but I heard him repeat it. Once, then twice, then again, becoming a series, a litany, a plea.

"A message?" I echoed, trying to stop him from spinning into another burst of anger.

Marnaigne nodded fervently. "The gods are sending me a sign.

Through Euphemia." He rose suddenly, his eyes darting about the room. "Something in my house is not right. Something in my realm is not as it should be. There's something I still need to do."

I took a step away, giving him a wide berth, as one would a dangerous animal. "I don't think that's what's—"

His gasp cut me off.

"Baudouin," he whispered. "I'm not finished with Baudouin."

Behind us, Euphemia's leg flopped heavily, kicking out at things unseen.

"Sire . . . you killed the duke this morning." I tried to keep my tone gentle, but it terrified me that he needed reminding.

"Yes." Marnaigne's zeal softened as his gaze drifted to the window.

I glanced back and forth between the king and his stricken daughter. Euphemia didn't have time for this.

I needed to get my valise. I needed to see if my black agar mixture would have any effect on Euphemia. But first—

"But I didn't kill all of him."

The king's words wiped away every bit of momentum I felt. I felt like a runner in a three-legged race, sprinting toward the finish line only to stumble and fall, caught on my partner's ankle. I narrowed my eyes, instantly wary. "What do you mean, Your Majesty?"

"Baudouin's seed. I haven't finished it all. I started," he said, turning from the window to pace, his energy frenetic. "I started this morning, but there's still more that needs to be wiped out. More that needs to be eradicated."

Bellatrice.

I shook my head, desperate to stop the direction of Marnaigne's thoughts. "No, Your Majesty. I'm certain Euphemia's sickness is not because of that."

He nodded. "It is. I can hear them whispering. *Kill the seed, save your daughter. Kill the seed, save . . .*" His pacing stopped, and as horrible as his manic frenzy had been, I found this sudden stillness even more alarming. "It's telling me to end it. Telling me to end her."

"Her?" I asked, still clutching the tiniest scrap of hope. Hoping I'd misunderstood, hoping the king wasn't completely mad, hoping that all of this could still be set right.

"That green-eyed snake," he hissed. "She lives under my roof, pretending she's one of us, pretending she's mine. And all the while she was plotting to undo me, plotting and scheming with her father." He breathed in sharply, aghast. "She killed Aurélie. She killed my wife. It was her all along. . . ."

"René," I said, all but shouting, trying to force him to meet my stare. "Bellatrice did not kill her mother. She has nothing to do with this. The gods have nothing to do with this."

"Then who does?" he snapped, his voice low and dangerous.

I swallowed the sob that wanted to rip from my throat. "People get sick. It's not a punishment. It's not a curse. It's just life. Some illnesses are cyclical. They come and go with the changing seasons and mutate. With all the warm weather recently, it could have . . ." I trailed off, sensing the problem with my logic. It didn't make sense. None of it did.

Euphemia *had* been whole and healthy only hours before. Now she lay shivering and sweating on her bedsheets, struggling for breath as more and more of the golden Brilliance wept from her skin.

Where had it come from? And would my tonic do anything against this new strain?

"I can't lose her," he said with grim finality, as if that was all he needed to do, as if this were any other edict he'd decided must be carried out. Proclaim it aloud and it would be handled. "I cannot lose her, Hazel."

"I know, Your Majesty. And I—"

"You have to save her. You have to cure her," he insisted, his eyes lighting upon me. It was the first time he'd truly looked my way since that terrible moment in the parlor before the ball.

"I will try to, of course. I will try and—"

"I don't want attempts," he snarled, cutting me off. "I want her well. Do that and I will give you anything you want. Money, jewels . . ."

"I don't need any of that."

I meant my words to be an assurance. I would do anything I could to save Euphemia, without question of payment. Seeing how tiny and frail she looked now undid me.

But when Marnaigne's eyes narrowed, hardening into small chips of blue, I understood how he'd heard them. He'd taken them as a refusal, as a play for something bigger, something more. Jaw clenched, he paused, weighing his next words.

"If you cure her, I will give you anything you want. Any*one* you want. Leopold," he added, throwing his son's name out as though it were nothing more than a bag of coins, a handful of baubles meant to bribe and entice.

I frowned in confusion. "Sir?"

He sighed, further explanation paining him. "Save Euphemia and I will see that Leopold proposes within a fortnight. You will be wed, and one day . . ." He sighed again. "One day you will be queen."

His words were madness. "I don't want that. I don't—"

"Oh, of course you do, Hazel," he snapped. "Everyone does. Girls clamor outside the palace grounds. Dukes travel from afar with their pretty daughters in tow. Scullery maids and kitchen wenches pour out of the woodwork, positioning and propositioning themselves to get closer and closer."

"That's not what I've done," I stated, my voice flat and cold.

Marnaigne snorted, unconvinced.

"It's not," I repeated with insistence. "You brought me here. You kept me here. I didn't even . . . I didn't even particularly like Leopold when I met him. I thought he was pompous and entitled and—"

"I've seen the way he looks at you," the king said firmly, and despite everything, my breath caught and a flush of heat broke over my cheeks.

Had he?

"Watching, watching, always watching. And I've seen the way you look at him," Marnaigne went on, his eyes flickering with too bright a shine. "So you do this thing for me, this *one little thing,* and he's yours. I will give it my blessing. I will welcome you into my family with open arms."

I nearly laughed aloud, stunned that he'd think I might wish to be any part of his family after all I'd witnessed that day.

"I don't want your bribes," I said, keeping my voice strong but even. It wouldn't serve me or Euphemia to spark his anger again. "I don't want Leopold, and I don't want to be a queen. But I will do everything I can to cure Euphemia. I care about her as if she were my own little sister. I don't want to see her sick or in pain. I . . ." Before I could stop myself, I reached out and fondly cupped her cheek. She looked so small and forlorn.

When the deathshead rose over her slumbering face, silent and leering, I was too surprised to make a sound.

"If you don't want it, that is your decision," King Marnaigne said, watching me with careful, guarded eyes, and I had the strangest sensation that he somehow knew what I'd seen. "But I will do *my* best to ensure you do *yours.*" His jaw tightened with resolution. "Starting with Bellatrice."

"Sire, no!" I cried in horror, spinning from Euphemia.

He was already in the hall. "If I cannot tempt your success, I will block any chance of your failure." King Marnaigne fumbled at the front of the door, and I heard a lock click. "If my daughter does not survive this . . . neither will you."

CHAPTER 52

I STOOD AT THE DOOR, TRACING ITS WOODEN GRAIN WITH my fingertips. I wanted to snort with laughter at how quickly everything had spiraled, to marvel that I'd ever thought I was in control to begin with.

I waited for the king to return and admit that he'd made a mistake, but the door remained shut.

I tried the handle, hoping, however foolishly, that I had heard wrong. I couldn't have heard the click of the lock, and I'd certainly not heard King Marnaigne threaten to kill me if I could not save his ailing daughter, then leave me without my valise or a single tonic or medicine with which to treat her.

Predictably, the handle did not twist.

"Sire?" I called. There would be no more *René,* no more pretense of familiarity with this madman. "Your Majesty?"

There was no response, and I slammed my curved palm against the door in frustration.

"Bellatrice?" I tried, knowing she could not possibly hear me, knowing she was dancing away her last few moments of normalcy.

Had Marnaigne already gone after her? Would she sense him coming? Would she be able to flee in time? Or would she be like me, unaware she was in a trap until it sprang shut?

"You can't keep me in here!" I howled, banging on the door again, over and over. I wanted to hear it shake in its frame, rattle and clatter and cause the whole castle to come running. But I could just make out the faint notes of a melody in the ballroom far below. The masquerade was still going on.

I hit the door one last time before giving up. Turning back, I restlessly scanned the chambers, searching, searching. I didn't know what I was looking for. A way to escape? Something to help Euphemia? A weapon with which to defend myself when the king returned?

There was no right answer. There was no one right thing to do.

I crossed to the princess's bed and perched on its edge, studying her. Brilliance pooled in all the recesses of her twitching face, down her cheeks and into her ears, along the dips of her clavicle.

How had she caught the Shivers? There'd not been a single case in months. I'd made sure that healers and doctors all over the capitol and surrounding areas were well stocked with black agar; that the pastes and tonics were sent to every province; that every village, however small, received instructions on how to fight it.

And it had been kept at bay. The reverents in the Rift burned sacrifices of gratitude each night, certain Félicité was finally showing a bit of favor after so many things had gone wrong.

And what I'd told Marnaigne was true: sicknesses were cyclical, often going dormant in warmer months when everyone was outside, breathing fresh air, eating newly grown greens and fruits, only to flare up again as winter set in.

But it was now spring. And no one around Euphemia had been sick.

None of that mattered. It didn't matter how she'd gotten sick. It didn't matter where or from whom. The Holy First had marked Euphemia with the deathshead. The little princess was meant to die.

If only I'd run when I'd had the chance. If only I hadn't stopped to have that one final moment with her. I could have been in a carriage halfway across the city by now. I'd have never known she'd gotten sick. I'd have never known I was meant to kill her.

Why?

Why hadn't I run?

Why was the Holy First giving me this assignment after nearly a year of seeing nothing?

My gift was gone, ripped away in a god's fit of castigation. Had I actually seen this deathshead or had it been a trick of the eyes, a moment of doubt brought on by too much stress?

Tentatively, I bent over Euphemia, bringing my hands to her face. I cupped her cheeks, heedless of the mess I was making, the Brilliance I smeared all over her and myself.

The deathshead appeared, covering her face, its skull a bleached white.

"Why?" I demanded out loud, an angry snarl, knowing the First would not answer. "Why now? Why her?"

I struck the mattress with my fist, lashing out at the bed because I could not fight a removed and aloof goddess. Euphemia made a small sound of protest and I wished I could take my outburst back, allowing her respite where I could.

I sat with her for a long while, watching her sleep, unable to offer help. I closed my eyes, listening to the husky rasp of her breathing. Had my valise been there, I would have made her a warm tea of jaggery and cumin, sprinkled with black pepper to help expel her congestion. I thought through all the ways I might try to treat her, all the remedies that would relieve her symptoms. But none of them mattered in the end. I had no supplies and one very insistent deathshead.

No matter how it would break my heart, I could not ignore it. The Holy First was giving me a second chance. She was giving me the opportunity to get back on track, to return to her and my godfather's good graces.

For Merrick's sake, I would not disappoint her again.

I sighed and opened my eyes, looking around the room for anything that would help me carry out this grim task. There would be no painless, easy slip into oblivion for Euphemia, not with my bag of potions and poisons so far from me.

My gaze fell upon the mountain of throw pillows she slumbered upon. There were dozens of them piled about. Ones covered in embroidery, ones beaded and ruffled. I picked up the largest of them, pleased to find it heavy with goose down.

Suffocation was a terrible way to die, but she was sleeping, at least, her eyes already closed. I'd hold the pillow over them and wouldn't have to see her look of betrayal. She'd never know it was I who'd done it.

Who'd killed her.

I sat back, hugging the pillow to my chest.

Could I kill her?

Snuffing out Kieron's candle had been brutally painful, but I hadn't seen him suffer. I hadn't heard his last gasps for air, I hadn't seen his limbs tremble and twitch. Truthfully, I wasn't sure what his death had even looked like.

Smothering Euphemia would not be like that. I'd see every

moment of it. I'd *hear* everything: the rustle of the bedsheets as she flailed, the frantic pounding of her feet as she fought to gain leverage, the terrible drop into silence. Those sounds would haunt me forever, even if her ghost could not.

I dug my fingers into the heft of the pillow, wanting to tear it apart. I hated the deathshead, hated that the First was back, asking me to do this. How much harm could this small girl possibly inflict on the world? How could it bid me over and over to kill the people I was meant to be closest with?

I wiped away a useless tear.

Tears could come later.

This was not the time to wallow. This was not the time to mourn.

I needed to be as pragmatic and efficient as possible if I was going to make it through the night with my own life intact.

I set aside my future murder weapon and examined Euphemia's room. Her chamber was on the fourth floor of the palace. The windows were unlocked and able to be swung open, but the parapet outside them was dangerously narrow, barely wide enough to stand upon tiptoe.

It would have to do.

Bellatrice's rooms were on the same side of the hall as Euphemia's. If I could make my way five windows over—or was it six?—I might be able to slip into her chambers and escape from there.

If her windows were unlocked.

If I could open them from the outside.

If I didn't fall to my death trying to get there.

If, if, if.

I pushed the worries from my mind. Little good could come from dwelling on all the things that could go wrong. I just needed to get into motion.

I needed to act.

Once I was far away from the palace, from this unhinged king, from the shell of this little girl, I could allow myself to fall apart. But not until then.

With a quavering breath, I approached Euphemia's side of the bed, pillow in hand. Brilliance had begun to spill from her mouth, running past her lips and down her chin in bold rivers of dark sludge.

"I'm so sorry, Phemie," I murmured miserably, lowering the pillow. "Please, please forgive me."

Across the room, I heard a squabble of loud voices shouting in the corridor, and then the door opened.

"No! Hazel! Stop!"

CHAPTER 53

Alarmed, I turned to see Margaux fumble past the guards flanking the entry. Once she was in, the door shut and the lock clicked back into place.

The oracle raced over and snatched the pillow from my hands.

"Don't—Hazel! Please don't!"

"What are you doing here?" I gaped, too surprised to put up a fight. "How did you know?"

"You can't do this," she said, squeezing the pillow tightly to her chest as if that was all it would take to stop me. "Euphemia is not meant to die. I had a vision."

Of course she'd known what I was about to do. Of course the Holy First had shown her. Nothing about this night was destined to be easy. I could almost hear Calamité laughing at me.

Except . . .

There was a prick of wrongness at the back of my neck, ticking, tapping.

"The Holy First sent you a vision?"

She nodded fervently, looking radiantly flushed, bursting with pious authority and hope. "She said that Euphemia was sick but that you're going to save her. She said that I'm to help you."

It didn't add up.

None of this did.

Merrick had made a bargain with the Holy First, allowing her to use me to save the lives of innocents. Why would she place a deathshead on Euphemia if she was going to show Margaux that I was meant to save her?

She wouldn't.

So who had seen the correct vision? Margaux or me?

I cupped the princess's cheek, watching as the skull blossomed over her. It was still there, staring up at me with the void of its empty eye sockets. Nothing had changed. My order was clear, even if Margaux was trying to muddle it up.

She could say the Holy First has declared the moon is made of pumpernickel and we all would have to believe it because no one can say otherwise.

Leopold had said that so many months ago as we returned from the Rift. He'd doubted Margaux from the very beginning, but I hadn't listened. I'd thought her an ally, a friend at court who was just like me. A thirteenth child, a marionette whose strings were pulled by our designated deities.

But what if Margaux had been the puppet master all along?

Just yesterday she'd talked the king into executing Baudouin and his family. What was she trying to get me to do now? I couldn't begin to guess what she was playing at, what her endgame was meant to be. But I knew I needed to be careful. I could give her no reason to think I suspected her of anything other than wanting the princess well.

Euphemia coughed, and a fresh wave of Brilliance poured from her mouth.

Margaux let out a sound of pained surprise. "Shouldn't you be treating her?"

I held out my hands helplessly. "In your vision, did the First show you how I'm supposed to save her? The king has locked me in here, and I don't have my bag. There's nothing I can do, and she's so terribly sick."

Margaux brightened. "But there is! I have your medicines!" She gestured to the satchel crossed over her chest with a long strap, hidden in the deep pleats of her layered robes. I'd not even noticed her wearing it till now.

I blinked in surprise. "Why would you have those?"

Margaux's smile was one of long-suffering patience. "I told you, the vision. I was at the ball—dancing with the prince, of all people—when I saw what was to happen. I knew you'd be trapped here, without your supplies." She frowned, a look of guilt crossing her face. "I took a bunch of things from your workroom. I hope I didn't make too much of a mess. I just wanted to grab whatever you might need quickly, so that you could fix all this." She motioned to Euphemia.

At face value, the story sounded believable, but it still clanged against me all wrong.

Margaux, dancing with the prince?

"That was clever thinking," I began slowly, unsure of how to handle this, what to do, what to say. "What did you bring?"

Margaux let out a sigh of relief and hoisted the satchel over her head. In her haste, part of the strap snagged at her neckline, pulling a button loose and exposing the hollow of her throat. It was the most undone I'd ever seen her. Her worry was palpable.

When I opened the bag, I was surprised to see it crammed full of vials and sachets, envelopes of herbs and powders. A whole chunk of black agar resin, a small mortar and pestle. Everything you'd need to treat someone with the Shivers, packed as thoughtfully and thoroughly as if I'd done it myself.

But Margaux couldn't have known the princess had been stricken with something that looked like the Shivers. Euphemia had been fine before the ball—a little fevered, a little bright-eyed, to be sure—but the Brilliance had not begun until she and I were on the dance floor. And I'd covered her face the moment I realized what was happening, racing her from the hall before anyone else could see and panic.

The only people who knew she was sick were me, the king, and the two maids he'd kicked out.

How had Margaux known?

"These are . . . These will be very useful," I said, rummaging through the bag and pulling out vials. Nothing within was an overt poison, nothing that would give Euphemia a quick death. I scanned my labels with a critical eye, pondering potential combinations. The pillow would probably be a quicker kindness.

"Such a blessing," Margaux murmured distractedly. Her eyes were fixed on Euphemia's chest, watching it rise and fall. "Are you starting treatments now? What can I do to help?"

She sounded in earnest, her concern most evident. There was an odd expression on her face, relief mixed with something bigger, darker.

Guilt.

My mind raced, trying to put together all the pieces I had, flipping them from this side to that, but I couldn't make everything fit. I couldn't see the full picture. Not yet. And I was running out of time.

I had no idea where the king was now, or if he'd found Bellatrice yet, but if there was a way, I needed to warn her. And I couldn't do it with Margaux watching my every move.

"Margaux?"

She looked up, dragging her gaze from the princess.

"How did you know Euphemia was sick?"

She frowned. "I told you. The vision."

I slowly shook my head. "I don't think that's true. I don't think any of your story is true."

She made an odd little noise, laughter mixed with disbelief. "Hazel, what do you mean? What could you possibly—"

"Euphemia isn't going to make it. If the Holy First had actually sent you a vision, you would have seen that. You would have seen me kill her."

Fear flashed through her eyes. "The pillow . . . I saw it in your hands when I arrived, but you wouldn't have really . . . Were you going to kill her? Euphemia? Truly?" She swallowed, waving her hands as if to waft the horrible thought from her. "It doesn't matter. I brought all the things you need to treat her. You have the medicines now. She's going to get well."

"Margaux, this isn't the Shivers. These medicines won't fix it."

For one slip of a moment, I could see her panic, her uncertainty. "They won't?"

"They could, maybe; I don't know. But what she has isn't the Shivers, and I won't—"

"Just fix her!" she demanded, striking the mattress with the thick flesh of her palm, her voice growing high and pitched with desperation.

We stared at each other with wide eyes. Margaux seemed as surprised by her outburst as I was. She let out a small laugh, running her hand up the side of her neck, fumbling with her neckline, thumbing a chain she wore as she sought to steady herself. Her fingers were trembling.

"I'm so sorry. That was uncalled for," she murmured, careful to regulate her tone more evenly. She raked her fingers through her hair, mussing the elaborate curls, and the necklace fell free.

A little bronze charm dangled from a matching chain. It sparkled in the room's candlelight.

My eyes narrowed.

Reverents of the Holy First wore silver. Margaux's fingers and wrists were covered in it, rings and bracelets all hammered from the finest sterling.

Bronze was the metal of . . .

The Divided Ones.

"What a pretty necklace," I said, keeping my voice light and innocent. "I've never noticed it before."

"Oh," she began, but stopped short, fingering the charm for a moment before tucking the chain away. As she parted the unbuttoned neckline of her robes, I saw a flash of red just under the hollow of her throat.

It was a line, thick and angry, and it looked like a burn or a welt.

Or one of the scars that covered my brother.

My brother, a member of the Fractured.

I glanced over the oracle's robes with fresh interest. Every inch of skin from the curve of her chin to the knuckles of her fingers to the tips of her boots was covered with layers and layers of thick fabric.

"An old family bauble," she said, patting at her bodice to make sure the necklace was well and truly covered. "I don't usually wear it, but since tonight was a special occasion . . ." She sighed, arranging her face into a look of contrition. "I'm sorry for yelling earlier. I'm just so worried about Euphemia. We need to—"

Without warning, I launched myself at her, knocking us both from the bed.

We fell in a tangled heap of twisted limbs as I fought against the long layers, trying to find the scar I'd glimpsed.

"Have you lost your mind? Hazel, what are you—" she started, struggling to defend herself.

I knew the instant she realized what I was doing. Her efforts to throw me off her escalated and she lashed out, swiping at me with curved fingers and flailing legs. One of her kicks landed a direct shot in my stomach and I doubled over, clutching my abdomen with one arm. When she tried again, I caught hold of her foot and hung on, flinging aside layers of gauze and brocade, ripping them in my attempt to reveal a long swath of bare leg.

I couldn't suppress my gasp.

Margaux's calf was broken into a dozen segments of mutilated flesh. Scars, thick and angry, crisscrossed her skin from ankle to thigh. The cuts were cruel and jagged, carved by hands that had been too small and too young to wield a blade so large.

"Oh, Margaux," I murmured, reaching out to her with sympathy even as I realized what the scars meant.

She flopped backward, trying to cover herself, but the scars could not be unseen.

"You're not an oracle," I said slowly. "Not for the Holy First. You're . . ."

"Fractured," she confirmed after a long, tense moment. She let out a curse, growling darkly.

I leaned back against the side of Euphemia's bed, suddenly exhausted. "You've been lying this whole time."

"No," she hurried to disagree, but then stopped short, looking lost and without a script to follow. Whatever her plan had been, it had not included this. "I mean . . . it looks that way, yes. But . . . I'm not Fractured. Not anymore . . ." She offered me a small smile, as if that confession was enough to regain my trust, to show me that we were on the same side.

I wasn't falling for it.

"Has anything you've told me ever been true? Are you even a thirteenth child?"

"Of course I am!" she snapped, wounded. "I'm every bit as special as you are. Even more so, truly."

There was something in her tone, in that imperious tilt to her head, that stirred up a memory I'd not thought of in years.

"I know you," I whispered, floored as I pulled that dreadful afternoon from the deep recesses of my mind. "You were the little novice at the temple in Rouxbouillet, that day when Bertie was sold off." My hands flew to my face, covering my mouth. "That was you!"

Margaux's lips parted. She looked as though she was going to deny it but then nodded. "It was."

I felt stunned into silence.

Her face curled in a sneer, all façades falling away. "You've no idea how much I hated you."

"What? Why?"

Margaux snorted. "That look right there, for starters! You're like a little woodland creature, all big-eyed innocence, fawning naiveté. It's sickening."

"Margaux, I don't know what I've ever done to offend you. I don't even know how I could have—"

Her hands balled into fists. "Just . . . being here. Just . . .

existing," she snapped, struggling to explain her resentment. "Our priestess wanted you so badly. It was all she could talk about." She pantomimed a spread banner. "'The Thirteenth Child Who Got Away.' When she already had me! And your brother! Oh—he was the worst!"

Her words rushed from her in a manic deluge. I felt each exclamation land on me like an assault.

"When he first arrived, of course, he had to take a vow of silence. One whole year of wordless devotion, of purifying your thoughts and mind and readying to serve your gods. But when his vow ended, all sorts of stories came tumbling out of him, and they were all about you. He was so proud, proud to have a sister chosen by a god. He was starstruck, I think, bragging about all the things your father had told him. The night that three gods came for you. The night you were chosen. The night the Dreaded End promised you all those extra years."

"Extra years," I repeated, dismayed that my father had understood Merrick's promise for me before I ever had. He'd told Bertie, and Bertie had gone on to tell Margaux. I felt a lurch of queasy dread in my stomach. That was *my* secret. That Margaux knew it felt terribly, terribly wrong.

"What do you need so many years for anyway?" she went on, the question falling from her lips with ease, and I suddenly pictured her in her chambers, asking it over and over as she paced, as she fixated, as she raged. "Why did your god give them to you but mine didn't do the same? It's so unfair. So infuriating. No matter what I did with my life, no matter how talented I was, no matter the great things I'd accomplish, at the back of my mind were all those extra years of yours, taking up space, pricking and prodding at me. So yes. I hated you," Margaux admitted. "You weren't living in a crowded dormitory, fighting for every scrap of attention, for a chance to be noticed. You weren't flaying yourself open, literally pouring out your blood to prove your love. You had blessings untold, and on top of everything, all those years."

"Margaux, I never asked for them. Merrick had it arranged before I was even—"

"Eventually," she went on, speaking over me as if my protests, my explanations meant nothing, "my anger and resentment built to such a fevered pitch that my lord finally took notice. Calamité came to me one night and promised that if I devoted my life to him alone, he would bless me too."

"But you're a daughter of the Divided Ones . . . of all their gods. How could you abandon the rest of them?"

Margaux shrugged. "What have they ever done for me? Calamité saw that I was special. He promised to reward me. So I accepted his offer. And he has."

She reached into the folds of her robes and withdrew the bronze chain once more, showing off the trinket.

"Where's your whistle, healer?" she demanded, her mouth open wide as she laughed. Candlelight winked off her canines, making her look as dangerous as a rabid dog. Without warning, she put the pipes to her lips and blew.

A low and familiar atonal rumble rang out, a call to war, a call to chaos and ill fortune. A call to the only god who ever came when beckoned.

Calamité.

CHAPTER 54

"MY LORD." MARGAUX GREETED CALAMITÉ WITH A deep bow of reverence.

"How is my favorite child?" he asked as the Divided Ones strode from a shadowy corner of the room and crossed to her.

She rose on tiptoe to press a kiss to his cheek without offering Félicité so much as an acknowledgment. "So much better now that you're here."

The Divided Ones turned, scanning Euphemia's chambers, their gaze missing nothing. I felt the moment Calamité's eye fell on me. "Hello, Hazel. I like your gown. Life at court seems to suit you."

I stared up at the god with a stony expression. "Nothing about this place suits me these days."

Calamité shrugged blithely and they turned to peer into the princess's bed, watching as she trembled. "My, what a mess she's made," he murmured, sounding pleased.

Something was wrong, I realized.

The Divided Ones were moving slowly, almost as if the air around them was too thick, holding them back.

They looked . . . sluggish.

"Good evening, Félicité," I called, noticing she'd said nothing since their arrival.

The room was quiet, too quiet by far. Usually the Divided Ones were always speaking, always talking over mortals, taking control of conversations, bickering with one another. But now . . .

"I'm afraid my sister can't hear you at present," Calamité warned me, abandoning Euphemia. "None of them can. It's just little old me."

I looked to the goddess's side. Since they had no pupils, it was always difficult to tell exactly where the gods were looking, but her gaze did seem to be especially unfocused now. Calamité shifted, his steps slow and measured, and I realized he was dragging Félicité's side of their body with him. She controlled nothing. She wasn't moving at all.

"What's wrong with her?"

"Nothing is *wrong,*" Calamité drawled, tilting their head so he might better look in my direction. "Perhaps everything is finally right."

"What did you do?" I gaped, unable to look away from Félicité's slack muscles. She looked like a cut flower left without water, wilted and shrinking in on herself.

"What did *we* do," Margaux interjected, sounding proud, and a sliver of dread sliced deep within me.

"You don't really think I'd spend millennia stuffed inside the same body as all my siblings and not find a way to secure a touch of independence? You've no idea how chafed I feel in here. So many gods, so little space." He shuddered, but only his side of their frame moved.

"Do they know?"

He laughed, stiltedly wandering about the chamber, picking up small trinkets and toys, examining them with interest before discarding them. Margaux watched, her mouth wide, smiling rapturously.

"Of course not. I once spent an entire afternoon along the canals of Boizenbrück, whispering treachery and plots into the ears of passersby, and a week later, as the citizens rose up and fomented revolution, I acted as surprised as the lot of them. Not a single one suspects a thing."

I let out a bark of laughter. "You can't possibly believe that Félicité won't catch on to this. She notices everything."

Calamité's eye flashed. "Do not forget to whom you speak, mortal. Just because I'm friendly to a thirteenth child does not mean we are friends. It does not make us equals. I am the lord of chaos, the great numen of turmoil. The earth and all its mayhem pay me homage, cast offerings of reverence at my feet. I hear praise in every cry of insurrection. My blood stirs at turbulence and panic and disorder. My acolytes sanctify me with their schemes, they venerate me with their gifts of sedition." His eye flickered over Margaux with cool appraisal. "Or they try their best to." He sighed testily. "What am I doing here, exactly? I specifically told you I didn't want to be summoned until the denouement."

Margaux's smile faltered before she gestured about the room, as if showing off a prize, grand and precious. "And here we are."

"This? This is your final act?" His tone was saturated with evident skepticism. "Where is all the fighting? No one is screaming, and not a single drop of blood has been spilt. The queen's bastard is alive, and if I'm not mistaken, Hazel still has both her candles." He cocked his head, horror growing across his features as he strained to listen to the noises filtering in from the rest of the palace. "There's a soiree downstairs. A party! Mortals are celebrating, happy and whole *and why did you bring me here*?"

Calamité's frame loomed large, scraping the gilt from the ceiling as his anger burst forth. His spine hunched to fit the space, bringing his splintered face unbearably close to my own. Waves of rage as tangible as fire radiated from his half of the body.

I felt the instinctual urge to drop low and beg for forgiveness, but I pushed the notion aside and stood tall. This was not my godfather, and for once, such ruthless anger was not directed at me.

Margaux, to her credit, only pressed her lips together, frustrated yet unalarmed.

"The plans did have to change a bit." She cast a look of scorn toward me. "But that doesn't mean we failed. We're just . . . adapting. You did say it was a good plan," she reminded him. "You commended it."

"You should have stuck to the original version," Calamité said, heat blazing from him once more. "Kill the queen, start the Shivers, let the king die, and watch as the world burns."

My mouth fell open, but before I could respond, from the far side of the chamber came a gasp, and our heads all snapped toward its source.

There, inconceivably, was Leopold, his jaw slack with horror, his eyes wide as he tried to take in everything happening. At his back was an open door, paneled to look like every other wall in the room. A perfectly hidden passageway.

Calamité beamed, relishing this new twist. "Your Royal Highness, good evening! Come, come in! What a most unexpected yet pleasant surprise!"

"What is going on?" Leopold turned to me, looking dazed. "Bellatrice says she's running away, and I heard Euphemia wasn't feeling well and there are guards outside her door, so I used the secret way in, and now there's . . ." He gestured toward the Divided Ones.

"Hazel?" He looked so painfully lost. I took a step toward him, unsure of how to explain any of this, but his gaze darted back to Calamité. "What are you doing here? The Divided Ones have no reason to be—"

"Don't blame me. I didn't ask to be summoned," Calamité interrupted, his half of their mouth grinning. "Poor little dimwitted prince. Your father opened your home to quite a wolf in sheep's clothing."

"Hazel would never have . . ." Leopold paused, then whirled toward Margaux, putting everything together. "You. What did you do?"

Margaux jumped as the room's attention fell on her. She looked mildly queasy, sensing that the last bit of her plan was unraveling into a big messy pile right before her very eyes.

"I? Nothing," she began. Her voice squeaked, breaking too high.

"Give it up, child," Calamité advised with a sigh. "You overplayed your hand and there's no way out now." His eye flittered toward the ceiling. "Such a waste."

"What did you do to the queen?" I asked, prompting softly, the words too terrible to speak at full volume.

"Nothing . . . much." Margaux's eyes darted from me to her god, then back to Leopold. "I . . . Well. Before she went out to ride that day . . ." She licked her lips. "I might have put a bit of oleander in her canteen."

I couldn't stop my gasp. "You poisoned her?"

She turned to me, her eyes impossibly round and pleading. "She didn't suffer. I didn't want her to suffer."

"Why?" Leopold demanded, his voice stony and loud enough to stir Euphemia from her slumber. She shifted uneasily in the bed, the muscles along her jawline twitching in staccato beats. "Why would you do such a thing? My mother was kind to you. She brought you here, made this palace your home. She—"

"It was regrettable," Margaux began, having the decency to glance down in remorse. "Certainly not personal. You're right, Aurélie always treated me well. She was lovely, without fault, truly."

Calamité broke into a laugh. "Other than that dalliance with her husband's brother, of course." He looked about the room, as if expecting us to join his mirth. He squinted at Leopold. "You do know that's the real reason your uncle left court, don't you?"

Leopold looked sick.

Margaux took a step forward, hands outstretched, as if to reassure the prince of her good intentions, then stopped short, thinking better of touching him. "It did not bring me joy, poisoning her, watching her go out on that fateful ride."

"Yet you did it all the same," Leopold muttered, voice dark as an approaching storm.

"For the greater good," Margaux explained. "For his good," she added, nodding toward Calamité. Her lips twisted, showing her sudden dismay. "For all the good it did."

"It was a promising start," Calamité offered.

"Your uncle was meant to have been blamed for Aurélie's death," Margaux explained, looking to Leopold. "Once she'd fallen from the horse, snapping her neck, I left a torn scrap of scarlet fabric near her body, with Baudouin's sigil stitched on it. It was supposed to start the war. Marnaigne was to strike first. Baudouin would retaliate. It would have been . . ." She paused, her eyes growing distant. "It would have been beautiful. A beautiful, calamitous ruin, the likes of which the world has never seen."

Calamité sighed, wistful over what might have been, but Leopold gritted his teeth. "No sigil was ever found."

"No," Margaux agreed miserably. "Your mother's maid never saw it. The foolish girl came across the body and panicked, trampling about, screaming her head off like some unhinged imbecile. By the time a game warden found her, the fabric had been smashed in the mud or lost in the grasses. I looked for it later, once the queen had been taken away, but it was gone, unrecoverable. So I had to adjust my plan."

"You've caused suffering and untold horrors, and for what?" I exclaimed, all but shouting. "For *him*?" I shot a terrible glance Calamité's way. He had the audacity to wink back. "You said she began the Shivers," I reminded him. "How? You don't just start a plague."

He shrugged, his shoulder rising and falling. "It's her gift; she can use it as she pleases."

"What gift? She's not actually an oracle, is she?" I turned toward Margaux. "Are you?"

She laughed. "Of course not. Who'd want to be saddled with a curse like that?"

Calamité reached out and cupped her chin, smiling fondly. "Margaux has been blessed with the gift of discord. She has an unusual talent for making a disordered mess everywhere she goes. Each time she uses it, she feeds me, venerates me. The more she uses her talents, the stronger I become. The stronger I become, the more time I can steal away from . . . well, all of them." He gestured toward Félicité's blank expression.

I studied the other thirteenth child with fresh eyes. "You truly started an entire plague?"

Margaux couldn't help but smile. "When my first attempt at revolution didn't work, I had to try something different. I traveled north, to Baudouin's duchy. It was clear his province was thriving.

Fertile farmlands, happy villagers. I tried to think up something that would disrupt that, something grand and dramatic for my godfather, something that would make it all fall apart."

"The Shivers," I prompted, tired of this conversation, exhausted with her expression of pleasure.

She beamed. "My eyes may not be able to predict the future, but my hands can certainly shape it. You don't think it coincidence the sickness runs gold, then black, do you?"

"Marnaigne colors," Leopold murmured. "I never . . . I never put that together."

Margaux smiled sweetly, unsurprised. "Of course not, Your Royal Highness. But Baudouin did. He immediately believed the plague to have been summoned by your family in an attack against him. So he rallied those around him who were left and began his march south."

Her cheery recitation horrified me. "Thousands of people have died because of you," I whispered.

"For *him,*" she reminded me. "Everything would have worked if I'd not brought you to court."

"Why did you?" I asked, curious. "You were poised for everything to go the way you wanted. Baudouin was stirring unrest, the Shivers was everywhere. Why tell the court you saw me in a vision?"

"She got greedy," Calamité supplied with a weary tone. "She couldn't execute her plans without wanting to bring you down as well." He rolled his eye. "I warned her it was a terrible idea, but some people just never listen."

"I didn't think there *was* a cure for the Shivers," Margaux said flatly. "I thought you would come and everything would still be terrible and the king would either sentence you to death or you'd get sick or—"

"This is exactly why you're in this mess right now," Calamité sang, and I wondered briefly if these confrontations were feeding him too, nourishing his hunger for chaos. "You used what should have been my crowning moment for your silly personal vendettas. You ruined—"

"I thought it would work!" Margaux snapped. "I had no idea she'd go and use one of her candles to save the king."

"Candles, what candles?" Leopold demanded.

Margaux blinked in surprise. "She never told you?" She glanced at me and the gleam in her eye turned cunning. "What other secrets have you been keeping from him, Hazel?"

"Don't—" I began, but she went right on, talking over me.

"Her god adored her so much he gave her three lives instead of one. Three candles meant to burn so very, very, terribly long. If anything should ever come of your disastrous little dalliance, she'll outlive you by nearly two centuries, I'd guess. Well, she would have." She *tsk*ed. "But she's only got one spare left now."

To his credit, Leopold didn't question the logic or the logistics of it. He simply believed.

"You gave up a life for Papa?" he asked, his blue eyes falling on me. "One of your own lives?"

His expression looked wondrous even as his words were tinged with horror, and I felt a flush of shame. He didn't know about my gift, my curse. He didn't know about the people I'd seen marked by skulls, the things I'd had to do to them. The things I was meant to do to his father, to Euphemia.

"It was the only way to save him," I said simply. It was the truth, even if it felt like half a lie. Hot tears pricked at my eyes. "His Brilliance was already darkening and I didn't have a cure yet, and I didn't want Euphemia to . . ."

Euphemia.

She was still lying there, soaking her bedsheets bronze with every twitch of her muscles, seized by an uneasy sleep and completely oblivious to everything happening around her, every dark deed that had been brought to light, every confession uttered.

I glanced at Margaux, putting the final piece of her twisted puzzle into place.

"You made Euphemia sick so I would use my last candle to save her, didn't you?"

The accusation landed in the room like a cannonball.

Margaux, suddenly wide-eyed and fearful, raised her hands in denial, shaking her head as she stumbled backward, darting behind an end table, a chair, anything that would put distance between her and the prince.

Leopold's cheeks flamed, hot spots of red burning across his face. He lunged at Margaux, but Calamité grabbed him first, and the pair crashed to the floor as the god struggled to restrain him.

"I will end you!" Leopold shouted, twisting to free himself. I'd never seen him fight like this, scrapping and wrestling, muscles straining as he sought to shove Calamité aside. This was not the languid prince of old but the battle-tested soldier.

Margaux, now cowering in the curtains of Euphemia's bed, kept shaking her head, denying everything. "I didn't. I swear to you. Not on purpose. It was so hot this morning at the execution. She was so thirsty and must have found the flask in my satchel. Leopold was supposed to drink it. I wanted him to get sick so that you'd waste your last candle on him. But Euphemia drank it instead. I never would have given that to her. Not Euphemia. I'll swear that on my life."

"Your life means nothing," I pointed out. "Your word is nothing.

Everything you've said has been a lie. Why should we believe you now?"

I rounded the corner of Euphemia's bed. If Leopold couldn't get to her, I would in his place. But a hand, fingers elongated and strong, shot out, stopping me. It grabbed my ankle and sent me stumbling.

"I've heard enough."

Félicité's voice boomed loudly through the chamber, startling us all.

On the other side of Calamité, the goddess had awakened. The Divided Ones' mouth opened wide as she stretched her muscles, wresting herself from whatever trance Calamité had kept her in. She flexed her hands, her fingers looking like the legs of a spider as she took back control, pushing their shared body up from the floor. Their spine rippled in a series of cracks as she straightened.

Calamité sighed, looking miserably put out. "Well, there goes that fun."

"Fun," Félicité echoed, rubbing her cheek. "You found yourself a thirteenth child of your own, Brother?"

He shrugged. "Perhaps."

"And gave her a blessing?"

On his side of their face, Calamité smiled.

The goddess peered down at Margaux and startled. "I remember you. You always were an appalling acolyte. Give me that."

Margaux made an attempt to cover her necklace, but Félicité snatched at the set of pipes, breaking the chain and crushing the necklace in her balled fist.

"This is terribly off-putting," she muttered, tossing the scrap aside.

Leopold let out a disgusted bark of laughter. "To put it mildly."

He too had gotten to his feet, but Calamité's hand was still heavy on his shoulder, holding him in place. He studied Margaux with icy hatred. "You will pay for this, for all of this. My mother, my sister. For every death you caused throughout the kingdom, whether on the battlefield or in the sickbed. I will see you pay."

Her eyes darted around the room as she searched, calculated. Even now, Margaux was trying to work out a way to survive this, to emerge unscathed. Her audacity was staggering.

"You know, I don't think you will, Your Royal Highness," she began. "Your father adores me. He trusts me. I've spent the last three years telling him the secrets of everyone at court: Yours. Your sisters'. Those of the entire gentry and every one of his advisors. I've proven my loyalty to him time and time again. He believes everything I say. All I need to do is whisper that it was Hazel who poisoned the queen, Hazel who made him sick, Hazel who—"

"Do you hear yourself?" Leopold demanded over her madness. "That doesn't even make sense. Hazel wasn't here for any of that."

"Perhaps not, but she could have had help from her secret lover . . . you," she murmured, her grin wide and wicked. She looked so triumphant. "That won't be too much of a stretch for the king to believe, will it, Leopold? You've been plotting this together for months, years. The timing doesn't matter; I'll make something up as I go. The pair of you will be executed by dawn and I will still be here. Still pulling every one of his strings." Her attention darted to Calamité and she offered him the smallest bob of her head. "I will fix this, my lord, I swear it!"

In a flash, Margaux was across the room, racing for the secret passageway. Leopold tried to go after her, but Calamité's hold on him was still too strong.

I turned to Félicité for help, but she only stared after the false oracle's retreating form. I felt any trace of hope within me deflate.

Calamité would never be punished. Margaux might be held accountable, but that wouldn't undo the deaths she'd caused, the chaos she'd created.

The only way to move forward was to fix what I'd done wrong.

The answer came to me in an instant, striking as bright and certain as a bolt of lightning from the sky.

I took the goddess's great hand in mine, drawing her attention. "Send me back to the Between."

"What?" she questioned, studying me curiously.

"Give me the godsight and send me back. I need to put a stop to all this. I need to set everything right."

She blinked, considering my words. "You'll clean up the mess my brother and his reverent made?"

"Now, just a minute—" Calamité started.

"As much as I can," I said, racing to talk over him. "I won't be able to undo the deaths she or the king have caused, but I can stop more from happening. Starting by killing the king himself. Send me back and I will make sure the deathshead is obeyed."

Félicité pursed her side of their lips, thinking it over with a terrifying divine stillness. "You certainly are your godfather's child," she murmured, then pressed one of her thumbs to my forehead, electrifying my senses and taking hold of my vision. "Perform your charge well, little mortal." She gave a meaningful glance over my shoulder to where Euphemia thrashed on the bed. "All your charges."

CHAPTER 55

When I heard the rush of the rapids plunging over the waterfall in the Between, I remembered to scrunch my eyes closed, keeping the painful godsight shut tightly away. Alone in the dark of my mind, I tried to orient myself, listening to where the falls were, hearing them echo off the back wall of the cave.

"You can do this," I whispered. "Kill the king and save the kingdom. Kill the king and save the kingdom."

I let out a long, calming breath, then took my first step toward Merrick's cavern.

"Kill the—"

"Hazel, wait!" When a hand fell on me, gripping my upper arm, I let out a shriek and involuntarily opened my eyes.

"What are you doing here?" I asked Leopold, aghast. "How did you—"

I had to stop, had to close my eyes as I crashed to the ground. My head pounded, too heavy to keep upright.

Looking at him through a god's eyes was the most terrible thing I'd ever done.

I could see every potential path his life might take, every iteration he could become. Every version of Leopold was superimposed upon another, magnifying his silhouette into an infinite image of possibility. He was a king: a good one, a bad one, one that was not much of either; he was a captain: at war, at peace, triumphant, imprisoned. He was a playboy, a father, a drunk, a monk, a widower, without family, so much in love. He devoted himself to the crown, to the gods, to earthly pleasures, to scholarly pursuits. On and on and on it went. It was too much to take in, too enormous for one mind to process or understand.

I let out a sob, feeling as if my head was about to burst.

"What's wrong?" he asked, kneeling beside me. He rubbed my back, offering comfort when I couldn't explain. "Hazel, what's happening?"

I leaned against his body, trying to ground myself in the solidity of his frame. There was only one of him here now—there was only this Leopold, my Leo—but I couldn't shake the memory of his multitudes.

"Why are you here?" I cried, fumbling to find his hand. His fingers were warm and rough and here with me in this moment. I gripped them fiercely, tethering myself to him. "How did you get here?"

"I couldn't let you do this alone. I didn't want you . . . I didn't want you to face whatever this is alone. When Félicité began to snap her fingers, I just grabbed your hand and didn't let go." He bent over my supine form, his lips brushing the nape of my neck. "Hazel, what's wrong? What's happening to you?"

"It's the godsight." I shuddered. "I see what they see. I see . . .

everything. It lets me know the lives of each candle, lets me find who I need to find. But with you here right before me . . ." I winced, feeling as though I might throw up. "I see too much with you."

His arms encircled me, his chest a comforting weight against my spine. I wanted to stay there, wrapped up in him, until my sight was once again mine, until this whole mess was over. But I couldn't. I was the only one who could end this. I was the one who needed to right the wrong.

"We have to get to the cavern before I lose the sight, before we lose this chance," I said, struggling to sit up, struggling to stand when all I wanted was to sink. Everything felt harder with my eyes closed. Every task took too long. But I couldn't bear to open them and see all those Leopolds again. "There's a crevice along the back wall. Do you see it?"

"Yes."

"Can you take me to it? Will you be my eyes, at least for a bit?"

He kissed the top of my head. "For as long as you need me."

We made our way into the tunnels. Leopold kept one arm tightly around me, guiding my steps, and every so often, I'd risk a peek through lowered lashes, making sure we were on track, making sure we took the right path.

I knew we'd reached the cavern when his breathing changed, growing sharper, full of wonder. "What is all this?"

"Lives," I said simply, squinting against their brilliance. "All of our lives."

There were fewer than I remembered, and my heart panged, thinking of those lost in the war, those who'd succumbed to the Shivers. The placement of the candles looked different too, and the aisle I recalled King Marnaigne's candle being down was no longer there.

"Stay behind me and don't touch anything," I warned. "If you should cause a wick to go out . . ."

I heard him swallow hard before he murmured his understanding.

We waded into the sea of flames.

With Leopold positioned squarely at my back, I dared to more fully open my eyes, inspecting individual candles as I searched for the king's. I led us down row after row, desperate to find someone within the king's orbit, but all I found were strangers living out their lives, completely unaware how quickly peril could topple their entire existence.

"What will you do when you find Papa's?" Leopold asked as I took us down a fourth aisle.

"I'm not sure," I replied, answering honestly. "There's so much I need to tell you, so much I need to explain, but there's not time. Just know that he was never meant to be saved. He's been living on borrowed time."

"Your time," he said, somehow understanding, if only a little.

"Yes," I whispered.

"I heard what you said to the gods. There's a deathshead?"

I bit my lower lip. We were going to have this conversation whether I was ready or not. "It's part of my gift from the gods. My curse, really. I see cures, but sometimes I also see the opposite. Sometimes I see when it's time for a person to die. Sometimes . . . I have to kill them, before they kill others."

He absorbed this. "You're going to kill Papa, aren't you? Blow out his candle here, killing him there."

I stopped in the middle of the aisle, feeling him at my back. I reached for him, finding his arm. "Yes. I'm sorry."

He was so quiet I nearly risked turning to see him.

Then, a small helpless noise.

"I . . . I didn't tell you before, but . . . Bellatrice has left the palace."

Relief rushed through me. "She got out?"

"I ran into her and Mathéo leaving the ball. She said Papa was after her, that Papa wanted her dead, and I didn't believe it—I couldn't—but then that god said the same thing, that Baudouin is her father. Do you think it's true?"

"It is."

Leopold sucked air through his teeth. "Papa will hurt Bells. If you allow him to live, he'll kill her, won't he?"

It hurt to answer. "Yes."

"And then you. And then who knows how many others."

Mutely, miserably, I nodded.

"What about Euphemia?" he continued. "Can she be saved?"

Tears began to fall. "I saw the deathshead on her too."

His intake of breath was sharp. "It was there? You really saw it?"

I glanced back, confused. "Of course I did."

Several versions of Leopold frowned, struggling to find their words, and I had to look away, feeling nauseous.

"I just wondered . . . With Margaux's gift . . . her chaos, her confusion . . . She said she wanted me to drink that poison so you'd use your candle to save me. Couldn't she be the one behind Euphemia's deathshead? What if it's not your gift you saw but hers?"

I froze, the possibility filling me with wonder. I'd never considered that the deathshead could have come from anyone but the Holy First.

My gaze fell upon the candles in front of me, and I caught glimpses of the strangers' lives. None of them was the king, and with a sigh of frustration, I went down another aisle, my insides feeling squirmy with indecision.

Could Margaux have made me see a deathshead?

"I don't know, honestly," I admitted. "I don't know how Margaux's gift works, but . . . I want to believe she could. I can't possibly understand why the Holy First would want me to kill Euphemia. It doesn't make any sense."

"It doesn't." Leopold jumped to agree. "So if it's not a real deathshead, not one of the kind you usually see, you could save her, right? Euphemia could get better."

I frowned. "In theory, yes, but she doesn't have the Shivers, not the normal strain of it, and I don't know if the black agar would work. Usually I see what the person needs—a cure, a treatment, *something*—but all I saw over her was the deathshead."

"And she's very sick," Leopold said slowly.

I nodded, my heart aching as I remembered the dark Brilliance pouring from her lips as she writhed. "Very."

"Papa was very sick too, when you gave him your candle, wasn't he?"

A wave of goose bumps broke over my skin. My words were colored with hesitation when I spoke, unsure of what Leopold was getting at, of what he was asking of me. "Yes, but . . ."

"Oh, Hazel," Leopold said, his fingers dancing over the curve of my shoulder blade. "No. I didn't mean that we should use your candle for Euphemia. That's not— I would never— No! No. You've given far too much of yourself for our family already. I only meant . . . if your candle once saved Papa . . . and that candle is going to be put out . . . couldn't we use his candle—your candle, truly—to save Euphemia?"

I hazarded a glance his way. Every one of the Leopolds looked so hopeful, so earnest.

It was an intriguing solution, one I wouldn't have thought of. *Could* a partially burnt candle be used to save another's life? Marnaigne's flame hadn't been burning for even a year yet. There was plenty of wick and wax, plenty of time left for Euphemia. And if it hadn't been a deathshead sent from the Holy First, if I had only seen some terrible vision that Margaux wanted me to see, then Euphemia didn't need to be killed, she needed a cure. One the king's candle would instantly offer her.

"We could try," I began. "But there's no guarantee it would work."

Leopold frowned, not understanding. "Blowing out Papa's candle here might not kill him there?"

"No. I know that part will work," I said, offering no further explanation.

I remembered the curl of smoke from Kieron's spent candle dancing into the dark of the cavern. I'd watched it until it had completely wafted apart.

Leopold studied me, questions burning in his eyes. "When all this is over," he finally said, with considerable care, "I can't wait to hear each and every one of your stories."

"They're not all happy," I warned.

He shook his head. "It doesn't matter. I want to know them all. I want to spend the rest of my life, however many years my candle has left, learning everything there is to know about you."

My eyes, already so full, began to grow wet with tears. Before I could think better of it, I grabbed his collar and pulled him to me, pressing my lips to his. I closed my eyes and kissed him deeply, thoroughly. I couldn't bear to look at any of his futures, to see him age and grow old with someone else at his side, but I could claim this moment as my own. I kissed him now, leaving my mark on every one of his futures.

My mind's clock, forever ticking the passing of each second, finally made me pull away. "Thank you," I murmured against his mouth, stealing one more peck, certain it was the last kiss I'd ever share with Leopold.

When all this was over, I was leaving Martissienes, leaving its court, leaving everything, including this beautiful boy who could never be mine.

"Please tell me exactly what I did," he said, his voice low with appreciation. "I need to make sure to do it over and over again, as often as possible."

"Leo . . ." When I opened my eyes, I didn't see as many versions of him as I had before. The candles' lives didn't stand out to me as bright or consuming. I sighed. "We're running out of time."

"We haven't tried this aisle yet," he offered, pointing.

I led the way, passing my gaze over each of the burning tapers, catching snippets of so many lives. When I saw Cherise bent over a set of Bellatrice's stockings, I wanted to cheer.

I stopped in front of the wide table. "Here. It's Cherise. There's Aloysius." I pointed to a candle, noticing with a pang that there was only an inch or so left of his wax. "Bellatrice," I said, finding a tall taper. I paused fretfully on hers. "She's not at the palace." I focused on her image. "She and Mathéo are in a carriage. They made it out. They escaped."

Leopold leaned against my shoulder, searching for a sign of his sister. "You can see her? Right now? Does she look all right? Is she safe? Is she scared?"

I watched her tip her head back as Mathéo kissed his way down the column of her neck, his hand sneaking under her skirt.

"She's fine," I said, quickly looking away.

I scanned the table, searching for King Marnaigne. It should have been easy to spot him, his candle was so tall and new, but it eluded me.

"Here's Euphemia." I pointed, seeing the princess writhe and struggle against her sodden bedsheets. Her flame burned high, making the wax run.

"Phemie," Leopold whimpered, watching his little sister's life burn up before his eyes.

"This is you," I murmured, gesturing to the candle beside hers. It was disconcerting to see Leopold in the flame, watching him move as he did beside me now, bending down to examine himself. Both versions moved in perfect unison.

"We have to find Papa," Leopold pressed, his eyes darting around the table as if he could make out the lives himself. "Phemie's candle is so thin."

I started at the top of the table, looking over each candle again, methodically, logically. I could feel the godsight leaving me, leeching from my system, and every last moment of it needed to count.

"Wait! Here he is, I found him," I said, catching a flash of the palace once more.

He was in the throne room. King Marnaigne looked furious, his face nearly purple with rage. He was yelling things I could not hear, stabbing his finger into a chest of blue brocade.

Margaux.

"He's upset with Margaux," I murmured, watching the scene play out. "He's shouting at her. She's crying."

"Good," Leopold said. "Maybe he's finally seen her for the snake she is."

The king grabbed her robes, hoisting her up till they stared eye to eye, her hands dangling loosely at her sides, trembling in terror. His face reddened, his mouth curling into a snarl as he called for the guards.

I pulled myself out of the vision and picked up Marnaigne's candle. It didn't matter what happened to Margaux now. Leopold could deal with her later, when he was king.

I froze, the magnitude of what I was about to do crashing over me like a wave.

I was about to make Leopold a king.

Without warning, Marnaigne's candle changed, its flame flaring, a burst of heat exploding from it. The taper instantly melted, turning to a river of scalding wax that ran down my fingers, burning my hands. I cradled the fiery liquid, trying to salvage something of my candle, but it was impossible.

"Leo!" I didn't know what I was asking of him, didn't know how he could help.

But before he could reach me, the flame winked out, and the king was gone.

CHAPTER 56

LEOPOLD AND I STARED DOWN AT MY HANDS, AGHAST.

The candle was gone.

Marnaigne was gone.

A cry of pain bubbled up from within me, releasing in a sob. The palms of my hands were burned and blistered. I could feel the last of the flame's heat embed itself within me. My fingers trembled, unable to open or shut. The spent wax had already begun to cool, hardening my hands into fists.

"He's gone." I gasped, tears falling down my face. Tears of pain, tears for Euphemia. So, so many tears.

"What happened?" Leopold asked.

"I don't know. The last I saw of him, he was yelling at Margaux. He looked so mad."

"He's dead?" Leo's voice was a mix of sorrow and anger, confusion and fear.

I wasn't sure how the puddle of wax could mean anything else.

"That's it?" Leopold stared at the blackened skim left behind, looking sick. "That's how his life ends? I thought when he died it would be . . . grand somehow. There would be a moment of importance, some sort of absolution or catharsis or . . . but he's just . . . he's just gone. He didn't even know it was coming."

"Very few people do," I agreed, feeling small. I flexed my fingers, trying to break the cooled wax off my skin.

"How did it happen?"

I swept my eyes over the table, trying to find anything that would explain what went wrong.

I found Margaux's candle quickly. Her hands were raised defensively against a squadron of guards. She held a knife, its tip red. A splotch of blood stained the front of her robes.

"She stabbed him," I whispered. "He was calling the guards and she must have stabbed him."

I couldn't imagine how confusing the throne room was at that moment, how full of anger and rage and fear.

Somewhere, Calamité was smiling.

One of the guards darted forward, thrusting his halberd at Margaux.

The knife fell from her hands, clattering uselessly on the floor. A splash of entrails followed.

Margaux's candle flared, its length melting with terrible speed until all that remained was a drifting waft of smoke. The last thing I saw was her staggering back, crashing atop the fallen king.

"She's dead too," Leopold said, putting everything together. "They're both dead. Margaux and Papa . . ." He let out a shaking breath. "Papa's candle is gone. . . . Euphemia's going to die, isn't she?"

"I don't know how to save her," I admitted.

I wanted to. I truly did.

I didn't want her to die.

Not because of Margaux and her mad devotion. Not to serve as a sacrifice for a god who wouldn't remember her life come morning. There were always new diversions for Calamité, for all of the gods. New things to hunger after, new schemes to plan.

Plans, plans, the gods always had so many plans.

I thought of Merrick, thought of all the things he'd planned for me, even before my first flame had been lit.

And suddenly, I had a plan of my own.

I took off down an aisle, darting through the walls of flames and smoke, making my way to the solitary plinth along the cavern's perimeter. My candle burned as solidly as ever, just as tall as when I'd last seen it. I picked up its unlit mate, marveling at how well made it was, how strong and sure it would be.

I glanced at Merrick's glowing orb of fire, burning silently above me.

"Thank you for giving me this life," I whispered to him, praying he'd hear me, praying he'd understand. "I know this is not how you wished for me to use it. I know it's not what you planned. But you did want me to do good things with my lives, great things. This is the very greatest thing I can think to do with it. Forgive me."

"Hazel, no!"

Leopold was just behind me, his arms up, holding a set of candles.

There was just enough of the godsight left to see they were his and Euphemia's.

"Leo," I began, trying to keep my voice level, my tone calm. "You need to set down your candle. Carefully," I added. "You can put it with mine, there." I nodded back toward the plinth. Back to where my one and only candle burned.

"What are you doing, Hazel?" he asked, and his words sounded so much like mine, steady and composed, as if he too were trying to defuse a situation gone wrong.

I showed him the unlit taper. "We'll use this for Euphemia. It'll wipe out all her sickness. It will save her."

Leopold shook his head. "If you do that, we play into everything Margaux wanted, and she'll have won." He took a step toward me and I felt the irrational urge to back away from him. "I'm not letting you shorten your life. Not for her. Not for us. The Marnaigne family has taken too much from you already."

"My life won't be short," I protested. "Look at all the years I have before me."

"And you'll have even more if Euphemia gets mine. Think of how many lives you'll touch, how many lives you'll save. Think of all the good you will do with those years. I've lived twenty already, and what have I done with any of them? I'll never accomplish half of what you will."

"It's not a competition."

"Hazel, I want to be more. You've made me want to become more. More than that entitled prince you met all those months ago, drunken and raving in hallways, as if he had any idea of what life was really like outside the palace gates. This is how I can do it. This is how I can do wonderful things."

"We'll do wonderful and good things *together*," I said, taking a wary step toward him, then another. "If Euphemia gets my candle, I can have a life with you. A real life, a normal life. I won't have to see you and your sisters and everyone I love grow old and die without me."

He froze, the light from the candles catching his eyes, brightening his face with a luminous beauty. "You love me?" His words were whispered, full of disbelief and hope.

He took a step closer, as if he couldn't bear for us to be so far apart. The candles were nearly within my reach.

Wordlessly, breathlessly, I nodded.

Leopold smiled. "Then this is so much easier."

"Leo, no!" Before I could stop him, he brought Euphemia's candle toward his. I lunged forward, holding mine out, and we crashed together, tumbling to the ground as we each fought to be the victor.

Here, just outside the cavern, it was so much darker, and I struggled against my failing godsight, trying to see which candle was where. Droplets of wax dripped over us as he struggled to keep Euphemia's lit, as he struggled to not burn us all.

"Hazel, don't!" he pleaded, twisting from my grasp, our limbs tangled. "Hazel, *please!*"

Leopold gasped as a wick sputtered out.

The smoke that followed curled up into my eyes, grasping like a skeletal claw. It was impossible for me to see. It stung my eyes, drawing tears, and everything looked so black.

Then, from that terrible darkness, a new flame sparked to life.

EPILOGUE

The Ninety-Ninth Birthday

WITH A PUNCH OF SHARP SULFUR, THE LITTLE match snapped to life, flame biting at its wooden stump, hungry for a wick to feed on.

"Another year, another year, another year has come," sang my husband, as hopelessly off-key as ever. He made his way to my rocking chair with careful creaking steps, balancing a plate in his gnarled hands. One lit candle poked from the square of dark spiced cake, a little ball of light pushing back the morning gloom.

"Please don't finish that song," I protested. "I may be many things, but 'done' is not one of them."

He smiled. "Thank the gods for that."

"Another year older," I mused.

The hands that took the plate from him were wrinkled and riddled with age spots. They trembled, far too much to be considered the tools of a skilled surgeon any longer, but they were still able to cradle great-grandchildren, could still pull weeds from the little herb garden I kept out back, and would hold on to the fingers of my beloved as tightly as I could muster.

"Ninety-nine," he said with wonder, pressing a kiss to my forehead.

His lips—much like his hair—had thinned over the years, over our decades together, losing the lush fullness of youth, but I found I did not mind. I loved them more now than I had when we'd met. They were the lips that had drawn wild kisses from mine during dark nights of passion and had murmured soft words of comfort in dark nights of grief. They were the lips that smiled at me each morning over breakfast and the ones so quick to scowl when we disagreed. I'd spent the majority of my life with those lips and considered them more mine than his.

The lips of my lover.

The lips of my best friend.

The lips of my Leo.

"You didn't sleep last night," he accused, falling into the chair beside me with a hiss of discomfort. There was a rainstorm making its way to Alletois, and we both felt it along every bone in our bodies.

He was right. I had not. Again.

I'd been feeling changes within me over the past few days, strange stirrings I could not put word to. My body had realized it before my heart or mind wanted to acknowledge the grim truth: there was not much time left for me in this world.

I did not want to spend any of my last precious moments asleep.

I'd spent them watching Leopold dream instead, remembering the moments of our life together. There were the big points—when we'd returned from the Between, my candle holding his life's light as Euphemia's burned clear and strong on his; when he'd abdicated the throne, favoring a life of humble service over dynastic rule. Bellatrice's coronation, our wedding day, the nights we'd welcomed our children to the world. The nights I'd ushered in others' children, set on dedicating my skills to the shepherding of new life, never again using them to bring death.

Sifting through my years, I was amused to realize that the best memories I had, the ones I longed to play over in my mind again and again, were the days of seemingly no importance, the ones full of laughter prompted by jokes I no longer remembered, rainfalls and sunsets, picking clover with my daughter, the soup Leo made one winter that still caused my mouth to water. Little snippets that looked like nothing but were everything, comprising the brightest threads in the tapestry of my extraordinarily long and altogether too-short life.

Ninety-nine years sounded so vast and yet was nothing: a wisp of breath, a flutter of moments, the hiss of a candle's flame.

I could feel my candle now, the little fire dancing upon a wick grown too short. I worried endlessly about when that light would extinguish forever.

What then?

Where would my memories go? Would there be a place to store them or would that be it—the whole of who I was, who I'd grown into, gone in the wrong second of a wayward draft?

I wanted to know if I'd see Merrick once more. I'd not laid eyes upon him since my nineteenth birthday, and it hurt knowing how much of my life he'd missed. I hoped he'd watched some of it, even from afar. The good parts, the bad parts, the parts that were neither but somehow both. Those beautiful, messy, wonderfully ordinary moments.

"Aren't you going to make a wish?" Leopold asked from his chair. It was hard to see him through the light of the approaching dawn. "The candle is nearly out."

"It is," I agreed, watching the little taper's wax melt all over the top of Leopold's spiced cake. I studied the struggling flame, feeling a profound kinship with it, and made no motion to dash it away.

I glanced back to Leo, a smile of chagrin ready at my lips, then blinked. I knew morning was nearly upon us, knew the sun was beginning to rise over the eastern field, spreading its rays wide and warm, but the room seemed darker now, the shapes around me dimming and growing soft and indistinct.

"Leo?" I asked, unsure if he was still there. I couldn't see him, couldn't feel the warmth of his presence.

But there was someone else with me in the dark. I could feel the air move over the shape of his gaunt frame, drift over the heft of his fine robe.

"There once was a very foolish god who lived at the heart of the Between," he began, and I felt tears prick at my eyes. His voice sounded just as I remembered, rumbly and deep, like the smoke of an autumnal bonfire, like the rich loam of blackened earth.

Like Merrick.

Like my godfather.

"Happy birthday, Hazel."

I reached out, fumbling to find his hands in the surrounding darkness. I couldn't see the bright shine of his red-and-silver eyes, couldn't see his inky silhouette, and I needed to feel him, needed to know he was finally here.

"I didn't bring a cake," he apologized. "I knew nothing I created would best dear Leopold's efforts." He let out a small laugh. "I never would have guessed spiced cake was your favorite."

My heart swelled. He *had* been with me, checking in, whether I'd sensed his presence or not.

"Where are we now?" I asked, wrapping my arthritic fingers around his even bonier ones. It was a terrible thing to be in such an all-consuming darkness. My eyes flittered through the void, restlessly searching for something to focus on. But there was nothing. "Does Leo know you're here?"

I heard him shake his head. "He thinks you've dozed off. He's taken the plate from your hands. Such a pity too; it looks like a terribly good cake."

The threatening tears spilled over my cheeks as I nodded.

"Hazel, I . . ." Merrick paused. "There are so many things I want to say to you, so many apologies I need to give."

"You don't," I promised.

"I'm so proud of you, so proud of the life you've made, the things you've done." His grip tightened. "Despite everything I did, all the trials I saddled you with, you became exactly who you were meant to be. It has been a privilege to watch you grow." His voice quavered, sounding wet. "Oh, my brilliant, bright, darling little Hazel."

"There's not much candle left, is there?" I asked.

"No," he admitted, tears choking the word. "And there's so much I need to—"

I squeezed his hand, silencing him. "There's nothing you need to do, nothing that needs to be said. I had the life I did not in spite of but because of you, because you thought me special enough to fight for, because you loved me."

"Love," he corrected. "Never past tense. Always present."

My throat felt full with wishes that wanted to be let loose and free. I wished I had more time, I wished Leo could be with us, I wished . . .

I swallowed them down.

A wish was nothing but a hopeful regret, and here, at the end of my life, I had none.

"There is one thing I'd like to ask of you," I started. "One small favor."

"Anything." He said it immediately, unconditionally.

"Will you stay with me till the end comes? Will you sit with me in the dark?"

I felt his tears fall on my hands, wetting them. "I will," he swore.

We sat together, quietly at first. I leaned my head against his shoulder and he gathered his robe around us both and it was the most peaceful, companionable silence I had ever known. My godfather, me, and the dark.

"Will it be like this always?" I dared to ask, then took in a quick breath as my eyes began to adjust, sharpening the shadows around us, drawn to the lines of highlights and limns. "Oh, Merrick," I whispered, awed. "Look at that wondrous light."

ACKNOWLEDGMENTS

One of my least favorite questions to be asked is "What made you want to be a writer?" There's no one exact answer, just a series of little life moments that snowballed into an avalanche. If my parents hadn't told me stories and taken me to the library every week, would I have grown up loving books? If I hadn't picked up that one story and read that one line, would I ever have tried to do what my favorite authors could? If my sister and I hadn't spent our childhood imagining fantastical adventures to play at, would I ever have wanted to create new worlds of my own? If I hadn't become a stage manager and sat through years of rehearsals, would I understand plot and pacing and dialogue? If I hadn't met that really cute and brainy guy, and if we hadn't gotten married, and if our incredibly amazing girl hadn't come along, would I still be in theater, content to manage others' creative endeavors? And if I hadn't been held by the collective decades of so many family members and friends who love and support and cheer me on, would I be here, writing this now?

No. I wouldn't.

Hazel's story has convinced me that there are no big moments in life. Every giant joy, every bitter heartache, is made up of all the little seemingly ordinary events that led to it. But oh, the wonderful life those little moments create!

It's impossible to thank everyone who helped make this book

sparkle as it does, but here are a handful of the seemingly inconsequential moments that brought it to life.

One morning in 2017, Hannah Whitten made a post on a silly social media site, asking if any writers wanted to swap their fairy tale retellings. After a long and weighted moment, I hit the reply button, and now we're stuck together forever.

Later that year, Sarah Landis hit a heart button on that same site and completely changed my world. You, Sarah, are absolutely the real MVP, and I'm forever grateful I'm on your team!

A little while later, a tree fell on a house in New Jersey, and Wendy Loggia stayed at home and had time to read a submission she'd just received. She's been reading (so very many of) my words ever since. There's no one else I'd rather hurl a ton of atmosphere and plot twists at!

Noreen Herits was assigned a debut book to publicize, and when she called to introduce herself, she somehow mentioned something about the royal family—who I have an irrational fondness for—and that debut author knew she was in amazing hands.

Back in 2020, Casey Moses was picked to design a bee-autiful cover for my second book. She and her team of artists (special thanks to David Seidman for this one!) went on to create so many eye-catching beauties.

Every day, a whole host of talented people sit down at their computers, pull up to their printing presses, or whip out their phones and pour out their magic. They polish my mistakes, shout about my silly characters, put my words on actual paper, and help me and my stories shine. Forever in debt to the wonders at Delacorte Press and Random House Children's Books. Y'all truly are my A-Team.

So many, many years before any of this, my mama took me to a Hastings Bookstore and bought a copy of Ann Martin's *Kristy's*

Great Idea. The next weekend, my dad got doughnuts and rented *The Neverending Story* from a United Supermarket. Days later, when I had the idea to make a *Fantasia*-themed Babysitters Club, my little sister, Tara, joined with an enthusiastic yes and went on to say yes to every one of my over-the-top ideas that followed. I cannot thank the three of you enough for all your love and for setting me up for a life of falling for fandoms!

In the spring of 2011, a ridiculously tall guy named Paul Craig took me out for dinner at a Thai place and did not laugh at me as I ate the shells of our edamame appetizer. Thank you for always having my back in all things.

Years later, that ridiculously tall guy and I were playing cards in a labor and delivery room (let the record state: I was winning) when our Grace finally decided she was ready to come on out. Of all the birthday stories I'll ever tell, Gracie-girl, yours is my favorite.

And just a little while ago, beloved reader, you picked up this book and became part of my story too. Thank you.

About the Author

#1 *New York Times* bestselling author ERIN A. CRAIG has always loved telling stories. After getting her BFA in Theatre Design and Production from the University of Michigan, she stage managed tragic operas with hunchbacks, séances, and murderous clowns, then decided she wanted to write books that were just as spooky. An avid reader, a decent quilter, a rabid basketball fan, and a collector of typewriters, brass figurines, and sparkly shoes, Erin makes her home in West Michigan with her husband and daughter.